D0050640

A Hollywood Education

A Hollywood Education

Tales of Movie Dreams and Easy Money

by David Freeman

G. P. PUTNAM'S SONS
NEW YORK

G. P. Putnam's Sons
Publishers Since 1838
200 Madison Avenue
New York, NY 10016

These stories are works of fiction.
The events described are imaginary and the characters are fictitious
and not intended to represent specific living persons.

The author gratefully acknowledges permission from the following sources to reprint material in their control:

Acuff-Rose-Opryland Music, Inc., for lyrics from "Bye Bye Love" by Boudelaux & Felice Bryant, © 1957 by Acuff-Rose-Opryland Music, Inc., 2510 Franklin Road, Nashville, TN 37204. All rights reserved.

Frederick Music Company for lyrics from "Do the Do" by Willie Dixon, © 1954 Frederick Music Company.

New Directions Publishing Corporation for excerpt from *Poems of Dylan Thomas* by Dylan Thomas, copyright 1939 by Dylan Thomas.

Published simultaneously in Canada by
General Publishing Co. Limited, Toronto

Library of Congress Cataloging-in-Publication Data

Freeman, David, date.
A Hollywood education.

1. Hollywood (Los Angeles, Calif.)—Fiction.
I. Title.
PS3556.R3844H64 1986 813'.54 86-1487
ISBN 0-399-13044-6

Printed in the United States of America
1 2 3 4 5 6 7 8 9 10

For Mark and Linda Freeman

Contents

Reporting the News

I am a reporter, a collector of fact and detail, an arbiter of truth and lies. Like many of my brethren, I've always known everyone's business but my own. I had been on the New York *Post* for two years, covering city politics, when the paper was sold to an Australian syndicate that transformed it from the last of New York's liberal, afternoon dailies into a combative tabloid with brash headlines: NIGHT KILLER STALKS BROOKLYN; NUN HAS BABY. My inclination was to quit. But the new management, needing somebody on the staff who knew the city, encouraged a few of us to stick around. In parts of New York, out of loyalty to the old *Post,* it was considered slightly dishonorable to read the new version, let alone write for it. To my surprise, instead of hating what the paper had become or being embarrassed to be associated with it, the immediacy of the new version charged me with energy and made me feel raffish and a little wicked. The *Post* wasn't going to win any journalism awards, but it was lively, rude, and fun to read. So I kept my job and I chased the fire engines, asked a few questions, separated the big lies from the little ones, hunted for connections, subtle or bold, then knocked out six hundred words for everybody to read on the subway. My star was in the ascendancy until I started making up the news.

The trouble began when the paper hired Chandra R. V.

Chandrahassan, the twenty-four-year-old heir to a Bombay newspaper fortune. He had been sent to New York and the *Post* to learn American reporting and editing before he went back home to run the family business. We called him the Maharajah. He was a pleasant-enough guy, but probably too naive and gentle of spirit to be a New York newspaperman.

I was subbing for one of the regular night editors who was out with the flu. It was a responsible job; getting it was a sign that I was on track with the new management. But it was dull. I preferred being on the street to sitting in the newsroom reading wire-service copy and rewriting what the other reporters filed. When I came on for my nightside tour, Marv Seligman, the city editor, rolled his eyes and warned me he had sent the Maharajah out to the South Bronx to cover a big residential fire because no one else had been available. Marv was my rabbi at the paper. He had hired and trained me. We were both veterans of the old regime—Marv for many years, I for only a few, but it had forged a bond between us. We both loved what Marv called "the New York hat trick of manly pursuits: newspapers, movies, and baseball." Marv was fifty-three, tall and angular, with a shaved head. The pressmen and drivers called him Kojak, but not to his face.

Night fires are a staple of television, so the story would be all over the eleven-o'clock news. We would have to find an angle that the television cameras missed. The thought of the Maharajah questioning the fire captain and survivors didn't fill me with optimism. It was almost ten-thirty when he called in his copy. He quoted a victim of the fire, one Calvin 16X Shabazz, saying, "Well, chaps, this conflagration is a nasty business but my family and I, we will persevere." I cut the quote, patched up the rest, and sent it through.

The next day when I told Marv about it, he said, "Last week I sent him out to cover that bank job with the hostages on Fordham Road. The cops nailed the guy and the Maharajah had him saying, 'I have been drinking too much alcohol and I regret the distress I have caused.'"

Now my eyes rolled. "What'd you do?"

"Same as you did last night. The poor bastard's in so far over his head he just makes up the quotes because he can't understand what anybody says. I'd fire his ass out of here, but I didn't hire him. It came from upstairs—all part of the Australian crawl. He'll get better. Forget it."

It was probably good advice, but I couldn't get those loony quotes out of my mind. The Maharajah's version of New York speech began to obsess me. As I look back on it, I think what got to me was that except for the unlikely diction, he would have gotten away with it. It wasn't a question of truth or ethics, but of skill. I began wondering whether reporting was anything more than finding someone to give voice to the reporter's own ideas. Risky thoughts for a man who traffics in facts.

At the time I was thinking them, I was going through a personal crisis. I was living with Beth, whom I honestly believed I loved. We looked like the perfect couple, everybody's favorite candidates for marriage. She was going to law school and we lived in her rent-controlled apartment (inherited from her mother) on Riverside Drive. No matter how promising our arrangements might have appeared, the truth was our life together had degenerated into a tense, sexless friendship. She was studying so hard that we agreed to put our emotional problems on hold until the end of the term. Somebody else might have just moved out; maybe I should have.

Under the new regime, the paper was always short of reporters and one of my regular tasks was to check the city edition of the *New York Times*. If they had a story we didn't, a frequent occurrence, I rewrote it and rammed it into the paper. This work should have been done by a junior reporter, but they took hours and I could knock it off in forty-five minutes. I just cut the *Times* piece, put some zip in the language, and that was that. The Maharajah's reportorial techniques were on my mind a lot (probably as a way of not thinking about my situation at home), when the absurdity of doing *Reader's Digest* versions of the *New York Times* came over me. I was rewriting a *Times* piece about designating a part of Staten Island a historic district. It was a four-graph story (twelve in the *Times*) and I included a fake quote from a nonexistent person: "Andrew McCarter, an enraged Staten Island property owner, said, 'You're going to make it impossible for anybody to remodel their house. I think it stinks.'"

Marv never questioned it. If he'd read to the end of the *Times* piece (admittedly quite a chore), he would have known there was no similar quote. He knew we hadn't covered the hearing. I took it as tacit approval; after that, the dam just burst. I began filing interviews that put words into mouths that had never opened. Reporters have been known to make up blind quotes. If a story says, "A prominent businessman close to the mayor . . ." and then the remark is a little too perfect, chances are the source is the reporter. That's a journalistic misdemeanor; I was trying to turn a newspaper into a forum for my imagination. It amused me when precious little else in my life did, but it put me on a collision course with the news business. Reporting was all I had ever done. I had always taken it seriously and been rewarded for my ability to do it. Maybe all the tabloid raucousness and general shoddiness of the paper were getting to me; but the very fact of reporting seemed absurd. What was the point of asking a cop what he thought about, say, closing the Music Hall or tearing down a brownstone? I knew full well he'd say, "It's the end of an era." It never failed. The cop always said it, I always wrote it down and the *Post* always printed it. All over the city people read it and muttered, "How true." At least that's what I imagined them doing. The thought of all those people saying "How true" kept bouncing around in my head. I kept hearing Claude Rains in *Casablanca* saying, "Round up the usual suspects."

I'd get my assignment in the morning—cover a speech by the mayor or interview a retired senator on his eighty-fifth birthday. I'd go through the motions of reading the appropriate clips and making a couple of calls to get additional background. Then I'd march out of the newsroom, notebook in hand, and go to the movies. I'd spend all day at the Variety Photo Plays near Fourteenth Street or going in and out of the theaters around Times Square. I'd turn up at the paper at five o'clock and write my story in time for the metro edition's seven-o'clock deadline. If it was a big story I'd read the wire-service copy; if it was local I might call a friend on another paper, or the press flack. It amazed me how quickly I could put a story together, whether I'd covered it or not. I didn't do that every day, but I did it a lot.

My ethical nadir, or my finest revolutionary hour—depending on how you look at it—came when I reported a story that never happened. My assignment had been to check with the police about an outbreak of purse-snatchings on West Forty-ninth Street. The police didn't know anything about it. That happened frequently. It might have been another precinct, or the reports might have been misfiled. Part of the job was to run it down and see if there was a story. I didn't bother. Instead, I wrote a three-graph piece that claimed two teenagers had knocked over a tourist from New Hampshire and stolen her bag, which had contained all her money, traveler's checks, and the only remaining photo of her dead pet dog. I quoted her as saying she still loved New York but now she wanted to go home. It ran in the first three editions but then got bumped to make space for a presumably actual murder on Amsterdam Avenue. When Marv asked me why the purse-snatching hadn't appeared in the *Times* or the *Daily News,* I said, "How should I know? The *Times* only covers out-of-town crimes and the *News* only cares who's winning the pennant." That sufficed for the moment.

When I was sitting in the movies, which was more and more of the time, I found myself playing around (in my head) with all the copy that goes into the *Post.* I imagined all the characters meeting one another and running together, taking on a new life of their own—so the guy who complained about the Staten Island Planning Commission (a guy I made up to begin with) turned up at the South Bronx fire. I was there too. When I asked Mr. Shabazz about losing his house, he said, "What a relief! That dump was full of cockroaches and I have insurance. I love starting over." Then the mayor heard him and said, "How true," and the killer-who-stalked-Brooklyn wandered by announcing baseball stats. I saw the New York *Post* as one gigantic imagined set of surreal connections—one story with continuing characters who leapt from column to column, checking up on one another. If this had been somebody else's imagination and I was writing a news story about it, I'd at least have suggested the possibility the guy was coming apart. Maybe I was, but I doubt it. I knew it was a fantasy and I enjoyed it. Even if I didn't think I was flipping out, I certainly knew I was taking big risks with my job. The daydreams were harmless enough, but not the chances I was taking the rest of the time. Did I want to get caught? Was I trying to get fired because I didn't have the courage to quit? Those questions bothered me; the hallucinations only amused me.

A friend had offered Beth and me his house in Essex, Connecticut, for a few days. Despite our problems, I knew if Beth could get away from her case books she could help me sort out what I'd been doing. I picked up a barbecued chicken and a few salads at Zabar's and walked home thinking about the weekend. Beth was twenty-nine—a late starter for law school. It made her self-conscious, so she worked harder than everyone else. She sometimes put in twelve hours when four would have been sufficient. It made her feel better but it wasn't always easy on us. I was looking forward to relaxing in the country and going for a walk out to the waterfall and along the Falls River. I'd tell her step by step what was happening—that at first it all felt like a lark. But it kept getting easier to do. I'd explain that I didn't like myself for doing what I knew was wrong, but even if it was awful and self-destructive, it was in the nature of an irresistible impulse. Beth would apply her logical mind to it and tell me what it all meant. I felt better just thinking about the weekend.

The apartment was one of the pleasures of our life together. New York real estate was such a grim business that six rent-controlled rooms in a solid prewar building was more valuable than a trust fund. It certainly was more comfortable than anything we could have afforded on the open market. As usual, books were stacked so high around Beth's desk, I couldn't see her. "Hello in there," I said, waving a chicken leg, knowing the aroma would entice her. She was wearing her usual work outfit of baggy shorts and one of my old blue oxford-cloth shirts. She allowed herself one cigarette an hour and all the Tab she wanted. As we devoured the chicken with our fingers, I asked, "Are you almost done with torts?"

"Yes. By tomorrow."

"I'll get off early. We can leave right after lunch."

"Where?"

"Connecticut. The weekend."

"I can't go to Connecticut," she said, surprised at the suggestion. "I have to do contracts."

"But you said you wanted to go. I've made the arrangements."

"I didn't say I could go. I said I'd *like* to. I still would, but I can't."

"You said very clearly, 'It'll be great to get away from these books.' It was on Monday when we had dinner at that Brazilian place on Seventy-ninth."

"No, I didn't. That's not accurate," she said, sounding like a lawyer.

"I have some experience in remembering what people say," I answered.

"Not what I say. I'm sorry. I think your imagination is running away with you."

Am I inventing Beth's quotes too? Why would she lie? Do I only hear what I want to hear? Or what I make up? It rattled me and made me wonder if I was less in control of myself than I thought. In the moment I realized that my hoped-for weekend was not going to take place, I also realized Beth was hiding behind those lawbooks because she too had qualms about our relationship. "It's okay," I said. "I'll say we can't use the house and thanks anyway."

"I'm sorry. Contracts is my hardest course."

"We'll do it another time."

Marv's antennae were very good; he was always on the lookout for treachery in the ranks. He knew something was wrong. He began bouncing my stories back with "What's the source?" scrawled across every blind quote. It hadn't yet occurred to him that entire stories might be bogus.

Finally, one evening after the second edition closed, Marv took me over to the China Bowl for a drink. The *Post* is downtown near the World Trade Center, not far from Wall Street. There are plenty of saloons but Marv was partial to the Bowl, which he always called the Nosh and Josh. It was actually a wretched Chinese restaurant, but as Marv pointed out to anyone who criticized the joint, "How tough do you think it is to pour Johnnie Walker?" Marv had been newspapering in New York for thirty years; he had been an editor for half of that. On his own time he was a closet intellectual. He was divorced, his kids were in college, which left him a lot of time to hang out at Carnegie Hall and read contemporary poetry. When Marv said, "I want to talk to you, let's go for a drink," it meant you were in hot water but there was hope. If he said, "We have some things to discuss, let's have lunch," it meant you were about to be either fired or promoted.

When we were sitting at the bar he started things off by asking had I seen any good movies. A twinge of fear jumped through me. But then I thought: He's got a hunch or he's heard a rumor and he's fishing. Reporters do that all the time. I nodded and mentioned a couple of films.

Marv sipped a little more Scotch and then slid into a discussion of how easy it was to burn out. "A reporter deals in other people's calamities. Everything's an emergency, so pretty soon nothing really matters—events pile up so fast, your mind can get cooked."

"I know that's right, Marv—derailment's a danger in the news business." I was trying to stay calm and relaxed, as if we were chatting theoretically.

"If you're losing interest in fact and developing a taste for the creative arts, maybe you ought to consider committing a novel or giving Hollywood a shot. Around here we exploit scandals. We try not to create them. How old are you? Twenty-nine? Thirty?"

"I'm thirty-two, Marv. And you know it."

"Don't worry. You'll still be young for another hour and a half."

"Is this a warning, Marv?" I tried to ask the question with a smile, but I was scared. "Warning" was a union term. The paper couldn't fire you without a prior warning and a memo to the shop steward.

"I want you to be a reporter full-tilt or not at all," he said, skipping over my question. "Don't confuse hard news with your imagination. It's not a warning. Yet."

That much was a relief. He must have seen how tense I was, because he relaxed a bit and dropped the prosecuting-attorney tone.

"Look," he said, calling for more Johnnie Walker. "I'm not your confessor. I'm your boss and your friend—not always compatible roles. I know what you've been doing—probably not all of it, but more than you think. I know you well enough to know you're going through hell over this—partly because what you're doing is wrong, but also because you don't feel guiltier than you do. You'd feel better if you were suffering over questions of integrity and honor."

"Probably true," I said, amazed at his ability to read my thoughts more readily than I could do it myself.

"You were on the *Post* when we were a real newspaper," he said, remembering the paper's glory days. "People trusted this paper; it was a necessity. We were liberals when that was a term of honor. The columnists were like relatives who made sense of the world. But that was when this was still a magic city, not a drug depot for junkies on a rampage or millionaires looking for restaurants."

"Say anything you want about me, Marv," I said, smiling, "but don't bad-mouth Nueva York."

"You know what you're guilty of?"

My face flushed red and I felt light-headed as a sense of what I had been doing came over me. "Letting you down, compromising the paper, shooting holes in my foot." I hadn't intended to confess to anything, but I guess Marv's saying I felt bad about not feeling worse made me want to come clean. I probably would have gone on to confess to being the night-killer-who-stalked-you-know-where, but Marv laughed at my earnestness and cut me off.

"No. That's not it. Not at all. Aside from wanting to create a little fiction, what you're guilty of is thumbing your nose at how pathetic this paper has become. You're not going to get any medals for it," he said, leaning in close. "But you can put your thumb to your schnoz a few times for me while you're at it." Then he lifted his glass in a toast. "To newspapers, the movies, fact, and fiction—may they all flourish. Separately." He drank and began to laugh. When I got my bearings, I laughed with him until the two of us were giggling at the absurdity of the whole thing.

"Thanks, Marv," I managed to say. Once again, he had explained myself to me. It was the first time I was comfortable talking about the paper since the day I made up the first quote.

"On the other hand," he said, with a touch of his prosecutor's voice returning, "however much I might appreciate the poetry of it, that doesn't mean I approve. In New York, if you muck around with facts you'll wind up in newspaper-jail. Do it in Hollywood, they'll probably throw money at you for it."

As Marv was praising me instead of putting me in leg irons, I remembered one of his theories about Los Angeles (every New York journalist had theories about California; at least Marv's were amusing). In this very Nosh and Josh he had once claimed that the true cost of living in Southern California was four IQ points per year. "Think about it," he had said. "You go out there weighing in at maybe one-twenty, which is high for a lot of these would-be sun bunnies, and you stay five years. You won't be able to find the airport to get back, even if you want to." At the time I had laughed. "All I know about the movies is how to go to them," I said, feeling better than I had in quite a while.

"Make it up," he said, sounding exasperated. "Say you're a screenwriter and you are. You think you need a license? Go out there and invent yourself. File free-lance at first. Interview the door-to-door phrenologists or the holistic lox slicers. Don't pipe anything," he said, meaning don't make up the quotes. "You're a reporter. While you're making your Hollywood bundle, take notes. When you've got a fix on the place, write about the daily life of the movie business." As Marv outlined his marching orders for me, waving his cigar and scattering ash, I couldn't help thinking he was recalling a plan he might have once had for himself. "Start with fact," he said, chewing the word. "Then add whatever you need to make it more revealing. It'll use your journalistic skills and put your piping impulse to better use. You might even get at some skinny version of the truth. If you do, send me a copy."

When I first started working for Marv I thought the world had lost a great shrink when he became a reporter. Not only did my poor hole-blasted integrity not feel quite so damaged, but the hard-nosed clarity of his thought helped me see my situation as a turning point, not a disaster area. Marv might be trying to manipulate me into quitting, but was that so bad? The real question in my mind was not should I get out of the news business—hell, I was already out of it—but did I have the guts to pack up and start over somewhere else? I had my share of Hollywood fantasies. That's mainstream for my generation, which holds that movies are the last romantic profession. But I'd never seriously considered doing anything about it. Hollywood always seemed like something other people did.

"Think about it," he said. "You can write to order, on demand. You're essentially a serious man, but you've got a silly streak in you. You know how the world works and you're ready to change with new circumstances. There's some agent on Forty-fourth Street who specializes in turning overworked, underpaid New York reporters into underworked, overpaid Hollywood screenwriters. I'll get you the name."

"Maybe. At the rate I'm going, I could finish off this paper before the end of the year."

He nodded and said I probably had a point, then hitched up his pants, brushed a little cigar ash from his jacket, and said, "Here's my other theory about California: threading that particular needle, which is to say, going West to try your luck, is the American walk. You go in a seven-forty-seven instead of a Conestoga wagon, but it's the same damn thing. If you hit, you can make a shitload of money. If you don't, you can still get a suntan."

I laughed and Marv ordered another round of Johnnie Walker. I hadn't known it before we sat down at the bar; maybe Marv had known it all along, but by the time my second Scotch was finished, I had decided to take the stroll.

Family Ties

When I first got to California I lived in the Chateau Marmont, a vast, clunky Norman pile of a hotel on Sunset Boulevard. The Chateau was cheap and easygoing, with airy rooms and a bohemian clientele. Some of the residents were semipermanent but most were transient—the working folk of the movie world, here for a few weeks to do revisions on a script or shoot a television pilot. I thought of the Chateau as a sort of halfway house while I tried to decide just how permanent my sojourn would be. I wasn't alone in my indecision. An actor who lived down the hall never bought more than two bottles of beer at a time, in case his agent called and he got to go home. When I realized I was in danger of developing a similar world view, I resolved to get out and find out where I was. At about that time a bit of good fortune came my way. A friend had been called back to New York by a show-biz combine that wanted him to produce a soap opera. "From what?" I asked.

"From the dust of the earth and one of my ribs," he answered.

I was feeling too unsettled and uncertain to question anyone's motives for doing anything. That my friend, a graduate of Harvard and of film school, a man of some wit and sensitivity, should be chasing a soap opera was not at issue. What he was leaving, he was leaving to me: a topless, slightly battered, bright red 1959 Porsche Speedster. It looked like a red vitamin pill, and even in Los Angeles, practically a shrine to German cars, it attracted admiring stares. I felt great in it. The car made me want to drive, and the more I drove, the more I came to know my surroundings and the more I felt as if I lived here. I drew strength from my little vitamin pill and I wandered on long exploratory expeditions. It rode low, hugging the road, and I felt as if I were sitting directly on the wheels. I could feel every bump and jolt in the highway. I frequently got reckless, weaving in and out of traffic, getting high on the vitamin pill's instant response to my foot on the pedal and my hand on the wheel. I pushed that car harder than I pushed myself. It was as if I'd come here to California, to the edge of the earth, and was daring God to throw me off, down to where only dragons thrive. I drove north to Ojai and south into Mexico on the coast road, and east, into the desert past Palm Springs, kicking up so much sand and dust that I could not see the road and I found myself speeding into the unknown. I dubbed the car El Vitamino and I spent hours in it, in a vaguely therapeutic trance. Except for the color, my little car was similar to the one that killed James Dean. I enjoyed the romance of the connection but mostly I enjoyed the speed. My new mobility helped me to see the place I found myself in with a greater clarity, but even so, much of what I saw and heard seemed to be in an elusive local idiom that I couldn't always translate.

I had assumed covering New York city politics would be adequate preparation for a world of easy money, hard people, and general all-around venality. But New York is only the powerhouse of the world; this was the movies, complex, stratified, and steeped in a moral inexplicability. To understand what was around me, to gain a sense of it, I had to interpret what I saw and imagine what couldn't be seen. In that way my Hollywood education took shape: part heard, part lived, and part invented. The men and women I met and came to know were my teachers and guides. Some led spectacular lives and I met them in glamorous circumstances. Others were struggling to make car and mortgage payments and might have been living in any suburb, working at any job.

I met Sheila Hill because an agent introduced us in the hope we might do business together. I was drawn to Sheila's intensity and her energy. But because I had split with Beth so recently, I wasn't much good at dating, which I think relieved Sheila. We became friends, not lovers. I heard her story in little pieces, over several years—part of it when we first met, the rest later, when I was more established myself and working at her studio.

Ken Becko had hired Sheila to be a production executive at the studio and for a while she was his protégée. He had to know where she was all the time, who she was having lunch with, and what she thought of every script that came across his desk. Sheila wasn't sure why it had turned sour. Maybe Becko had wanted her to fall in love with him so he could have the pleasure of saying no. It made sense: he was the head of a studio, and saying no is what studio heads do best and most often. Whatever the reason, Becko, who had once been so solicitous of Sheila, was hard on her now, cool and distant, and her future at the studio seemed shaky.

Sheila's life and career seemed so unsettled to her that for anyone to be jealous of her, let alone the president of the studio, seemed ludicrous. But Sheila had one thing Ken Becko didn't have, and she couldn't share it with him. Sheila is the third generation in her family to work in the movie business, and to Ken Becko, whose father was born in a shtetel in a part of Eastern Europe that has vanished from the earth, Sheila's family seemed like royalty, her life charmed.

Benjamin Hill Sr., Sheila's grandfather, was one of the titans of Hollywood's glory years, a producer who once accumulated Oscars, mistresses, and money the way less-driven men might raise dogs or grow vegetables. He's eighty-three now and although his mind is still penetrating and his wit cutting, he's confined to a wheelchair. An electronic larynx has replaced the silky voice that once ruled Hollywood. The body lost out to a stroke, the throat to cancer, probably a result of the Montecristos he could never resist. It can't be easy to be such a man's son. Sheila's father, Ben Jr., is also a producer, but his productions are mostly television pilots for series that don't get on the air. He's an alcoholic and a man whose only pleasure seems to be irritating his current wife. For Sheila to take her place willingly in that generational parade was not a casual decision. Of course there were professional advantages to being a Hill, but if she didn't do better with the hand she had been dealt than her father had done with his, she knew there would be no mercy for her in Hollywood.

That Ken Becko was jealous seemed unlikely to Sheila, but there could be nothing else. Money, sex, and power were Becko's trinity and he hadn't wanted sex and he already had more money than she did. It had to be his belief that she had a free ride, that she could be powerful without working at it, without manipulating the world. Sheila knew full well she didn't get her job wholly on merit. Becko had hired her precisely because he wanted to use her family's name and connections. Sheila never pretended otherwise. She only had to look around her at all the second-generation also-rans spending their middle age chasing parental shadows, to know that if she was going to trade on her name it had to be while she was young. Her own father was a vivid example and thoughts of him were never far from her mind. Sheila tried to love him and understand him, but Ben Jr., so dark and bitter about his own father and his career, so distant and opaque, never made it easy.

Sheila dreaded Monday mornings, which was when something called the Creative Group met in Becko's office to discuss new projects. Unlike the full staff meetings, which were too large for anything to get done, the smaller meetings were only for Becko and his four production executives, a collegial group supposedly anxious to give one another the benefit of their opinions. Sheila didn't mind the give-and-take, the pledging and refusing of support. It was the time she resented. Monday morning was when she needed to be on the phone, because weekends in Hollywood are spent reading scripts. Sheila wanted to get to the agents, actors, and directors as soon as possible.

As Sheila approached Becko's office, the small talk that preceded these meetings drifted into the corridor. Becko was saying, "I've ordered a couple of the Corbusier sofas from Al in New York. Classic Corbu lines are what the room needs. I'm getting the buttery brown leather." Sheila believed Becko cared more for his office than anything except hit movies. When he was made president, he had knocked down the walls of the adjacent offices to make a gigantic room for himself. He was always apologizing for the furniture, explaining it was only temporary and he was in the process of remodeling. He spent a lot of time studying floor plans and conferring with decorators. When studio executives get promoted or change jobs, they always remodel their offices. It's a good way to show power quickly. But Becko had been in his job for several years and he was still moving the furniture around and buying expensive sofas. Sheila knew it was his neurotic need to fuss and adjust things, endlessly trying to control them—scripts, movies, furniture, or his staff. Becko was forty and he wore beautifully cut Italian suits. There was always a sharp crease in his pants and usually a silk square in the jacket pocket. It should have been perfect, and it wasn't bad, but if you looked at Ken Becko as often as Sheila did, his wardrobe often felt contrived and self-conscious. His power as an executive came largely from his having been the champion of several unexpected hits. Becko had said yes to *American Made,* a cop movie that every other studio had passed on. It grossed eighty-five million dollars and won two Oscars. That was the biggest one, but there had been several others, and no matter what else Sheila thought of him, she knew better than to underestimate the man. He seemed to work all day and all night. It reminded Sheila of grade school, when she assumed her teachers lived at the school, because they were there when she arrived and there when she left. She composed herself, put a smile in place, and walked into his office.

In these meetings, Becko stayed behind his desk while Sheila and her colleagues sat drinking coffee, hoping they wouldn't spill any on the sofas. A woman who had once been a court stenographer kept track of the wisdom. Becko began the meeting announcing he wanted to buy *Days Without Nights,* a dog-eared romance that was in turnaround at Fox. The story department had liked it, and the producer was a pal of Becko's named Hugh Held. There was no other important element in the package, which was unusual, since Becko usually wanted to know everything but the names of the ushers before he'd spend money. But no one was about to argue with the boss before they made their own pitches. So Hugh Held and *Days Without Nights* went on the studio's active-project status list and Becko turned to Sheila.

Sheila was pushing a novel called *Roll Away,* about the return of a kidnapped child. A sweet little boy had been stolen from his parents and abused and twisted about for two years. Then he was returned home. And that's when the real trouble began. The difficulties he and his family had adjusting to one another after what had happened were the heart of the book. It was a first novel, still in manuscript, which meant it could be optioned for very little money. Sheila had lined up Leo Sattler, an established screenwriter, to write the script and now needed permission to make both deals. Sattler was expensive, but Becko had once been his agent and liked his work. She'd given the book to Sattler's agent at William Morris with the understanding that if Leo said yes, the studio would meet his price, which was one-hundred and twenty-five thousand. All the pieces were in place, assuming Becko would go for it. If he didn't, then Sheila would be in the position of having made a promise to the Morris office that she couldn't deliver. She didn't even want to think about what particular pound of flesh they would exact if she had to renege. On Friday Sheila had circulated the story department's coverage of the novel so it could be discussed today. God knows if any of them had bothered to look at it, but it was her choice of Sattler that turned out to be the problem.

"He's so discursive," Malcolm Bockstein said. "The book is already too Proustian, if you ask me. Don't you think an action-oriented writer would be more appropriate?"

"Proustian? Oh, come on, Malcolm. Nobody wants to make a long dull movie in which nothing happens," Sheila answered, regretting it instantly. Bockstein prided himself on his taste and sense of literature. He was hauling out Proust not because he cared if *Roll Away* was Proustian or not, but to remind everybody that he was so well-read. He pushed the same crap as everyone else, but he wanted his colleagues to recognize that his own sensibility was far more elevated. The game was to humor him, not argue meaningless literary distinctions. "Of course Leo's script will be more action-oriented than the novel," she said in a conciliatory voice. "That's why we're hiring him. I don't want to shoot the novel. I want the central situation—a story about a family torn apart by outside circumstances. I mean, the kid is walking down the street one day, and then boom, everybody's life is changed forever."

"Pu-leeze," from Billy Andrews, the studios trash-and-flash expert. "We all know 'stolen child' is a euphemism for some faggot kidnapped the kid and turned him into a little queen. Gay people will resent it and all the breeders out there won't get it anyway." So Billy boy was lining up with Bockstein. God knows what that's about, Sheila thought.

"Don't fight, dears," Becko said, smiling. "At least not on company time."

"Right," Sheila said. "Leo used to be your client, Kenny. You know what he can do."

"He's a lovely guy, but he can be long-winded. Let me take another look at the coverage on the book," Becko said, trying to get rid of the problem.

"Kenny, I'm dealing with the Morris office here. I need a yes right now or I'm going to lose Leo. Paramount wants him for a rewrite and if we don't move, he's gone. He wants to do it but he won't wait."

"I don't make our decisions based on Paramount's schedule or pressure from William Morris," Becko said icily. "I'll look over the material and let you know."

Sheila suffered in silence, knowing that he'd never look at the coverage, and she'd have to hold the Morris office off one way or another till she could think of a way to ram it past Becko.

Bockstein began going on about a pitch he had heard. It was yet another teenage romance. This one was in outer space, or maybe it was just in the future. One of Sheila's secrets was that science fiction put her to sleep. There was always somebody saving the universe from a fate worse than the loss of the universe. Except for the kid angle this one didn't seem one bit different from all the other science fiction Bockstein pushed. Bockstein presented the teenagers-in-space story like a legal brief, no detail too small or too tedious. Sheila didn't give a damn if the studio put it in development or not, but it would be too transparent if she was the first one to attack it. That fell to Marty Coslowe, the studio's resident lefty. Coslowe was supposedly a big radical in the late sixties. Sheila always suspected he had spent the sixties drinking beer in some fraternity house and then bribed somebody to fake an FBI file on him. In the seventies Coslowe had gained fifty pounds and gotten into the movie business. He could be counted on to find political messages in everything. At least in public. In private he was as hungry and lowbrow as the rest of them, looking for star vehicles and pimply teenage farces.

"What's a thing like that really about?" Marty asked rhetorically. "Escape. Right? But they're escaping to nothing. There's no third act unless they're going someplace they at least think is better than Earth. I think it's unfinished."

As Becko listened to the debate he pursed his lips and made involuntary sucking noises as if he was trying to pull every idea in the air to himself. He did it all the time and to Sheila it always sounded as if he was saying "gimme, gimme, gimme."

Bockstein suffered his anger in silence as he prepared a judicious response. Sheila saw her opportunity for revenge and moved fast. "It has some potential," she said. "The concept is clear, the sides are drawn." Becko looked at her, knowing full well she wasn't about to praise anything Bockstein was promoting, at least not today. "The problem is it sounds like a segment of *Star Trek.*" Sheila had never been able to watch an entire episode of *Star Trek,* but she knew Becko was always afraid of trying to sell a story you could see for free on television. "I mean, you can practically see Shatner getting the *Enterprise* ready to go find the kids. 'It's our duty, Mr. Spock. Meet me on the bridge,'" she said, imitating the show and making everyone but Bockstein laugh.

"Only if it's done badly," Becko said. "That it evokes *Star Trek* is one of its virtues. The story has legitimate room for special effects, and the clarity of the central situation gives it a mythic simplicity. It will appeal to ticket buyers if not to movie executives," he said, looking at Sheila. "I think it has potential. How much will a step deal cost?"

"Seventy-five for a draft and set of changes," Bockstein said, smelling victory.

"Who's the writer?" Becko asked.

Sheila couldn't believe it. He was going to go for it. Becko didn't think it was a good idea. The only thing he ever truly thought was a good idea was Clint Eastwood in something with thirty million in overseas advance guarantees. No, Becko was going for this to send her a message. But she couldn't deny that Becko's analysis was right. The bastard, she thought. He's doing his penetrating-critic show to irritate me, not because he believes it or even remotely cares about it. The man is all technique, she thought, and not one bit of real feeling. The writer Bockstein was pushing was Barbara Ellis, a sitcom writer who probably couldn't even read a 120-page script, let alone write one. It had to mean Bockstein was sleeping with her. *Plus ça change*, as Bockstein would probably say. Sheila glanced at her watch hoping this thing wouldn't go past noon, so she could make her phone calls before everybody left for lunch.

When she got back to her office her secretary had already gone, so Sheila kicked off her shoes and plunged into a container of yogurt and a script. Sheila had learned to read a script in less than an hour. She skimmed the directions, ignored any references to the camera, and concentrated on the dialogue. Hundreds of badly written, illogically conceived scripts had taught her to read fast. If the thing didn't grab her right away, she figured it wouldn't grab an audience either, and she discarded it. If there was coverage from the story department, she used it to keep track of the plot. When Sheila first got this job, she had hoped every script would be good. Now she was relieved when they were bad, because she didn't have to worry about saying no. At first she had lingered over all but the worst ones, looking for some seed of buried talent, some hint of a vision. But two years of internal studio politics had eroded that sense of hope. The hardest scripts were the ones that were pretty good but not great. If she passed, someone else might say yes; then if it was a hit, Sheila would look incompetent. Some of the scripts had bright covers and crisply printed pages that all but smelled of someone's hope and ambition. Others with torn pages and coffee stains looked as if the creators had already given up and probably had already been read by most of Sheila's friends and enemies. Now she often found herself thinking: Well, it's good but Becko won't like it, or even if he does go for it, how do I keep it from being taken away from me and assigned to someone else? Sheila hated the cynicism she knew was growing in her and she fought against it by trying to look at every script as if nothing but the story and the characters mattered. It wasn't easy. When the yogurt was gone and she was working on a Tab and a cigarette, Grace from Business Affairs knocked on the open door.

"Sorry to bother you, Sheila. I brought you the memos on *Roll Away.*"

"Thanks, Grace. How's Jason?" Grace's twelve-year-old son had been in the hospital with a double hernia, unusual in one so young. Jason's misfortune had been the occasion of one of Becko's few effective jokes. In a full staff meeting, he said: "Grace, I always knew you were a ball-buster, but this is ridiculous." Even Sheila laughed.

"He's coming home tomorrow. We're pretty excited." Grace couldn't be more than five years older than Sheila. A twelve-year-old, Sheila thought. Plus a little girl and a hardworking husband. Sheila sometimes mused about Grace's situation. Her job was to keep track of all the contracts and deal memoranda that went in and out of the studio. Grace always seemed astonished to have such a responsibility, as if she never expected to be in charge of anything more complex than a car pool. There didn't seem to be any question of greater professional ambition and Grace seemed untouched by feminism. Grace had introduced her husband to Sheila once. "Pleased to meet you," he had said, as if he had been rehearsing the words for days. But he was strong-looking and solid. He had something to do with furnaces. Whenever Sheila found herself idealizing Grace's domestic life, she remembered that Grace was always tense, almost brittle, as if one more contract would shatter her. When Sheila wondered if she would ever know the pleasures of sweet domesticity, she reminded herself that a good man and children didn't seem to be nearly enough to make Grace happy.

After she finished the script, Sheila opened the interoffice envelope to look at the *Roll Away* memos. Except that Grace in her rattled state had given her the wrong documents. Sheila had the deal memo for *Days Without Nights,* the project Becko was so high on. Deal memos aren't secret. Any executive can look at them, but they're so dry people rarely bother. If they want a specific fact, they ask Grace to look it up. In movie studios people are usually too busy to be curious about anything that doesn't concern the crisis of the moment. But Becko was so much on her mind, Sheila paused to have a look. The script Becko liked had been owned at one time by Paramount as well as Fox. Between the two studios, seven hundred thousand dollars had been spent. The figures, surely inflated, made Sheila laugh. Paramount was claiming the project had cost them four hundred thousand. And they wanted every penny of it back right now before they'd release the script. They'd probably settle for fifty grand out of net profits. Eight different screenwriters had taken a whack at the thing over the last five years. "Jesus," Sheila muttered aloud, thinking that the first draft was probably the best of the bunch. Becko's chum Hugh Held was down for a quarter-million-dollar producer's fee and fifteen points. Sheila stared at the document for a moment. It was couched in the usual blah-blah-blah of accountant's babble. But it clearly said "fees" and "points." "And?" she said aloud to no one but her can of Tab. Quite a deal. As she read further, she saw that Held's points were tied to the gross and that his profits cut in so early that Mr. Hugh Held would be earning money—in addition to his quarter-million-dollar fee—before the studio ever recouped its investment.

She put her shoes back on, and enclosing the Held memo in some other papers, ambled down the hall to the Xerox room. She was glad her secretary was at lunch. This was one to handle personally.

While she was figuring out the machine, a lost, slightly stoned Chicano messenger wandered in. "Hey, pretty lady, where they got the story department?"

"What?" Sheila snapped at him, regretting her tone as soon as the word was in the air. The kid was culturally and intellectually incapable of realizing that calling her "pretty lady" was not the way to win her heart. She told him how to find the story department and he smiled what he probably thought was a sexy smile and left. Calm down, she thought to herself. I'm a woman at the Xerox machine. What's he supposed to think? She gave the original of the Held memo to Grace's secretary and exchanged it for the right one.

The house on Summit Drive in Beverly Hills, not far from Pickfair, was built by her grandfather in the mid-thirties. It's now presided over by Sheila's father and Laura, his third wife. They gave dinner parties that always sounded better than they turned out to be. The menu was invariably fish or veal. Ben Jr. just drank Scotch all evening, but everyone else was given first-rate Napa Valley chardonnay, whether they wanted it or not. For a while, right after she had married Sheila's father, Laura gave advice to her guests about cholesterol and eating healthy food. Mercifully, the lectures stopped when Laura acquired new enthusiasms, but the no-red-meat regimen continued. Laura kept index cards on what dishes she had served to which guests, lest somebody be given baby salmon and endive salad twice in the same lifetime. Laura never quite understood that the food was not the reason her dinner invitations were sought.

Sheila drove through the gates a little past eight. She sped up the long curving drive, past the fountains, and toward the vast Spanish house with its graceful arches and tiled walkways. "Oh God, I hope we're not too late," she said to Ross, her date. "I really don't want to hear about how I never get here on time."

"My dear," Ross said, looking at the house, once celebrated in books and magazines as one of the most lavish in Hollywood, "I think we're about thirty years late for the primo squad." Sheila always laughed at Ross's gay patois. She could follow about half of it, but she usually got the general idea. "I don't know why you put yourself through the Becko-blender," he said, waving to a stray Mexican houseboy. "You are born to shop."

"Easy, Ross," she said, smiling. "We don't have all that much. We used to. But not now."

"Then get it on credit. I mean, ultra-gold-card." Ross was the ideal date for these dinners. She could ignore him and he'd be fine, or she could play like they were a couple and he'd hardly notice. He was an agent and he could discuss any issue that was likely to come up; as a semi-in-the-closet gay, Sheila knew that on Summit Drive, at least, he wouldn't act effeminate and he wouldn't make a pass at her. She called him her no-fuss, no-muss escort.

This was to be a small dinner, so drinks were in the library, in the shadow of the portraits of Ben Sr. and Sheila's grandmother Ida, who died while Sheila was away for an unhappy year at the

Ethel Walker School in Connecticut. The first sign Sheila had shown that she might succeed in the family business was the way she used her grandmother's death to change schools. Sheila was genuinely upset at the loss, but she cranked up more tears than she actually felt and told her parents that if she had been at home she could have spent time with her grandmother. And now she'd never be able to do that. The next term they enrolled her in the Westlake School in Holmby Hills; Sheila never went to boarding school again.

The portraits were done in 1939, when Hollywood and Ben Hill were both at their absolute peak. He and Ida were young and wonderfully beautiful. They were just sitting there in the paintings, which had been done by Russell Patterson, but Sheila had always imagined her grandparents as having just come in from the polo field at Will Rogers State Park in their Hispano-Suiza. A few years ago when the Los Angeles County Museum was thinking about mounting a show of Patterson's Hollywood portraits, Ben was asked if he'd lend the paintings. He refused to consider it; without them the museum felt they had no show. The idea was scrapped.

Sheila knew more about her grandfather from reading about him than she ever learned from being with him, a condition she always assumed was normal until she was in high school. In addition to producing his signature films, which were elegant, glossy drawing-room comedies, he had done a series of cheap but lucrative westerns at Republic Pictures and several big-budget musicals at MGM. When he was young he had been notorious for the actresses he pursued and kept. One book Sheila had read while she was in junior high school claimed Ben kept several young women in adjacent rooms at the Beverly Wilshire Hotel, and then each evening worked his way down the hall. But when his wife died, he surprised everyone and just dropped them all. He withdrew into his house and when his health began to fail, he lost interest in an active part in the movie business. Although he never said it, his son was surely his greatest disappointment and his granddaughter his greatest hope.

Sheila kissed her father hello and saw he already looked a little drunk. Laura came fluttering in, doing what Sheila always thought of as a Loretta Young imitation. Sheila introduced Ross and extricated herself to say hello to Gilbert Rollins and his wife. Rollins was a novelist and journalist who was doing a piece about the Hills for *Esquire*. Sheila had canceled several dates with him, and asking Laura to invite him to dinner was her way of letting him know she wasn't opposed to the story. Sheila could see Rollins' eyes darting around the room, trying to absorb everything, doing an inventory of the paintings, and inspecting the damn furniture, a lot of which had been there since Sheila's childhood.

"You can take notes if you want, Gil," she said. "We're used to writers in this house."

"I can keep my notebook in my pocket during dinner. But this room is revealing. In the new Hollywood there are always bound scripts and movie posters in every room. There's not one bit of movie memorabilia here."

Great, Sheila thought, we're old-money because we haven't had a picture worth fussing over in ten years. But instead she said, "I suppose that's right, Gil. I see why you're the writer. Have you met everybody?"

"I have. My wife and I came early and I had a talk with your father. I appreciate your help, Sheila." As she was considering what kind of story would come out of an interview with her father, Ben Sr. was rolled in, which meant dinner could start.

Jackie Weller was Ben Sr.'s contemporary. He had retired twelve years ago and no matter how hard people tried to persuade him to come back, he stayed retired. Sheila couldn't imagine Weller dragging himself before the cameras like Cagney or some of the others who kept coming back for more when common sense should have told them they'd had enough. But that wasn't about to stop Ross from trying. Sheila could see him eyeing Weller, looking for an opportunity. Ross was seated next to Laura and she was speaking intimately to him. Laura always flirted with Sheila's dates, gay or straight. Tonight she was going on about God. Laura had her little enthusiasms, but religion wasn't usually one of them. Maybe she'd been born again since Tuesday, when Sheila had last seen her.

"At first I didn't take it seriously," Laura was saying to Ross, who was listening politely. "But then I heard what these ministers were saying. They're always on the cable. This one was saying, 'If you could have God with you all the time, around the clock, why wouldn't you want it?' Then I thought, if I want it, I can have it. That's one of the best things about God." Ross nodded as if he was going to give that a lot of thought, and when Laura poked her Buccellati fork at the chanterelle mushrooms on her plate, Ross locked his eyes on Jackie's and began his pitch. Sheila knew Ross didn't have a script in mind, but if Jackie would give him the tiniest sign, Ross could conjure it into an enormous series of deals.

"If you would go back to work," he said without a hint of gay jargon, "it would be an inspiration to senior citizens everywhere. Plus I can get you gross points from box-office dollar one. You would have approval of everything—script, director, final cut."

Weller listened and then in the international accent that once was East End London and for a while in the fifties was imitated by every man who spoke English and wanted to sound elegant, said, "Dear of you to offer, and if I change my mind you'll hear. But I'm retired. Right, Ben?"

Ben Sr. adjusted his electronic larynx and growled, "Who the hell would give gross points from box-office dollar one? For anybody. Including an old war-horse like this?"

Despite the lack of encouragement, Ross pushed on. "Mr. Hill," he said, "if your participation would be an inducement to Mr. Weller, and if it pleases you, perhaps you'd be executive producer."

"Oh, hell. I can't even look at pictures anymore, let alone make the damn things."

That caused Ben Jr. to lift his glass and propose a toast. "To my father," he said, his voice a little slurred, "and his view of moviemaking, an occupation written on water. Perrier, to be precise." Laura laughed at her husband's toast a little louder than she intended and in a voice more shrill than she knew. Sheila had once seen her stepmother sitting alone in a rocking chair in a bay window looking out over the grounds. As Sheila approached, she saw it wasn't the chair that was rocking, it was Laura. She was crying. Sheila could only guess at what slight, what drunken rudeness from Ben Jr., or what private ghost had caused the tears. Laura's in such pain all the time, Sheila had thought, wondering if everybody winds up sitting in the window and crying.

After the toast, as the guests began to eat again, Ben Sr. turned to Sheila. "Come with me," he growled, rolling his chair away from the table. Sheila excused herself and followed her grandfather out onto the patio.

Ben rolled his chair to the cabana at the far end of the pool. Sheila rejected the chaise he pushed toward her and instead sat at his feet by the edge of the pool, the way she often had done when they were both younger. In the cool evening air, they could smell the jasmine and bougainvillea and watch the lights from the house reflect off the water. For a moment Sheila was content to just sit with her grandfather, looking at his gray herringbone jacket. It was cut for him in London at Anderson & Sheppard when she was a little girl and it still smelled of cigars, even though he hadn't smoked one in fifteen years. Ben fiddled with his larynx again and asked, "What is it?"

"What do you mean?"

"You've been trying to catch my eye. Now you've got it." Sheila showed him the copy of the deal memo. He looked it over, snickering at the size of the fees. "Well, once again it pays to be the boss's friend. Who's Hugh Held?"

"The boss's friend, all right. Look at the fee and the points."

"This thing's a mine field," Ben muttered as he skimmed the document. "Big fee, big piece of pre–break even gross. Becko ever give that before?"

"Not to Hugh Held. Not for marginal material that's got so many tracks on it."

"Who else knows?"

"That's the thing. I don't think anybody. I only saw it by accident. Becko sort of brought it up in a meeting, but nobody exactly grilled him about the costs. He made the deal and filed the memo. Who's going to check his memos? He's the president."

"President means nothing. They've debased those titles so much that anything less than vice-president sounds like a clerk. What about Harry Geller? Or Bill What's-his-name? They're his superiors. Where are they?"

"In New York. It's pretty clear what's going on here."

"How much you think he's kicking back?"

"Fifty grand. Seventy-five. Maybe more. Who knows?"

"He's a fool."

"Becko's not stupid. It seems like a big chance for not much money. Could I be reading it wrong?"

"No. You're not," he said with a finality that did not invite discussion. At eighty-three, there were very few surprises about human nature and the movie business left for Ben Sr. "You can't be certain its money he's getting, but he's getting something."

"I need to be sure," she said, allowing her grandfather a glimpse of the terror she felt at even the possibility of misjudging what Becko had done.

"I'm sure," he said, managing to suggest that his certainty would be sufficient for them both. "Nobody does this only once. The question is, what do you need from him?"

Sheila thought about that for a moment. "It's tough. He's very hard on me on all kinds of stupid things. I have trouble getting routine things through. It uses me up."

"Think bigger."

"I want green lights on a couple of projects. It's what I'm supposed to be doing. Getting pictures made. I've got three scripts now, better than what he's making. He stops things because they're mine," she said, her pent-up anger and discontent pouring out. "The agents are going to get wind of it, and I'll be isolated."

"It doesn't matter if your scripts are good. The machinery of a studio is set up to perpetuate itself. Occasionally a movie slips through on merit. But not often."

Her grandfather's ability to formulate and give a voice to her own inchoate thoughts always comforted her. If it was so, and no one who had ever been around a studio would doubt it, then why bother? she thought. Why not go into the wide world and feed the hungry or join the Peace Corps and bring movie deals to the disadvantaged? Instead she said, "How do I play it?" letting what was left of her innocence fall at her grandfather's feet.

"You have to be subtle. Ask him about this picture," he said, tapping on the deal memo as if it were the film itself. "Hint that you know a bit about it. And about his friend Mr. Held. Drift back to the money a few times. He'll get the idea. Make it clear that you're on his side in this. That sometimes you have to stretch the rules to make things happen. Some crap like that. Then mention that Harry Geller's coming here for dinner."

"Is he?"

"Why not? Find out when he's going to be out here and I'll invite him. It'll remind Mr. Becko you have access to his boss."

"He already resents the family. He thinks I've got a free ride."

"If he already resents it, all the more reason to use it. You think he'll resent it less if you don't?"

"I don't know what he'll do," she said. "Because I don't know what he wants."

"You think *he* knows?" Ben said, his voice tinged with contempt. Ben's ability to subtly shade the electronic growls that were his voice always surprised Sheila. He can turn absolutely anything to his advantage, she thought. He gets cancer, and not only does he beat it, but now people have to listen to him more carefully than ever. "He's just jumping around and sucking air," Ben said, "trying to get whatever's out there."

"That's Ken Becko, all right," Sheila said, admiring the way her grandfather could sum up any person or any situation, quickly and accurately.

"You know, of course, everybody in the picture business is addicted to something," Ben said.

"Becko's addicted to himself. Not drugs, anyway. He wouldn't give up the control."

"That kind of addiction is for amateurs. The real players want to be consumed by something of their own devising—deals, work, power. You think they were any different forty years ago?"

"Probably not," Sheila said, knowing he was right and wondering about her grandfather's addictions.

"You understand what Becko is addicted to, don't you?"

"Me," she said, surprising herself. But when the word passed her lips she knew it was true.

"Now you're getting to it," he said. "I assume they taught you Shakespeare at one or two of those schools. 'When love begins to sicken and decay . . .'?"

"He's not in love with me," Sheila protested.

"But he's addicted to you, or he was," Ben said sharply, like a prosecutor with a sure conviction. "To what you are. Who we all are. Your wisdom was not to sleep with him."

"How do you know I didn't?"

"You didn't," he said, as if Sheila could not have kept such a thing secret from him. "I'll tell you what you did, and if I'm wrong I'll shut up. You found a way to hint that he was attractive to you. That it was a possibility."

Ben was right, of course. Sheila had kept her relationship with Becko a working one. She had flirted a bit and disliked herself for it. The irony of it was that at first she did find him attractive. Maybe it was his power over her or his formidable intelligence, or just that they were thrown together so much, but Sheila had been a tiny bit interested. But she didn't say that to her grandfather. She just asked, "Then why did he turn on me?"

"Because he's an addict," Ben said, knowing he was right. "Mercurial. Not logical. Excessive. High-flying. Hard-crashing. Becko doesn't know who he is or where he's from." Ben was silent for a moment, savoring the logic of his argument. "You know who you are, Sheila. Don't lose sight of it."

It was midnight when Sheila dropped Ross at his West Hollywood apartment. "Good night, Ross," she said. "I hope it wasn't too boring."

"My dear, I intend to claim I'm in discussions with Jackie Weller about his comeback. Who cares if it was boring?" As he got out of the car, Sheila knew Ross would wait till she drove away, and then he'd probably go down to Santa Monica Boulevard to cruise the bars and find a little trouble.

Sheila owned a tiny house in Nichols Canyon filled with furniture from the house on Summit Drive and planted with acacia and night-blooming jasmine. The sofas, chairs, and end tables were from the thirties and the moderne look made her little house fashionable. When friends who don't have families with rooms full of unused deco furniture asked where she got her things, she usually lied and said secondhand shops in North Hollywood. She'd lived in her house almost six years, most of the time—but not all of it—alone. A few years ago, for a difficult and intense six months she lived there with Derek. They met in New York, where they were happy together; for a while they had been happy in Nichols Canyon too.

When Sheila graduated from Westlake, she finally managed to leave home for Sarah Lawrence. Derek was two years ahead of her there studying acting. He quit in his third year and moved to New York so he could audition and try to start a professional career. Sheila did a lot of commuting between the Bronxville campus and Derek's apartment on the Lower East Side. She loved him, and although the rest of the world found Derek difficult and prickly, no one doubted that he was a fine actor, possessed of great intensity and the gift of impersonation. Unlike most young actors, Derek got work. Not Broadway, but showcases and limited runs of new plays in church basements and storefront theaters. Sheila went to the performances and then they would talk long into the night, analyzing and dissecting Derek's work. A lot of what Sheila knows about acting she learned from Derek. When she graduated they packed up their lives and moved to Los Angeles. It was easier on Sheila, which they had expected and talked about, but it was harder for Derek than either of them had anticipated. He said that he found it difficult to adapt his bold theatrical style to the more minute naturalistic demands of the camera. Sheila had always accepted Derek's view of acting as more considered than her own. But the trip west had changed more than their address. For Derek, New York was real life. For Sheila it was an interlude before she returned to Los Angeles. On her home ground Sheila felt more assured; she was quicker to take issue and argue with Derek. In New York if Derek had made the claim about the differing acting styles, Sheila would have all but taken notes. But in Los Angeles she laughed and said, "Every New York actor who comes out here says that."

"I'm not every actor," he had snapped at her.

"You can't expect to be Brando overnight," she told him. "Your technique is fine. You're a realistic actor on stage or screen. You make it sound like you're an opera singer or something."

"I know what I am," he said, glowering at her.

"Your trouble is, when the camera comes close, it shows a different person than the one you think you are. You can't hide.

It's not your technique you don't like, it's yourself. That's what the camera shows." It was their first argument because it was the first time Sheila hadn't accepted Derek's opinions, whole and without question.

Sheila tried to ease the tensions Derek's professional problems created by borrowing money from her father for the Nichols Canyon house. In the end it didn't help the romance, but Los Angeles real estate being what it is, the house tripled in value. When he began to have trouble with his career, Derek wanted and expected Sheila to use her family connections to help him. They hadn't talked about this before, but they both knew it was always a possibility. In the past Derek hadn't had any need for the help. Now he did, but it came when her own career was a problem, what with people watching to see if she'd follow her father or her grandfather. That's when Derek and Sheila began to fight about more than acting theories. He couldn't bear being so unknown, and he withdrew, scattering papers and clothing everywhere and sleeping for days at a time. When he awoke and looked at the mess he had created, he called Sheila selfish and spoiled. He said she didn't know anything about the world. He called her smug, and that word came back to her and caused her pain on sleepless nights. After six years she could still hear Derek's voice telling her she was refusing to help him because she wanted him to fail, that was the way she thought she could control him. He said he hated Los Angeles and he left in anger. But instead of going back to New York, he went all the way to Europe, where he stayed. He learned Italian and two years ago did a well-received Hamlet in Rome. The *Herald Tribune* said Derek had learned to weep in Italian.

On those sleepless nights when she thought about Derek, she wondered if she should have tried harder, if she were a smug rich kid and nothing more. Sheila called these thoughts her late-night punishments and they came on nights when she'd had too much coffee or too many Kenny Becko problems. She'd tried Dalmane, brandy, marijuana, and warm milk to get to sleep. None of it worked and she'd learned that until she'd thought her sad and painful thoughts, given guilt the free run of her soul and mind, until she'd shed a few tears, there would be no sleep for her. Just accepting that fact had made the insomniac nights a little easier to bear. Sometimes she wondered if it was Derek she missed or just a man. She could have dates and escorts when she put some effort into it, and not only gays or the seemingly endless married men who chased single women in Hollywood with a perseverance that Sheila found awesome. She met eligible men. The lawyers and agents, the writers and directors she dealt with were mostly men. A lot of them were straight and single. But her life was so tightly organized and scheduled that dates were difficult. It was okay to juggle days and times for dinners and screenings with people you knew well, but for a new romance to blossom, leisure is everything and that was exactly what Sheila didn't have. As she was thinking her dark thoughts, she wondered if it was possible for her to succeed without becoming as cynical and corrupt as Ken Becko by the time she too was forty. She vowed that it wouldn't happen to her. But she also vowed not to let Becko push her around, or she could well wind up like her stepmother, crying in the window. Sheila knew from the venom she felt that she had taken a big step on the march to forty. She hoped the tears wouldn't make her eyes red in the morning.

Her mind roamed back over the conversation with her grandfather. It had been only a few hours ago, but it seemed distant and far away, like a memory. Sheila realized that when she talked with her grandfather there rarely was a personal word, not so much as an "Are you happy?" between them. When they talked about that sort of thing, the conversations were forced and tentative. But when her grandfather counseled her in business, then the Hill bloodlines really showed. Business is what made him happy, and like it or not, Sheila was the same.

The next morning Sheila put on brown linen slacks and one of her blazers over a red silk blouse, an all-business outfit, at least in Hollywood. She wanted to look attractive, but not self-consciously sexy and certainly not too rich. She had considered a skirt, but decided it looked as if she was trying too hard.

Sheila could tell how her stock with Becko was doing by how long he made her wait for a casual appointment. She had called his office and asked if she could have a few moments to talk about *Roll Away*. Becko's secretary told her to come down right now and she could get in. But once she was in his office, Becko began to take phone calls, casually chatting with agents and producers, an activity he sometimes called "buffing up my relationships." Sheila just smiled politely and waited the bastard out.

"All right," he said when he felt Sheila had waited long enough. "I've looked over the coverage again." Hah, Sheila thought. He never looked at it in the first place. "I like the story," he said. "I agree with you."

"Good, Kenny. It's promising, but it's difficult stuff. We have to get a quality writer on it."

"I'm not so sure about that. I think it's pretty routine. Why go for Sattler? He's so expensive. Some kid can do it for scale."

"I don't agree. Leo's good. He'll get it right. Otherwise in three months we'll be looking for a rewrite, then the damn option'll run out. In the end it won't be as good and it won't be any cheaper. Besides, we'll want a big director for this and it'll be easier if the script's got a brand-name writer." Sheila called to Becko's secretary, asking for a Tab. Keep it casual, she reminded herself. Don't get excited.

"I don't know. Leo's scripts never get made," he said, looking down at the papers on his desk, a sign that he was getting tired of this discussion.

"Nobody's scripts get made," she shot back at him, a little more harshly than she should have. "What's that got to do with it? He'll get it right. If not on the first draft, on the second. I can probably get him to put in another set of changes. That would give us Leo's first draft on a story we know, plus two rewrites for one-twenty-five. We'll have a big five grand in the book, and we'll have a shooting script in hand before the novel's in the bookstores."

"I'm just not sure, Sheila."

Nobody says no to this deal, she thought. No question, he's saying no to me. "All right. Think it over. But let me know." That ought to surprise him. Let him think I'm not going to fight.

"I will, Sheila." Becko was about to dismiss her and just let *Roll Away* drift off and disappear.

"I ran into your friend Hugh Held," she lied, opening up the subject and suggesting she had a personal relationship with Hugh Held that Becko didn't know about.

"Yeah," Becko said. "He gets around."

"And I looked over the script. *Days Without Nights.*"

"You want to supervise it?"

"Not particularly. I will if you want me to. I thought the deal was kind of rich."

"Those costs won't stand up. We'll pay Paramount and Fox out of profits. Maybe a little cash on principal photography."

"I meant Hugh's deal."

"You and Hugh talk about his deal?" A little edge was creeping into Becko's voice.

"Big fee. Lot of points that cut in early," Sheila said, sounding relaxed again.

"He's a very good producer. Packages well."

"Seemed odd to be getting a fee that size in addition to the points. I don't know why I'm bothering you. I should ask Business Affairs about it."

"How odd did it seem?"

"Maybe there are some details I don't know, but I would think the most your friend could command would be one-fifty guaranteed, every penny of it against a more moderate definition of net profits. But a deal memo doesn't always tell the whole story, does it, Kenny?" Becko's mouth grew tight and he didn't say anything for a moment. Then his buzzer rang. Sheila always suspected Becko had a button at his foot that would make the damn buzzer ring whenever it was convenient. He told his secretary he'd call whoever it was later.

"Why don't you go ahead and make the Sattler deal," he said in a calm and even voice.

Great, she thought. A first offer. I've got him scared. "Fine. I will."

"Okay. Now I need to make some calls, so if you'll excuse me . . ."

"I just need another minute, Kenny."

"About what?" he said coolly, trying to stay airy and unconcerned.

"Even without the fees and early points, I have difficulty understanding the scope of this deal. I've researched it and I can't find where Hugh Held has ever received quite such a large fee. Against profits or not. Did I miss something?"

"Don't fall into the executive's trap of resenting the fees the talent gets. If that's what you want, I'll understand and help you convert to a production deal." He said it calmly, as if she had come to him for advice.

"It's this specific case, Kenny. Your friend Hugh Held's case," Sheila said, refusing to move off the point. She tried to appear relaxed, but she could feel the blood pumping through her veins.

Becko was quiet as he assessed the possibilities. "I think your fantasy life is working overtime."

"Maybe so, Kenny."

"What you're implying is not true. But as you well know, even a suggestion of these allegations from you and then the toothpaste is out of the tube. I'll lose, right or wrong. Is that what you're after, Sheila?"

"It's a question of right or wrong. I agree with you there," she said.

Becko was quiet again. Sheila knew there were very few cards left to play. Whatever he was going to do, this was when it would happen. "If you must know," he said, "the *Days Without Nights* deal was initiated by Harry Geller. I carried out his instructions. This is his deal." Geller was the real head of the studio, the corporate boss in New York. Becko was saying: If you insist on poking around in this, be ready to go to the top. A wave of terror rolled over her as she considered the possibility that it was true and not an improvised lie.

"Well, that makes it easy," she said, keeping her voice soft and her gaze steady. "Harry's coming out day after tomorrow. My grandfather's having a small dinner for him. It'll give me a chance to talk it through with him." Her throat was dry and she had to squeeze her toes to keep her foot from tapping. "He can tell me the details himself."

"I think you're due for a raise, Sheila. We haven't talked about it before, but it's your turn."

Wow. No more small talk, not even the veneer. I've got him. "Fine. Glad to hear it," she said, uncurling her toes. "But you don't become a studio executive for the money."

"Oh? Why do you become a studio executive?"

"To make pictures. That's what I want."

"I see. Any particular picture? Or just in general?" When Becko got sarcastic it meant he knew he didn't have a negotiating position. It can't be easy to be Ken Becko, Sheila thought. He's in a state of anxiety and high tension all the time. Now this. Plus who knows how much more is buried in all the other deal memos. Then she caught herself. Stop thinking about his problems. Give him even a tiny opening and he'll step right on your head, just mash your skull under that Gucci loafer. Don't hesitate. Move on him hard.

"I want to be able to move on the Sattler deal, and I want a go on three pictures immediately," she said in a relaxed voice. "I'll keep them all below ten million. Each one comes out of development. *Lifeline, The Dawning,* and *Winners and Lovers,*" Sheila said, naming projects she had been working on for months, each one stalled at Becko's desk. It was Becko who had taught her that when you make an outrageous demand, you just say it, shut up, then count to ten and smile till the other guy says something. So Sheila, who always knew how to learn from her mentors, smiled at the boss.

"I think that's all possible," he said evenly, as if announcing the three pictures had been his plan all along.

"Glad to hear it, Kenny. I think with all those pictures working, I ought to have a more appropriate title."

"What would you suggest?"

"I would suggest that after the announcement of the pictures, I be named a vice-president of the studio."

"You're pushing it, Sheila."

"Oh, I don't know. You can talk it over with Harry at the dinner. You will come, won't you? It'll be small. A nice, relaxed chance to talk."

"Fine."

"I'll let you know the day. Nice to see you, Kenny." Sheila put down her Tab, excused herself, and went back to her office. She returned a few phone calls, went to lunch with an agent, and by four o'clock, just because she felt like it, she canceled her dinner plans and went home.

She got into bed early, read a few scripts, and then for a treat ate a chocolate-chip cookie and flipped through a copy of French *Vogue.* Her browsing was stopped by a full-page picture of Derek on the stage in Paris. He was dressed in a scarlet doublet and black tights and he was playing Antony, a part he adored. Sheila's thoughts floated back to New York, to the tiny apartment on the Lower East Side where they lay in bed on cold nights while Derek read Antony's speeches to her in his rich, rolling voice. "Let Rome in Tiber melt, and the wide arch of the ranged empire fall! Here is my space." She looked at the magazine for a long time, running her fingers over the cool paper, remembering the heat of his touch. Even in the glow of the day's triumph, she felt a twinge of sadness and the ache of loss. As she studied Derek's brooding face, so dark and malevolent, she could imagine how contemptuous he'd be in public of this fashionable magazine and how ecstatic he'd be in private to see his picture in it. It made her smile and think how difficult and strange the world is. When she couldn't, or wouldn't, use her family's strength to help Derek, for whom she had felt selfless love, she lost him. When she used that strength on the dreaded and hateful Becko, she was victorious. It made her sad and happy, all at once. The tears that came were gentle and cleansing. As she thought about Derek's triumph, her own loss seemed to diminish and a sense of abiding pleasure washed over her. Schadenfreude, her grandfather would probably call it. Sheila smiled and toasted Derek silently, wondering if his success made him happy. She closed the magazine and eased into a deep and comforting sleep, contemplating the pleasures of family ties.

Deus ex Machina

When I was living at the Chateau, it wasn't fashionable and it certainly didn't have room service or even a restaurant. I got in the habit of walking over to Schwab's pharmacy for breakfast. Schwab's was as close to historical tradition as anything in Hollywood got. Everyone knows the story of Lana Turner being discovered there, sipping a cherry Coke. Cynics always said it never happened. I met her once and asked, was it true? She was in her sixties at the time and gorgeous. She laughed her sweater-girl laugh and said, "Of course it's true, darling. Everyone was discovered there. Don't let anyone tell you different."

Schwab's had a counter and a room next to it with about twenty-five yellow, Naugahyde booths with Formica tabletops. Breakfast was its specialty. If you turned up there a few mornings a week, you'd run into everyone you knew. Some mornings, when I didn't feel like talking, I sat at the counter, read the trades, and drank too much coffee. The waitresses were all out of a 1950s dream of a coffee shop. They called you "hon" or "dearie" and told you if the melon looked good. They asked the writers how their scripts were coming along and the actors about their auditions.

A lot of deals were cut in Schwab's but I think Steve Terzarian and I were the only ones who actually wrote a script there. We did it in the round booth in the corner, while Big Edith, the German waitress, kept the coffee coming. Steve had to browbeat me into doing it—I was in Hollywood to launch a new career, not to get involved in a flaky deal with an untried director. But Steve was persuasive and it was the closest thing to an offer I'd heard. He had in mind a yarn about a sensitive psychopathic killer who falls in love with his victims. We sat there each morning accumulating pages until we had a draft. I figured that would be that, another unmade script. But Steve and his partner, Jerry, who was to co-produce it, actually managed to make the movie. It took us ten days to write the thing; it took Steve and Jerry a year to raise the money. They pleaded with all their relatives and affluent family friends. They begged near-strangers to invest in the picture. They sold the European and cassette rights in advance at terrible terms to get enough money to start shooting. They used their credit cards to pay caterers to feed the cast and crew. They shot on the streets without permits, and in the film's big stunt, they smashed up Steve's father's station wagon. They took serious personal risks to make the movie, which was finally called *Cry I Am*. It wasn't bad, despite the title. Like so many first films, it went straight to cult without doing any real business along the way.

The irony of *Cry I Am* was it did more good for me than it did for Steve. The credit was enough to get me some real jobs working on scripts for the studios. But Steve and Jerry floundered. One of the most difficult things for a young director to do is get a second picture—if the first one fails. It takes an act of great will to get a studio to put millions of dollars into the hands of someone who hasn't done it before, but that's nothing compared to getting them to do it again if the first one doesn't turn a profit.

Steve never gave up. He wrote scripts and kept plugging away until he had *High Flier*, a thirteen-million-dollar adventure story about barnstorming stunt pilots. Through an agent's wizardry, and Steve and Jerry's persistence, *High Flier* had a star and a green light. Steve would direct, Jerry would produce. So they were feeling good. While they were in Schwab's having breakfast, Steve showed Jerry an invitation he had received. It was for his twentieth high-school reunion, in a place deep in the San Fernando Valley, out where the kids talk about going to Los Angeles the way kids in Queens talk about going to "the city."

"Look at this thing," Steve said, waving the invitation. "They tell you the menu for the reunion dinner. Like that's the reason somebody would go."

"Surf and turf?" Jerry asked, smiling.

"Listen," Steve said, reading from the invitation. "'After cocktails al fresco on the football field, your reunion class will adjourn to the Charter House motel for dinner. You and your spouse will have a choice of entrées and two vegetables, featuring home-style potatoes.' You believe it? The whole invitation is about ridiculous food. That place is always thirty years out-of-date. You want to know what they'll be eating at the fiftieth? Look at what people are eating right now. Then you'll know." The more Steve read the invitation and thought about the menu possibilities, the more irritated he got. "For the al fresco cocktails, I'd bet on terrible wine and pigs-in-a-blanket with toothpicks. What a two-bit, low-rent dump that school is," Steve said, signaling for more coffee.

"It's where you went to high school," Jerry said, hoping to calm him. "It's just a fact. Not worth getting upset."

"I'm not upset. I'm in awe. What do you have to do to get more coffee?" he said, more loudly than necessary.

"Take it easy," Jerry said, holding up his cup so that Dorothy could see it. "I thought you liked high school."

"Yeah, yeah. High school was okay." Steve smiled at Dorothy as she poured the coffee. "Should I go to my high-school reunion?" he asked her, enjoying the cheekiness of the question.

"Sure," she said. "Remember Norma, used to work the counter at lunch? She went to hers."

"How was it?" Steve asked.

"I don't know. She never came back."

Steve laughed as Dorothy walked away. He resolved to leave her a big tip.

"Go and be a big shot in front of the captain of the football team or whoever you were jealous of," Jerry said.

"You don't get it. I don't care if the president of the class just got out of San Quentin or if the cheerleaders weigh three hundred pounds. None of that. I was okay in high school, considering it's the hardest thing on earth, except raising money for pictures. That's not why I'm hesitating."

"Just do it and stop torturing yourself," Jerry said, knowing it was what Steve wanted to hear.

"Maybe. Maybe not."

"You got a go picture. That's better than being thin. Everybody'll be a grown-up. You're not the only one who doesn't have acne anymore."

"No. They're still sixteen. Every one of them. It's a total time warp. I come from the high school of the mind," Steve said, feeling silly and a little ornery. "A voice is telling me to drop in on them from out of the clouds and show them the terror of my ways. I want reunion blood." He held up his hands and wriggled his fingers like a vampire.

Jerry laughed at his friend's fantasy and said, "Go. You might even have a good time."

"I can have a good time in Hollywood."

"So what do you want?" Jerry asked, exasperated.

"Revenge."

"What for?"

"It's high school. That's reason enough. I want to knock them dead just to see them die."

"Guess that about says it."

"Not quite. We both know I'm going. The question is, how?"

The helicopter hovered several hundred feet above the field and then began to descend. On the ground, bartenders, waiters, alumni, friends, and enemies all looked up into the sky as the helicopter sank slowly toward them. The lawyers, doctors, bankers, and shopkeepers, assembled to reminisce and compare lives, gawked like stage rubes looking up at tall buildings. The helicopter settled just inside the goalpost, its whirring blades kicking up a private windstorm. The women held their skirts and their hair or clutched their wide-brimmed hats. The men looked amazed and unbelieving when Steve appeared in the helicopter's door, grinning at his classmates. He was dressed in the film director's uniform of jeans, running shoes, bush jacket, and baseball cap. He got out casually, or as casually as a man could be who had gone sixteen hundred dollars in debt to hire a helicopter. He was followed by a woman called Lilly, a perfect blond, slim and feral with the face of an ice queen. Then Jerry stepped out, looking very serious, carrying a clipboard with the boss's schedule. Lilly spent her time looking adoringly at Steve and hanging on his arm. She was an actress who was hoping to be cast in *High Flier*. Her arrangement with Steve was sort of a contemporary casting-couch deal. No sex was involved—people give that away. Hers was to be a performance, an audition. She was to look exquisite and be polite but distant to all the other men. She was always to look worshipfully at Steve as he worked the crowd while the helicopter sat idling in the background. Jerry was to stay a step or two behind Steve, keeping an eye on everything, speaking to no one, trying to give the impression that he was a combination majordomo and bodyguard.

Steve shook every hand that was offered, saying, "Hi. How are you? Great to see you." He was careful never to let his eye betray any knowledge of the person he was greeting or of the past they might have shared. They were all strangers to him now, these people he had laughed and cried with in homeroom and study hall. After all, unlike them, he had spent the last twenty years being glamorous, on helicopters, in exotic locations, and with women like Lilly at his side.

He allowed one slight betrayal of emotion when he got to Cynthia, the not-entirely-forgotten heartthrob of his teenage years. If Cynthia had sinned against Steve in the long-ago, she was guilty only of the classic high-school transgression of refusing to sleep with him. Steve hadn't exactly been smooth and debonair at the time, but he didn't care to remember that now. True to his present occupation, Steve refused to recall any details but the ones he wanted. All he could summon up was that Cynthia had said no. Everyone said no at the time, but only Cynthia had seriously considered saying yes. Steve allowed his eyes to linger and his hand to grip Cynthia's thirty-eight-year-old hand a little longer in the unisex shake he used for everyone. "Cynthia," he said, reading her name tag, speaking more softly than the "Hi-how-are-you?" voice he'd used on everyone else. "You look wonderful."

"Steve, this is my husband, Bill," she managed, barely able to speak. Bill, who looked like his mouth was dry, extended his hand and said, in the flat accent of the San Fernando Valley, the accent Steve had spent twenty years losing, "Pleasure to meet you, Steve.

I've heard a lot about you." But Steve kept gazing at Cynthia until her cheeks were flushed. He moved on, shook a few more hands, and then permitted Jerry to whisper something in his ear. Steve gave the crowd a worldly shrug, as if to say: "So little time." Jerry went first, then Steve guided the glorious Lilly back onto the helicopter. When Jerry and Lilly had vanished, Steve leaned out of the door and waved good-bye to his classmates, like a President on his way to Camp David. Then the helicopter lifted off and ascended into the clouds.

When *High Flier* began preproduction, Steve was able to reimburse himself for the cost of his reunion trip. He charged it to "location scouting," which, as he pointed out to Jerry, in a sense it was. Twenty-two months after the reunion, *High Flier* played at the triplex in the shopping mall near Steve's old high school. A group of his classmates arranged a theater party to see the film on the first night it was shown. When Steve's credit, "Directed by Steven L. Terzarian," appeared on the screen, everyone applauded. They all recognized Lilly and cheered when she made her first entrance. *High Flier* was a modest success, not as big as Steve and Jerry had hoped, but big enough for them to make a deal for another picture. Cynthia's husband, Bill, began to follow the grosses in *Variety*, to see how Steve's career was faring. After Cynthia had seen the movie, she wrote Steve a sweet note telling him how much she had enjoyed it. She spent a long time on the letter, worrying about what she should say and trying to strike the right tone of casual affection. Steve was pleased when he read it and meant to reply, but he never did.

The Presto Brothers

For a brief time I was an agent. I got the job at Schwab's. One of the regulars, who ran a small agency, had watched Steve Terzarian and me write *Cry I Am* in the corner booth. He offered to make me what he termed "an agent trainee." He knew I was out of work and when he asked if I was interested, he said he liked my "methodical approach to screenwriting." I think he meant I showed up every morning with a sharpened pencil and always glanced at the check before I paid it. My theory in taking the job was that I'd never get anywhere in Hollywood unless I had an understanding of how deals work. Suffice to say, agent trainees were not overpaid. In the six months I spent there, I came to understand a bit about the intricacies of deals. I also learned about the agents themselves and how they think. What I discovered was this: agents deliver bad news so often that they learn to put their own emotions at a distance. It put me in mind of doctors who have to tell people they have a dire illness. I saw the clients, many of them gifted, sensitive people, at their most emotionally exposed. The question of how much money you're going to get, or whether you're going to get any at all, tends to push decorum aside. For the first month, my job was to hang around my boss's office and listen to his phone calls on an extension. I spent weeks doing that. The idea was I would see how he operated and then I could do the same. I was to say nothing and hear everything. I was a spy in the house of deals and I was better at it than I would have imagined.

Maury and his brother Eugene grew up in the Bronx, on the Grand Concourse. When they were children, in the 1940s, the Concourse was a place of grandeur and stability, and middle-class Jews worked hard to attain it. That Bronx no longer exists; it is vanished forever. When Maury and Eugene were young men, full of ambition, possessed of little doubt, and newly come to the West, they had jobs in the mail room at the William Morris Agency. Maury and Eugene, who were still more alike than not, learned the movie business by reading and examining all the contracts, letters, deal memoranda, and scripts that went in and out of the agency. They spent their free time mocking the senior agents, contemptuous of what they took to be the inadequacies of their elders and looking for ways to advance themselves and launch dazzling careers. In those days, the brothers were lean and hard and ready for anything life might throw their way. They were a team, and if you spoke to one, it was like speaking to both.

The boys had grown up at the movies. Dora, their mother, took them to the Loews Paradise when they were little, and later, when they were bigger, she knew she could send them there on the subway on Saturday morning and they would be safe and content all day. They were so happy there at the movies that once, when Maury was ten years old, he refused to leave. He hunkered down in his seat and said he wasn't going to get up. Eugene, who was two years younger, kept repeating, "Mau-reee, c'mon." He said it loudly and brought the wrath of the ushers down on them both. Dora had to be called and she came to the theater, lifted Maury up out of his seat, and took her sons out of the theater. Maury was calm during it all, but Eugene cried all the way home.

When the brothers were a little older, in junior high school, they still went to the movies a lot, but they also performed a magic act together. They called themselves the Presto Brothers and they loved card tricks. They practiced in their room for hours until they could do one-handed cuts and fancy shuffles. They imagined themselves riverboat gamblers in brocade vests, sailing down the Mississippi River, fleecing the rubes and outsmarting the law. At school assemblies and in their synagogue, the Presto Brothers turned water into wine and pulled colored scarves out of the air.

When they got to California, the brothers recognized it might take a while to conquer the movie business. Maury and Eugene believed that in Hollywood you had to look good, dress right, and be seen in restaurants that were too costly for mail-room salaries. Dora's second husband, their stepfather, had been in real estate in New York before he died. He was usually one step behind the money, but the boys had learned about property from him. Soon after they started at the Morris office, they were buying and selling land, leveraging modest sums of money with the bank, and making collateral "out from the mirrors," as Dora said to them on the phone in a disapproving voice that Maury and Eugene knew masked a proud smile. Everyone who knew the brothers recognized they were very smart, and even if they were so ambitious as to be a little overbearing, they both had the saving grace of dearly loving Dora.

When they were established as agents, the representatives of famous actors and celebrated directors, and Dora was elderly, they sent her money and frequently went back to New York to make sure she was all right. Dora's health was good, but she was seventy-eight years old. She refused to have live-in help. "A girl to clean, okay. Once a week. No more," she said. "This isn't Hollywood yet." Maury and Eugene rented the adjacent apartment and installed a practical nurse, called her a "companion," and told the woman her duties included keeping them informed of Dora's condition. The brothers badgered their relatives to go up to the Bronx and look in on Dora and take her out to dinner. If you weren't good to Dora, Maury and Eugene, the font of money for the family, would cut you off.

Maury and Eugene pleaded with Dora to come live in Los Angeles, where they both had big houses. What neither of them had, however, was a wife. They both had been married twice, but those women were gone now. Dora had accepted her first set of daughters-in-law with love and enthusiasm. Her sons had brought their wives, soon to be the mothers of Dora's grandchildren, all the way to the Bronx to visit. Even after the divorces, and until the women remarried, Dora spoke regularly with both of them. She referred to them as "Maury and Eugene's real wives." She had tried to know and accept their replacements, but those marriages collapsed too. The girlfriends Eugene and Maury kept were not the sort they could expect Dora to approve. And she knew it, so she stayed on the Grand Concourse. Then one of her friends, Mr. Potosky, a man of her age who had lived in the building since Maury and Eugene were children, was mugged on his way to the synagogue. Mr. Potosky's hip was broken and it hadn't mended. Dora knew it never would.

When word of Mr. Potosky's "accident," as Dora called it, reached Los Angeles, Maury and Eugene blew their collective top. They were hard, persuasive men who were used to getting their way. This time Eugene went to New York and laid down the law. He and Maury would continue to pay rent on the apartment; it was rent-controlled and inexpensive. Dora could come back for visits in the spring and fall, but from now on she was to make her home in the West. Dora cried and complained, but life and time had turned parent into child and child into master. Maury's daughter, Caroline, who was only sixteen, but very responsible, went to New York to help her grandmother pack the clothes and photographs she wouldn't leave behind. Although she had been to Miami on the train with her second husband, this was Dora's first airplane flight and the longest journey she had made since she had arrived in New York from Russia, when she was her granddaughter's age. She would never have done it, no matter what her sons wanted, if Caroline hadn't been along to help her.

In California it was decided she would stay at Eugene's. He lived in Bel Air on a lovely green hillside. Above the main house, a little higher up the hill, there was a guest cottage and it was to be Dora's. Eugene promised that if it would make his mother happy, he would make her corner of Bel Air over to look as the Bronx once looked. Maury offered, only half-jokingly, to put in a candy store and get some actors to pretend to be old Jewish men who could sit on benches and complain. Dora said that was ridiculous and it would ruin a perfectly good house. She would be fine, thank you very much. And she was. Dora spent a lot of time by herself watching television or taking the sun on her little deck. "Better than Florida," she said of it one day, which made her sons beam.

She would amble down the brick path to the main house when her grandchildren, Caroline and Gene Jr., were there. When she felt like being alone, she could go back up to her cottage. She telephoned New York a lot, always careful to call after the rates changed; despite the presence of maids and gardeners, Dora always swept her patio, watered the plants, and cleaned the cottage herself. All in all, it seemed to be working and Maury and Eugene were relieved.

The weather in the canyons of Bel Air is not always friendly. If there's a lot of rain in the winter, in the spring there will be more vegetation, thick green yucca and flat broad acacia along with enormous jade plants and cactus, twenty times the size of the ones you could buy in New York and keep in a little pot in the window. It was lovely to look at but it could burn in the fires that came with the Santa Ana winds in the fall, hot, dry, wicked winds that came in from the desert and were like nothing that had ever been seen or felt on the Grand Concourse. And that meant the land would be bare and scorched, so that when the rains started again, mud slides were always a possibility. The rain made the air fresh and clean and gave Dora something to tell her friends in New York about. "It's a regular fire plug here with the rain—for days it goes, then nothing. The boys were right, moving out here was a good idea."

Dora settled into her new life and with her granddaughter Caroline's help arranged the photographs they had brought from New York. Dora told Caroline about life in the Bronx and about the magic act her father and uncle had performed when they were children. Caroline was interested in the stories, but what fascinated her most were the pictures of her own grandfather, whom she had never known. The photographs had been taken in the 1930s and were now brown and curled with age. To Caroline they looked like something from another century, something from a history book. Dora enjoyed getting to know her granddaughter and she even tried to make peace with her sons' bachelor lives. "You think I don't know what goes on?" she would say when her sons were vague about where they were going for a day or two. "You think I'm going to be shocked? I'm from Odessa, where the shtarkers come from. You can't shock me."

On a rainy, wintry day, Dora was sitting in her little cottage. Maury was in New York chasing deals and Eugene was in Palm Springs with one of the women he didn't introduce to Dora, when the hillside began to slip down toward the cottage. Dora's hearing was weak but she was usually quite alert. The mud pushed its way through the windows and doors. It crushed the back wall and swallowed up the cottage. Dora suffocated and was probably killed very quickly, which was a tiny comfort to her sons. She had managed the Odessa waterfront, the Russian Revolution, and the Bronx in its decline. She had buried two husbands, but after six months of Southern California, she died beneath the soil she had resisted so long.

Even though the brothers were devastated by their loss, they fought bitterly about it. Maury blamed Eugene for the catastrophe. "You knew it was a possibility, and you let her stay up there," Maury said, attacking his brother and accusing him of murdering Dora as surely as if he had shot her with a gun.

Eugene said it was a terrible, terrible accident that no one could have foreseen. "If you're blaming me, it's because you feel guilty yourself," Eugene said in a moment of unusually perceptive insight. "We're both responsible and nobody's responsible, so just shut up." But Maury wouldn't shut up, and neither would Eugene. Their families and business associates assumed the anger and recriminations would ease, but instead the tension between the brothers grew. They couldn't see one another without arguing about who bore responsibility for their mother's death. The result was that Maury and Eugene, who had once been as close as men could be, didn't speak to one another for four years. In his righteous anger, Maury left the agency business and became a producer. He got married for a third time; not a word passed between the brothers. Maury threw himself into his new career and treated every deal as if it were his first and his last. He became even more successful than he had been before Dora died. Eugene, who did indeed feel a little blameworthy, but not nearly so much as his brother had said, lost some of the drive and ambition that had made him successful. He remained an agent and eventually opened a small agency of his own. Without his brother to prod and goad him, Eugene began to take a more relaxed view of life. Eight years after Dora's death, the brothers were able to do business together. Maury hired some of Eugene's clients from time to time, and that required them to speak on the phone. A de facto, enforced peace was established, but they rarely saw one another, and when they did, it was uncomfortable for them both.

Grown gray, in his late middle age, Maury was a difficult, contentious man, well known for his toughness in negotiations. Deal-making was Maury's art, his passion, and he was famous for his cool nerves and nearly compulsive need to come out on top in any deal. No matter what the stakes, Maury was always ready to put everything at risk if he thought he could improve his position.

Eugene's career has been steady, if not spectacular, and he played golf at the Hillcrest Country Club three times a week. He had two young agents, Bobby and Jennifer, working for him. They studied all the contracts and letters and had their sights set on big careers. Eugene knew they were as contemptuous of him as he and Maury had been of the senior agents at the Morris office twenty years before. He once overheard them gossiping. "When they were starting out, Maury was an agent too," he heard Bobby say. "They were both ambitious."

"Maury, I can see. But Eugene?" Jennifer said with doubt in her voice.

"Absolutely."

"*Qué pasó?*"

"I don't know. I guess Maury never could get along with anybody and Eugene just went off to the land of putters and five irons."

Eugene had wanted to go to them and say it was a lot more complicated than they knew. But then, he thought, they would ask a lot of unpleasant questions that he'd rather not think about. He let it pass and went back to Hillcrest.

Maury hadn't produced a really big hit, and that was a disappointment, but he'd made films in the United States and Europe steadily for twenty years. A few of his pictures had been good enough to play continually on television and in revival houses. But most of them were of the moment and were now forgotten. Maury never tried to kid himself about what he was doing. He always understood when he was making a picture only because he needed the action and because the deal was good even if the script was not. His marriage to Ellen, a handsome, serene woman with short blond hair and a realistic view of the world, has been the calmest and the best of the three.

It was Ellen's second marriage; she loved her husband and was determined to make it work. She had been through some rough times and was glad to be married and to be solvent. Ellen worked hard at taking pleasure in Maury's skills and passions. She could accept his stridency and occasional obstinance. After the break with his brother, Maury's greatest personal scar was his estrangement from his daughter, Caroline. She was in her early thirties; she and her father hadn't spoken in many years. Caroline hated the way Maury blamed her Uncle Eugene for her grandmother's death. That's when the rift between father and daughter began. Everyone said Maury's personality changed then. Within a year, he refused to give Caroline's mother any more alimony. Then he cut off the payments to his second wife. Even when the court ordered him to resume payments to both women or risk going to jail, he wouldn't do it. "The hell with them both. They don't deserve a penny," is all he would say. Because he was rich, and her mother was not, Maury was sure Caroline would come back to him. But his behavior disgusted Caroline and she decided to stay with her mother. She became a schoolteacher and she wanted nothing to do with the movie business or her father. When she was mentioned, Maury's mouth would get tight and he would call her "my ex-daughter."

In recent years Maury had specialized in television movies—MOW's, as they're called in the trade, for movie-of-the-week. Maury's personal favorite was about a middle-class woman who was a compulsive shoplifter. Another was about anorexia nervosa. Maury was very good at spotting trendy problems and illnesses. He was developing scripts about child molestation and teenage pregnancies when he himself got sick.

Because of his toughness, Maury had made a lot of enemies, but no one wished him the illness that befell him. He was fifty-seven and he was diagnosed as having an inoperable and particularly unpleasant cancer. When Maury went into Cedars-Sinai Hospital, everyone around him tried to be upbeat and encouraging. Maury swore he would beat it, but in his heart he knew he would not come out of the hospital alive. Maury pondered what to do with his remaining days, but no matter how hard he tried to fathom the difficult and complex circumstances that had been thrust upon him, the situation he faced seemed addressed to someone else. Maury decided to make a deal for a movie about the last weeks of his life. He knew he would be criticized, that others might not approve, but it was his life and his death, and work was his only solace. His secretary was too upset to assist him, so Ellen stayed in the room at Cedars to help when Maury began to make the calls announcing the availability of the rights.

He saw quickly that he would not be able to handle the negotiations by himself. Sometimes he felt strong enough, but he was frequently ill from the chemotherapy, or not readily available to take phone calls. He knew that if he was seen as negotiating from weakness of any sort, the idea of selling the film rights to his own demise would be called ghoulish and no deal would be made. If the sale appeared to be a cool, rationally made decision, then the movie would feel possible, ideal for television and maybe even theatrical release. Despite his condition, Maury could think clearly about this; he wanted very much to win. He knew that the cancer would have the final victory, but he wanted a last triumph for his business.

From the time he entered the hospital, Maury pretended his purpose in being there was to enhance the value of the film rights. It was his way of coping with the terror. Psychiatrists would call it denial. Maury called it good business. For a while Ellen tried to handle the phones. She had been an actress before they were married and she was good enough at pretending she was an efficient secretary, handling the boss's affairs, so long as Maury could coach her and tell her what to say. But for negotiating and selling, Ellen was inadequate and Maury couldn't put himself in a position where he might have to tell a buyer he couldn't talk now because it was time for his radiation treatment.

Without her husband's permission or knowledge, Ellen told Eugene about his brother's condition and about his plan to sell the rights. She asked Eugene to come to the hospital, make peace with Maury, and either talk him out of the plan or help him with it. "Because, I tell you," she said to the brother-in-law she hardly knew, "I just can't do it. It's all I can do not to fall apart. You have to help, Eugene. You really do."

Eugene knew he would go to his brother, but he was uncertain how to do it. When Maury called first, Eugene was relieved. "Have you got a good doctor?" he asked.

"The best. Tops in the field."

"Good. That's good." Neither of them mentioned the fact that they hadn't spoken in years. "How are you feeling?"

"Tired. From the treatment. It's to be expected. You heard what I'm doing?"

"I did. Any luck?"

"Luck's the least of it," Maury said. "There's a sale in this. It's a lock for the tube and very possibly a feature. What do you think?"

Eugene knew his brother would never ask for help, no matter how much he wanted it. "Can I do anything?" Eugene asked.

"Maybe," Maury said, as if the idea had never occurred to him.

"I'd like to come see you. Would it be all right?"

"Yeah. Sure," Maury answered, as if it were nothing special. "Come on over. We can talk about it."

At a time of crisis like this, it would have been difficult for anyone to say no, and for Eugene, no matter how much bad blood was between them, refusing his brother now was just not a possibility. So he left his business in the hands of Bobby and Jennifer, who were solemn and respectful about Maury, but glad to have the opportunity to take over the agency, even temporarily. Eugene set up an office next to Maury's bed without trying to argue the wisdom of negotiating from a hospital room. Eugene had phones with buttons and a second line installed. "I want to see those buttons glowing and beeping," Maury said, looking confident for the first time in a while. Ellen went back to her role as phone answerer and Eugene took over the negotiations. "Identify yourself," Maury told him. "Say you're head of business affairs for me."

Eugene had a little trouble with the system at first. Negotiating wasn't a problem; he'd been doing that for years. It was Maury, lying ill and frail in the bed right next to him. Maury kept whispering orders. Whenever there was a silence on the phone, whenever Eugene was listening rather than talking, Maury demanded to know what the other guy was saying. Eugene tried to make it easier by having a speaker phone installed so Maury could hear everything. But hospital noises kept intruding and Eugene had trouble concentrating. Maury hated the idea that the doctors, nurses, and orderlies who came in and out of the room could listen to the phone calls if they cared to. To solve the problem, Eugene called in a favor at one of the networks and they provided a special headset for Maury so he could listen to the negotiations and still keep them private.

Because it was a production office with only one production, there were frequently times when the phone didn't ring. The brothers both knew that these periods of silence were very likely the last time they would ever have to talk. Eugene wanted to use the time, but he and his brother had been estranged for so many years that it was difficult. It was Maury, always more aggressive, who tried to talk to his brother. Maury found himself thinking about their father, who had died in Montefiore Hospital when the brothers were children. "Remember how we went to see Dad when he was sick?" Maury asked.

"Sure I do. It was in the summer. Every day we took the Jerome Avenue train and got off at Mosholu Parkway. We walked from there," Eugene said, glad to take refuge in manageable memory.

"You know what I remember about Montefiore?" Maury asked, without wanting an answer. "The lines on the floor. Follow the yellow line, or the blue line, or the red. I liked that. She said you couldn't get lost that way." That was as close as either brother could come to mentioning their mother.

"I don't remember that part," Eugene said. "I just remember Dad with the IV thing in him. We thought they said ivy. So we called it poison ivy. Remember?"

"No. All I remember is that thing sticking in my father's arm. It scared the shit out of me."

"Yeah," Eugene said, recalling the time of their father's death. "He was thirty-nine. A kid."

"In a way, I've had a free ride."

"No, no. In those days, they couldn't do anything. Now they got all this," Eugene said, gesturing to the modern equipment. "It's a completely different situation." Maury really wasn't comfortable talking about it, and that was okay with Eugene, because he too really preferred talking about the deal. And when there was nothing to say about that, the room fell silent.

Because time was short, and to show the people they were negotiating with just how serious this venture was, Maury ordered Eugene to hire a film crew to come in and shoot general coverage of what Maury called "the situation." In the film there would be an actor playing Maury, but real footage of Cedars-Sinai in action, the modern equipment, the other patients, and the staff would be valuable as background. Eugene called a few of the cinematographers Maury had worked with over the years, but they were all busy and none of them could or would change their schedules. He spoke to Mishko Volavich, a Yugoslav Maury had helped get into the Los Angeles local of the cameramen's union. Mishko seemed genuinely sorry not to be able to help, but he was busy preparing a feature. "Maybe is for Shtoon-ey," Mishko said, in the accent that seemed to get thicker the longer he stayed in Hollywood and had to deal with agents and producers. Stoney Daniels was Mishko's camera operator, his second in command, who wanted to move up to director of photography.

"It breaks my heart," Stoney said when Eugene told him Maury was in Cedars. "I'm really sorry, but I have to tell you, it's kind of risky for me."

"No, no," Eugene said. "It's not contagious. I'm in the room with him all the time."

"I mean careerwise," Stoney said. "If I had more credits maybe, but for my first shot it can't be TV. I want a feature."

"Maybe you could do it under another name," Eugene suggested. "It's his last deal."

"I wish I could, partner. It's a terrible thing," Stoney said, with enough emotion in his voice that Eugene almost believed him. "You give the slugger my best. He'll understand."

Eugene told Maury that the problem was no cinematographer could work with a nonunion crew, and the cost of hiring a full union team was so high as to be prohibitive. Maury, who probably knew the truth anyway, said, "The hell with them. Use video and transfer it to film, then blow it up to thirty-five-millimeter." So Eugene asked his son, Gene Jr., who was now in his early twenties, and enamored of video, to bring his portable video equipment to the hospital and act as an ad hoc second unit. Gene Jr. arrived at Cedars with two of his friends who were to handle the lights and sound. Eugene explained the delicacy of the situation and Gene Jr. assured his father that all three would be sensitive to Uncle Maury's condition. The boys were thrilled to have the opportunity and were quite impressed with the seriousness of their mission. Eugene told Ellen privately, "You know, this video business is a little strange. It's not going to enhance the value of the rights one bit, and it's not going to make it easier to sell."

Ellen understood better than Eugene that her husband's need was to do something, anything, that might make him feel in control. "As long as the video stuff doesn't get in the way," she told him, "just let them do it."

With Eugene on the phone and Maury in command, they got several offers, but each one was for an option against a big payment when and if the film got made. The best of the option offers was for five thousand immediately against fifty thousand later. Maury wouldn't consider it. He demanded that Eugene push on and negotiate for a flat-fee buy-out with profit participation. He wanted the money in his hand while he could still feel it. With Maury's mind on the negotiations and his pain, Ellen asked Gene Jr. how she could reach his cousin Caroline. Ellen called and introduced herself to the stepdaughter she had never met, who was only nine years younger than she was. Ellen tried to be direct and to speak without euphemism, but it was hard for her. She began by telling Caroline she had difficult news. "Your father's very sick. He's in Cedars."

Caroline was silent for a moment as she tried to absorb the words. "Cancer?" she finally asked, knowing that it was and trying hard to keep her voice steady.

"Yes. There's not a lot of time left."

"Has he asked for me?"

"He wouldn't be your father if he did," Ellen said. "But your Uncle Eugene is here and they're getting on all right. I think he'd like it if you came." Ellen spoke so plainly, and without trying to manipulate, that Caroline liked her immediately and trusted her. She said she'd come down to Los Angeles from Santa Barbara, where she lived, whether Maury asked for her or not. She came the next day, expecting a death watch, or perhaps some last desperate measures to keep her father alive. Instead, she found her Uncle Eugene on the phone conducting business and her father dictating a film treatment about his illness, which he thought would enhance the value of the rights. Caroline had been thinking about what to say, how to greet her father, and how frank to be in discussing the past and the present. She was determined to be clear and as forthright as possible. Instead she had to shield her eyes from the bright lights that Gene Jr. and his video crew were using. The activity confused her. Her father and uncle were acting as if there were no illness, not like two men who had barely spoken since she was a teenager. "Hi, Daddy," was all she could manage before the painfully apparent reality of his sickness made her forget her speech.

"Hi, kiddo, I'm glad you came."

"Of course I came," she said, struggling to maintain her composure, determined not to upset him.

"See what you've got to look forward to, where your genes will get you?"

"Shh," she said, and sat on the edge of the bed and held his hand, gently stroking the pale, parchmentlike skin. Each time she tried to tell him she was sorry that he was going to die and sorry they hadn't been close, Eugene would interrupt with a new bulletin or a phone call, and Maury would ask Ellen to help him with his earphones, so he could listen. Caroline finally left in confusion and sadness, promising to call every day. When she was gone, Ellen said, "You were hostile to her. She wanted to make up." It was the only criticism Ellen had made of Maury from the time of the diagnosis till now. She meant it, but then was sorry she had said it. Maury ignored it.

Despite their video equipment, Gene Jr. and his friends managed to insinuate themselves into the hospital's routine without disrupting anything. Eugene was proud of his son's ability to manage in such difficult circumstances. Eugene saw him talking to a pretty Filipino nurse named Flora, who had asked about Maury. Gene Jr. told her that his Uncle Maury was a film producer. She nodded and asked what that meant. "They find the stories, you know, that some guy dreams up, or some book, any old thing," he explained. "Then they hunt around and find how to turn it into a movie that you go see." Flora nodded her understanding and seemed quite interested, so Gene Jr. asked if she had a boyfriend. She didn't, and he offered to take her to a movie to point out some of the technical things she might not be aware of. She agreed that was a good idea and the two of them began going out.

As Maury's body was wasting away, Eugene seemed to get stronger. Once the speaker phone was gone, Eugene lost his nervousness and did the most effective negotiating he had done in years. When he wasn't on the phone, he was telling his son what shots to get, suggesting angles, and urging the boys to stay longer and shoot more. Eugene's phone voice took on an intimate urgency; everything he said had an immediacy about it. He almost cooed into the phone, making promises and demands, sounding outraged and hurt if what he considered a legitimate offer wasn't forthcoming. He didn't think about golf, he didn't think about his other clients. He just stayed on the phone, demanding, cajoling, offering, and refusing. As Maury lay disintegrating next to him, Eugene pushed on, feeling younger. Maury was not a man easily moved by sentiment. He mistrusted any emotional response he couldn't count, but he was moved by his brother's enthusiasm; it was a measure of just how sick he was that he didn't resent it.

By the second week of negotiations, with Maury becoming very frail, Eugene had two production companies on the hook, but neither one would budge from their option offer. Maury ordered Eugene to hold out for thirty-five thousand in cash. Eugene wanted to accept one of the offers, for fear that if they didn't make the deal quickly, the buyers would lose interest. "The heat is now," Eugene said. "In a couple of days it could be old news." But Maury felt certain that by playing one against the other he wouldn't have to settle for an option deal. He made Eugene hang tough and refused to consider less. Maury said he could feel the opposition folding, he knew they would come around.

But the cancer wouldn't wait. Maury died before the deal could be closed. At first Eugene wanted to keep negotiating. He didn't see why he had to volunteer the information about his brother's death. If he were asked directly, "Is Maury alive?" well then, of course he'd have to say what had happened. But so far the only thing anybody had asked about was the price.

Eugene called Groman's Mortuary and made arrangements for the funeral. The next day, when Maury's obituary appeared in *Variety* and the *Hollywood Reporter,* the buyers stopped calling. Eugene didn't have the heart to call them. Maury was buried next to Dora at Forest Lawn. Eugene felt wobbly when he looked at the grassy space next to his mother and brother and remembered that spot would someday be his own. He leaned on Gene Jr., who steadied him and helped him sit in one of the folding chairs under the canopy that Groman's had provided. When Maury was lowered into the ground, it fell to Eugene to drop the first bit of earth into the grave; it made him weep. He was crying for his brother and for the years they had lost. He had tender thoughts about their mother, remembering how it was when they were all younger and everything seemed possible. He thought about the Bronx and Bel Air hillsides, about his father, gone so long, and about his own son, who would someday be the one to drop the first dirt on his own grave.

Eugene mourned until grief became memory, and then, slowly at first, he began to play golf and look after his business. Bobby and Jennifer had enjoyed their autonomy too much to be subordinates again. They took several of the clients and opened their own agency. To take their place, Eugene hired an ambitious young man just out from New York who wanted to learn the agency business. In the time of Eugene's sadness, he decided there should always be fresh flowers on the graves of his mother and his brother, and there always were.

Another Bottle of Petrus

One of the advantages of living at the Chateau was I could pack up and leave on short notice. That was also one of the disadvantages. I was never certain I wanted to be in Hollywood at all. So from time to time I'd store the few items I had accumulated in the basement of the Chateau and go back to New York. I'd drop by the *Post* to see Marv and say hello. The reporters, in their newsroom state of perpetual adolescence, called me "Hollywood" and outdid one another asking dopey, ingenuous questions. A sports reporter asked if I'd brought my surfboard; the guy who took over my old job of monitoring and condensing the *Times* asked if I could get him a date with Candice Bergen.

I hadn't spoken to Beth in a while. She'd passed the bar and I had heard she was going out with her contracts professor—the one she used to complain about. I wanted to see her, but not enough to call.

My reasons for all this back-and-forthing were no doubt neurotic, but I claimed (to myself and anyone who asked) that I was going to New York to work in the theater. And sometimes I did just that. On one of my more extended excursions, I wrote a play for a gloomy but earnest storefront theater on the Lower East Side. The venture went well enough, and as a result of some federal arts grant, the play moved a few blocks uptown. I wound up being profiled in the *New York Times* in one of those articles asking where-are-the-new-young-playwrights?

Barney Harris, a producer I had worked with a few times, asked me to meet with him and Moon Dugan, who at the time was a very big star. This was a few years ago and Moon is dead now, cancer in Mexico. He tried some trendy cure that amounted to coffee enemas and thinking good thoughts and he died in an adobe hospital, his insides rotted from the Camels he smoked for thirty years. When I met him, if he knew he had the disease, he wasn't saying. Barney told me to read a play called *The Outsider*. As it happened, I had seen the play when it was done on Broadway. It was by Edward Lopat, a minimalist playwright who went in and out of favor with the critics. Lopat is dead now, too. He died in an absurd traffic accident in Knightsbridge about a year after Dugan died. He was crossing Sloane Street with his oldest daughter when a motorcycle hit him. He died in St. George's hospital a few days later, without ever regaining consciousness. Death has done wonders for his reputation.

The meeting was at Barney's office in Century City. I had flipped through the play that morning and rather liked it. It was about a man who intrudes on the lives of two women, each of whom may or may not have been his lover. It was mysterious and full of unexpected drama. I assumed Dugan wanted to make a movie of it and wanted me to adapt it. It seemed like a long shot, but if you were a screenwriter, working for Moon Dugan couldn't hurt. I was sitting out in the hall waiting to be called into Barney's office when an overweight man with a reddish beard extended his hand and said, "Hi, I'm Moon Dugan." I drew a blank for a moment—Moon Dugan had a tight, muscular face and a lean, hard body, a movie star's appearance. This guy looked like a Humboldt County dope farmer. After a moment of confusion, my wits returned and I said something like "Of course you are," shook the man's hand, and followed him into Barney's office. Moon wanted to do the play as a film, all right, but Lopat had already done the screenplay. Moon needed some changes and Barney had suggested me. Moon wanted the man to be an American so he could play the role, and that meant changing the language to a looser, more colloquial American speech. I didn't see why that couldn't be done. After all, the character is an outsider—that's the title of the thing. So long as the two women were still English, the guy would be all the more of an outsider. Moon thought that was dandy—like all movie stars, he liked it when you told him what he already thought, but you framed it better. Did I think the language could be changed?

"Well," I reasoned, "if you're going to make him an American, you can't very well have him sipping tea and eating cucumber sandwiches. You either do it or you don't."

Moon smiled and then Barney told me why I was there, and it wasn't to do the rewrite or the script. "Do you think you could persuade Mr. Lopat to make those changes?" Jesus . . . People write Ph.D. theses about Lopat's use of language. Normally the producer or the star would do this himself. But one look at Moon Dugan's gut and it was pretty clear why he didn't want to go out in public. Barney didn't say why he wasn't going himself, but it was probably because he thought Lopat wouldn't take him seriously. An important part of all this is that Moon and Barney were ready to pay me ten thousand dollars plus the cost of the trip to undertake this mission. As we discussed it, I guess I was a little standoffish, not as a ploy, but because I wasn't sure I could pull it off. They had picked me because I had written plays, one of which had been done in London, and I was a screenwriter. Great. To Moon and Barney that might certify me as an intellectual, but to Lopat I would surely be some sort of rude American joke foisted on him by Hollywood. Moon must have sensed my discomfort and doubt. He began to back off, saying maybe he'd better wait till he was free and could do it himself. Translated, that meant get someone else, or wait till he'd lost enough weight and then bring Lopat to Hollywood. I could feel the whole thing slipping away, so I had to come up with something big, fast. I said, "Let's make it double or nothing. If I succeed, and bring back the revisions, the price is twenty grand. If I fail, keep your money." You'll never get anywhere in Hollywood if you're not ready to gamble all the time, and Dugan, who was a famous poker player, loved the idea. Barney began to cough and hem and haw, but "double or nothing" were the magic words to Moon Dugan. So we made the deal on a handshake and a grin and I was off to London to see just how seriously Mr. Lopat would take me.

Since it was on Moon Dugan's ticket, I flew to New York, took the Concorde to London, and checked into the Connaught. Lopat was coming in from the country to meet with me. His secretary wanted me to know that was a concession. I thanked her, as if I didn't realize Mr. Lopat was avoiding the alternative, which was to invite me down to his house in the country, where I wouldn't leave till I got what I wanted or he threw me out. So we were both staying at the Connaught and, I suspected, about to run up some serious room-service bills. I had met Lopat once a few years earlier in New York at some junior playwrights' bash. He was in town and he came by to be held in awe by a group of hopeful dramatists. We were all tongue-tied in the presence of the great man. It was a room full of writers acting a lot more sensitive than they felt. Lopat's response to it all was to mumble and talk so quietly that nobody heard anything he said.

I was to meet him in the grill at half-past one. I had checked into his background. He was from Manchester, working class. He'd gone to Cambridge, Clare College, where he read history. He was fifty-two, a CBE, and a knighthood was a possibility. His politics were Tory and his plays were often very good. He'd been married a few times and God only knew what I was in for. I read his screenplay of *The Outsider* on the plane. It looked to me as if he'd taken the play and had it retyped with a lot of what somebody took to be cinematic touches. The dialogue and the structure were mostly unchanged from the stage version, but the characters regularly saw their faces reflected in champagne bottles, pools of water, and once, I think, in a mustard pot. The sun seemed to rise or set gloriously in every third scene. Maybe he'd been to film school since I met him. All this was on my mind as I waited at the Connaught bar.

He arrived about twenty minutes late, and he came in bowing, nodding, and begging pardons in the English upper-class manner. I guessed the Manchester childhood was only a bad memory. He was with a woman so beautiful she made my eyes ache. Her name was Vera and she was French. So the author turns up at the

Connaught with a French mistress. Mr. Lopat, I realized, was going to play this one full-tilt. "Hello, hello," he said. "So sorry to be late. I do hope you haven't been waiting long?"

"No, no," I said, matching his double hello with my double no. "Think nothing of it." I could see the subtitles running across my stomach: "Okay, you've shown you've got the power, now let's get on with it." He introduced the glorious Vera and we went to the table. I don't know why I felt such resentment toward this man—of course I know why. I was jealous. He was a celebrated playwright, an author. I was kicking around Hollywood doing rewrites and I had come halfway around the world to talk him into making a hash out of a fine play so Moon Dugan, if he could lose weight, could turn it into a bad movie.

Before we ordered lunch Mr. Lopat studied the *carte des vins* as if it were the Upanishads, discoursing about the virtues of claret as opposed to anything grown in Burgundy, Italy, or, God forbid, California. He let me in on the little secret that Petrus was an excellent wine as he ordered a thirty-two-year-old bottle of the stuff. Maybe that was Vera's age. The wine steward went off to hunt for the bottle and it was clear that Mr. E. Lopat was some piece of business. The man had English tailoring, European manners, and now he wanted some American money.

After a few glasses of the Petrus, with Vera's smile pinning me to my seat, Lopat began to talk about what he took to be the central problem of adapting his play to the screen. "You know, my boy, the process is extremely difficult. I suffered—oh, yes I did. It was as if I were asked to give birth to the same child twice." Maybe it was the way he guzzled the Petrus, or maybe it was the glare from Vera's Cartier bracelet, but I began to see subtitles on Lopat's stomach, too: "I don't give a damn what Moon Dugan and all the princes of Hollywood think. And you, laddie, you just keep pouring the great wines of France." That was a very good sign and I started to get hopeful. "The screen is so literal," he said. "I try to be, if I may say so, more poetic. I'm not interested in the conventions of naturalism. I prefer suggestion and symbolism. One can hardly photograph the pages of a play. We must seek out the cinematic, the pictorial." When his little speech was finished, he smiled, absolutely pleased with himself. It made sense, sort of. But it certainly didn't address the specific problems of turning this English play into a Hollywood movie.

"Moon became interested in *The Outsider,*" I said, sipping Petrus and ignoring the chops that had arrived—always good to ignore the food at these lunches, it suggests you eat in places like this so often that you hardly notice—"because he feels like an outsider. He doesn't live in Hollywood and he rarely comes to Los Angeles." Subtitle: "He spends all his time in Aspen because there's more cocaine there than anyplace but Bogotá." "Moon has an actor's sense of your play, an intuitive feel for it." Subtitle: "Moon Dugan never even read the thing. It was explained to him and he said yes because he thinks you're a highbrow and that's what he wants the world to think he is." "His fear, and I think you'll agree it's a legitimate one, is that his audience won't accept him as an Englishman."

"Umm," Lopat said, stroking Vera's arm. "The bottle seems empty."

I signaled for more Petrus, wondering if even the Connaught Grill had more than one bottle on hand. Lopat's contract called for a large bonus if his script was used and he got screen credit. So for a man who drinks Petrus and has a friend like Vera, a big production bonus is going to be very important. "Moon hopes that you can stay involved, but if you say it can't be done, Moon's willing to drop the project right here. No hard feelings." Subtitle: "We both know who the real power is in this. Do what he wants or forget the money."

"I want to help make it a success," he said, a tiny trace of fear on his face. "I suppose the screen does require language that is less rhetorical . . . more accessible . . . colloquial. Some of the long speeches might be more effective if a bit were pared away. One must find visual equivalents. It's all so wretchedly real on the screen, so literal, what with all the streets and the trees and the teacups. It doesn't permit irony, does it?"

"That's a wonderful analysis of the problems. I'll quote you. I hope I do it justice." Subtitle: "Sounds like a graduate student gone berserk. The man's worried. If I just talk art and think money, I can win." "I think one way to proceed would be for me to sketch in the changes, using American idioms and my own sense of

Moon's voice. I wouldn't presume to write your script, but it would give you something to react to." Subtitle: "I'll do it and you can pretend to change it and we can be done with this charade."

"Well, I've never collaborated before. I . . . I . . . I . . ." He's hauling out the Cambridge stutter. I guessed that meant I'd got him.

"I wouldn't presume to be your collaborator. I'm going to propose a few specific changes. You will of course be free to accept, reject, or alter them. Perhaps we could meet again tomorrow to review the changes?"

"Fine Fine. Shall we have a bit more wine?" I signaled for another bottle of Petrus and Vera laughed, a little tinkling laugh of a sort heard only around bottles of the best Bordeaux.

I spent the rest of the day and much of that night rewriting the script. It was mostly a matter of changing the "I says" to "okays," and giving the man some "How do I get to the train station?" lines. In Hollywood, often enough the work isn't hard; it's getting the job that's the problem. I resolved to claim that all the changes I was proposing had Moon's approval. If Lopat hesitated, I would say that I was Moon's plenipotentiary in this matter and if the changes were not made to my satisfaction, Mr. Lopat could forget about the movie ever being made. The funny part of it was, the more I thought about Lopat and his pretensions, the less I liked him; yet each time I read his script I had more respect for him—not as a screenwriter, God knows, but as a dramatist. With only a few words and without appearing to try, the man could make shimmering characters. But the world rewards playwrights with prizes and laurels; it rewards screenwriters with truly interesting sums of money.

Lopat was to come to my room in the morning. If I prevailed, we would work until I had a script I could take back to Los Angeles. He came rolling in about noon, looking as if he and Vera hadn't been doing much sleeping. He asked for a drink and I poured him some coffee.

"Well, from the look of this room, I daresay you've been hard at it. Hmm?"

"I've roughed in some of what Moon would like." I handed him the script with my penciled alterations. He stared at them, pretending to read, nodding, and mumbling under his breath.

"Well, yes then. You seem to have done it, haven't you?" The irritation in his voice was unmistakable.

"Not at all," I said quickly. "This is meant as an indication of the direction. Your hand is yet to be felt here. I certainly—"

"Now, listen here, you're a clever-enough fellow. You can't expect me to race through this. You'll recall what Valéry said: 'Art is never completed, it is abandoned.' Well, I'm not quite ready to abandon this particular bit of art. I would like something to drink that doesn't come in a cup."

I was calling room service for a pitcher of Bloody Marys when it dawned on me that what Lopat wanted was to stay in London with Vera for a while, living it up courtesy of Moon Dugan. "Let me suggest something," I said to him as sincerely as I could. "Suppose you take the pages to your rooms and think about it for, say, a week. Then, based on your thoughts, we can either change it a bit or deliver it as it now stands."

"Interesting idea," he said, flipping through the pages again. "This is a deceptive task. It looks simple enough, but it's quite easy to mar the rhythms if one isn't careful. It may take some doing."

"How long do you think the doing will take?" I asked as I went to the door to receive the drinks. The bellman poured while Lopat studied the pages.

"I think I could complete the work in, say, two weeks?"

"I'm sure I can persuade Moon of the value of taking your time. Is it possible for you to stay in London while you work?"

"Umm," he said, a trace of a smile appearing. "I suppose I could arrange that. The Connaught is satisfactory. You'll continue on here as well?" I nodded yes and Lopat finished his drink and mine. We agreed that I would send a photocopy to his quarters so he could begin work. I called Hollywood later that day and told Barney we were working hard and that I estimated Lopat would need about two weeks and that if the two of us just stayed at the hotel, which Lopat was willing to do, I could bring a finished script back with me. Except for Lopat's agent, who demanded additional payment for his client's incidental expenses, there were no objections.

After that I saw Lopat twice in the bar and once in the barber shop. He was always courteous; Vera was always on his arm. He never mentioned the script, and two weeks to the day later, he checked out and I took the manuscript I had revised the first night back to Hollywood to collect my twenty thousand. Barney was satisfied, but Moon Dugan, who by then must have had the first intimations of the disease that would kill him, never looked at it.

Muscle Burn

Mornings at Schwab's were run by Virginia, a flinty, birdlike woman who was almost eighty and who didn't suffer fools. Virginia took messages for itinerant actors, kept the cash register, sold the cigars and doled out the New York papers. The *New York Times* didn't always arrive—storms in the Midwest and fog over Denver were the usual excuses. There's a regional edition now, printed locally, but in Schwab's heyday, Virginia was the woman to see if you wanted the *Times.* The *Post* turned up a few days late and I found it easy to ignore. A three-day-old tabloid, even one I once worked for, is only amusing. I considered the *Times* a necessity. Every morning about eight, when I walked over from the Chateau, there would be a group of ill-tempered New Yorkers, mostly writers, drinking coffee and waiting for newspapers. For a scheduling reason that the airlines claimed was a result of deregulation, there was no Monday delivery. Virginia contended that the *Times* didn't come out on Monday. I pointed out that the Monday edition arrived on Tuesday. "It comes out on Tuesday," she answered testily.

"Out here, maybe," I said. "But in New York—"

"Of course out here. Where do you think you are? Don't be thick." Then she handed me the *Los Angeles Times* and *Herald*

Examiner. "Look at these," she said. "It's the same news and you know it."

There are a lot of New Yorkers in Hollywood and the adjustment isn't always easy. Some come in the grand style, others arrive in leaky Chevrolets. Not all of them long for their hometown newspapers; but all of them eventually go to the gym in pursuit of the trim good looks they assume will be easier to achieve here than in the East. I went for a while; that's where I met Tommy. At the time he was an unhappy man who was considering writing off California as a bad mistake and going back to New York. He didn't and he never regretted it.

Tommy had been in Los Angeles long enough to know he should park his old Chevy a block away. He weaved through the German cars parked on the street and glanced up at the towering palms as he walked the rest of the way to the Beverly Hills reunion of Brooklyn high-school alumni. The invitation said "Bring your accent," and it had made Tommy laugh. He was in Los Angeles to be an actor. In New York he had taken some classes, had appeared in two commercials, and had taken his optimism west, but his supposed career was going nowhere and he knew it. Mostly he went to the gym.

The reunion was at the home of Sidney Dellinger, who was a big deal in the record business. Tommy wasn't sure exactly what Mr. Dellinger did, but from the look of his house, he did it pretty well. It was an enormous Spanish house, with gates and guards. Tommy had been in Los Angeles for eight months and this was the first time he had been near one of these big Beverly Hills joints. He filled out a Midwood High School name tag and slapped it on his shirt. He didn't fill in the class year because he never graduated.

There were easily two hundred people on the grounds behind the house. With a tennis court and rolling lawn, it looked like a public park to Tommy. He recognized the Brooklyn types, milling about, sipping drinks, and reminiscing. He smiled at the sight of so many Jewish, Italian, Irish, and even a few black faces, all jabbering at one another about Atlantic Avenue, egg creams, and Pee Wee Reese. When they were kids they would have been kicking the shit out of each other, he thought. True to the invitation, Brooklyn accents—urban, nasal voices, just like his own—were in the air. He might not know any of these people, but he'd bet they were self-conscious about their accents. Not today, though. He accepted a glass of seltzer from a Chicano bartender who was working beneath a sign that said "No Perrier Allowed." The Dellingers had rigged false fronts of a Brooklyn street, like a movie set. It looked like Flatbush in the 1940s. There was even a little boy appointed to stand in front of one of the brownstones and yell up to a third-story window, "Hey, Ma, t'row me down a quarter." But he was a California child, with no memory of Brooklyn, and he kept wandering away to try the egg creams.

"Which would you rather have, a bagel with a schmear or a bialy?" The woman offering him the choice was wearing a white linen skirt and a floppy hat. Tommy could see a few tendrils of frosted blond hair poking out beneath the brim. "They also have charlotte russes, but they might be gone."

"I'm okay with this," Tommy said, holding up his glass of seltzer.

"So how long you been out here, Tom?" she asked, reading his name tag.

"Eight months. How about you?"

"Fourteen years. I came out with my ex-husband. When we split, he went back. I decided to stay. I actually like it. So what do you do?"

Tommy was enjoying her brash directness and her loud voice, which in this crowd didn't seem so loud. He knew women like this, and he knew when he answered her question, she'd disappear. "I'm an actor. I'm looking for work and I go to the gym a lot."

"Hey, well. Good luck." And she was gone.

Later, he listened to an argument about the configuration of the handball courts in Brighton Beach and a squabble about how many stops there were on the Canarsie line. He was about ready to leave when he saw a guy he had spoken to at the gym. "Hey, how are you?" Tommy said, offering his hand.

"Hey, Nautilus, how you doing? How about this stuff, huh?"

"Al?" Tommy asked, reading his name tag.

"Yeah. I'll tell you something. Dellinger, he's from Bensonhurst. Came out here after the army, didn't have a nickel. I didn't know you were from Brooklyn. What you do out here, anyway?"

"Nothing good yet."

"I thought you were a coach."

"I just work out."

"No kidding? You know more about it than those jokers at the gym, any day. Hey, got to go."

It was true that he went to the gym to stay in shape. He was naturally well-muscled, but it was also because he didn't have anything better to do. Given the state of his acting career, working out was his only solace. Instead of leaving, he lived in one room above a garage in Laurel Canyon and his money was running out. He didn't want to think about that now. He got another glass of seltzer and tried to figure out which one was Dellinger. A lot of the crowd looked rich and they made Tommy aware of his clothes. At a glance, he could see that the party was divided into natural fabrics and synthetics. The all-cotton crowd didn't talk to the polyesters. By luck he was wearing a cotton shirt.

The guy who had to be the host was talking to a dozen people who stared at him as if he were the pope. Tommy was too far away to hear what Dellinger was saying, but it looked like the others were trying to grab onto the words as if they were souvenirs. Touch Sidney Dellinger's words and maybe something will rub off. Dellinger was very short, a middle-aged guy, but even from this distance Tommy knew those eyes saw everything. He edged nearer for a closer look. Tommy knew he was as legitimate a guest here as any of them, but he still felt like a fraud who had slipped in under the tent.

"Yes, yes," Dellinger was saying, a broad smile on his face. Up close, Tommy could see his face was lined and creased. Dellinger had silvery hair, combed straight back. He was wearing an old Brooklyn Dodgers warm-up jacket that was frayed enough to be a real one—not some fake silk job, tricked up for rock stars who had never been near Ebbets Field. Tommy stood on the fringes of the circle and listened. Some of the others spoke, but it was Dellinger, the host, the rich man, the success, who held them by the power of his deeds. "The right idea is important, but it has to be right for the time and place," he was saying. "A lot of it is luck. It was wide open out here back then. We recorded in a studio over on Vine Street and pressed them at a factory up in San Francisco. I took the records around to the stations in my fifty-one Merc. Nobody made albums, it was all forty-fives, with the big hole. I just liked the beat and hoped other kids would too. I guess they did." The others laughed and repeated, "I guess they did." Tommy backed away, thinking how amazing it was that Dellinger had come here, to this place, with nothing, and now he had all this. It was a Brooklyn dream of California, and Tommy was one of the dreamers.

The reunion had made Tommy edgy so he went to the gym to work the tension out. An aerobics class had already started on the second floor. Tommy slipped in late and stayed in the back. The instructor was a leggy blond who was prancing around, shouting conflicting instructions that nobody could hear because her rock-and-roll tape was so loud. Probably stoned, Tommy thought. And showing off. Maybe it was seeing all those established people at the reunion, or maybe just the words "came out here after the army, didn't have a nickel," but Tommy's street instinct told him that this class of sweaty, humiliated, confused people was an opportunity if he could just figure how to take advantage of it. He pondered the possibilities before he left to go down to the Nautilus room.

While he was working out, he overheard a conversation about a guy named Greg Tishman who was planning to climb Mount Everest. Greg was a studio executive who had taken a leave of absence to attempt the mountain. The next day, Tommy gave the Nautilus coach twenty bucks, which he could hardly afford, to mention to Greg that old Tommy over there was an expert in conditioning for mountain-climbing. All Tommy knew about mountain-climbing was that you needed strong legs and a mountain. When Greg asked him about this special conditioning program, Tommy said, "Yeah, I know a little about that. What's on your mind?"

"What do you think about Nautilus?"

"Better than nothing, but if you want to climb a hill, you got to work on those legs, right down to the ankles."

"Ankles too?" Greg asked, clearly interested.

"Hey, you're goin' six miles straight up where there's nothing to breathe but yak farts. You better be on pneumatic pumps," Tommy said, pointing to Greg's calves.

Greg sensed the possibility of an advantage and he wanted it. "What do you suggest?"

They began with an hour at Greg's house in Nichols Canyon, no charge. When Greg saw he was making progress, he formalized the deal and began paying Tommy to conduct private workouts. There were other exercise coaches who would come to your house. Some of them had fancy traveling equipment—one of them, the ex-wife of a movie star, came with a traveling gym in a van. Tommy didn't have anything like that so he just modeled his style on a drill instructor he had suffered under at Parris Island when he was in the Marines. Tommy made Greg's muscles burn. He just wouldn't stop when Greg said he couldn't do another fifty sit-ups. The more Greg suffered, the better he thought it was, and then he worked all the harder and made progress. Tommy began sculpturing Greg's legs, which were indeed getting hard as pneumatic pumps.

Greg couldn't stop talking about his hot new exercise coach. He mentioned it to his friend Jay, the publicist. Jay too wanted to be lean and mean instead of flabby and short-winded. Jay never paid for anything if he didn't have to. He flacked for a couple of restaurants and they picked up the tab for his business lunches. In exchange for the workouts, Jay offered to put Tommy's name in the columns and get his business going. Tommy didn't hesitate. A week later *Variety* and the *Hollywood Reporter* were writing about "Tommy's training techniques that allow you to focus on and alter any part of your body." When the phone started ringing, Jay told him to call the business Muscle Burn.

After the first item in *Variety* appeared, an English secretary called to make an appointment for her employer. News of the cult of the English secretary hadn't reached Tommy's one room in Laurel Canyon. Her accent intimidated him. "Mr. and Mrs. Robinson would like you to come to the house," she said in a brisk, clipped voice. Later Tommy learned "the house" meant it would be a very big house. "Our house" meant something more modest.

"Our place" meant an apartment. Tommy took down an address on Ladera Drive. Common sense told him this wasn't the milkman calling, but the only Robinson that meant anything to a Brooklyn boy was Jackie. Jay explained that Sam Robinson was a television producer with four hours on prime time and a wife who goes to lunch. He told Tommy to charge sixty bucks for a half-hour and to leave a bill with the secretary or the butler, or failing that, mail it. "Don't take a check like you're the Sparklett's man. And give diet advice. You know, eat mangoes or papaya puree."

"I hate that stuff. Bird guts and rabbit crap."

"Then say that. They're all diet-happy. Keep your eyes open."

Tommy felt uneasy driving his old Chevy through the big wide gates at the Robinsons'. A Mexican maid led him into a den. The walls were papered in a dark green plaid, the bookshelves filled with leatherbound scripts. The maid asked if he would like anything. He was thinking about asking for a half-million-dollar loan when the silver-haired gentleman of the house strode in, hand extended. "Tommy? I'm Sam Robinson. Good to see you. Let's boogie." Tommy shook Sam's hand and looked at the man's Universal Exerciser machine, and said, "That's okay for general work, but you can't personalize a program on that stuff."

"Okay for off-the-peg but now we're talking bespoke, that it?" Tommy didn't have any idea what the man meant, so he just nodded. Tess Robinson in a bright red Gilda Marx spandex leotard walked in.

"Can I play too?"

"Okay," Tommy said in his everyday voice. "Both of yous then, down on the mat."

"Don't you use music?" Tess asked.

"I use my voice. You know what a sit-up is?"

"Of course," Sam answered.

"Then hit it!" Tommy boomed. "Let's rock and roll!" His voice turned dark and mean as he counted the sit-ups, double-timing in sets of twenty. He screamed the numbers, biting off the words. "One-two, make it hurt, three-four, burn some more."

Tess Robinson stopped after the first ten. But you don't get four hours of prime time on the air by quitting easily, and Sam was not about to be outdone by mountain-climbing Greg Tishman. When

Tommy got to fifty sit-ups, he barked, "On your back, legs in the air." Sam rolled over and put his legs up, perhaps expecting to do the bicycle, an exercise beloved of the stoned aerobics teachers. Tommy reached over and pulled Sam's legs back over his head until his spine cracked. "Lift your tush! I said lift it!" Sam Robinson couldn't lift his tush, no one could. Tommy kept screaming, "I said lift it!" He slipped his hand under the small of Sam's back and pushed. Mr. Robinson's face was turning red but he stretched and lifted. At the end of the thirty minutes Sam Robinson was trembling.

"Great workout," he managed to say as he lurched toward the bathroom. When he heard Sam vomit, Tommy knew he was onto something.

Thirteen months after he had arrived in Los Angeles, Muscle Burn was a fact of Hollywood life. Jay owned twenty percent; Tommy owned a condo in West Hollywood. Instead of the old Chevy he drove a silver BMW with a license plate that said MUSCLE.

Tommy met Jay at Ma Maison once a week to discuss strategy. He left the BMW with the parking valet and walked past the line of Rolls-Royces that were always displayed in front, their noses aimed at Melrose Avenue as if they were about to drive away pulling Ma Maison with them. Tommy never felt comfortable, but Jay insisted he be seen there. The only part of these lunches he liked was watching the constant traffic of slim, long-legged women who paraded through the patio in silky dresses that rolled across their hips when they walked. Tommy hated Ma Maison's food because he never knew what most of it was. They always sat at Jay's table, number two in the patio, a prime spot from which Jay could survey the room.

"Hey, kiddo," Jay said as Tommy arrived. "Who'd you brutalize today?"

Polite lunch chitchat was not Tommy's specialty. No matter. Jay could keep a conversation going with a rock. A waiter came by with menus and the recitation of the day's dishes. Tommy let him go on about the osso bucco and the blackened redfish, then cut him off with, "Double steak, medium rare."

"I'll have abalone, broiled, no butter, and a glass of the white burgundy. Glass of wine, Tommy?"

"Bubble water."

"Bring us a bottle of Pellegrino as well." The waiter backed away as Tommy let out a silent sigh, glad to be through the ordeal. A man in a cashmere blazer and a year-round tan stepped between the white ceramic ducks that decorated the pink-and-green patio and came over to the table.

"Now, here's a pair," he said, shaking Tommy's hand and slapping Jay on the back.

"Artie! Artie!" Jay said. "You know Tommy? This is Artie Kamel."

"Know him? He kicks the shit out of me twice a week. How are you, Tommy? They feeding you right in this dump?"

"I hear it's a go at Fox," Jay said, before Tommy could answer.

"The go is for nine. I bring it in south of eight, Fox puts the difference in prints and ads. Barry loves it. Tommy, I need to switch my Tuesday to an hour earlier. Can you do it?"

"Tuesday? I don't know . . ."

"He can do it," Jay said, not allowing Tommy to hesitate. "Where's the shoot?"

"We're moving the whole thing to London. The fuckin' pound is collapsing and I can save twenty percent going in and ten coming out. Got to go."

When Artie was gone, Jay said, "What an asshole. The guy's packaged thirty pictures, every one a dog. He's zero for thirty."

"How am I supposed to switch his Tuesday? It'll mess up everything."

"Tommy, Tommy, when are you going to learn? He doesn't want to switch. He just wants to know you'll turn your schedule around if he asks. If he really wants to switch, a secretary'll do it."

"Jesus," Tommy muttered. "How'm I supposed to know that?"

"Don't worry about it. I want to do some TV. I'm putting you on Merv. You'll do a workout."

"Everybody'll see what I do. I'll put myself out of business."

"They'll want you all the more. You see the way Artie Kamel looked at you?"

"That guy lives in a house looks like B. Altman's. I kick him around but I don't know what he's talking about."

"You're like a shrink. They tell you what they don't like about their body, you fix it. You're a shaman."

"Just talk in words I know," Tommy said, wishing his steak would arrive.

"Hey, look. Jack Lemmon," Jay said, changing the subject. "That's what you need, some real old Hollywood type." Jay waved to Lemmon, trying to signal him to the table, but Lemmon didn't notice.

"What am I going to do with Jack fuckin' Lemmon? I don't have no more hours in the day."

"The hell with him. He hasn't had a hit in years."

"I don't know, Jay," Tommy said, full of doubt. "All I do is kick a little ass. I don't know what these people are talking about half the time."

"Let me tell you something about these people. All they want in the world is to be classy and have good taste. They're just a bunch of circus clowns who made some money."

"They're millionaires! I'm a wop from Brooklyn. I mean, the houses they got and their fuckin' diets and the dames—Jesus! All the time, it's goor-may this and goor-may that and what kind of food to eat. I mean, what the hell's going on out here?" Tommy blinked, surprised at his own outburst.

"It's Hollywood," Jay said. "Enjoy it."

"What about getting me in a series? Or a feature? What happened to the acting?"

"Not yet. Don't mess with your edge. That's real. The rest is fantasyland. Trust me on this one." Tommy wasn't so sure, but lunch arrived and Jay got up to talk to a producer at the other end of the patio. Tommy cut into his steak, glad to skip the sideshow around him.

Tommy's first morning appointment was in Benedict Canyon with Jack Sanderson, an agent at the William Morris office. Tommy parked his BMW next to Sanderson's Jaguar with the license plate 10PRCNT. Sanderson's house was high-tech, a metal catwalk running the length of the living room. There was a large steel sculpture of a yogurt container near the door. Tommy ignored it and stopped to glance at a treadmill rigged with a video projector. Sanderson used it to practice cross-country skiing while tapes of snowy mountain trails were projected in front of him. When Tommy first saw it, he said, "Bag that crap when I'm around, or I won't be." Now the contraption just sits unused, at least in Tommy's presence.

At the pool, Sanderson was talking to New York on a cordless phone. He was sprawled on a sofa that had been fashioned from a Philippine pig trough, made comfortable by a large pillow with "More Eclectic Than Thou" embroidered on it. "Little late, aren't you?" Sanderson said, putting down the phone.

"Don't look like you lost any weight," Tommy shot back. "On your belly, and hit it!" Sanderson sprawled on the redwood deck and started doing push-ups. Tommy barked the count and snapped a rolled towel above the man's backside. If Sanderson got too high, he got zapped. "Fingertips," Tommy snarled; Sanderson switched to fingertip push-ups. Tommy stepped up the speed, yelling out, "Clap in between." Fingertip push-ups with claps between are for professional athletes and soldiers. After twenty minutes, Sanderson was quivering at poolside. "You're a pussy," Tommy snorted. "Your gut is what you deserve. You don't work, you'll never look no different than your sorry self. This is a waste of my time. Fuck it. I'm going."

"Wait a minute. Take it easy. I've got some time coming up, I'm going to get on track."

"When I'm not here you don't do shit. You got to show respect for what I'm teaching or what's the point?" Tommy said, a hurt look in his eyes. They bantered back and forth, with Tommy threatening never to come back and Sanderson trying to make a compromise. Finally Tommy agreed to give him another chance. Sanderson looked relieved.

Mark Collins was as near as an actor can get to being a star without being one. He was twenty-four and had played the lead in two teenage hits, which made his price eight hundred thousand dollars a picture. But the public had only a vague idea who he was.

Tommy saw him five mornings a week, courtesy of Helen Markel, the producer of Mark's next picture. Helen, a woman in her late fifties, had instructed Tommy to "Make that kid a hunk. Get him so every little girl in the audience gets squishy." Because he didn't ask for Tommy's services, Mark was a little different from the other clients. Tommy had learned to soften the verbal abuse. During their first session, when Tommy told him, "Eat dirt," Mark just laughed.

As Tommy walked up to Mark's rented house in Santa Monica, two exhausted-looking young women wobbled their way toward the street. Inside, the air was heavy with the odors of sex and drugs.

"I can't hack this," Mark said, sprawled on a sofa.

"Yeah, you can. We'll do it all laying down."

"Hey, man, I'm wrecked." Tommy was unsure if he should bully this guy into the session or try to reschedule. Mark signaled to him from the sofa. "I got an idea for you," he rasped. "Come here."

"Yeah?" Tommy said, sensing something weird.

"I'll give you a thousand dollars to split. Tell Helen whatever she wants to hear. Tomorrow we'll get back to it. I promise." No Brooklyn boy ever got a better offer and Tommy couldn't suppress a grin. "On the table," Mark muttered. "My wallet. Get it." Tommy flipped him the billfold and Mark fished out a wad of hundred-dollar bills. "I'll see you," he groaned. Then he turned over on the sofa and fell asleep.

Tommy's first afternoon session was Panos, a production executive at one of the studios. They held the workout in his office. Panos spent his first session propositioning Tommy, who politely refused. "But you're so gorgeous," Panos kept saying. "Don't waste all that on women." Unlike men rejected by women, Panos didn't pout or get angry. He did suggest that Tommy open a gay division. "You know, 'Pecs by Pete,' or whatever. You'd make a fortune." Tommy just laughed, put a broomstick behind Panos' back, and made him do one hundred and fifty intense, high-speed twists and stretches.

After the workout, Panos beckoned Tommy toward his

bathroom. Tommy hesitated. "Oh, don't worry, nothing like that." The bathroom had a marble counter where six lines of flaky, ivory-colored cocaine were laid out. "I can cut it right on the marble. Very convenient." Panos leaned over and snorted two lines. "Umm . . . Almost as good as blond boys. Only way to fly."

"No, thanks."

"Now, look, Snooks. Don't say no to this. You're not in Brooklyn anymore. What's the point of coming to Hollywood and treating it like your mother's house? Snuffle up."

Tommy thought about it for a moment. The man had a point. As he was considering, Panos rolled a hundred-dollar bill into a straw. Tommy leaned over the marble counter and inhaled a nose full of Hollywood's most famous candy. As Tommy snorted, Panos couldn't resist patting his behind. In a few minutes Tommy could feel the blood in his veins and he began to talk rapidly. "I can see my heart," he said. "I can see it pumping. Look at it! Oh, my God!"

Panos laughed, delighted. "Now maybe you'll listen to me when I suggest new adventures."

"I don't mind this." Tommy dropped to the floor for twenty-five one-armed push-ups, then rolled over for a series of high-speed sit-ups.

It amused Panos for a while, but then he got bored and started making phone calls. "Careful, darling, you're likely to crash," he said, flipping through his Rolodex.

"I'm fine."

"You know what they say about coke, don't you? When you're up, you do what you really want. I usually grab ass, you do exercises." Panos laughed at the absurdity of it and Tommy started doing push-ups again. Panos giggled, leaned down, and ran his hand across Tommy's thigh. Tommy was too stoned to care, and too happy doing his push-ups to pay any attention. His interest in men was minimal, but he was so high, so wired, and Panos was so easygoing about it, that Tommy didn't object. He didn't exactly participate, but he stopped exercising and let Panos stroke him. As he was about to sink his mouth onto Tommy's crotch, Panos looked up at Tommy's indifferent face and said, "Close your eyes and think of England." Tommy didn't get the joke. He went along just to see what all the fuss was about.

Tommy had planned to go to a party that night but by evening he wasn't up to meeting new people. He flipped through the scrap-book Jay's secretary made for him, looking at his clippings. The go-round with Panos had upset him. He barely remembered the details, but the fact of it made him uneasy. I'm like some girl who says she got drunk and now she don't remember a thing. He put the cassette of his talk-show appearance into the video recorder and watched himself with Merv. When he'd seen it all the way through, he watched it again. In the morning he told Panos it would be better if he found another trainer.

The next day Tommy put his troubles out of his mind and got on the road early, determined to push his clients into health and strength, no matter how hard they fought it. He drove out to Coldwater Canyon for a session with Carol Button and Steve Miller. On the way, Tommy mused that these canyons were filled with couples like Carol and Steve—shiksa actresses from the Midwest and their hard-charging husbands, New York Jewish guys who were always the girls' lawyers or agents.

When Tommy arrived, Steve was on the phone talking to Tokyo, making a deal for Carol to model sportswear for Japanese television commercials. He waved apologetically to Tommy, indicating he couldn't take the session. Carol, in denim bib overalls and no underwear, greeted Tommy at the kitchen door. "It's just me. Okay?"

"Let's see what's in there first," he said, heading for the Sub-Zero refrigerator, about to make a surgical strike. "What's this?" he snapped, holding a tinfoil duck.

"Left-over duck salad from the Le Dôme. They wrapped it like that. Cute, huh?"

"Bag it," Tommy said, tossing the duck into the garbage. "This?" he asked, holding another tinfoil packet.

"My salad from somewhere," she answered, not at all surprised to see Tommy going through her refrigerator.

"Birdfood. I want red meat in this house. Eggs."

"Steve's worried about the cholesterol."

"Doctor talk. It's all bullshit. Eat protein. Let's go. Poolside."

"Can we do it in the media room? So I can have music?"

"No. It takes away from the work."

"It could be a learning experience. For personal growth and all, we should be more gentle."

"No pain, no gain," Tommy said, ending the discussion.

At the pool, he loomed over Carol, screaming in her ear, using fear to send her through the series of exercises. After twenty minutes, when Carol was sweating and struggling to keep up, her husband came out to the pool. Steve was from Brooklyn too, and although he was older and richer than Tommy, the two men always circled one another, each certain he knew the other's secrets. "How's she doing?" Steve asked. Carol was too involved to talk and Tommy was working. Steve was not a man who liked to be ignored, certainly not by the help, no matter how celebrated or how true a son of Brooklyn. "Double session for me next time," Steve said, a tiny edge in his voice.

Tommy backed off from Carol and glanced up; his eyes told Steve to wait just another minute. "Ten laps. Move it! Then pull-ups at the edge. Come on, hit it!" Carol peeled off her denim overalls, startling Steve.

"You wearing a suit?" She ignored him and dived in, naked. It rattled Steve but Tommy stayed detached. He was more interested in firming Carol's flesh than fondling it. While she was cutting through the water, doing her laps, Tommy finally turned to Steve.

"Double session is bullshit. That's gym talk. Ninety-five percent of what you're going to get, you get in thirty right minutes."

"You're the coach," Steve said, watching his wife.

"Get it smokin'!" Tommy screamed. "Make it burn." Carol kicked in, raced back to the edge, and started to pull herself up out of the pool. Tommy knelt and put his palm on her head, pushing her back down. "Hands on the edge and pull up fast." Carol pulled herself up until her breasts were level with Tommy's eyes. He shoved her back down into the water, yelling, "Again, faster." Steve watched, trying to decide if he should stop it, join it, or ignore it. The man was an agent, and true to his profession, which teaches stay away from personal trouble at all costs, he chose the last.

From Coldwater Canyon Tommy drove out the Pacific Coast Highway to the Old Malibu Road and Tanya Reisenbach.

Tommy's late-morning clients were actors and actresses who, when they're not working, tend to sleep late. Tanya had a television series for several years and now she lived very well on the syndication income and her fantasies about a feature career. Tommy parked in front of her house and for a moment listened to the Pacific, a few hundred feet away. Tommy had spent a lot of his childhood at Coney Island, but the Pacific, so vast and blue, with its insistent rolling waves, always amazed him. While he was considering the water, Tanya honked and drove up in her red Fiat convertible, license plate HOTSY. She parked in her driveway, waved to Tommy, then jumped out of the car with a bag of groceries. Tanya was wearing her morning uniform of a black leotard, cut high on her thighs, silver spandex tights, and lavender wool leg warmers that drooped and sagged, unlike any part of her body, which was as firm and tight as thirty-four-year-old flesh could be.

"Want to see what I got?" Before Tommy could tell her he didn't care what she had, she spread the groceries on the hood of her car. "Fertilized eggs, brown long-grain rice, and a jicama. Okay?" she asked, hoping for his approval.

"What's this garbage?" he asked, poking the jicama. "Eat meat. You don't stoke the furnace, the engine don't go."

"Meat is poison," she said petulantly. "I eat fish and veggies."

"Birdfood! Let's go to work." Tanya left the groceries on the car, certain that someone in her employ would pick them up, and led Tommy through the house. Tanya's living room opened onto the ocean. It was furnished with white deco scallop-back chairs and sofas. There were big pillows by the stone fireplace, and bits of colored glass, and wind chimes hung in the windows.

"If I ate as much red meat as you, what about my alkali-acid levels?" she asked, glancing at herself in a mirror.

"You worried about the moo cows? What do you think they're for? To eat and make shoes out of."

"Maybe if I doubled my lecithin and took more vitamin E . . ." Her voice trailed off, lost in diet thoughts.

"Protein is everything," he said flatly.

"I want to check out my new diet with you," she said, oblivious of his contempt for the food she ate. "For a meal, only one food group. If I have grapefruit, I don't have bread. Sometimes I have rolled oats. Is that okay?"

"Those eggs you got, they're good," he said, leading her through the French doors to the patio.

"My nutritionist says not to mix, but my psychic says eat more melon before noon. My dry cleaner says eat big in the morning and less as the day goes on." She sprawled on an exercise mat as the wind from the Pacific rolled in.

Tommy took her through his standard drill of butt burns, broomstick twisters, and leg rolls, and when he barked the orders, Tanya's skin tingled. As Tommy headed for the end of the session, he went to work on her arms. "Get the oranges," he said, making it sound like Brando telling Maria Schneider to get the butter. He put them in the crook of her arms and ordered her to curl until the oranges broke and the juice ran down. The oranges were the final exercise, and when her arms got sticky, Tanya always invited Tommy to lick the juice. He always did and they always wound up in her bedroom amid stuffed animals and Liberty-print pillows. Tommy always sent her a bill and she always paid.

By midafternoon Tommy was finished with his beach appointments and he went back to Hollywood to put Jay through his paces. Jay usually threw a mat on his office floor and exercised until he got bored with it, which was about fifteen minutes after he started. "I want you to go see Olivia Callender," Jay said, trying to catch his breath. "You know who she is, don't you?"

"Yeah. When?"

"It has to be tomorrow morning and you're going to have to spend all day. Probably all week. You don't leave till she's buffed up."

"Wait a minute. I got a schedule here."

"I'll call your clients. We'll say you have the flu and don't want to infect anybody."

"It's going to screw up everything."

"Tony Keller's got some idea for her," Jay said, mentioning a prominent television producer. "He thinks she could make a big comeback. It's possible. Olivia's a little on the weird side. Eccentric."

Olivia Callender had been a big star when Tommy was a kid. He remembered her in costume dramas, with her long neck and high cheekbones. She always played haughty aristocrats, and men were always fighting over her. Tommy parked in front of a rambling old Spanish house in Mandeville Canyon and stepped into the midst of several barking dogs.

"Hello," she said, answering the door with two more dogs yapping behind her. "Ready if you are." She looked about fifty-five, with puffy cheeks and a sallow complexion. She was still Olivia, no doubt about it. She was wearing a caftan, and Tommy thought she must be a blimp under that thing, why else wear it? Her house was simply furnished and even Tommy could tell that no decorator had ever been near it. He sank into an old down sofa and watched Olivia pour jasmine tea. After a few minutes, Tommy realized that for the first time, he was comfortable in a client's house.

As they sipped the tea, Olivia explained she had been dieting for six weeks and was feeling better than she had in a while, but she was flabby. "When I was younger, I never had a weight problem. I swam a lot, so I was in good shape. My life is different now." For a moment Tommy thought she was going to talk about her life. That's what actresses did all the time. But she changed her mind and said, "I'm told you're the man to help."

Olivia was the first Hollywood figure Tommy had encountered whom he had liked from the first moment. In the time they worked together, she never raised her voice, never tried to impress him or browbeat him. From the start he knew he could hardly bark commands at her or call her a scumbag. The woman was a lady and it made a gentleman out of Tommy.

It was true she was flabby and a little overweight. The worst part was she carried herself like a fat person. The first morning, they worked at an easy pace. Tommy found himself doing the exercises with her. If he told her to do fifty tummy tucks, he did them as well. If he wanted her to stretch her spine, he stretched his. The pace was less furious than he was used to, but she was sweating, and Tommy knew that meant it was working. During one of their breaks Olivia asked him about himself and his business. He told her about growing up in Brooklyn but he didn't have the nerve to say he really wanted to be an actor. She was interested in whatever he said and she even told him a little about herself. After her divorce she had sort of retreated into this house and her animals. Now, finally, she wanted to get back to work. It was a relaxed conversation and Tommy didn't worry about how he was going over or if he was saying the right thing.

The afternoon session included a three-mile run and a hike up to the top of the hill behind Olivia's house. A couple of the dogs trailed after them and when they got to the top they soaked up the afternoon sun. "I think you're going to be okay," Tommy told her.

"How long do you think it will take?"

"If we work like this, you'll feel tone in a few days. By a week you'll look different."

"I don't know if I can take a week of it."

"Sure you can. Part of it, I can't help you with."

"What's that?"

Tommy thought for a moment about how to say his answer. He thought he'd rather die than insult this woman, but he was here to do a job and he wanted to succeed as much for her as for himself. "You have to think different than you do," he said finally. "You walk around like a fat person. You think you're dumpy."

"Well, I'm not exactly a water sprite."

"I keep seeing you in those movies. The way you stood. It was, I don't know . . ." His voice trailed off into his memories. He was quiet for fear of hurting her feelings.

"Proud?" she asked quietly.

"That's the word. I can help you firm up. You do the rest."

"I'll just have to act." She said it without any self-pity, but Tommy wondered why she should have to fake pride.

He spent a week with Olivia, from morning till evening, stretching her, massaging her muscles, pushing and bending her back into shape. By the end of the week her skin had a glow and she had put aside the caftan. It was a victory for both of them but Tommy knew he would miss their talks and the serenity of her house. He wasn't exactly in love with her. She was older, and nothing in their time together had suggested romance. It was that he felt comfortable with her, and that made him realize how uncomfortable he felt the rest of the time. On their last day together Tommy said, "If it's okay, I'd like to come up an hour or two a week. To make sure you're on track." Then he added, feeling awkward, "And to see you." He explained he'd have to charge for the current week because he'd put his other business on hold for her. "But from now on I want to just do it. You know, no charge."

Olivia laughed and told him she was flattered but of course she'd pay him. They could be friends and he should come for lunch or a talk whenever he liked.

"I don't have a lot of friends," he said, feeling embarrassed to say it.

"Why on earth is that?"

"I just work and I only see the people I work around. And they're not . . . well, you know."

"I do know. Would you rather be doing something else?"

"Not right now. I like to be right here."

"I mean with your life."

"I want to be an actor," he said, not worrying that she would laugh at him. "It's hard."

"It certainly is. I don't know if I'm the best person to give this kind of advice, since everybody seems to think I've made a mess of my life, but if that's what you want to do, shouldn't you try it?"

"Your life looks pretty good."

"All I mean is, eventually we all become some version of what we want to be. We don't always know the steps, but I think that deep down what I want is to be pretty much what I am. Not completely, but I've made the life I want. Maybe even the one I deserve. If you want to be an actor, you'll find a way."

"I took some classes. I don't sound right is one of the problems."

"Not true. You'd have trouble playing classical roles, but you're ideal for the movies. Don't let anybody tell you different. You sound like city streets and that's just fine. But it's hard to know. You're doing well at something and I think it gives you some pleasure. At least being successful makes you feel good. That's okay. Why fight something that gives you pleasure?"

"Because something else might give me more."

"And there you have the dilemma of modern life. My answer to it was to drop out totally." She shrugged as if to say: You'll have to find your answer your own way.

No one had taken him quite so seriously before. He knew that even if nothing more came of it, he'd always feel better. He thanked her and then overcame his shyness and asked what she had been doing since she stopped making movies.

"Not much. I wasn't a drug addict or anything like that. I didn't even mean to be a dropout. The business all got so difficult. Everyone at each other's throats all the time. The actors were all so self-absorbed and the producers were so vile. Then we had all that craziness about auteurs, and the directors decided they were gods. All the writers were docile as mice and getting ulcers. I just hated it, so I said: Why do it if you don't like it? Why not just quit? Everybody said, 'You're too famous to quit.' Then my marriage came apart, and I didn't feel like seeing anybody, and the next thing I knew, it was fifteen years later."

Tommy knew he had just heard the truth, unadorned. He drank it down like a thirsty man. "I hope this works out for you," he said.

"I do too. It's a series. If I get it, I would play this sort of grande dame. When they called, I knew I wanted it."

"You'll get it."

"You're dear to think that, but an actor never knows. That's our real burden. I want this job, and if I don't get it, well, I'll be sorry. Briefly. Then I intend to put it out of my mind. I'm not going to let these people tell me if I can be happy. You can do that too."

"Maybe I can," he said. "Sometimes I think I totally lost control of this thing." Then he told her all about his business and how it started, how he had just screamed at people because he couldn't afford equipment. Olivia laughed and told him she thought that was wonderful, just what Hollywood deserved. It made him feel good, and he wanted to pour his heart out to her, tell her about Sidney Dellinger, who came out here without a nickel, and look what he became, and about Panos and how bad it had made him feel. He wanted to tell her he was unhappy and confused and maybe she could make it better. But he didn't let himself go quite so completely. All he managed was, "Jay wants me to write this book about exercise. He keeps sending these writers around. I don't know what the hell they're talking about. I keep saying: I can't write it, I don't know how. Then Jay sends over more writers. Five guys already. All they do is work out with me, then have lunch. They don't want to write the book either." Olivia started to laugh and then Tommy was laughing with her. The dogs began to bark and dance around them and it was the first time he had found his business problems funny.

The next day Tommy and Jay had lunch at La Toque, which was less intense than Ma Maison but where the menu was too nouvelle for Tommy. Jay had persuaded the chef to make Tommy a six-egg cheese omelet. Jay wanted him to expand the business, to franchise his name and techniques. "It's just a matter of getting used to the idea of not taking care of every detail," Jay said, taking a bite of his confit of duck. "Very big indeed."

"What happened to the idea of me being in a movie? We don't talk about that anymore."

"It'll happen," Jay said. "But not just any picture. When the right one's here, I'll know."

"It could be great. I play myself. We go around with me to all my sessions and I talk right to the camera while I kick ass. I could do it," Tommy said, forgetting his omelet. "It opens on me waking up. I do my own workout. Nobody's never seen nothing like it. Two hundred sit-ups, bam-bam-bam. One-armed push-ups, bam-fuckin'-bam. Then we cut to me doing some pussy drill on a client and the guy's falling apart over fifty sit-ups. See? I'm tough all right, but where I'm really tough, the fiercest guy going down, is on me."

"Thought about it, haven't you?" Jay said, ordering another glass of cabernet. "Sounds like a documentary."

"No, no. A feature. Only it's about me and I'm in it. I act all day right now. So why not?"

"You go make some movie and you're out of business for six months. Think the choo-choo waits around here? Forget it. Three guys'll take your place before you get film in the camera. Relax. You were a big hit with Olivia Callender. She told Tony Keller you were great."

"She's the good one. She going to do the show?"

"Hard to say. They're talking to some other people."

"They're always talking to some other people, aren't they, Jay?" Tommy raised his voice a little, without meaning to. "No matter what fish is in the barrel, you're always looking for another one. Ain't that right?"

"Take it easy," Jay said, surprised at his anger.

"The thing is, I don't even like screaming at people all day. It's stupid."

"That's you, huh? Screamer to the stars."

"I want to be in a movie," Tommy said, with an ache in his voice.

"Picture this," Jay whispered, leaning close, taking advantage of Tommy's pain. "Every city in the country has a gym called Muscle Burn. Coaches that you personally train lead the workouts."

"It'd turn out like all the other gyms, which are crap completely."

"Except it'd be yours. Don't be stupid. You can always be an actor. How many chances like this you think you're going to get? Listen to me on this. You're hot enough right now for your clients to finance the expansion. Ten guys with fifty G's each who want in on the ground floor. The rest will follow. You only get that while you're hot. You understand?"

"I don't know how to raise money. How am I going to ask these people for that?"

"Schmuck, you don't have to do anything but what you're doing. We get this thing rolling, you'll be pulling down half a million a year. For no work. Then, if you still want to be an actor, you can name your terms. I don't believe you. In sixteen months you can buy all the actors you want. They're all for sale and you know it."

"Not all of them."

"Yeah, yeah. This is Olivia Callender talking, right?" Jay said, reading his mind. "It's all that get-in-synch-with-yourself crap. That woman's got a screw loose. She didn't come out of her house for three years. They had to send the dogfood in. You going to let her give you advice?"

"Olivia Callender has more talent and more brains in her little finger than every one of your fifty-grand guys put together. She's got different standards and it don't matter what you think."

"Yeah, yeah," Jay said, trying to get the conversation back on track. "She's a wonderful human being and I would be too if I was at peace with my inner self. Okay?" Tommy looked across the table at Jay and saw him grinning. It was the smile of a man who knew his argument was persuasive. "Trust me, Tommy. I might not love little animals and all green things, but I know what to do with heat. I can turn it into an empire. Your empire. Did I mention half a mil a year for no work by the second year?"

"Yeah, Jay. I think you mentioned it."

"It can be done. You have to be ready. No hesitation. I can set it up. Now, what are you going to do?"

There was still a corner of his heart that wanted to refuse the whole thing, but only a little corner, and he nodded yes. It was only a tentative nod, but as Jay's smile got bigger, the nod got more vigorous and then Tommy said to Jay, "Make the deal. Let's raise the money."

Sometimes Tommy got a little drunk on the visions Jay conjured. Even though he'd said yes, he was worried that he'd painted himself into a gilded corner, and no matter what Jay said, he'd never get to be an actor. But he was in Hollywood, where there were always possibilities. Tommy knew that when he was feeling confused he could go out to Mandeville Canyon and talk it over with Olivia. She'd help him sort things out and make him feel better. In the meantime, he still woke up early, ate a steak and six eggs, and when Jay wasn't torturing him, he spent his day torturing Hollywood.

Bob Hope's Writers

A lot of the work I did in Hollywood was rewriting and doctoring other people's scripts. I didn't realize it at first, but part of my feel for rewrites was a result of my background as a reporter. Scripts are different from newspaper stories, of course, but there are similarities. To revise a script you have to decide what the script is trying to say and if it's worth saying. You have to ask yourself if the characters are credibly drawn, and if so, are they interesting enough to spend two hours with. Newspaper work involves similar judgments—of course, on a paper the subjects and events are (presumably) real and actual; in a script they're whatever you make them. A few years of covering the passing parade had taught me facility. Because it was all so ephemeral, I was quite used to jettisoning pages, starting over, or having someone else revise and update my work. Most scripts that get shot in Hollywood have been through sets of drafts—for the studio, for the director, again for the star, and again for the budget. Most screenwriters shudder at the thought of it; it seemed a natural procedure to me.

During the time I was playing doctor to damaged scripts, I worked at the studios. I'd be at Warner's for a while, and then shift over to Paramount for a few months, and then to Universal or Fox, playing the circuit, as I liked to call it. I had lunch at all the commissaries and got to know a lot of actors, directors, producers, and other screenwriters. But each time a job was completed, I'd have to pack up and leave. I was always in some stage of moving offices. Given my transcontinental bent, it seemed important to feel settled, if for no other reason than it might encourage me to stay in one place. I decided I'd have to have my own office, where the lease wasn't dependent on the head of production or the time it took to beef up a second act.

I took a pleasant room in the Writers and Artists Building in Beverly Hills. The building was in an architectural style of an earlier era. Instead of a front door, there was an open arch and a set of stairs that led to the offices. The offices locked, of course, but anyone could wander down the corridor. The assumption of the architect must have been that neither weather nor intruders were a problem in Southern California.

My room looked out onto the street and had a view of Hunter's Bookstore, which was a constant temptation. My neighbors were two comedy writers who had seen *Cry I Am,* the cult film I wrote in Schwab's. Because they also knew I had once covered city politics in New York, the guys next door thought of me as a combination of Noël Coward and Walter Lippmann.

Bert and Harvey had been at the business of writing comedy for three years when they got the job that led to writing jokes for Bob Hope. The three years had been harder on Harvey than Bert, who didn't have anyone else to support. Harvey's wife, Freda, worked at the phone company and although she didn't complain, she wasn't crazy about being married to an underemployed comedy writer. Harvey, who could always make Freda laugh, had been a schoolteacher in Chicago when they met. His dream, which he shared only with Freda, had been to go to Hollywood and try his hand. "I know I'm funny, and you know. But what does it mean if I don't ever test it?" She had encouraged him and they had moved west so Harvey might find out if he could be funny for a living. Only now that he was doing it full-time, his wit seemed forced and studied. He talked about comedy a lot, theorizing about what was funny and what wasn't, but nobody was laughing, least of all Freda. Bert was a bachelor and so if he was morose in the evenings, he just stayed home and ate Lean Cuisine. Bert and Harvey met in Hollywood when they were each trying to launch careers.

They liked each other and found a shared sensibility, so they decided to become partners. They spent their days in the W&A Building, trying to be funny, while next door I worked on my scripts and wondered why there was never any laughter on the other side of the wall. If they didn't have an assignment, which was most of the time, they worked on proposals for television series or treatments for movies. When they weren't productive they walked over to Nate and Al's Delicatessen and sat around with the retired and out-of-work comics, drinking coffee and schmoozing about the difficulties of it all.

The chance to write jokes for Bob Hope came from Bert and Harvey's first real job, which was to punch up the script of a film that was already in production. They were to add jokes and polish the dialogue. In addition to being paid, Bert and Harvey got to spend their days on a film set. They got the job not through Mitchell, their agent, but because one of the guys at Nate and Al's had recommended them, and because they were willing to work cheap. The picture, called *The House Moron,* was independently financed, but Charlie, the producer, had a distribution deal with MGM. That meant Mitchell could claim his clients were working for MGM, which was sort of true. They went to the film's location each day and sat in the director's trailer writing jokes about a man who had to stay home and mind the kids while his wife went to her job as a welder. There was a subplot about a beautiful exercise teacher who was also a drug dealer, but Bert and Harvey ignored that and concentrated on jokes about an adorable but still masculine guy making a mess in the kitchen.

Bert and Harvey worked hard and everybody laughed at what they wrote. The actors were so glad to be working, they just said whatever dialogue was put in front of them. Bert and Harvey were paid twenty-five hundred dollars when they started, with another thousand due when they completed the job. After they banked the first check, Harvey and Freda and Bert and his date, the makeup woman from the picture, went to the Imperial Gardens, a Japanese restaurant where the management would give you a good table even if you weren't famous. The four of them ate sushi and drank a lot of sake. When Bert took his date home, she invited him in and he didn't leave till morning.

After *The House Moron* was finished, Charlie told them what a great job they had done and how he couldn't imagine ever shooting a picture without calling in Bert and Harvey to punch up the script. "Guys," Charlie said, "my problem is cash flow," which meant he didn't have the money to pay them. "The thing of it is, you wrote so great, we had to shoot it all. So now I'm over budget. I'm sick about it." Mitchell threatened to enjoin the picture, but Charlie had a solution that he was sure would be satisfactory. Charlie had made deals with the manufacturers of household appliances to use their products in the movie. In the kitchen scenes there were several gags with the dishwasher—gags that Bert and Harvey had written—that showed how lovable and inept the hero was around the house. In one of the gags, he washed his socks in the dishwasher and in another he put the groceries in the trash compactor. Charlie had cut a deal with Kitchen Aid to provide the appliances. The film was to include a couple of shots with the brand name prominently displayed. Charlie had made deals for almost everything in the film. He was driving a new Thunderbird because everyone in the film drove Ford products. Ford wouldn't give Charlie the Thunderbird outright, but they had given him a twelve-month lease and insurance. The kitchen appliances were his to keep and his solution to the cash-flow problem was to offer the stuff to Bert and Harvey. He also promised to do everything he could to get them screen credit and gave them five net points. Since it was either take the deal or spend the rest of their lives chasing Charlie through the courts for a thousand dollars, they agreed. They were each given their choice of three major appliances. Harvey as the married man went first. He selected the Hotpoint double-door refrigerator, the Kitchen Aid dishwasher, and a set of copper pots. Bert went for a Westinghouse microwave oven, the trash compactor, and a GE oven and range. Mitchell got a Mr. Coffee machine and a food processor.

Bert and Harvey were disappointed not to get the money, but the idea of the whole thing turning into some crazed version of *The Price Is Right* amused them enough to ease the pain. They were able to use the experience in a comedy monologue that Mitchell sent to Bob Hope's company as a sample of their work. Mitchell told the Hope people that Bert and Harvey were just coming off a picture at Metro and the monologue was the sort of thing they could do. Now, if Mitchell had been any kind of an agent he would have known that Hope rarely hired free-lancers. Hope's writers, most of whom were almost as old as their boss, worked for him exclusively. Hope was getting ready to do a series of campus shows and thought he should have some younger writers in on the job. It had been some years since Bert and Harvey considered themselves young enough to be collegiate; to the Hope organization, they were practically adolescents. The deal Mitchell struck for them wasn't much. They were to submit jokes that would work on college campuses, and any that Hope laughed at, he would buy. If he didn't buy any, they would be paid a modest kill fee and that would be that. As Mitchell pointed out, if he did buy, they could bill themselves as "Bob Hope's gag writers" and they would be in great demand. So Bert and Harvey burrowed into their office to work up the jokes. They stopped going to Nate and Al's for breakfast and had sandwiches sent in for lunch. They worked furiously for ten days and came up with several pages of wisecracks, one-liners, and ideas for sketches. Their only instructions were to remember that at each college, Hope would be onstage with the homecoming queen or the student-body president, so he would always be provided with a local straight man.

Question: Bob (or Mr. Hope), how do you manage to keep up your hectic schedule?

Hope: I play a little golf, I eat right, and I use industrial-strength Geritol in a drum.
(laugh)

It's true I have done a bit of flying. I'm the only guy I know who's been in the air longer than the smog.
(laugh)

I fly so much the airlines issue me a season ticket.
(laugh)

But I want to tell you, the campus sure has changed since my day. I remember when the homecoming queen was a girl.

Mitchell personally delivered the jokes to Hope's office at NBC. What Bert and Harvey didn't know then, but have since learned, is that for Bob Hope to use three or four jokes out of, say, seventy-five, is not bad. His regular writers call him Piggy because he demands so many jokes and uses so few. So when Mitchell told Bert and Harvey that Hope was taking two of their gags they were disappointed. It meant they were to be paid, which was good news, but it was hard for them not to feel let down. Then Hope's office called and said the boss liked the stuff so much that he wanted the boys (he was already calling them "the boys" even though he'd never met them) to work up some sketches for his next NBC special. Mitchell pointed out that in comedy writing, this was the big time. They had done well on the campus shows. Now they were being given an opportunity which could mean big salaries. Mitchell was already pricing Porsches.

The trouble was, Bert and Harvey had worked so hard on the campus gags, they were having real trouble writing more. And the sketches, which had to include other characters, were doubly difficult. How could you write a sketch for Hope and, say, Ann-Margret, before you knew if it was going to be Ann-Margret, or Angie Dickinson, or Joey Heatherton, or maybe some starlet they had never even heard of. It was tough and Bert and Harvey were stuck. Hope expected pages fast and they knew if they didn't deliver, they were out. "I mean, it's one thing to be a blocked novelist," Bert said, "but a blocked gag writer?"

"Let's just give him the ones he didn't take from the campus gig. He'll never remember," Harvey said.

"We do that, we'll be right out on the street."

"We're practically on the street now," Harvey answered testily. They weren't exactly fighting, but it was tense between them.

Bert was losing sleep over the problem. He would sit up late and watch all the talk shows, hoping for inspiration. About two in the morning he found himself staring glumly at something called *Night-Owl Comedy,* which was mostly reruns of sketches from other shows. It was on a cable station and for the most part it was the bottom of the barrel. As Bert was watching, the show ran a Bob Hope parody, from SCTV. Apparently it was a staple of the show, but Bert had never seen it. When it started, he knew he had found the answer to their problem. He called Harvey, woke him, and told him to tune in. They watched simultaneously and talked on the phone as the sketch played. It was called "Bob Hope's Desert Classic," but instead of being about the Palm Springs golf tournament Hope promoted every year, it took place in the Sinai Desert and Hope played golf with Yasir Arafat and Ariel Sharon. It was very funny and Dave Thomas, the guy who played Hope, was uncannily accurate. For the first time in weeks Bert and Harvey could laugh about Bob Hope.

The next morning Bert and Harvey knew exactly what to do. They would stop trying to write for Bob Hope, and begin writing for a parody of Bob Hope. They wouldn't go so far as to put Yasir Arafat into the sketches, but instead of trying to create Bob Hope jokes, they would just loosen up and mock the whole thing. They both agreed that Hope had been doing what he does for so long he had become a parody of himself anyway. Instead of trying to fight that, they would embrace it. Mitchell had told them to work up some football gags, because Hope was negotiating with Joe Namath to be a guest star on the show.

Locker Room—Coach's Office

Namath as the coach is on the phone.

NAMATH

This is Coach Namath speaking.

Applause from the audience.

I'm sorry, you're just not mean and tough enough to play for me. Thanks for calling us, Mr. T.

Suddenly a football comes crashing through the window.

SFX: *breaking glass.*

Hope enters wearing an old-fashioned football uniform and leather helmet.

Applause from the audience.

NAMATH

Who are you?

HOPE

I'm your new place kicker, Bob "Big Foot" Hope.

Hope holds up his right leg, revealing a giant shoe.

Audience laughs.

HOPE

How do you like my Muck-a-lucks?

Audience laughs.

HOPE

I got them from Zsa Zsa's closet.

Audience laughs.

NAMATH

Where'd you learn to kick like that?

HOPE

I was first string at Southern Geriatric.

Audience laughs.

HOPE

Then I was at Flagstaff, Arizona. And then Winona, Kingman, Barstow, San Bernardino . . .

NAMATH

You mean . . .

HOPE

That's right . . . I got my kicks on Route 66.

Audience laughs.

Namath shakes Hope's hand. Cue music. Cut to commercial.

Harvey thought it might be too extreme, but Bert said if anything, it wasn't enough of a parody. He wanted to add more Zsa Zsa jokes but Harvey insisted that would anger Hope rather than amuse him. They gave the sketch to Mitchell, who was relieved to get anything from them.

The next day Mitchell called to say, "They love it. Hope says it's great. The funniest thing he ever saw. You hear me? Bob Hope loves it! He loves you guys. You're his new favorite writers!"

"That's great," Bert managed to say. Harvey was too stunned to say anything.

"The only thing is," Mitchell added, "since it's a sports sketch, can you put in some hockey pucks?"

"Yeah . . . I guess so," Bert mumbled, unsure if Mitchell was making the first joke of his life.

"A couple more little things, too," Mitchell said. "They're having trouble getting Namath, so change it around for either Reggie Jackson or this girl golfer, I forget her name."

"But that's impossible," Bert said. "Reggie Jackson's a baseball player. It changes everything."

"What golfer?" Harvey asked, panic settling on his face.

"That's what they want. And they want it in the morning. Just do it," Mitchell said, with the clear implication that if they didn't, they could say good-bye to Bob Hope.

Bert and Harvey stayed up most of the night revising the sketch. They bickered about the impossibility of the task, and argued about the unfairness of it. By dawn they were sick of each other and of the whole business. They had written a sketch in which Hope said, "Hi, I'm Bob 'Big Stick' Hope," and wore an enormous baseball glove that he said came from Michael Jackson's closet. In the mystery-golfer version he said, "Hi, I'm Bob 'Big Club' Hope," and lugged a big golf bag which he said was "Liz Taylor's jewel case." By the time they gave the pages to Mitchell so he could rush them out to NBC, they had both passed through disgust and misery and settled into a kind of gallows humor. Bert said, "We wrote for Bob Hope and for a while there he liked it. That's not so bad, right?" Harvey just nodded glumly.

By the end of the day, word came that Hope was thrilled. He thought the rewrites were among the finest he'd ever seen and he wanted Bert and Harvey to know he'd be calling on them again. Mitchell saw to it that word of their success got around. The *Hollywood Reporter* ran an item that said Bert and Harvey were "a hot new duo of comedic scribes and wouldn't you know it, old ski nose has them all wrapped up." NBC offered Bert and Harvey long-term contracts and so many comedians wanted them to write material that they had to farm out some of the work to their friends at Nate and Al's. At first Bert and Harvey had a little trouble adjusting to their sudden prominence, but when Freda quit her job at the phone company and Mitchell ordered a Porsche, they decided not to question the fortunes of war. They hired an accountant named Norman to keep track of their money and a secretary named Greta to answer the phone, do the typing, and laugh at their first drafts. Harvey stopped theorizing about comedy and joined the Friars Club and Bert forgot about Lean Cuisine and began dating actresses. They moved to a suite of offices down the hall in the Writers and Artists Building and settled down to write jokes and sketches and pursue their careers as comedy geniuses.

Runaways

> *You can live a long time in Hollywood and never see the part they use in pictures.*
>
> —Raymond Chandler, *The Little Sister*

When the Porsche was running right, which was by no means all the time, I would take it into the desert, traveling fast. The Mojave, with its long, empty highways, lends itself to high-speed driving. When the Porsche was going flat out, with nothing in sight but saguaro cactus and tumbleweed, I began to think I was part of the car, a mechanized centaur flying through the desert. At the very moment I felt like an extension of that red machine, I realized this aimless speed was only another version of my trips between New York and California. Maybe the realization was enough, or maybe the wind and sun purified me, but after a few hours in the desert, I felt less compelled to go to the airport and get on a plane. I still felt a need to go back to the streets, only now the pavement didn't have to be three thousand miles away.

The sun and the wind were fine by day, maybe even necessary, but at night I craved the demimonde. The little red Porsche was my ticket, racy-looking certainly, but topless and dented enough to be more raffish than luxurious. It interested everyone but threatened no one, which helped me talk to people who weren't in the movies and didn't expect to be. I became a nighttime habitué of Yucca Street and Ivar, of Las Palmas and Cherokee. The car was my passport, my translator, and I came to know parts of Hollywood that weren't in the guidebooks. I learned about the Almor and Danny's not from my own nocturnal wanderings but from an acquaintance named Graham who tried to make a documentary film about Hollywood's street life. Graham could never crack the subject and his film was abandoned. My old tabloid instincts kept me hanging around the trouble zone, getting to know Sunny and her friends. Every reporter knows if you spend enough time with people, no matter who they are, eventually they'll tell you what they have to say. I spent time with Sunny and after a while she told me her story.

Sunny rolled over in her bed at the Almor Motel and considered waking up. The clock, not that she noticed, said noon. She fumbled for last night's joint, looked around, and then realized Mick wasn't there. That wasn't necessarily bad news. Maybe he was out earning money, and then Sunny could spend the day in bed. She decided to get up anyway, just to see what was going on. She slipped on tight shorts and a halter and left the Almor to look for Mick and get some breakfast at Danny's Oki Dog, the street-corner stand where she and Mick ate their meals and met their friends.

As she left the Almor, the day manager glanced up at her, a trace of a sneer on his face. But the rent was paid so Sunny didn't flinch or avoid his gaze. When she hit the street, a teenage boy in a pickup truck honked at her. She ignored him and kept moving. When she passed the Egyptian Motel, which is where Sunny and Mick used to live until they were thrown out for being underage, Sunny saw two older hookers she sometimes talked to. They were standing on the corner, dressed for business.

"Hey, give me a break here, will you?" one of them said. She was a black woman about thirty, twice Sunny's age.

"What's your problem?" Sunny asked her.

"I got to make a few dollars quick, you know what I'm saying? I don't need no cute little white meat standing around. Okay?"

"Okay. I'm out of here. You owe me," Sunny said, smiling to

herself, since she had had no intention of working the corner anyway.

Sunny arrived at Danny's a few minutes later and sat at one of the picnic benches on the patio, with an I-haven't-had-my-morning-drugs glaze on her face. She glanced around at the kids who were nursing french fries or nodding out, until Mick came rolling in, shirtless in white tennis shorts, his long blond hair looking dirty and matted.

"Hey," Sunny said, smiling. "Where you been, Mr. Mick? Got any money?"

"I'm wasted," he answered, making a faggy pout to let her know what wasted him. Then he offered her a handful of money.

"Well, all right! It's breakfast time," she said, sending Mick to the counter to order the french fries, which, with the occasional teriyaki burrito, were the staple of their diet. Mick was a year or two younger than Sunny. They met at Danny's and teamed up. They offered each other a little stability in a life that didn't provide much, working the same streets, often standing in a pair at the corner of Santa Monica Boulevard and Vista Street with their thumbs out, the Hollywood sign of availability. Men in cars always stopped, some for Sunny, others for Mick. There were plenty of customers for both. "So what happened last night?" Sunny asked in an unconscious parody of the housewife's question of how was your day, dear.

"Some dudes came by and we went to this house. There was his own Space Invaders up there. Cool, huh?"

"You holding?"

"No. We had meth, but it's gone."

"Meth? You didn't save me any?"

"It's up that guy's nose."

"Oh, man! Me and that spade chick, we just goofed. Mr. Convertible was around. Meth? Oh, man . . ."

Sunny and Mick stayed at Danny's nursing their fries till the transvestite who policed the patio and whom the kids called Carta Blanca, for the beer he always drank, saw their plates were empty and told them to buy more or split. They decided to walk over to Hollywood High to try to score some drugs. Sunny and Mick weren't interested in attracting business just yet. Until they had gotten high, neither of them wanted to get into a passing car and unzip a stranger.

As they were about to leave Danny's, Mick saw a camera crew on the corner of Santa Monica and Vista. Film crews on the Los Angeles streets are a commonplace, so Sunny and Mick were only casually interested.

"What's that?" Mick asked.

"Making a movie," a girl about Sunny's age, named Sharon, said. "About runaways."

"They pay?" Sunny asked.

"Maybe. Carta Blanca busted 'em," Sharon said. "Threw their ass out."

"Come on, Mr. Mick. Let's go be movie stars." They walked casually toward the camera crew. Sunny noticed four adult men and a woman. A van was parked on the street and the crew had some equipment, but not much. Even Sunny knew this was a small-time operation.

As Sunny and Mick drifted past, one of the filmmakers approached. "How you doing?" he asked in an easy, unthreatening voice. He was a paunchy, intelligent-looking guy with a full beard streaked with gray. "You guys were in Danny's, huh?"

"We weren't doing nothing," Mick said.

"Do you know what a documentary movie is?"

"I think you're going to tell us, right?" Sunny said, taking the upper hand.

"My name's Eugene. We're making a movie about places like Danny's and the kids who hang out. That's you, right?"

"Put him in it," Sunny said, pointing to Mick. "He's a movie star."

"Okay. We'll put you both in it. A documentary means it's real. Not made up. I'll ask you some questions. You'll answer, and that's it."

"Great," Sunny said, starting to walk away, pulling Mick with her. The film crew walked along with them. When Eugene nodded, the cameraman began to roll film. The young woman in charge of sound pointed her microphone at Sunny and Mick. Sunny smiled at the attention as they walked down the street, camera crew in tow. "How much?" she asked.

"I'll buy you lunch. How's that?"

"We already ate. Where's this supposed to be happening?"

"Wherever you guys go, we'll go. Where you headed?"

"The park," she said, pointing to Plummer Park, not because they were going there, but because it was nearby and Sunny had second thoughts about attracting so much attention on the street.

Sunny and Mick hung out at Plummer Park because Jewish Family Services provided lunch for the elderly Russian Jews who congregated there to play pinochle and chess, talk, and soak up the sun. Sunny and Mick could usually hustle a sandwich or a bowl of soup. As they walked into the park, the old Jews looked up, curious about the new arrivals. Enough of them spoke English so they figured out what was going on. "Hey, hal-oo. The movies," one of the men said. He grinned and gestured awkwardly, as if he was having trouble translating his gestures into English. The less assimiliated ones had the frozen smiles of guests at a party where they don't know anyone. Their eagerness dissolved when they realized the camera was rolling. They moved away quickly, out of camera range, hiding who knows what Russian secrets.

Sunny and Mick sat on a bench and let Graham and his crew make their movie. Mick said little, but Sunny enjoyed bantering and sparring with this guy. "So what's your name?" he asked.

"Rudolph," Sunny said, pointing to Mick. "I'm Jackie."

"Great. This is Ted, Martha, and Bill," Graham said, introducing his crew. "So how long have you guys been going to Danny's?"

"Is this coming out on the TV?" Mick asked.

"It might, Rudy. Can I call you Rudy?"

"Huh?" Mick asked, already forgetting his alias.

"Yeah, you could call him that," Sunny said. "Is it going to be on TV?"

"We won't know for a while yet," Graham said.

"So what other movies did you make?" Sunny asked, deciding to take control.

"I made a doc about dirt-bike racing out in the Valley," Graham said, about to start running down his credits for her.

"You ever do any for MTV?"

"No. But I like to watch it. You watch it a lot?"

"Can I look in the camera?" Mick asked.

"Sure," Graham said, glad to do a favor for his new friends.

The cameraman turned the eyepiece to Mick and let him peer through. He saw Sunny through the lens. "Hey, Sunny, you're a movie star."

"Shut up, Rudolph," she said, but then asked for a look herself.

"Let me tell you a little about documentaries, the kind of movie we're making." Graham spoke quietly, patiently, trying to win their trust and confidence. Sunny listened, aware he was attempting to ingratiate himself, and tried to see what was in it for her and Mick. "What we do is look for a subject that we think is interesting, then we make as much film as we can of it. We try not to change things for the movie. We want to make a record of it. So, like, if we decided you would be an interesting subject for a movie, we would follow you around and film all your activities. Understand?"

"Hey, do I look like I'm from Mars? I know what a documentary is."

"Good. I just wanted to make sure."

"Whatever we do goes in the movie?" Mick asked, less certain than Sunny about documentary films.

"That's right, Rudy."

"X-rated!" Mick yelled, starting to take some interest.

While the camera crew shot establishing footage of the park and the Russian Jews, Graham gave Sunny and Mick sandwiches and Cokes. As they ate, Graham spoke his narration into the mike. He talked in a quiet, urgent voice, as if he were telling secrets. "They used to come to New York from the provinces to storm the worlds of art and Broadway, all those eager young faces. A few did. Most didn't. Now they come to Los Angeles to get on a game show or join a band. Some of them are very young, runaways, and some of them fall between the cracks. They congregate at Danny's Oki Dog, home to every kid hustler, junior junkie, and teenage hooker in Hollywood. It's the schoolyard and clubhouse for the out-of-control set and it's a long way from Archie and Jughead's malt shop. They've come to Hollywood for drugs, endless music, and because it's there. They get into the kind of trouble you never get out of. Not ever. This is their story."

When his crew had shot all the background footage they needed, and Sunny and Mick were looking restless, Graham turned back to them. "How long you guys been around here?"

"I don't know," Sunny answered.

"You like it?"

"It's okay. This all you're going to do?"

"It'd be great if we could just follow you guys around for a while," he said, making his move. "We'd try not to get in your way. Just shoot a little footage of your day. What do you say?"

"I don't know. We have to go to school," she said. "The teachers might not like it."

"Where do you go to school?"

"Hollywood High," she said, naming the school near the Almor, the only one Sunny was aware of.

"Well, why don't you let us try it for a while. If you don't like it, that's okay. We'll call it off."

"How much?"

"Tell you what, we film you the rest of the day, and I'll give you twenty bucks at the end."

"For both of us?"

"Sure."

"Just you?"

"The crew has to be there too."

"Boys and girls?" she asked in her coy, available voice.

"No, no, Jackie. We have a misunderstanding. All we want is to film you. Like we're doing right now. But wherever you go."

"Right," Sunny said, not caring what he called it.

"You understand? Rudy, do you? Nothing more."

"Okay," Mick said, not following the discussion.

"Hundred. Half now, half at the end. Otherwise we're out."

"It's a deal," Graham said, handing Sunny two twenties and a ten.

When the cash was in her hand, she nodded to Mick, and the two of them bolted, dashing out of the park. As they ran off, the crew filmed their retreating figures.

Hollywood High, at the corner of Sunset Boulevard and Highland Avenue, has its share of teenage trouble and some of the girls work the street at lunch hour, but when the last bell rings most of the scholars don't go home to the Almor Motel. Sunny and Mick arrived as school was letting out and the kids were milling about on the front lawn. A few of the straighter ones moved away when they saw Sunny and Mick, doing as their parents instructed. But a rougher sort, a boy in full punk drag, including a Mohawk haircut, headed directly for them. Sunny and Mick were stars in this guy's orbit.

"Heeey . . ." Mohawk said in greeting. Sunny nudged Mick, which meant: You deal with this jerk.

"Hi," Mick said in the girlish voice he used for his tricks.

"What's happening?" Mohawk mumbled.

"We're looking for that guy. You know."

"Ain't been around."

"Well, where is he?" Sunny asked, impatient with Mohawk and edgy around so many straight contemporaries.

"Heard he got busted. I don't know," Mohawk said, shaking his head at the imponderable mystery of the dealer's whereabouts.

"You got anything?" she asked, her patience wearing thin.

"I could get you a couple of jays, maybe."

"Oh, fuck that. Let's split," Sunny said, taking Mick's hand.

"We're going to party later," Mohawk said, trying to entice them. "Be some heavy dudes there."

But Sunny and Mick weren't listening. They turned up Highland, past the sign announcing auditions for the school's production of *Annie Get Your Gun,* heading for the football field and track. A few joggers were panting their way around the quarter-mile loop and the Junior ROTC was running through its maneuvers. The army was a ragtag bunch, mostly Chicano and Asian students who marched about carrying wooden rifles and answering to a fifteen-year-old drill instructor.

"They got girl soldiers," Mick said, looking over the little army. "That one's a chick, see?" he said, pointing. Sunny shrugged, indifferent to the gender of the troops. They watched the soldiers march about for a few minutes, then Mick wandered away to look for the elusive dealer. When Sunny was alone, one of the joggers, a guy about forty-five with silvery show-business hair and an expensive jogging suit, trotted over to her.

"Playing hooky?" he asked with a smile.

"What?" she answered a little sharply, probably because she didn't know what the word meant, but with a touch of a smile because Sunny can't be completely rude to business, even if she doesn't need it at the moment.

"Go to school here, do you?"

"Run around in circles here, do you?" she answered, mocking his speaking style.

"I don't need any shit from you, little girl," he snapped, the pleasant veneer gone and his Hollywood soul showing.

"Hmmm," she purred, hearing the sort of voice she understands best. "Yeah, I'm a student here. Biology."

"You get A's?"

"I get fifty bucks."

He laughed, enjoying her sassiness, but then either lost his nerve or just changed his mind. "Maybe another time," he said, regaining control of the conversation before trotting away to continue running in circles.

On the other side of the field, Mick was standing in the midst of three teenage boys large as football players. They didn't look friendly and Sunny sensed the souls of bikers. Mick, who was so pale and frail in his tennis shorts and bare slender chest, seemed to be okay, but even in an age of gay lib, boys like Mick got beat up by boys like this. Sunny knew her presence in that little circle could exacerbate the problem. She hesitated for a moment, unsure of the most prudent move. Then she saw one of the giants poke a finger at Mick's chest. That meant no more time for rumination. She strolled toward them, no fear on her face, just her rock-group smoldering look. The ringleader was standing very close to Mick, making little kissy face noises. The other two stood around looking numb.

"Hey," Sunny said. "So what's going on?"

The big one turned, and seeing Sunny's available look, forgot about Mick. "Well, fuck me," he said.

Mick backed away as quietly as he could; Sunny stepped a little closer to the giant. Up close they didn't look like actual bikers, just big dumb high-school boys in denim and leather.

"So?" she said, putting herself between Mick and his tormentor. The big guy tugged at his groin and stared at Sunny, probably thinking about throwing her in the bushes. "You guys know where we could score?" she asked, more interested in keeping up the patter than doing business. But the big guy wasn't interested in chat. He sneered and yanked Sunny to him, pulling her by the hair.

"What are you going to do?" he muttered, running his hands over her.

"Lighten up," she said, smiling. "Take it easy." She reached down and put her hand on his crotch. He backed off, amazed at her boldness. While he was confused, Sunny grinned and gave him an extra squeeze. "Maybe I'll see you later," she said, and backed away, taking Mick's hand and steering the two of them out of there. They walked back toward the track and the relative safety of the joggers who were still running in their endless loops.

Sunny and Mick walked up Highland, away from the school, planning how to score some speed, but only managing to wander about, listless in the hot afternoon sun. A few drivers honked and slowed down, but since they already had money, Sunny told Mick to ignore the cars. They headed toward a burnt-out storefront on Ivar Street that was filled with illegals, mostly from Mexico. It was known as Tijuana Chica, Little TJ. Cars from all parts of L.A. pulled up in front and Mexicans ran out to curbside to sell drugs. It was mostly marijuana out on the street, but inside, for those with nerve enough to enter, there was stronger stuff. What Sunny wanted were amphetamines, speed, that would get her heart pounding and her soul sailing. "I don't want to go in there," Mick said, while he and Sunny stood across the street watching the cars pull up and make their buys.

"Come on, we'll go in the downstairs. Let me talk."

"Okay," Mick said, without much conviction.

Inside Tijuana Chica, in what once might have been a salesroom, a dealer had set up a booth covered with chicken wire and makeshift bars. Raggedy children in soiled diapers wandered underfoot. There were no lights, but a few shafts of dusty sunlight came in through broken windows.

"Hey, Paco," Sunny said to the young Chicano behind the chicken wire.

"What chu want?" he muttered, looking Sunny and Mick over.

"Want to go flying up in the sky."

"How I know you ain't cops?" he said, laughing at the ridiculousness of these two being police.

"You got it?" Sunny asked, forgetting to laugh with him.

"Got the green? Got *dinero*?"

"Got the crank?" she asked defiantly.

He produced a fistful of red pills shaped like footballs, not exactly what Sunny wanted, but they'd do. He had enough in his hand to send both of them to the sky, all day, all night, and the next day too.

"How much?" she asked, unable to keep her eyes from widening.

"What chu pay?"

"Dollar a pop?" she said, too excited to negotiate.

"Sold to you," he said, laughing. Sunny nodded to Mick, who took out the roll and peeled off bills until he got to thirty dollars, where Sunny told him to stop. The dealer took the money, riffled through it, counting it again, and then grabbed Mick by the wrist and squeezed. "Hey. *Rubia . . . Maricón,*" he sneered. "What you give me now?"

"Come on, Paco," Sunny said. "Just give us the stuff."

"Why you call me Paco, bitch?" He reached out with his other hand and snared Sunny by the neck, yanking her to him. When he had both of them, he knocked their heads together, hard. "I don' give you nothin' . . ." he said, and knocked their heads together again. It made their eyes blur; Sunny was too dizzy to know what to do, but it didn't matter because Paco only wanted the money and the victory. "I know what chu are. Get out or get cut." He let them go and they didn't have to be told again. Forgetting their money and the drugs, they ran out of Tijuana Chica. One of the toddlers looked up at them and gurgled as they hurried back to the street and the sun.

By six o'clock Sunny and Mick were at the corner of Hollywood Boulevard and Las Palmas, low on cash. This used to be the main corner for runaways and teenage hustlers, but then the *Los Angeles Times* started running articles about it and the cops cracked down. But that was a few years earlier, the Ice Age to Sunny and Mick.

They knew if you were a kid on the street, Hollywood Boulevard meant trouble. Even adult hookers got busted, and there was no telling what might happen to Sunny and Mick if they got caught. They stayed close to the buildings, hanging back in the shadows until the traffic lights changed, then they darted across the intersections, looking for safety. When an LAPD black-and-white cruised by, they slipped into a doorway or a parking lot, hoping they wouldn't get thrown out before the cops passed.

An hour later, they were on Sunset Boulevard in West Hollywood, where the danger wasn't the cops. These corners were filled with adult women soliciting, and Sunny and Mick had to look out for the pimps. "They'll beat you bad, maybe cut you. So look out," Sunny said, instructing Mick. This part of the evening was a busy time for the business of the street and there were little clusters of brightly dressed hookers, black and white, standing on the corners. To get across and stay clear of the pimps, who were always lurking, Sunny and Mick had to head west, staying on the north side of the street, leaving the south side to commerce. It took them out of their way, but neither of them was in a mood for more trouble. At Fairfax, Mick wanted to stop at the Thrifty Drugstore for an ice-cream cone.

Inside Thrifty's, Sunny headed for the cosmetics counter while Mick played a couple of games of Ms. Pac Man and then drifted down the aisles. He was trying to steal some candy, but his shorts were too tight to hide the bag. As he pondered his dilemma, Sunny arrived with the cones. "Buy it if you want it," she said of the candy, a touch of the maternal in her voice. But Mick lost interest when he saw the ice cream. "Chocolate's all they got," she said, handing him his cone.

In the parking lot, as they were leaving Thrifty's, a rangy black man in a jogging suit stepped out of nowhere and pushed Sunny up against a car.

"What you be doing, girl?" he asked, gripping Sunny's arm and ignoring Mick.

"What?" she asked, ingenuously licking her ice-cream cone, trying to appear suburban innocent, despite her little-girl-whore outfit.

"I got enough problems round here. Stay off these streets."

"We're going home."

"Yeah?" he said, doubting every word of it, but still not absolutely certain. "Who's this?" he asked, pointing at Mick. "Leave it to Beaver?"

"My little brother. I'm baby-sitting him."

"I baby-sit you. I take you home and ream you out till you can't walk. You like that? Huh? Do you?" He squeezed her wrist and pushed his knee between her legs, hard, grinding against her. Sunny tried to look surprised and baffled, as if nothing like this had ever happened before.

Mick looked much more frightened than Sunny. "I'm going to tell Mom," he said.

"What's this faggot asshole?" the black guy said, noticing Mick.

"We're supposed to be home," Sunny said again, trying to take advantage of the man's momentary interest in Mick.

"You just shut up, you hear me. Just shut up. You come round here again, be the last time." As he said it, he smacked Sunny across the bridge of her nose. The cartilage made a dull ripping sound as it cracked. Then he turned and punched Mick in the crotch. He spit at them both as they turned and ran, putting distance between themselves and the Thrifty parking lot, the ice-cream cones forgotten. They moved fast, staying on Fairfax, not bothering to keep to the side streets, hurrying toward the open territory of Santa Monica Boulevard.

"That hurt," Mick said. "He hit me hard."

"Me too," Sunny said, touching her throbbing nose. A purple bruise was forming.

"Is it broke?" Mick asked.

"I don't know. Go to Danny's. Sit down for a while. I'm going to make us some money," she said, her face set and grim. They separated at Santa Monica Boulevard and Fairfax. Mick headed east for a little comfort, and Sunny stood on the corner, looking sultry. It was seven-thirty, when a lot of men were on their way home from work, so she didn't have to stand long. A Mercedes-Benz 450SL pulled up, stopping a few yards ahead of her, making her come to him. Sunny knew not to make it too easy. She strolled slowly up to the Mercedes, letting him check her out in the mirror but making him wait. The driver was a bearded movie-business sort in flashy clothes. There was a phone in the car.

"Get in," he said, hard and humorless.

Sunny looked him over. No cop had a car like that. "So?" she said as she sat next to him.

"So I want head and I don't want any grief. How old are you?"

"Hey, it's cool. Got fifty bucks?"

"I'll give you thirty. If you don't want it, good-bye." The guy was probably an agent with a compulsive need to bargain, but Sunny was in no mood to haggle.

"Okay," she said.

"Where?"

"I got a room."

"No, no. No motels. In the car."

"Behind Gio's on Sunset, then."

He nodded and took off toward the parking lot. As they drove, Sunny stroked his leg, letting her fingers curl into his thigh. "How the fuck old are you?" he asked again. Sunny didn't answer, leaving her age to his imagination. At the parking lot behind Gio's, he pulled the car into a dark, private corner, where Sunny performed the agreed-upon act. The gentleman shoved two twenties at her and told her to get out.

On the way back to Danny's, Sunny stopped at the Fountain Grocery Mart and bought a Coke to wash the taste of her customer out of her mouth. She moved back toward Santa Monica Boulevard on the side streets, avoiding the traffic and trouble. The sun was beginning to set as she ambled along the north end of Vista Street, past the rows of masonry bungalows filled with retired insurance men from the Midwest and frail ladies who carry parasols to shield themselves from the sun. No one stopped Sunny there, or even noticed her. Despite her throbbing nose, she enjoyed the solitude and the calm.

When Sunny got near Danny's, she started to feel better. Just seeing the glow of the lights on the patio, and hearing the noise, comforted her. When she turned the corner, she saw Eugene and his film crew, still hanging around, trying to talk to the kids in the parking lot. She hesitated, but then decided the day had been too hard to worry about these guys. She strolled toward Danny's with her I-don't-care-what-you-think look in place.

"Jackie. How you doing?" Graham said, ambling over to her with his crew in tow. "Good to see you." The camera was rolling again but Sunny wasn't interested. She was tired and she wanted to see Mick.

"Okay," she said, as she kept walking.

"Where you been? What's going on?" His easy, relaxed voice told her he wasn't going to give her a hard time about running out on him. She recognized the voice of a man who wanted something from her. She heard voices like that all the time, and it didn't much matter what they wanted—a go-round in the front seat of a Mercedes or an interview with a film crew. It was all the same, just men wanting something from her and never paying nearly enough for it. "You hungry? Rudy's over there," Graham said, pointing at Danny's.

"Yeah. I'm kind of tired. Let's get together later."

"Sure. I want you to think of me as your friend. I'm on your side, Jackie. If you need anything, all you have to do is ask. We'll be around a lot, and whenever you're ready, I'd love to talk. You understand?"

"Okay."

"You keep the money from this afternoon. Even if you don't want to talk to me. It's okay."

"Okay."

"I have one favor for now, though. Tell the kids in Danny's that it's okay to talk to me. Would you do that? I'd really appreciate it, Jackie. And I think you owe me one."

"Okay."

At Danny's the evening was starting to roll. The flashy cars were pulling in and out of the parking lot as the drivers looked over the talent. Mick was glad to see Sunny because he'd been borrowing money to pay for his french fries. He hurried over to her, holding out a balled fist. "Look," he said. "Look what I got," as if it were his report card, filled with A's. He opened his hand, revealing a dozen large white pills.

"Yeah," she said, smiling and heading up to the counter to order some more french fries. "Floaters, huh? Where'd you get 'em?"

"This guy, he was real nice. We went up to his house. He had like every kind of pill. Your nose still hurt?"

"Not for long," Sunny said, popping two in her mouth.

"In around no time, you'll feel great," Mick said as Sunny washed down the pills with a borrowed Coke. Another girl, about Sunny's age, asked for one. Mick gave it to her, took another himself, and then gave them out to any other kid who asked.

A black Trans Am pulled into the parking lot and sat idling. The driver, a lean, hard-looking guy about thirty-five with a shaved head and a fierce mustache that said this wasn't an accountant, rolled down his window and called to Mick. But Mick was feeling too good now and they already had some money, so he turned away. The guy saw two other boys, both as thin and young as Mick, and maybe because Mick turned him down, decided to take the pair. "You and you," he barked. "Come here." The boys were new around Danny's and a little scared, but after a whispered word they got in and the car drove away.

Sunny took more of the white pills until she couldn't feel her nose anymore. She and Mick stayed around Danny's for a couple hours, eating french fries and talking with their friends about the latest drug scores and the events of the day. Sunny told about the trouble at Tijuana Chica and the run-in with the pimp in the Thrifty parking lot. About eleven, after Graham and his crew had given up for the day, Sunny and Mick floated back to the Almor, feeling loose and relaxed. In their room, they watched television for a while and then fell asleep curled in each other's arms.

Monkey Business

There are two kinds of independent producers. The high fliers who get the big fees and are often as famous as the actors they employ and the marginal hustlers who work out of phone booths and try to stay ahead of their creditors. The difference between them is one hit.

While I was working for the studios, jumping from one lot to another, an entirely predictable side effect was that my value as a screenwriter to the marginal independents went up. The idea was that if these fellows could hire someone the studios hired, their chances of making a studio deal were improved. Another side effect, as the agents pointed out, was I could charge them more than the studios paid me. So whenever studio jobs weren't there, or weren't interesting, I would go around and meet with producers who were holding movies together with charm and adrenaline.

Harold, who had high ambitions, got into the movie business making a documentary about an invasion of Haiti. He gave some would-be revolutionaries money to buy boats and rifles and then filmed the results. He was aware there was a certain moral murkiness in that, but he preferred to think of himself as politically involved in the third-world struggle. He had a camera crew on a beach in Florida when the little ragtag army of expatriate

Haitians launched. The film was never finished because the army went aground in Key Largo and the Haitians just drifted off. After that Harold lowered his sights and made a lot of money producing low-budget movies only demented teenagers ever saw. Of course, Harold wanted more—so he spent his time chasing new investors and new ideas.

While Harold was in Georgia negotiating for a remake of *The Georgia Peach,* he visited the Primate Center near Atlanta, where he met Nana, a signing baby gorilla. Harold was enchanted. He couldn't stop thinking about making the story of a baby gorilla who could carry on a conversation. Nana had been taught a few hundred words and she could make connections among them, so Harold was able to say, "Well, Nana, how are you on this gloomy, rainy day?" Nana would make several signs that translated as "Nana doesn't mind the rain, it feels kind of cozy." At first Harold, true to his Hollywood soul, assumed it was a stunt and he would soon be asked to bet money or in some way be tricked. When Harold was certain Nana was exactly what the scientists said she was, he forgot about the remake of *The Georgia Peach* and flew back to Los Angeles and went to work.

Harold needed a screenplay, fast and cheap. The Writers Guild minimum for a script is thirty-five thousand dollars, but Harold never paid more than five. He roughed in a story himself, then hired Walter, a docile screenwriter who was glad to get the work, to "rewrite" it, the minimum for a rewrite being considerably less.

Harold's story was about a mysterious disease sweeping through a little town in Georgia. Nana, the signing gorilla, had to leave the town, go to the nearest doctor, report the news, and lead the doctor back. Harold took Walter to lunch at the Cadillac Café, a punk-chic hangout with an inexpensive menu and a lot of atmosphere, and told him, "Keep the focus on Nana and the kid and keep the locations down."

"But why does Nana live in the town? I mean, it's pretty weird, isn't it?" Walter asked, poking at his Chinese chicken salad, doubtful about his ability to make dramatic sense of the idea.

"I don't know," Harold said, a bit of irritation showing. "Maybe she was visiting friends at the zoo. If you have trouble with the details, just steal *Lassie.*" Walter considered that for a moment;

then, with his writer's need to codify everything, said, "I think it's a good idea. Hollywood loves chimps, gorillas, and monkeys—*Bedtime for Bonzo,* Tarzan, those Clint Eastwood movies. I think it's because the little guys are always credible—you believe them, no matter what they do—and they're still theatrical. That's a tough combination."

"Absolutely," Harold said. "I couldn't put it better myself. Now, let's get to work." Harold rode Walter pretty hard, calling him several times a day, dropping by unexpectedly to look at the pages, and demanding that Walter turn out eight finished pages a day. After two weeks Walter was punchy, but Harold had a script in hand, which meant he could go to work. Harold drew up a budget showing he could deliver the picture for nine hundred thousand dollars, nonunion. With the budget, Walter's script, and some videotapes of Nana chatting with the press, Harold went to the major studios for financing. No major will finance a nonunion production, but there's nothing to stop a studio from distributing a nonunion picture. When the film is in hand, the studio pays the unions to put the union seal on the prints. It's costly, but not as much as having the unions involved from the beginning. With the distribution agreement, Harold went to the banks to get a line of credit. The big banks wouldn't touch it, but the First Bank of West Hollywood, a newly organized firm that was known as the gay bank (because that's what it was), needed the business and said yes as long as Harold put up the equity in his house in Coldwater Canyon as additional collateral.

Harold flirted with the idea of directing the picture himself, but worried that if he did, no one would look after the money. So he settled on Curtis, who had done the most successful of Harold's teenage pictures. Harold persuaded Curtis the way he had persuaded the gay bank, by repeating the musings of Walter the screenwriter, embellished slightly and delivered with enthusiasm. "Hollywood loves gorillas," he said. "Think about it: King Kong, J. Fred Muggs, *Bedtime for Bonzo.* Everybody loves monkeys—plus, this one can talk! Clint Eastwood makes chimp pictures. We do it for a price, nonunion, and it can't miss. Gorillas are the only actors who are always believable and always theatrical. Plus we've got a great one lined up." Curtis liked the speech and he needed the work, so he signed on for a deferred salary and a piece of the profits.

Six months after Harold first saw Nana, *You and Me* was ready to roll. Fast as that was, it wasn't quite fast enough, because Nana was now committed to do a *Sixty Minutes,* and after that, a documentary about the Primate Center. Harold and Curtis talked it over and decided that if they waited for Nana, not only would they lose part of the human cast, but the deals for the Georgia locations might not hold. Curtis pointed out, "Availabilities are everything, even for a monkey." The Primate Center was able to provide a substitute baby gorilla named Candy, who didn't have as large a vocabulary as Nana and wasn't as adorable. Candy was still a gorilla and so she was hired.

Shooting began on a peanut farm in rural Georgia. All movies begin shooting with high hopes, so for the first day of *You and Me* Harold invited the local people who were to be extras to the set to visit and meet the actors. Candy behaved beautifully, signing with strangers and looking generally benign. Harold gave an interview to the local paper and said how excited everyone in the company was to be in Georgia. He explained that movies with gorillas were always popular because gorillas were always believable and still theatrical. Harold talked about King Kong, J. Fred Muggs, the Nairobi Trio, *Bedtime for Bonzo,* and the Clint Eastwood movies. The local paper ran a photo of Harold, Curtis, and Candy.

Candy wasn't as good at acting as she had been at greeting strangers. The problem was she wouldn't do a second take. "The monkey's worse than Sinatra," Curtis said, referring to Sinatra's well-known refusal ever to do more than one take of any shot. No matter how much Curtis or Harold coaxed, no matter what treats they offered, Candy wouldn't repeat anything. That's no way to make a movie, so Candy was fired on the second day of shooting and replaced with another gorilla from the Primate Center. This one was named Lucy and she was very cute, but she hated the crew and bit an actor. Lucy had to be sent back to the Primate Center too. The production was in motion and for Harold to close down would mean he would be in debt for every cent spent so far. That made him determined to push on, even though the reason for making the movie, the participation of Nana, the wonder gorilla, had long since evaporated. In his desperation, Harold sent photographs of Nana to Western Costume in Hollywood and had them stitch up a baby gorilla suit to look like Nana.

When the suit arrived, Harold declared it adequate to the occasion and put it on a local ten-year-old boy who showed promise. The lad didn't do badly. He would trot around in the gorilla suit and Harold would hold up cardboard signs telling him what to do with his paws to approximate signing. They had lost a few days of shooting time, but now, with the child in the gorilla costume, Harold thought he could still pull the whole thing off. What he hadn't foreseen were Georgia's child-labor laws. There was a time when a producer could ignore such things, but now every state has a film commission to promote location shooting and welfare workers who look into the labors of children on movie sets. The rules were so onerous, and the enforcement so strict, that Harold found it barely possible to proceed. On top of that, the child began to sneeze, apparently developing an allergy to his costume.

There was talk of hiring a midget to replace the little boy, but Curtis thought they would be better off with a trained movie-business gorilla, who would know how to take orders. Curtis suggested Mr. Jiggs, the gorilla who had starred in *Hello Again,* a hit of a few years ago about a gorilla who ran a roadside vegetable stand. Curtis felt Mr. Jiggs could finish the picture and they could still use a lot of the footage of the little kid in the gorilla suit. Harold agreed and got on the phone to Hollywood to line up Mr. Jiggs. But Mr. Jiggs was in Mozambique shooting an aspirin commercial and wouldn't be available for a month. Mr. Jiggs's agent suggested Albert, an orangutan who had been the stand-in for the Clint Eastwood movies. The problem was that an orangutan, no matter how well trained, would not look like a gorilla, and all the footage they had shot would be worthless. But if Harold didn't deliver the picture, he'd be in debt to the gay bank for the rest of his life. He asked how big Albert was. The answer was, slightly larger than the gorilla costume. So Albert was hired, and with his handler, flew to Georgia to take over the role. Harold cut off the costume's feet and told Curtis to shoot Albert from the ankles up. With Albert dressed in the gorilla suit, the picture was ready to resume shooting. The biggest problem was, Albert didn't know how to sign. Also, inside the costume Albert was disoriented and couldn't do much more than stand around. He did, however, look adorable, which gave everyone hope.

Harold was nothing if not flexible, so he brought Walter out from Los Angeles to rewrite the script as they shot. Each day they would film, and each night Walter, Curtis, and Harold would scheme to reduce the amount of signing Albert had to do, yet still keep the story coherent. They had to change it from a tale of a heroic signing gorilla who saves the town into a story of a little boy who has just started training his pet baby gorilla to sign, when the gorilla is kidnapped. Everyone hunts for the gorilla, and during the search, the little boy gets lost in the woods. The gorilla escapes from the kidnappers, finds the little boy, who is suffering from exposure, and takes him to a farmhouse where the farmer is deaf. The gorilla, using the very, very few words he can sign, explains the situation to the deaf farmer. Then the gorilla goes for help, saving the little boy, and if they can work it in, saving the town from an epidemic left over from the first draft.

Curtis was able to keep the picture on schedule, but one night, when everyone was restless from too much night shooting, the crew showed up wearing gorilla masks, seven burly grips in ape faces. Harold, Curtis, and the actors laughed, but it spooked Albert. Even after the crew took off the masks, Albert ran around in circles for almost an hour and wouldn't put on his costume until he had been fed an extra meal.

During the third week of shooting, an officer from the bank came to Georgia to check on his firm's loan. He inspected the budget, met the actors, and was charmed by Albert. He was able to report that despite the delays, everything seemed to be proceeding, and he kept the line of credit open. Harold brought the picture in a little late and a little over budget, but close enough to the forty-two-day shooting schedule that the bank was satisfied.

After seeing the rough cut, the studio's sales department didn't think they had *Star Wars,* but they did think *You and Me* was quite touching. Harold told the head of the sales department, "We're in the tradition of *Bedtime for Bonzo* and Clint Eastwood. A baby gorilla is adorable, believable, and always theatrical, and at this price we're all going to make money." The studio had a problem with a fourteen-million-dollar sci-fi western that was playing to nine hundred mostly empty theaters. The exhibitors were yelling for a substitute, and the head of the studio thought the charm of *You and Me* might solve the problem. Honoring the agreement, the studio wrote out an advance check to Harold for a million-six. Harold paid the bank, took care of the deferrals to Curtis and the actors, and then took Walter, the screenwriter, to Le Dôme to begin discussing the sequel.

The Burning Porsche

The dinner was for a friend, a studio executive who had once been my agent and was now about to be a groom. We were in the upstairs room at Mr. Chow's in Beverly Hills. There was a bankable director, a couple of writers, some producers, a lawyer, and a guy who I think was a big shot in distribution. And Teddy, who was hot enough to burn. The man was breathing hits and wrapping Porsches around trees. He'd wreck one, stagger away, and order another. He'd gone through five of the damn things. His life was like a fevered movie dream. Live hard, live fast, make millions.

We made a few toasts to our friend, ate a lot of sesame prawns and Mr. Chow's seaweed, gossiped, talked about deals and grosses, and made a fuss over the chardonnay. Except for Teddy, who came late, looked stoned, and kept jumping up to go to the bathroom. In Hollywood that means one thing, and it isn't an upset stomach. After the fifth trip to the loo in two hours, he had white dust dribbling from his nostrils. Nobody else wanted any, or, so far as I knew, ever used the stuff. But Teddy couldn't get enough. The party broke up about eleven. By then most of these hard chargers were anxious to go home to their wives, their television sets, or whatever. It was a school night and this was a room full of good boys. Teddy boy, however, was ready for more. More cocaine maybe, but mostly for more deal talk, which is the true drug, grail, and lubricant of Hollywood. He had been dancing around a script of mine for some time and now he wanted to talk. Okay. Getting scripts into production occupies a certain amount of my time and Teddy can do it, so I was game. I figured we'd go down to the bar and have a brandy. We did, and then, as we were leaving, Teddy decided he wanted to talk some more. He certainly didn't want to go home. The one time I was in his house, it contained very little furniture and a lot of records, videotapes, half-eaten pizzas, and German pornographic magazines.

We wound up sitting in his car, the Porsche of the moment, on Brighton Way, a little side street in Beverly Hills, near Mr. Chow's. As we sat there and talked, Teddy kept the engine running and the cocaine coming. Despite his altered state, the discussion was pertinent—casting, directors, budget, script problems. He talked fast all the time, and when he was on coke, his words rushed out, blurred but not confused. Watching him shovel the stuff into his nose made me feel as if I was watching the scene from across the street. The more loaded Teddy got, the farther away I felt. Maybe it was the drug haze, but watching him like that made me remember how I first met him.

He turned up in Los Angeles fifteen years ago, to go to UCLA. He came from South America, which didn't make him your typical freshman. His family had lived in Bolivia for three generations. His grandfather left rural Georgia during the Depression, because he'd heard there was work to be had in a tin mine. The tin business worked out and the family had been there ever since. Grampa's sons married South Americans, so Teddy had olive skin, spoke Spanish, but his features were gringo.

He left La Paz when he was eighteen, carrying a change of clothes and three pounds of creamy, flaked Bolivian cocaine. The media and professional athletes hadn't yet discovered the drug, but even if it wasn't so celebrated, it was certainly illegal. For Teddy to have brought in that much, and then to have sold it once he got here, must have taken the same combination of courage and idiocy that informed his activities from then on.

Before he got to Los Angeles, Teddy's knowledge of the United States had come from books, magazines, and movies. He always resented his parents for not having arranged for him to be born a little closer to the Polo Lounge. He used to get angry when his friends complained that someone else had been born rich or with some imagined social advantage. "They don't know shit about being born wrong," he once said. "All you people went to Camp Run-a-Muck together. All I ever did was kick Indians and look for Nazis." To Teddy, everyone in Hollywood, which is very much a city of outsiders, appeared to have grown up together, gone to the same schools, and taken bar-mitzvah lessons in a big group.

He didn't last long at UCLA, but the cocaine opened a few nonacademic doors for him. He sold some of it, but he gave a lot of it away. It was his calling card; he used it to meet Hollywood high fliers. As a result, he got a job as an assistant to a record producer and manager named Jack Robbins. I'm sure all Teddy did was supply drugs and watch Jack maneuver. In a few months, Teddy was about to start stealing the clients, signing them to his own management contracts. He might have pulled it off, but Jack was indicted for income-tax evasion and his business fell apart. Teddy lived on the beach for a while and dealt drugs, until he landed a job in the mail room at a studio. Six months later he was an assistant to the head of production. God knows what pharmaceutical inducements were involved in getting him from the mail room to the outskirts of the executive suites, but he was there when I met him.

I was working at the studio then, rewriting some long-forgotten script, and Teddy and I used to hang out. We'd go to lunch or run movies we wanted to see. Teddy's education was hit-and-miss. He was widely read but there were frequently things he didn't know. If the question was even vaguely literary, he always assumed I'd have the answer. He'd come trotting over to my office to ask something like "What's a pathetic fallacy?" or "Quick, name me some Norwegian novelists." If I didn't know, I told him where he could probably find the information. For my part, I liked hearing about growing up in La Paz. Not exactly Tom and Huck, but we were friends.

I left Hollywood and went back to New York for a while to see how the *Post* was managing without me and to try my hand at the theater, so I lost daily touch with Teddy. I had heard about some of his promotions, so I wasn't surprised when I read that he was head of production. By then I was back in Los Angeles, where it didn't hurt to be an old pal of the boss. He sent me books to adapt and called on me to rewrite scripts. Although I did a lot of work for him, I didn't see him all that much. He had begun the lunatic behavior that was excessive even for him. Late at night, to unwind, he would cruise around Hollywood in his Porsche and pick up the hookers who worked the street. He'd take them two at a time and bring them back to his house, where he'd spend the night slapping them around. He always gave them lavish sums of money, no doubt charged to the budget of somebody's movie. There was probably sex involved, but so far as I could tell, the violence he could perpetrate was his only pleasure. When he was through with them, he'd call a cab and make them wait on the street while he got a few hours' sleep.

He was in the top job at the studio for about a year when the corporate bosses in New York got wind of his nocturnal activities and Teddy was pushed out. He converted his contract to a producer's deal and hit the ground running, doing what he was put on this earth to do. He took a script called *City Boy* off the shelf, hired four writers, and started dictating changes. He took over four sound stages and put four directors to work, each on different scenes. Only Teddy had the whole picture in his head. He steered the actors from one stage to the next, yelling something like "This is the scene where the kid gets to town and doesn't know anybody. He comes on to the waitress because he can't pay for lunch. Get your thumb out of your mouth and let's make a movie." At the same time, he haa teams of editors working around the clock. Teddy would trot from one cutting room to the next, supposedly coordinating the activity, but mostly yelling, demanding, and pushing everyone to work faster. For a three-week stretch he never left the studio and very likely never slept more than an hour or two at a time. When he wasn't on a stage or with the editors, he was on the phone negotiating music deals or trying to calm down the unions, who weren't crazy about his working procedures. Seven weeks after he started the rewrite on the script, he had an answer print in hand, and two weeks after that *City Boy* was in nine hundred theaters. It grossed sixty-five million dollars and Teddy never looked back.

By one-thirty in the morning, Teddy and I were still sitting in his car on Brighton Way. The script we were talking about was a love story about a younger man and an older woman, set at a newspaper in San Francisco. He's twenty-three, a reporter. She's thirty-five and married to the publisher of the paper.

"Thirty-five! That's geri-fucking-atric. What is this, a movie-of-the-week? I want rock and roll, you're giving me a waltz."

"Make her thirty." I shrugged. "To a twenty-three-year-old, she's still different. The Other. That's the point."

"You don't get it, do you?" He inhaled more cocaine and his voice took on a black street sound. "You listen to me, bro, 'cause I know," he said. "It's tight skin that brings 'em in out there. Wet dreams and pussy schemes."

I laughed and asked, "What's that, the Bolivian Dozens?"

"Think who's buying the tickets," he said in an exasperated voice. The black patois was gone for the moment. "Kids in a high priapic state, that's who," he said triumphantly. "Tune in on it, man, or else you're going to be a writer all your life." As he yelled out his view of life and commerce, his accent shifted to the New York streets, and he sounded like a Pitkin Avenue wise guy. "If you're old, you stay home and, I don't know, play hide the salami or tube out. If you're young, you go to the Bijou or the triplex down at the mall. Where's your head, boychik?"

It's probably true that everyone invents his own voice and personality, but Teddy always seemed to be working on several at once, like a ventriloquist who was both master and mannequin. He called it "trying on hats." The black sound was meant to appear mean and street-wise. The Yiddish touches were developed to deal with older colleagues and to suggest an intimacy with his contemporaries. Sometimes he would get precise and sonorous. My theory was, he thought that's what an Oxford don sounded like. Another favorite was the shit-kicking good old boy just in from the farm. That one usually included a burp and a request for a beer.

He spooned out some more cocaine and let his voice shift back to his own unaccented English. He began to wave his hands, rewriting my newspaper script, painting a movie in the druggy, close air of the Porsche. "He's sixteen. She's twenty. Her father's the publisher of your newspaper and he's a copy boy or a delivery boy. Why does it have to be a newspaper, anyway? Nobody cares about that shit. Fuck this movie. I want to do one about dope. Put it on a marijuana farm. Two thousand cannabis sativa plants in Oregon and the National Guard comes down with choppers and flamethrowers. Search and seize. Scorch the earth and nuke the dopers. Your boy rises up, organizes the kids, and offs the Guard. Put in the romance if you want, I don't give a shit."

He went on like that, inhaling cocaine, jumping from one subject to another, changing voices, laughing and attacking. By two-thirty I felt myself getting positively sleepy. When he saw me trying not to yawn, he once again offered some of the white powder. Cocaine is usually consumed with a grander purpose than merely staying awake, but there wasn't any coffee around, so what the hell, I thought. "Sure," I said. "I'll have some. Thanks."

"Welcome to modern times," he said, and passed me the little bottle. Whatever else it might do to you, like wreck your mind, ravage your body, and destroy your mucous membrane, the stuff will make you feel great for a few high-energy minutes. I could feel the top of my head starting to lift off. My mouth was dry and going numb and I was starting to chatter. For a moment or two, I got a sense of what it must be like to be Teddy. He's in this state all the time. And he's been like this for years.

For a while Teddy was mixed up with John-Michael Pedigo, who was sort of a producer and sort of a gangster. No one knew for certain just what John-Michael's mob connections were, but Teddy had found him useful in straightening out the occasional union problem or speaking firmly to an agent who wasn't fast enough in doing what Teddy wanted done. So far as anyone knew, John-Michael never actually did anything to these people, but his voice carried a certain perceived authority.

An agent named Glickman once made a big mistake with Teddy, and John-Michael was called in to straighten it out. Glickman's career wasn't going well and his boss had assigned him the suicide task of selling an inexperienced writer to Teddy for a rewrite job on a television pilot. Teddy told Glickman not to bother him with such ridiculous proposals. But Glickman was in a bad spot and he called and begged. Finally, to shut him up, Teddy said, "Give me a copy of the kid's best script."

Glickman was worried that his client was too green and Teddy would reject the guy's work. So he took another script, one of the many that were on his shelf, and inserted a fake title page with a new title and with his client's name on it. He sent that script to Teddy's house as a sample of his client's work. If Teddy had read the script as he had promised, Glickman might have gotten away with it. But Teddy gave it to one of his assistants, an ambitious young woman who was always looking for ways to impress her boss. She recognized the script as one Glickman's agency had already submitted. She was pleased to tell Teddy what had happened. Teddy sent word to Glickman that he was not amused. He let Glickman squirm for a few days, then turned the matter over to John-Michael Pedigo for adjudication. No one knows for sure what happened after that, but Glickman resigned from his agency and wasn't seen for several weeks. There were rumors that he was dead, but then he turned up again, looking for a job. No one would touch him until he got up the nerve to call Teddy and plead for help and a recommendation. Teddy surprised everyone and made a few phone calls for the guy and got him back in the agency business. I guess he figured Glickman had suffered enough.

I didn't snort as much cocaine as Teddy did, but I certainly had more of it than I had intended. We sat in his car talking and planning until almost four o'clock. That wasn't the longest conversation I'd ever had with him. Once, when he was running the studio, he called me about a script I was working on. He called at ten at night and he didn't hang up till five the next morning. Here in his car, whether he knew it or not, he was using script talk as a way to talk about his life.

"Start fast and hard and loud and then stay that way," he said, telling me how the movie ought to open. "Don't let up for two hours. Story problem? Character logic? Fuck it. Turn up the music and dance."

"That's the answer to everything?" I asked as I accepted more cocaine.

"Everything!" he yelled, his hands gesturing, his voice rising. "You don't have any idea what this country wants. I'm on the outside. I can see it whole."

"You ran a movie studio. You're a producer. You're not an outsider. Your fantasy is that you're on the run, escaping from . . . what?" I asked, hoping he might say.

"I know what America wants, because I had to learn it. You were born here, you can't see."

"What does the country want, Teddy? Educate me."

"Sex. Loud music. Hot clothes. Drugs. Fast cars. Did I say sex?" he asked, laughing.

"No other questions or interests in the wide world?" I asked, giving in to a coked giggle. "Emotional doubts or romantic confusion? Home and family? Understanding of your life? Science? Politics and religion?"

"We'll open two pictures," he said, loving the subject. "Side by side. One's called *Sex, Drugs, and Death,* the other's called *Mom and Dad Go for a Walk.* Now, where you going to put your money, white boy?" He was laughing, charged by the argument and the drugs.

"Of course people respond to the sensational. But that's not all they respond to."

"Fine. You do movies about milking the cow." He was shouting again, reveling in what he knew was wisdom. "I'll do ones about fucking and getting loaded. See you at the finish line." The cocaine was running low and he was measuring it out. "Look," he said, about to jump to some other topic, using an inner logic only he could know. "I'm not really a Bolivian, but I'm a citizen of goddamn Bolivia, which is a lifetime sentence. I wasn't anything I could identify for my whole life. The result is, I spent the first eighteen years wanting what I didn't have and couldn't get. I am a stone expert on knowing what everybody wants."

"Your background is genuinely weird," I said. "I'll give you that. But it's a real-enough thing. You ought to see a shrink. Your subconscious must be like a mine field."

"What subconscious?" he said indignantly. "There is not one

thought, not one desire, not one urge that I don't act on. Shrinks are for people who don't know how to do that and want to give up and live with the boring results."

"The Libidinal-Pharmaceutical School of Psychoanalysis is founded! Free your id with drugs and movie money," I shouted, feeling the cocaine.

"I'm the prophet and founder of it," he yelled. "And I'm in the process of working my way through every car, orifice, and drug in Hollywood. Plus making more money than anybody else. Ever."

I laughed at the truth of it as he handed me the little bottle for a final toot. I dished out the last granules, and as I was ramming that old devil coke up my nose, a Beverly Hills police cruiser pulled up next to us and a cop asked if everything was all right. I froze. My life was finished. My career was over. I was going to die. Teddy boy—and I guess this is why he is an effective producer—took the little bottle and spoon from me. He palmed, then pocketed them both, and smiled at the two cops, saying things were just fine, but if they happened to stop at a coffee shop, he'd be very grateful for two regulars, no sugar. They nodded, saluted, and pulled away. I should have guessed it. We were in a forty-thousand-dollar car and we were neither noisy nor messy, the only absolute felonies in Beverly Hills.

After they left, I declared our meeting over, announcing that I had to go home. But Teddy was much too high to quit now. He wanted to go to Probe, a gay disco in Hollywood, just to see what the naughty boys were up to. When I passed on that, he suggested the Lhasa, an after-hours dive, where something was bound to be happening. But my brush with the law and common sense made me want to go home and nowhere else. Teddy pouted and implied if I didn't want to hang out with him, maybe he didn't want to do the movie after all. It was clear he wasn't at his best. I urged him to go home, and then left myself.

He was in Encino when it happened. It was about an hour after I left him. I don't know what he was looking for in Encino, but the police report said he had been doing ninety down Balboa Boulevard. He clipped six parked cars, bounced off a telephone pole, and went through the display window of a lighting store. His Porsche flipped over, bounced off a wall, and slammed into a display of floor lamps and chandeliers, all of which were as lit up as Teddy was. Ripping through all that wiring set the shop on fire. The car burned too, just like in the movies. There were drugs and alcohol in his system and a lot of second- and third-degree burns on his body. The police arrested him and took him to the Sherman Oaks Hospital Burn Center.

When I heard about it, I drove out to the Valley to have a look. The block was cordoned off, so I walked down Balboa Boulevard. It was early, but it was already hot and the smog made the air thick. The fire engines were still there and a crowd had gathered to watch a tow truck pull Teddy's car back through the broken window to the street. A teenage boy who was studying the operation said to me, "The burning Porsche. Definitely superior. Stay tuned for the slo-mo replay."

I went to see him as soon as visitors were allowed. As I drove to Sherman Oaks, I was feeling vaguely guilty about the accident. Not that I caused it, although I might have prevented it, or at least delayed it. I half-expected him to be on the phone making deals, or yelling in his various voices, treating the nurses like waitresses. But he was in bed, covered with bandages. An IV was dripping some chemical into his system and various dials and meters kept track of his vital signs. Flowers, telegrams, baskets of fruit, and get-well cards were shoved in corners and piled on tables. I smiled at him and said, "You're all over the papers, you know. *Variety* called you an 'indie impresario.'" He nodded slightly, but didn't say anything. "Remember the first script we worked on?" He didn't answer and I wasn't sure how well he could hear under all that gauze. "I'll give you a hint," I said. "It had mummies in it."

"Yeah," he finally answered in a soft voice that I had never heard before. "It was when that King Tut crap was around." He lapsed into silence again and I decided not to make any more jokes.

I wanted to thank him for not mentioning to the police that a great portion of the drugs in his system were taken in my presence. But all I managed to say was, "Is there a lot of pain?"

"There's supposed to be. But I don't know," he said through the layers of gauze in a drifting voice. "They'll probably make me go to AA or some drug clinic." He seemed to be shutting down, closing up the shop. Then a nurse came in and asked me to leave so she could change his bandages.

He was in the hospital for two months, and even then the skin grafts weren't completely successful. He had to keep going back as an outpatient for a lot of dermatological problems. The pigment of the new skin kept changing, and growths and tiny tumors grew on his neck and scalp. They were all benign, but they kept reappearing and had to be cut out each time. He always seemed to be waiting for a biopsy report. The medical problems consumed his energy for a while and I figured this thing would change him as surely as leaving La Paz had done when he was a younger man. His life really was like a movie dream and I found myself wondering how the drama would play out. I thought about it a lot, and in the script I wrote for him (in my mind), he was never quite the same after the accident. In my version, all that manic energy evaporated, as if the burning Porsche had consumed him. But that was my movie. In the movie he wrote for himself, the skin grafts finally worked and the tumors stopped appearing and Teddy got repaired. He bought another Porsche, started producing movies again, and picked up his life as it was before the accident, only more so. As usual, his script got made.

Walking Through the Fire

The idea of the unhappy screenwriter is part of American folklore. The impoverished-but-pure playwright or novelist sells out, goes Hollywood and spends his days by the pool and his nights in debauchery among vulgarians who hold him in contempt. The obligations of art are forgotten as he loses his soul and earns vast sums writing Flipper movies. He grows old and bitter among his shopping centers and tax shelters, hating himself and regretting what might have been.

In fact, screenwriting is a complex, exacting craft that requires one to assume many voices and to accommodate a singular vision to group practice. It's attempted by many and accomplished by few. The reason the pay is high is called the law of supply and demand. But that doesn't mean screenwriters are a jolly lot. Some of the unhappiness comes from not getting their scripts made, or on the occasions that they do, having no control over how the scripts are shot. Screenwriters are also frustrated and unhappy because whole studios, producers, and directors tend to regard them as interchangeable; the writers like to think of themselves as unique.

A producer with more money than sense once hired another writer and me to rewrite the same script simultaneously. I guess his plan was to use whichever scenes he liked best. I discovered it by a fluke. I called the producer's office about a routine matter and the secretary called me Claude. When I corrected her, she said, "Oh, yeah. That's the other one on this."

Since I'd heard of only one Claude in the Writers Guild, I rang up, introduced myself, and we compared notes. Our employer had filed contracts for each of us for separate projects. Except it was the same script with two different titles. It was a clear violation of the working rules, and our first thought was to lodge a complaint with the Guild. When we cooled off, we decided to take advantage of the situation. We got together, compared our work, and discussed the problems we were each encountering. It improved both scripts, made them easier to write, and it was a terrific way to get to know the man, who became a good friend.

Claude, the unhappy screenwriter, agreed to go to the fire-walking lecture because his friend Mae, the British publicist, had heard about it in her yoga class. Mae was convinced that walking on hot coals was just the ticket to make Claude less cynical and more able to embrace life's mysteries. Before she heard about fire walking, Mae, who tended to be enthusiastic, had tried tantric yoga, psychic nutrition, and flotation tanks. Although Claude sat in the occasional hot tub, for the most part he thought of it all as Melrose Avenue mysticism. But to be a screenwriter is to be flexible, and Claude recognized these endeavors as nonalcoholic and relatively uncrowded ways to meet people. So when Mae urged him, Claude agreed to go along. "Let's combine it with exercise," he said to her, "and go fire jogging."

But Mae was not about to be deterred by a joke. "Now, listen here," she said in the clipped accent that seemed to grow more British the longer she lived in Los Angeles, "fire walking is real. People have done it."

"People have gone over Niagara falls in a barrel," Claude answered. "That doesn't make it worth doing. Can this guy teach walking on water? There's a skill that'll get you somewhere."

"You can see film of it. They walk on hot coals. Barefoot. There's more in this world than your experience, you know."

"I don't doubt somebody can do it," Claude answered. "The question is, why would I want to join them?"

"Surely," she said, "a screenwriter can see the advantage of learning to endure pain without suffering."

At the Holiday Inn in Santa Monica, Claude and Mae listened to Garth, the guru of fire walking, explain that walking on hot coals was largely "a matter of using neurolinguistics to claim the warrior within you." Claude had long ago learned to discount the rhetoric these people used. If you had any respect for language you couldn't listen to their words. But that didn't make the ideas wrong. Garth showed a videotape of two barefoot men walking over hot coals. The cuffs of their trousers were singed, but the soles of their feet unburned. What interested Claude most was that the fire walkers didn't look like mystics, but like the people you see at the Irvine Ranch Market carefully selecting fresh produce.

Some years ago, before he was a screenwriter, Claude had known moderate literary success. He had written two novels. The critics liked the first one, but not the second. The recession of the early seventies made it hard to publish books that weren't likely to sell, and although Claude wrote several more, each better than the previous, they were not published. Eventually he stopped writing them. He moved to Los Angeles and pursued the movies. No one produced his scripts, just as no one published his novels, but because writers get paid in Hollywood whether or not the movies get made, Claude was well off financially, but a frustrated man. Over the last decade he had tried marriage, marijuana, and irony, none of which brought him satisfaction.

One of Claude's scripts, a love story called *Passing Fancy,* was sold to MGM for a great deal of money. But the management that bought it was fired; the management that followed was considering it, when it got fired too. The current set didn't say yes and didn't say no. Claude brooded about it and schemed ways to buy his script back. One problem was that the script had picked up so much studio overhead through the years that it was valued at several times what Claude had been paid. *Passing Fancy* had become a corporate tax write-off instead of a movie. Claude had listened to countless suggestions and critiques of his script. He'd made adjustments and corrections, deepening the characters and clarifying the action. But no matter how much he revised, no matter that the script had become the Platonic ideal of *Passing Fancy,* it still didn't get produced. Several of the stars and directors who admired it have hired Claude to write other scripts. He said yes often enough to support his mortgage and alimony payments.

After the introductory lecture at the Holiday Inn, Mae had gone on about how charismatic Garth was and how she just knew fire walking was "a valuable opportunity to turn fear into power." Her easy enthusiasm irritated Claude. He snapped at her, "It isn't some restaurant, you know, some new kind of sautéed goat cheese."

"Just what's wrong with inner peace? All you care about is making jokes. At my expense."

"You sound like an English parrot. 'Polly wants hot coals. Polly wants inner peace. More moral certainty, please,'" he said, imitating her English accent and flapping his arms like parrot wings. After that, Claude didn't see much of Mae but his outburst made him realize he was more interested than he knew in learning about walking on hot coals.

After the fight, and without Mae, Claude signed up for the three seminars with Garth. At the end, for those who wanted it, there was to be a fire walk. Garth told his students, "You can overcome your fear of fire, and therefore your fear of anything, if you alter your belief system. You believe fire will burn. And it will. But if you believe you are more powerful than fire, it will not burn *you.*"

After the first seminar, Claude, Garth, and a few others went out for a drink. Claude learned that while he had been in New York writing all those novels, Garth had been in an ashram near Benares pondering large questions. It was there he had learned the secrets of fire walking. The thing Claude liked the most about Garth was that he wasn't naturally charismatic at all. He had forced himself to become a public speaker. Offstage he was tentative and a little awkward. Words, which came so easily to Claude, were more of a struggle for Garth. Claude's glibness, the very quality that made it possible for him to make movie deals, was the thing he liked least about himself. Even though others called him articulate and honored him for it, in his heart the quick and easy voice felt unearned, a private badge of self-contempt, achieved by putting his technical skill above any belief. Claude could make his voice anyone's, which is the dramatist's skill, but he had done it so long for money or expediency, and so rarely for ideas that were his own or that moved him, that he was afraid his own voice had disappeared. He had cared about his novels, and no one noticed. Except for *Passing Fancy,* he didn't much care about his scripts. No one seemed to notice that either, but at least he was highly paid. There wasn't much solace in those paychecks, which was why he was unhappy. But there was some, and in this life, Claude always felt, we take what we can get. To Claude, Garth's awkwardness meant the man truly believed in what he said; otherwise, why go through so much difficulty to say it? "Whatever else he is," Claude said later, "the man is genuine. He isn't trying to sell me anything he hasn't already personally bought."

On the night of the last seminar, they gathered on the beach in Santa Monica. A man with a video camera was there to record the event. When Claude arrived, the coals were already hot, a ten-foot-long trail on the sand, running down to the blue Pacific. Garth, Claude, and two more would-be fire walkers stood barefoot and holding hands in a circle at the head of the fire. Several well-wishers milled about nervously. Garth reviewed what he had taught: "When you're about to make your walk, trust your instincts. If a voice says 'don't,' listen to it. The only people who get burned are the ones who are afraid they'll get burned."

Garth led the group in a long chant: "Let your mind go. See what it finds. Bring it all home." For an hour, while the coals grew hotter, they repeated the phrases, until they became a mantra, taking on a life and rhythm of their own. As the chant intensified, Claude could feel himself changing, or at least the things around him seemed to be changing. The coals didn't look bright to him; the observers seemed to fade from his view. The chant filled his brain and gave him a paradoxical sense of being both empty and filled with an elusive power. Garth added a few oms to the chant, and then turned away from Claude and the others and walked into the fire. When he got to the end, he turned, and, still chanting om, opened his arms to his students. Claude, who later said he couldn't remember any of it, turned and without thought, perhaps in a neurolinguistic trance, followed Garth into the flames, crushing the coals to ash beneath his feet. He moved more quickly than Garth and he didn't chant om, but he did walk on the fire.

Later, when he watched the videotape of himself, Claude declared it more like fire running, but there was no doubt he had done it. The tape showed Claude was glassy-eyed, that his feet touched the coals eight times, four times for each foot, and that when he was across, he fell into Garth's arms.

When they had completed their walks, and the video camera had taken close-ups of their feet, which were dirty but unburned, they all went to Gypsy, an Indian restaurant in Santa Monica, where they ate tandoori chicken and drank Indian beer. Garth toasted the fire walkers and asked how they felt when they came out of the flames. "A little giddy, I guess," Claude said. "It's hard to remember exactly."

"I feel protected," Garth said. "That's the best word I know to describe it. People say to me, if they can walk through the fire, then nothing will ever frighten them again. But I still feel frightened a lot. The difference is, I never feel frightened of being frightened." Claude just drank his beer and sat quietly.

When the tape of Claude walking the coals was shown on the local news, the television show *Lifestyles of the Rich and Famous* wanted to interview him as the fire-walking screenwriter of Hollywood. Claude said no to that. Instead, he tried to take pleasure in the glimpses of serenity that came to him from his accomplishment. He walked the coals several more times and indeed did begin to feel more at ease.

Mae was so impressed that she chose to forget his rudeness and wanted him to go to a pychic with her to see if he had been a fire walker in any of his previous incarnations. Claude declined, but he was glad to see Mae again. He found it easier to accept her enthusiasms. In his pleasure, Claude lost a little weight and the creases around his mouth began to fade. He wasn't as harsh to Mae as he had once been, and that pleased them both. Mae wanted to know how Claude felt now that he was able to fire-walk so easily. "And please," she said, "just tell me, don't make a joke about it."

"For a moment there," Claude answered, with no inclination to make a joke, "I thought: I can walk through fire. I can do anything. A lot of that goes away pretty quickly, but some of it stays. I guess it's true, I'll never be quite the same." Mae smiled, privately thrilled at the changes in Claude that she had helped to shape. "But I'll tell you," he said, when he saw her glowing, "don't order a halo for me yet. Not everything's changed. MGM still won't take my phone calls. No matter what I do or how hard I try, I still can't get *Passing Fancy* made."

Above the Line, Below the Line

All of Hollywood is divided into above the line and below the line. It's a budget term that has become a sort of sociological shorthand. On studio budget forms, money for profit participants is separated from money for those who receive a straight salary. Above the line means writers, directors, producers, and principal actors—people who are likely to drive German cars and live in Spanish houses. They tend to talk about making a film. Below means crew, technicians, and supporting cast. They're likely to drive vans or pickup trucks and live where they can afford the rent. They usually say they're working on a show.

I was at Paramount rewriting a script about a troupe of daredevil stunt drivers who went around the country crashing into one another and driving through walls of fire. For background I talked with a few Hollywood stuntmen. We met at Duke's coffee shop in the Tropicana Motel, which is sort of a below-the-line Schwab's. Our conversations sometimes lasted for hours. They were storytellers, ready to talk about the lunacy of their profession until they were exhausted from the telling and I was high from the hearing. It was from his colleagues, over fried eggs doused with hot sauce and ketchup and later while eating tortilla chips and salsa and drinking Mexican beer, that I heard Bucky's story.

Bucky was up at Lake Arrowhead, on the set of a television show about lumberjacks. The gag he had been hired for was a fall from a tree; if he did well, it could lead to steady work. In the story, one of the characters is high up in a tree, topping it, when he falls. Another tree, being cut at the same time, also falls and just misses him. Bucky never got the plot details quite straight. He just concentrated on the gag, which in this case didn't look too bad. It was a straight drop, seventy feet. As long as he stayed clear of the falling tree, it would be up, down, and out, which was just fine with Bucky.

He had spent two hours supervising the placement of the cardboard boxes he'd fall on. The younger guys used air mattresses or foam, but Bucky liked the old way, several layers of industrial cardboard cartons. Each box was three feet deep, and he stacked four of them, so there was plenty of cushion. There wasn't a lot of landing surface, but space was crowded in the woods. It's still a piece of cake, Bucky thought as he started to put on his padding. At the last minute, the producer of the series, another young hotshot with a beard, came over and told Bucky not to wear the padding, to take the dive bare-chested, or else it wouldn't match the shots of the actor, who was playing the scene shirtless. "No way," Bucky said. "That's seventy feet. You can't take that height without pads." The producer nodded and walked away. A few minutes later, the production manager strolled over and told Bucky that was it for the day. They were going to make other arrangements for the tree gag. Bucky was stunned, and then he saw his spotter, a twenty-year-old named Junior, going up the tree, with an idiot grin on his face. He was bare-chested. "I hope to hell he's got insurance," Bucky muttered as he packed up his gear. Before he left, he turned back to watch the shot from far enough away so no one could see him. Junior did it all wrong. It looked like a swan dive, as if he were going off a diving board, which is ridiculous and not the way anybody ever fell out of a tree. The other tree came down exactly right, and Junior hit the cardboard properly, but Bucky thought it looked stupid. Later, he heard the producer loved it.

On the drive home, Bucky put a Springsteen tape on and turned the volume way up, trying to let the music make him feel a little better. He reminded himself that on the set the stuntman's word about safety is supposed to be law. No matter what some kid producer thought. What the hell did they let the actor play the scene without a shirt for? They knew the tree gag was coming. Where the hell was the script girl on that one?

Bucky had been having trouble getting work lately. There seemed to be so many young guys coming up, guys who were ready to lower their price and do any damn thing without proper preparation, like this crap with the no shirt and Junior. Just last year, he reminded himself, his picture had been in *California* magazine, in a story about stuntmen. Bucky kept a copy in the glove compartment of his Ram Charger. He pulled off the road to have another look at it. The clipping was starting to yellow and the folds were becoming tears. He noticed it was actually two years ago, but it was still great. Whenever he was feeling down, he took it out and read it aloud to himself: ". . . somewhere there might be a quiet, reflective stuntman who would rather have been an astronomer, but for the most part they tend to be hard, strong men who think of themselves as courageous, even heroic. But their courage isn't in service of king and country or damsels in distress, it's more likely for a TV show about exploding cars and people who run in and out of burning buildings. But stuntmen do have nerve, everyone on a movie set knows that. Strong, raw nerve."

Bucky was born and grew up in Malibu, where his father once owned a lot of property. Not the Malibu of the Colony or the Old Malibu Road, where the Pacific regularly washes away the million-dollar real estate. Bucky was from the hills, the Santa Monica Mountains, on the other side of the Pacific Coast Highway. Until recently, few people lived in the hills; the temperament of the residents was right-wing, redneck, and unforgiving. It's changed a bit now and the population of what the real-estate people call the Malibu Hills is a bit more heterogeneous. Bucky straddled the two camps. He was old Malibu by birth and therefore a little strange to the new money. As a stuntman, he was in the picture business;

that made him suspect to the people he grew up with. Stuntmen are certainly part of the movie business, but they are a breed apart. No producer, director, or writer really trusts someone who crashes cars and jumps out of windows for a living. Bucky's response to the dilemma of not quite fitting into either of the camps was to hunker down with his family, retreating into his status as an old-timer. When movie people in Malibu ask how long you've lived there, they usually mean how many months, not how many generations.

Bucky's wife, Marlene, stayed home in Malibu all day tending to Billy, their six-year-old son. Marlene cooked, cleaned, mended, and tended. When Bucky wasn't crashing motorcycles or staging brawls, he added on to their house. The main house, the part that had been there the longest, was the first house built on Bucky's road. Over the years, Bucky had added rooms and outbuildings so that the place sort of rambled in an eclectic style. Bucky was proudest of his pool. He put it in the ground himself. He dug the hole and poured the concrete. He set the tile in an intricate pattern of different shades of blue and he installed the filter. Bucky believed in self-reliance. He always said a man who can't fix his own car, or his own plumbing, or who can't build a swimming pool, is no man at all.

The day after Bucky's problems up at Lake Arrowhead, his friend J.T. came by for a visit and a little smoke. He was wearing a T-shirt that said "Bag the Dialogue, Let's Wreck a Car." J.T. had been a stuntman until a few years ago, when he broke several bones in his leg. It never healed properly and although J.T. still takes an occasional fall if the money's right, he usually works as a grip. Marlene knew her husband was upset about something, but he hadn't yet told her what and she knew better than to ask. She was glad J.T. was around, because even though they'd probably get stoned, J.T. was funny and she could count on him to put Bucky in a good mood. Marlene had made a meatloaf and there was plenty of food, so she asked if J.T. wanted to stay and have supper.

While Marlene cooked and fed little Billy his dinner of Spaghetti-O's, Bucky and J.T. sat in the living room getting high. In her kitchen, Marlene kept a rack filled with herbs and spices she bought in the supermarket, like the ones in the homemaker magazines. She'd had the bottles for years so that any flavor they might have once possessed was long since dead. But it was satisfying to her to display them in her kitchen, and when they had company, like J.T., she sprinkled the bottles over the food, pleased to think she was treating her family and guests right.

During the meal, Bucky and J.T. laughed and told stories about an actress named France.

"That was her name, France. Like the country," J.T. said. "She had a mouth on her. All the time giving orders. She was the star of the show, but she wasn't a star, per se."

"That's right," Bucky said. "Never knew your name, always saying, 'Oh, please, I need my purse. It's in my trailer.' And she was always drinking Tab. Real bitch on wheels." The combination of the marijuana they had been smoking and the memories of France made both men laugh uncontrollably. "We got her, didn't we?" Bucky said.

J.T. turned to Marlene and said, "Old France goes, 'Oh, please, put gas in my car.' She had this stupid VW Rabbit convertible she thought was so hot. So Bucky goes, 'Sure thing, Frances. Glad to.'"

"So me and J.T., we filled her tank, all right. With Tab, which she was always drinking," Bucky said. "We just dumped a six-pack in. We told her it was a new kind of gas and now she'd get better mileage and it would reduce the wear and tear." Bucky and J.T. laughed again at the memory.

Marlene didn't think it was all that funny and she wondered if it had wrecked the Rabbit, but telling the story had put Bucky in a better mood, so she let it pass.

About two years earlier an artist named Elmo Driver had bought the house across the road from Bucky and Marlene's. Elmo was well-known in the world of museums and galleries. His work was sold in London and New York; people who knew about these things knew about Elmo, but it was all news to Bucky. Elmo's house was a simple frame place that had been unchanged for twenty years. Elmo needed a studio. That's why he moved to

Malibu. He worked on a large scale. His paintings were often eight feet high and twice as long; he needed a lot of room. The architect who had helped Elmo design his studio was celebrated for using raw construction materials in his buildings and for making furniture out of cardboard. It was high-tech to readers of art magazines; unfinished to Bucky, who occasionally read *Road and Track* or *Soldier of Fortune*. The studio's walls were made of corrugated steel. Bucky had assumed that stucco or perhaps siding would eventually go over the sheets of steel, so that the new studio would blend with the older part of the house. He himself spent two years building his pool, during which time someone might have considered it an eyesore. But Bucky finished the job. Completely. It wasn't until an article about Elmo's studio had appeared in the *Los Angeles Times* that Bucky realized what he saw out his window was it. The finished product. To Bucky it was an insult. Until he had a famous artist for a neighbor, Bucky had always taken a relaxed, live-and-let-live attitude toward life.

When photographers from glossy magazines came to shoot the studio, Bucky threatened to shoot them. He would stand out near the road with his hunting rifle slung over his arm. The art lovers and high-tech fans who drove past had their eyes locked on the corrugated steel and rarely noticed Bucky. If they saw him, they just took him for a bit of local color. The little road Bucky had lived on for years began to get busy, with art students coming and going. Bucky began to worry about the marijuana plants he grew behind his house. He didn't see the situation as a clash of cultures, he saw it for the abomination he knew it to be. Elmo was oblivious of any offense or difficulty his studio might have caused. When a newspaper or magazine made unfavorable mention of it, Elmo professed ignorance and astonishment that anyone might find a corrugated-steel building unattractive. Mr. Driver wanted nothing to do with fashion and he would have been just as happy if the photographers never came around. He liked the steel because it was an inexpensive way to get the space he needed for his work. Elmo had no interest in Bucky or old Malibu. In fact, Elmo had grown up on a ranch in Colorado and was quite handy with hammers and saws. His own brothers still lived on the ranch. Only Elmo had gone away, to Europe, New York, and now Malibu. Had he known Bucky had built his pool by hand, Elmo would surely have been impressed.

One afternoon, when Elmo had been away for a few days, Bucky went across the road to see if he could have a look inside the studio. From Bucky's side, all that was visible were the steel walls. "Maybe I should take a can opener over there," Bucky said to Marlene before he set out.

"Don't try to go inside, okay?" she said as he left.

Bucky walked through the weeds and along the steel walls, running his hand over the corrugated metal, looking to see if it was some sort of an illusion, like a movie set. He certainly couldn't see anything more than he had already seen from his own house, at least not in front. But Elmo's living quarters, which were in a part of the old house that had been gutted, faced the rear of the property and had plenty of windows. The first thing Bucky noticed was a second-story bathroom. It had a glass wall. From where Bucky was standing, he could see right into the john. It faced the hills, but Bucky could look right at the toilet.

After he had gotten over the shock of Elmo's bathroom, Bucky peered into what he guessed was the living room, not that you could tell. Part of the room was apparently the kitchen, and part was the living room, and no wall divided the two functions. There were several large canvases on the wall that Bucky assumed were examples of Elmo's work. Each one had geometric shapes emerging from large fields of color. They weren't to Bucky's taste, but compared to the bathroom, they were easy enough to take and not nearly as bad as he had expected.

"The goddamn toilet is in the window," he told Marlene when he got home. "You can see it. Anybody standing in the back could see right in," Bucky said, still amazed.

"Well, I'd never use it, no matter what," was Marlene's reply.

After his inspection of the studio, Bucky referred to Elmo as Rembrandt or, sometimes, Toilet Brain.

Life at the studio was quite active, what with Elmo's children, ex-wives, and current mistresses coming and going, along with the art-transfer truck bringing and taking the enormous canvases. It made the little dirt road busier than Bucky could bear. After a day jumping out of windows and off exploding bridges, he would spend his evenings brooding about the monstrosity next door. Late at night, when he had smoked a bit of his marijuana and sipped the Wild Turkey he favored, Bucky would go outside and shoot his rifle at the stars. Sometimes he'd lower the barrel a bit and fire in the direction of Elmo's studio, sending the bullets just over the steel roof and into the hills beyond. Elmo, for his part, continued to be oblivious of the consternation he was causing. Bucky wasn't the only resident angry at the presence of the studio; he was just the nearest. There was a kind of grass-roots rebellion brewing, with a lot of loose talk about how the planning commission must have been bribed. A petition of recall was planned, but nothing came of it. So Elmo just kept painting, quite happy with all the room he had created for himself. Elmo kept an apartment in West Hollywood. During one of his marriages he had used it for assignations. When he grew restless with the isolation of rural Malibu, he would drive into the city for a few days. Bucky, Marlene, and little Billy weren't people with two addresses, so they couldn't escape when they got tired of looking at their neighbors. Marlene suggested that Bucky try not looking at it, averting his eyes. That, as Bucky told her, was running away. And Bucky didn't run from anything.

After the winter rains, the corrugated steel began to rust, changing to a patchy, dirty red. Elmo, like every artist who ever drew breath and paint, thought that was just terrific. He used words such as "patina" and "chiaroscuro" to describe the look his studio was acquiring.

Fires come to Malibu the way the swallows come to San Juan Capistrano—regularly and without fail at the same time every year. The movie people in the million-dollar houses hired Mexicans to hose down their roofs while they themselves moved into the Beverly Wilshire Hotel or went to their apartments in New York. In the hills, the residents soaked the roofs themselves; if it looked particularly dicey, they might take their valuables and go stay with cousins who lived in safer places. The more prudent ones always kept the brush cleared from around their houses. Elmo had never even planted a lawn. He had just let it run wild. Among the weeds were wild violets and columbine. Elmo thought it was beautiful. To Bucky it was an unweeded garden and it disgusted him.

Bucky had always been among the last to leave when the fire department cleared the neighborhood. Always a little reluctantly, Bucky had packed Marlene and little Billy into the Ram Charger and moved in with J.T. up in Ventura County. J.T.'s house was small, but they had never had to stay more than a few days. This year, in the face of the high-tech studio, Bucky was feeling more than a little ornery. This was his turf and he was making noises about not leaving. Marlene didn't know what to make of her husband's obstinance, but she knew she was in for trouble.

It happened often enough for people to know what to do, but never often enough for them not to be scared when flames were scorching the hillside. The fire-department helicopter was overhead warning everyone to evacuate the area. Sheriff's vans swept the streets with the same message, clearing people out before dark.

When a sheet of dark smoke was visible in the distance, the fire department did its usual final patrol of the streets, telling everyone to leave immediately, reminding them to turn off the gas and round up all domestic animals. Elmo wasn't even home. He hadn't been there in days. The mail was just stuffed in his mailbox. Bucky was contemptuous of him, of a man who ran from danger. Bucky had fantasies of torching the studio and blaming it on nature. Only his doubts that the damn thing would even burn prevented him.

When most of his neighbors were gone, and the fire was still a few miles away, Bucky stood out by the road, straining to see into the distance, watching for the first flashes of orange light against the evening sky. One of his neighbors, who was late in leaving, drove past in his pickup truck and called out, "Everything is on fire."

"So what?" Bucky shouted, refusing to move as his neighbor's truck disappeared up the road and the fire burned its way closer. All Bucky could think about was how impossible the stunt business had become. He hadn't worked much lately and the phone wasn't ringing. The hell with them, he thought. And the hell with the fire, too. He wasn't about to run from it. That was the coward's way out, the way Toilet Brain would do it. No, Bucky was born here, he was of this place, and he wasn't going to leave, not because a helicopter told him to, not for some fire, and not for some artist in a tin studio.

Marlene, who questioned very little, stood waiting for whatever would come. She stroked little Billy and watched for the fire. She knew it would consume brush, trees, and the occasional unlucky house. It was a crapshoot, eating up one house, skipping the next. There would be no pattern to it, only the serendipity of destruction. Bucky stayed out by the road, staring into the distance, until he could see the fire itself. It was made of light, yet it blocked out light. The flames were like a vast orange ball rolling toward him; it might have been the sun itself, fallen to earth. It was near enough so all three of them could feel its heat. Bucky knew the paint on the walls of the house would begin to bubble. Awestruck at the power rolling toward him, he said, "I am become death, the destroyer of worlds." It was from the Bhagavad Gita, and Bucky had heard it when he was a stunt double in a mini-series about India. The line had stuck with him, but Marlene didn't know that. She only knew a big fire was coming fast and her husband was behaving strangely. All she could think to ask was whether they were going to leave and what should she take. Bucky told her to put on her bathing suit and to put one on Billy. Marlene didn't question the order, she just did it, glad to be taking some action.

While they were changing, Bucky sprayed his roof again and then went to the garage and dragged out the tank of oxygen that he used for welding. Rabbits, rodents, and a few stray dogs were running across the fields and the road, moving on instinct, staying ahead of the fire. Marlene and Billy joined Bucky at the pool. It's hard to know when stuntmen are scared. They usually affect great calm, saying they're scared all the time and that only amateurs claim otherwise. For most of them—certainly for Bucky—the greater the danger, the calmer they appear.

When the fire was whirling through Elmo's overgrown front yard, consuming the weeds and wild violets, Bucky ordered his family into the swimming pool. He gave his wife and son each a scuba mask with a hose connected to the oxygen tank. He took a third for himself, dropped the tank into the pool, then they all plunged into the water.

The fire scorched Elmo's yard, burning the hated weeds. Although the flames licked and charred the corrugated steel, the studio really was fireproof. Flames leapt above Bucky's roof, dancing over the pool like random celestial light. Cinders and ash fell into the water, hissing and disintegrating, while Bucky, Marlene, and little Billy stayed at the bottom, breathing their oxygen and watching the fire above through the scuba masks. Bucky swam to the surface and saw the fire skipping over his property. When the flames were past, gone to cook someone else's house, a house where the owner didn't believe in property with quite Bucky's conviction, he guided his family back to the surface. When they came out of the water and Marlene saw their house had been spared, she cried with joy and thanked God and her husband. Bucky knew he had done the right thing. He felt strong and good about himself. He had been tested by fire. He had faced the flames and he had not run away, not taken the coward's way out.

The next day, when the police allowed people in again, Elmo came back to Malibu to see how his studio had fared. When he drove up, relieved to see the structure still standing, he waved to Bucky in a neighborly gesture. For the first time Bucky strolled across the road to say hello to Elmo. They shook hands like soldiers well met after a battle. They talked about the fire and how lucky they both had been. Elmo asked a few questions about being a stuntman and then proposed a big party to celebrate the end of the fire. Bucky was hesitant until Elmo mentioned casually that he would invite all the producers and studio executives who collected his work. "They love to come out here," he said. "They think they'll get a better price if they buy the pictures off my wall."

That weekend, a stream of people from the movie business drove out to Malibu to have a drink or two and talk about the fire. Elmo ordered several trays of sushi from a Japanese restaurant and Marlene provided tortilla chips and a dip made from sour cream and powdered soup. Marlene was nervous about going into the studio and she made sure little Billy used the bathroom before they left home. She did the same. At the party, Bucky talked to Ike Harris, a producer he had worked for a few years ago. When Elmo saw Ike and Bucky talking, he walked over and put an arm around each one. Elmo, who was a little drunk, told Ike that Bucky had stayed right through the fire. "He saved his family and kept an eye on all the other houses. He's a hell of a guy, Ike." Ike was very impressed. He and Bucky talked about fire prevention because Ike was working on a pilot for a television series about a rural volunteer fire department. Later, Ike asked Bucky if he would consider becoming stunt coordinator on the show. Bucky nodded slowly and allowed as how that might be an interesting proposition.

The Senator and the Movie Star

Schwab's was unchanging; that was one of its pleasures. It was soothing to turn up every morning in a place where the customers and the menu were always the same. Even temporary repairs at Schwab's became venerable. When an earthquake broke the big windows that looked out on Sunset Boulevard, old Leon Schwab, the head man, made some noise about it being a good time to redecorate. Instead he put up plywood and left it there for months.

Trying not to gawk at movie stars was an honored tradition at Schwab's. The unspoken idea was, we're all so used to glamour that a star's presence doesn't turn our heads. It wasn't true, of course. People tried to stay unimpressed, but the occasional participation of a star in the dance of the Schwabaderos made the less famous feel reassured that they were in the right place, connected, even peripherally, to success.

I continued to have breakfast there every morning, but as my own career moved forward, I often had dinner at Morton's, a restaurant where the regular crowd is so high above the line that the air gets positively thin. Any night at Morton's, there are movie stars and the heads of studios. The Morton's crowd, which needs less assurance that they're doing things right, is far too famous to have a policy about gawking. Maybe if Fidel Castro walked in, heads would swivel, but only if he was wearing his green fatigues and handing out Montecristos. Reactions to fame might differ in Schwab's and Morton's, but as in all of Hollywood, movie celebrity was a fact of life. Earn your bones in some other racket and then come visit Hollywood and people can get very excited.

Because I had once covered politics, I was often invited to the social-political parties and dinners that are common in Hollywood. In the months before election time, candidates from other states turn up in Los Angeles to make pitches for campaign contributions and to hustle movie-star endorsements. Unless the candidates were from New York I rarely knew them, but once in a while their staff members were friends of mine. Like the candidates, the aides were curious to see Hollywood. One of them, a former journalist who had become a political consultant, wanted to be taken to Morton's for dinner so he might see the movie-business powerful dine. It was there, from him, that I first heard the story of the senator who came to Hollywood.

As he flew to Los Angeles for the fund-raiser, Frank Talifero was trying to keep thoughts of losing the election from his mind. He reminded himself that getting elected to the Senate the first time was the hard one. Six years ago he had had trouble raising money in his home state. Going to Hollywood on a money-hunting expedition would have been a waste of time. But the guy ahead of him on the Commerce Committee was probably going to get beaten, the chairman was seventy-six and looking to retire. With a little luck, in two years Frank could be chairman. That made him important to Hollywood because Frank was a man who knew how to pick his causes; when he knew he was going to give something away, he was always interested in seeing what it would bring.

Maurice Trumpelman had run three studios over the last eighteen years. When other studio heads changed jobs it was usually seen as a sign of turmoil or even personal trouble; for Maurice Trumpelman, each shift seemed to make him more powerful. As a child called "Mickey Trent," Trumpelman had appeared in several movies. He had been under contract at MGM all through his adolescence and attended school on the Culver City lot. As a young man, dissatisfied with the uncertainty of the performer's life, he had reclaimed his name and become a lawyer. Now he was the most feared and respected of the studio bosses. Not yet fifty, he was said to have already lived several lives. Trumpelman was the only studio chief who devoted time to public issues outside the direct concerns of Hollywood. He was active in Democratic-party politics and could be counted on to raise money when it was needed.

Trumpelman liked the senator, and if they weren't exactly fishing buddies, they could talk to one another and they could do business. Maurice Trumpelman made a point of getting to know every Democratic senator. They were all glad to meet him because they knew Trumpelman as a tough but realistic man with clout who delivered funds to candidates he approved of, in or out of California. Frank was looking at a tough campaign for his second term and he had turned to Trumpelman for help.

"Jesus, Trump," the senator had said on the phone. "This character could beat me." The senator's problem was an astronaut who wanted his seat. "He's already got more aerospace money than he can count, and his recognition factor in the state is almost as high as mine."

"When he opens his mouth," Trumpelman said, "the people will see through him."

"I wish I could agree with you. I need your help."

"I understand. Why don't you come out here? I'll put something together. We can do it at my house."

"That's great, Trump. I appreciate it. I really do. It'll give us a chance to catch up." As the senator hung up his phone, he buzzed one of his secretaries to ask which issues were of interest to Trumpelman of California. There had been several phone calls and some correspondence, but Trumpelman spoke in such discreet tones that Frank couldn't remember what the man had wanted. If he was going to ask him to raise money, Frank thought, he'd better know if he could deliver whatever the hell it was Trumpelman was after.

With their children in college, Maurice and Maia Trumpelman's Holmby Hills mansion was too large for the two of them, but they kept it because it was ideal for entertaining. After twenty-three years of marriage, Maia put political brunches together faster than it took to eat the food. For Senator Talifero, Trumpelman asked his wife to go all-out. He called the heads of three other studios and asked them to attend. "We'll make it bipartisan, Fritz," he had said to Fritz Porter, who was a Republican and the head of a rival studio. Fritz had once been Trumpelman's deputy and might have been his heir. Fritz was a Democrat in those days, but when he found an opportunity to run his own shop he had jumped ship, politically and professionally. Trumpelman had never forgiven him, and as a result Fritz lives waiting for the revenge he knows will someday come.

"Fine, Trump. We'll be there," Porter said.

"We'll raise some money for him," Trumpelman said, "then give the senator our shopping list."

The brunch was on a Sunday afternoon and seventy people turned out, which was everyone invited. Even the most high-powered people in Hollywood took the Trumpelmans' invitations very seriously. Most of the women were in white slacks or white linen dresses; their husbands wore silk sport jackets or cashmere sweaters slung casually over their shoulders. They stood around the pool sipping white wine and the occasional Bloody Mary, while the senator, in a blue suit, moved among them. With his big, solidly packed frame he seemed to gather each guest to him as he shook hands and made small talk. When the senator smiled, his mouth stretched back to show his gleaming teeth and he looked boyish. He kept his silvery hair cut short, which gave him a no-nonsense look. The blend of youthful high spirits and serious lawmaker was his charm. He discarded his jacket, loosened his tie, and worked the crowd.

When the guests were on their second drink, Trumpelman introduced the senator, who began to speak, quietly at first, almost shyly. He talked about the ferocious financial problems facing the country and about the social dilemmas that budget cutbacks created. He spoke about what it once meant to be a liberal and what it no longer meant. He told his listeners, "Today everyone is a fiscal conservative, and any politician who claims that as a special attribute isn't saying much. The trick to it is to know how to spend what little we have effectively. Of course we need a strong defense. But that's not to say we must give the Pentagon whatever it wants. Of course we don't want homeless people, hungry in the street. We are a compassionate and practical people. But that is not to say anyone should be able to get welfare because it's easier than getting a job." He spoke for twenty minutes, keeping steady eye contact with all the expensive-looking, suntanned people grouped around him. When he was done, everyone applauded and offered toasts.

"Oh, hell," he said, unconsciously imitating Jimmy Stewart. "Enough of this. You know why I'm here. I need your help in two ways. You're all opinion makers. Like it or not, it's the truth. I want your good opinion and I want you to spread it around. Second, as you know, I'm about to enter a political battle with a very tough opponent. People will vote for an astronaut because they've heard of him or because he's been in outer space. I won't say this to the press and I ask you not to quote me." Frank dropped his voice and drew them into his confidence, performing as well as any actor. "Politics can draw some weird ones, and this guy is one of the strangest. He's probably psychotic and he belongs in outer space. The man is dangerous. He could be in the Senate and the country will be the poorer for it. That is not to say I couldn't be replaced. I hope it doesn't happen, but there are worthy opponents. This man is not one of them. I need your financial support to beat him."

They applauded again. Freddie Ordway, one of the competing studio heads Trumpelman had invited, buttonholed the senator and began talking about Latin America. Ordway, unlike Maurice Trumpelman, cultivated the press and public and was frequently quoted in the papers and interviewed on television. Trumpelman almost never spoke in public, preferring to remain aloof and mysterious. As Freddie spoke, Frank made the appropriate responses, hoping he wouldn't be asked a factual question he couldn't answer. Freddie, the only bachelor among the moguls, had come to the brunch with Gwen Carrol, an actress who was in the process of becoming as famous as actresses can be. When Freddie introduced her to the senator, she shook his hand as if he were the minister and this was church, then tugged at her white silk blouse, pulling it tight over her breasts. Frank could have sworn the woman's nipples winked at him from under the silk. Senator Talifero didn't have a lot of time to go to the movies, and if the truth were known, his taste in films ran to westerns made before 1955. But even Senator Talifero recognized Gwen, the Midwestern farm girl who had become a goddess. With her white porcelain skin and red hair that looked hot enough to heat a room, traffic stopped for Gwen Carrol, even the traffic around Trumpelman's pool.

"It sounds like you're running on the commonsense ticket, Senator," she said, locking her eyes to his.

"Be careful, Miss Carrol, or I'll be running after you."

She laughed and touched his arm lightly, about to up the flirtation ante, when Trumpelman joined them. "Excuse me, Gwen. Sorry to interrupt. Senator, if you would come with me for a moment." Frank hadn't heard Trumpelman approach. The man seemed to glide from place to place. His feet touched the ground, but the soles of his shoes were never scuffed.

"Maybe I'll get to see you later," Frank said to Gwen, thinking he wouldn't mind seeing her alone.

Trumpelman led the senator, Freddie Ordway, and Fritz Porter to his study, where Jack Morris, the fourth studio head, was on the phone. Morris was the least polished of the bunch, a loud, slightly vulgar man who was likely to break into inappropriate laughter at any time. Porter and Ordway, like most studio executives, were former agents. Jack Morris, like the men who founded the movie business at the beginning of the century, had started in the garment district, a cloak-and-suiter. Morris was the toughest dealmaker of them all and anyone who underestimated his brains or his resolve was making an error. These men had already made substantial personal contributions to Frank's campaign, and all but Fritz Porter, the Republican, had shaken down their associates for donations. They were hard and often brutal men, but collectively, at least in private, they sometimes got jokey, wisecracking, because there was no accountability except to one another.

As the senator entered the study, he was thinking that it was easy to ask businessmen for donations. They always gave and they always told you straight out what they wanted in return. Socially conscious liberals were the tough ones. With those people, you had to read their minds to know what they really wanted and expected. As the senator greeted the four Hollywood bosses, he didn't think he'd have to do much mind reading.

"Gentlemen," Trumpelman began, "I've explained part of the situation to the senator and he's kindly agreed to discuss it with us now." Frank had been to enough of these sessions to know that the key words were "part of." That meant these hotshots wanted something they hadn't told him about. The supposed price of their support was ironing out some trade problem with video cassettes.

Trumpelman began by reviewing the situation. "We can't stop people from copying cassettes. It's probably healthy in the long run for them to do it, on a limited basis. It creates interest in movies and allows more people to see them. Up till now, it's been relatively difficult to copy the things. You need two machines and some technical skill."

"A minor irritant," Fritz Porter said. "But the Japanese are now producing a single home video machine that can easily copy the tapes."

"I don't quite understand," Frank said.

"Let me try to explain," Trumpelman said. "The Japanese are already marketing, in Japan only, a home video machine with two ports. That means you put one cassette in one port, and play it in the normal manner. At the same time, putting a blank cassette in the second port, you can make a copy. All the consumer needs is a blank tape."

"I see," Frank answered judiciously. This isn't going to be so bad, he thought. Standing up against the tide of Japanese imports will be popular at home. "I recognize the problem," he said. "But keeping products off the domestic market can be tricky. It's easy to be accused of restraint of trade. Are any of these machines for sale in this country yet?"

"No," Trumpelman said. "And we wish to keep it that way." He handed Frank a document. "This will outline our position and give you the necessary specifications and information."

"Fine, Trump, thank you. I have some leverage with the Japanese. I might be able to help. Any domestic manufacturer going to start making them?"

"No," Trumpelman said with a finality that suggested no domestic manufacturer would dare. "Now, the second issue is a related one."

Here it comes, Frank thought. Maurice Trumpelman's reason for throwing a party. "Yes, Trump, what else?"

"Fritz will run it down for you," Trumpelman said.

"The cassette market is huge and getting bigger. But nobody is buying them," Fritz said, beginning quietly. "People rent them. Cassettes aren't like books. Nobody but a few collectors wants to own them. People don't browse through them or keep them on a shelf," he said, nodding toward Trumpelman's bookshelves. "People rent them for two bucks and return them the next day. We don't see one penny of it. Neither does the talent."

As Fritz Porter spoke, Frank noticed that among the books on the shelves there were two framed photographs of Maurice Trumpelman as a child. In one he was sitting on Clark Gable's knee; in the other he was smiling up at President Truman.

"The talent is going to start looking to us for a piece," Freddie Ordway said as he bit into the last of the plate of strawberries he had brought into the study with him. He ate each berry precisely, biting it in half and sucking the portions through his teeth.

"The problem," Trumpelman said, "is the doctrine of first sale, which as you may know is part of the copyright act." Trumpelman looked at the senator to see if he had any idea what the doctrine of first sale was.

"Yes, Trump," Frank said. "I'm familiar with it." If Trumpelman was pleased or surprised, he didn't show it. "It holds, I believe, that a book or a cassette can command a royalty only once. Rentals are exempt. The law was intended to encourage inexpensive lending libraries."

"That's right, Senator. That's the law. We want it changed."

"Isn't this the issue that caused a strike?" Frank said, casting back through his mind, trying to recall the various Hollywood labor disputes of the last few years. "Didn't the writers go out over this one?" As he said it, Frank realized he had made a tactical error. He had asked a question because he wanted to know the answer, and with this crowd, as in a court, you didn't ask questions unless you already knew the answers. The last thing Frank needed was for Maurice Trumpelman to start doubting him.

"The writers are crazy, irrational," Jack Morris snapped. "A bunch of waiters and guys who want to be directors. They split hairs like it's the Talmud in the shtetel. They strike, it makes them feel powerful. The only reason they haven't walked over this one is, they haven't figured it out yet."

"But they will," Trumpelman said. "And we have to be there first. We'll give them a piece out of our end. The other guilds, too. But we have to control the pie."

The whiff of Jewish self-loathing made Frank uneasy. He was usually at pains to distance himself from racist remarks. If the language was harsh enough, he left the room. But the Jews were a different story. He assumed Jack Morris was Jewish. What Jack had said was harmless enough, and probably true, but if a gentile were to say it, God knows what Morris would think or do. Frank let it pass. "It's a tough one, fellows," he said, considering the problems. "We're talking about legislation here, an amendment to the Copyright Act. Could take years."

"We need it faster than that, and we're prepared to do what's necessary to get it," Trumpelman said.

"Let me be blunt. Your timing stinks. It's an election year for me, that's why I'm out here asking to turn your friends upside down and shake out their pockets."

"What's involved?" Fritz Porter asked, uninterested in Frank's argument.

"It gets proposed in subcommittee in the new session. I can help you there. Even if I don't propose it, I can ram it through. Then the committee as a whole. With a little horse trading, that can be done too. Then the floor, and we have to line up votes. If I try to do that in an election year, it'll absolutely blow up in my face. The libraries, and that means the school boards, are going to scream. It's a royalty to you, but it'll be a tax to everybody else."

"Can we win on the Senate floor?" Fritz asked, still ignoring Frank's point.

"You count heads and you find out. I provide you with a list of the persuadable senators who are on the fence. Your job is to persuade them." Frank looked at the bunch of them and thought: They're listening to me like they're watching a movie. Guess they're in the right business. "The next problem is the House.

That's a larger and less predictable bunch. The House is going to take a big lobbying effort."

"How big?" Jack Morris asked.

"I suggest you form a war chest and hire a coordinator," Frank said, avoiding the question. "It has to be a registered lobbyist. Your congressional liaisons or the Motion Picture Association can probably do it. Let's not kid ourselves; election year or not, I can't get it through the House committees, and I can't promise you the President will sign it."

"We'll take care of the House," Trumpelman said tartly. There were plenty of congressmen standing ready to help Maurice Trumpelman. Senators were a little harder to come by and he and Frank Talifero both knew it. "How soon before it can be gotten out of committee?" Trumpelman asked.

Frank was about to say before the century's over, but Trumpelman never joked, so Frank just said, "It should be coordinated with the House. When they're ready, the Senate bill should be in hand. A better way for me to be effective on your behalf would be to take it slowly until after the election. Somebody else can propose it in subcommittee and I'll keep an eye on it, but I have to distance myself for now."

"Fuck that," Jack Morris said. "You either quarterback this thing or you don't. Part-time won't work."

"You guys have a stake in my election, now you're asking me to get behind what amounts to a new tax. It's kamikaze."

Without knowing it, each man in the room looked to Maurice Trumpelman to adjudicate the impasse. "No one expects you to commit suicide on this issue, Senator. However, as you point out, a lot can be done without you going public on it just yet. We'll provide what it takes to activate the subcommittee. You do the same." Trumpelman's words left no doubt in Frank's mind that if he delivered on this one, these guys would turn on the Hollywood money fountain and never turn it off.

Outside at the pool, Frank worked the crowd again, smiling and laughing, keeping his eye out for Gwen Carrol. Sandy Keltner, a producer Frank had known off and on over the years, was planning a small dinner that night in Frank's honor. Frank was wondering if he could get out of it and just go back to his hotel, where there were several hundred pages of Senate reports he had to plow through. Sandy was talking and Frank was nodding and reacting appropriately, but he wasn't listening and he certainly wasn't hearing, until Gwen Carrol's name floated by. "I'm sorry, Sandy, what did you say?"

"I said, Trump noticed you talking to Gwen and thought you might like to have her come to dinner tonight." Sandy said it in a matter-of-fact voice but in a low tone so no one else could hear. Frank knew that if he wanted to chase women in Hollywood, Sandy was his man. But he also knew that it showed once again that Maurice Trumpelman missed nothing. Having Gwen Carrol at the dinner was the only reason Frank could think of to attend; his political instinct told him to be careful.

"Wonderful actress," he said, nodding yes. "What time is dinner, Sandy?"

"I'll have you picked up at seven-thirty."

"Remind me of some of her movies."

"The big one is *In the Evening Calm*. She was nominated for best actress and she should have won. It's a love story. I produced it. Did fifty-six million domestic and eighty-eight worldwide."

"Got it. Thanks."

Sandy Keltner lived in a modern house, built in the thirties, in Beverly Hills. Sandy had filled it with art-deco furniture and contemporary paintings. The house had been photographed many times and featured in *Architectural Digest*. Sandy was proud of it and enjoyed showing it. As Frank was sitting in the living room having a drink with the other guests, he noticed a color photograph in a silver frame sitting on the piano. It was a picture of Sandy and himself on a sailboat. The photo forced Frank to remember that he and Sandy Keltner had once spent a week sailing in the Caribbean. It was several years ago and Frank couldn't recall the details of the trip, but he was relieved to finally realize how it was he knew his host. "How is it I look younger in this picture, and you look the same?" Frank asked, grinning.

"It was my boat, Senator, that's why. You don't look so bad," Sandy said, putting his arm around Frank.

"That was a time, Sandy. Boy, I miss those days," Frank said with a dreamy look in his eye, as if he were yearning for the footloose past with his pal. Frank glanced around and saw all the guests were suitably impressed. He knew he had now paid whatever social debt he might owe to Sandy Keltner.

Invitations to dine with the senator were doled out with an eye to future favors. There were several producers, each of whom was an émigré from New York. They were a thuggish bunch, probably brutal, and certainly money-mad. Their wives, except for one, were all blonds and younger than their husbands. Surely, Frank thought as he looked around the room, these were second or third marriages. Only one of the producers appeared to be married to a woman he had known before he became rich. Her name was Ruth and when Frank spoke to her, he saw she was the crankiest, most contentious person in the room. The man who stayed married to her was the most neurotic of all. There were two screenwriters at the table, also ex-New Yorkers. They were dressed in lightweight tweeds, as if in imitation of the professors they had once hoped to become. Frank never got their names straight. They seemed nice enough, but trivia-crazed, and obsessed with baseball. They engaged one another in a running debate about the starting lineup of the 1953 New York Giants.

Gwen Carrol showed up late and unapologetic. She was wearing tailored slacks and a loose silk blouse. Her red hair was pulled back and she had put on only a tiny bit of makeup; she didn't need even that. While Frank tried to catch her eye, Sandy Keltner strolled into the living room and said, "Why don't we see if there's any food in this joint." He grinned and steered his guests toward the dining room.

Gwen was seated next to Frank and he found her easy to talk with. She joked and seemed relaxed, which was a relief to him. Most people worry about sounding intelligent or making a good impression when they meet a senator. It's tedious, and one of the reasons Frank rarely remembered social encounters. "No calories tonight," Sandy announced, as Mexican waiters moved around the table with the first course, a cold cucumber soup with sprigs of mint floating on the top. Sandy lifted his glass, which was filled with Cakebread chardonnay, and offered a toast to the guest of honor. "My friends, I couldn't be more pleased than to have the various strands of my life all meet here tonight. To Senator Talifero." Sandy sipped his wine and then said, "Put in your requests for a night or two in the Lincoln bedroom, because you're having dinner with a future occupant of 1600 Pennsylvania Avenue."

When the guests drank to him, Frank glanced at Gwen and thought he saw a smirk on her face. As he stood to respond to the toast, it occurred to him that this woman, in addition to being breathtaking, just might be smarter than he had assumed. "Sandy," he began, his glass held up, "that is, how shall I put it, wildly optimistic. I guess that's how you get all these movies made. Think big. But the only office I ever think about is the Senate. Doing what I can for the country from where I am. That and getting reelected." The guests laughed and applauded and Frank sat down, thinking: They're rich, they're good-looking, and they know how to make a deal. Why can't I be from California?

The waiter spooned a coulis of yellow pepper over a paillard of veal so white it looked painted. There was an exquisite arrangement of barely steamed tiny onions, baby asparagus, and small sweet carrots, all too delicate for a sauce; each vegetable as perfectly formed as nature permitted.

"What do you make of the local grub, Senator?" Gwen asked. "You miss bear meat and beer or whatever it is you people eat in Washington?"

"Why do you keep making me smile?"

"I don't know, the only other times I've seen you is on the news, and you usually look very serious." She made her face dour and did a deadpan imitation of Frank's press-conference voice. "'There are enough weapons in western Europe right now to destroy the continent several times over. It is not a policy of deterrence, but of madness.'"

Frank laughed and recognized Gwen's performance as an audition. She can have the job, he thought. "You know, I'm a great fan of yours. *In the Evening Calm* was terrific. I lost a lot of money on that. I gave odds you'd win the Oscar. You let me down." She smiled, wanting to believe him, but determined to enjoy it even as she knew it to be the lie that it was.

Frank was about to ask for salt, which was not on the table, when he remembered this was California, where salting food is a social gaffe on the order of breaking wind. The woman on his right, the wife of one of the producers, caught his eye and began talking about animal acupuncture. "It's not at all understood," she said. "Animals are very delicate and can't always take medication. A good veterinary acupuncturist can accomplish more with needles than a regular vet with pills."

"That's fascinating. I wasn't aware of it," he said, slipping into the unconscious overdrive he employed when people like this woman started talking.

"Animal acupuncture has been used successfully on all sorts of animals. Even tigers and elephants. There's a case of a camel who had cancer and was put into remission through acupuncture."

"If there's literature on the subject, you should send it to me," he said, cutting her off. "Just care of the Senate. I'll read it and shuffle it to the right people." Before she could crank up again, an endive salad with porcini mushrooms was served.

Sandy announced the Italian mushrooms were to give the meal an international touch, "so Frank won't think we're as provincial and chauvinistic about our food as we actually are." While the table was oohing appropriately, Frank turned back to Gwen, and as he did, she let her toe graze across his leg beneath the table.

"Are you and Sandy going to make another movie?" he asked, not caring about the answer.

"I suppose," she said. "What I'd really like to do is take some serious time off. I just keep making pictures back to back. It's an odd kind of work. If you don't have fun making a movie, it usually comes out wrong. But if you have too much fun, that's not good either."

"I know what you mean. I sometimes wonder what the hell we're doing in Washington. Half the time I think we're running in circles." As he spoke, Frank dropped his hand beneath the table and rested it lightly on her knee. She moved her legs apart slightly and his hand slid up her thigh. She opened her mouth a little and her tongue touched her upper lip.

During dessert, while the guests were picking berries out of a fruit tart, ignoring the crust and the custard, a second wave arrived to meet the senator. As Frank was shaking hands and listening to the political views of a European director, he saw Gwen starting to leave. He glanced at his watch and realized it was past eleven. Damn, he thought as the director was talking about European attitudes toward Latin America. Where's she going? When the man took a breath, Frank excused himself and tried to catch her before she left. It wasn't easy. Each step took him past another guest, each of whom wanted his ear. "Just a second," he said brightly, and stopped Gwen at the door, where Sandy was speaking to her. "I want to say good night. I enjoyed talking with you."

"Yes, it was fun. How long are you here?"

"Till tomorrow."

"Umm. Then good night, Mr. Senator," and she was out the door.

For a moment he was about to follow, but Sandy spoke to him with some urgency. "Please, Frank. Say something to each person here." A room full of killers, Frank thought to himself, all here to meet me. Talk to them, learn some names. Do your job. For the moment Gwen Carrol was out of his thoughts and he plunged into the politician's task and had a conversation with everyone in the room, speaking their names at least twice, listening to their views on nuclear power, the federal budget, the arms race, and whatever else they had read in the paper that day. Before he left he went into the kitchen and shook hands with the waiters, the cook, and the cook's helper.

The next morning at the Beverly Wilshire, he had room service bring him breakfast and he stayed in his robe working his way through the papers in his briefcase and conducting his business on the phone. He spoke to his office in Washington a few times, took calls from other senators or their aides who were soliciting his support for one bill or another, and talked to his wife, who asked how the fund-raiser had gone and reminded him they were having twelve people for dinner the next evening, constituents from their home state. He wanted to speak to his daughter, but she was out playing soccer. "That reminds me," his wife said, "Karen wants you to get her lime-colored sweatpants from a store in Los Angeles. Can you?"

"Sure," Frank said. He loved his wife and he supposed he missed her, but it was his daughter, Karen, that he thought about.

She was twelve and Frank adored her. As every newspaper and magazine in the world had reported, Frank and Barbara Talifero had lost a son some years ago. He was eight, he got leukemia and died, and even now Frank couldn't bear to think about it. The tabloids had covered the story in detail, calling the child "the senator's son with the poison blood." The terrible sadness of the loss was part of Frank's political legend and he knew it, but he still wouldn't permit it to be discussed in even a remotely political context. And that had become part of his legend too. "What's the shop?"

"Esprit. It's in West Hollywood. Try to get them with the name of the place on the leg. Okay?"

"Sure. I'll get the concierge here on it. Lime sweatpants from Esprit. Medium. Tell Karen to call me when she gets home."

He called down to arrange for the purchase and the man at the desk said they were holding a package for him. A tiny shudder raced through him. Public men couldn't open unexpected packages without a little fear. At the Senate, every envelope was X-rayed before it was distributed. At home they were always careful, and if an envelope or a package looked strange, it was put aside and taken to the office to be inspected by the guards. "Where's it from?" he asked.

"MGM. I think it's papers or a script or something."

"Okay. Send it up." It's Hollywood, all right, he thought. They think everything's a script. "And you'll get somebody on the lime sweatpants, right?"

"Yes, Senator. Right away."

A few minutes later a bellman came up with a manila envelope. Before Frank could open it, the phone rang. It was Candace, his secretary in Washington, calling again. He opened the envelope while she outlined changes in his schedule. As Candace spoke, he murmured his assent to each change, until a pair of red panties dropped out of the envelope and fell at his feet. "Did you write it down, Frank?" Candace asked.

"Yes. I have it," he said, without any sense of what she was talking about. With the panties there was a sheet of ivory-colored stationery engraved with the name Gwen Carrol. It read "I enjoyed meeting you last night." It was signed with her initials.

"Frank? Are you still there?" Candace asked.

"Yes. Absolutely. Anything else?"

"No. Do you want to be picked up at the airport? Or what?"

"I'll get a cab. I might have to take a later flight. I'm not sure yet." When he got off the phone, he examined the panties, holding them up to the light and twirling them around his finger. There was no return address except for MGM's, and he knew she wouldn't have a listed phone. He shuffled through his papers and found his sheet of Los Angeles contacts and phone numbers. He dialed Sandy Keltner's office. The secretary who answered said Mr. Keltner was in a meeting. "I won't take but a minute," Frank said. "Please tell him Senator Talifero is on the line." When Sandy got on the phone, he repeated Frank's name a few times, calling him Senator. That meant he was impressing somebody. "Sandy, I want you to do me a discreet favor. I'd like to speak to Gwen Carrol and I need her number."

"Yes, Frank. I see. Let me go to another phone." Frank could imagine the song and dance Sandy was giving the people in his office as he excused himself. In a moment Sandy got on and gave him her private number. "She has a place up in Coldwater Canyon and one at the beach—that's where she is now. She's the only one who answers this number. No maids, nothing. She's great, Frank. Enjoy."

"I just want to say good-bye to her. I appreciate everything you've done this trip, Sandy. I'll give you a call from Washington." He was forty-eight years old. He had been in the United States Senate for five years. His face had been on the cover of *Newsweek* and he had been around the world more times than he could remember. But as he dialed her number his pulse was racing, and he felt about sixteen. "Gwen? Frank Talifero here."

"Well, Mr. Smith comes to Hollywood. How are you today, your Majesty, your Senatorship?"

"Just fine, your Starship. I got your CARE package. It's great as far as it goes, but I'd love to see the rest."

"I don't understand."

"When can I see you? How about right now?"

"Whoa, here. Slow down. Explain, okay?"

"Your envelope and its contents arrived and I'd like to discuss it further."

"I didn't send you anything."

Her airy denial gave Frank a fleeting twinge of panic, but true to his profession, he pushed on. "Okay. Let's have dinner."

"Tonight? I can't tonight."

"Gwen. Change your plans. I'm changing mine."

"Okay."

Her house was in the Colony, a high-priced collection of narrow beach houses. Gwen's was on the water and although she didn't know how much it was worth, her accountant listed it at two million dollars. Frank's cab passed through the Colony gate, but only after the guard checked with Gwen by phone. Great, Frank thought to himself, first the cabdriver, now the guard. I might as well take an ad in the paper. The hell with it, he thought, remembering the red panties. He had stuffed them in his pocket before he left the hotel; from time to time on the drive out to Malibu he had put his hand in his pocket to touch them.

She greeted him at the door, wearing tennis shorts and a baggy sweater. This woman would look sensational in a Mao suit, he thought. "Hi," she said. "Well, you look the same as yesterday. That's a comfort. Like a drink?"

"Sure. What are you having?"

"Mineral water, but don't let that stop you. Believe it or not, there's actual liquor here. I smuggle it in, in white wine bottles," she said, poking around at the bar. "Want a Scotch?"

He nodded yes and said, "You always make me laugh, do you know that?"

"Is that good or bad?" she asked, handing him his drink.

"It's great. It reminds me I have a sense of humor." They sat on a sofa looking out through glass doors that opened on a patio. Beyond were the beach and the Pacific, vast and soothing and lit by the moon. "Where shall we go for dinner?"

"Oh, stop it, Frank. We can't go out, unless you want it on *Good Morning America*. We can go for a walk on the beach and I'll make us something later."

"Sounds great."

"You can be the second guy in the history of Malibu to walk on the beach wearing a tie."

"Who beat me?"

"Jerry Brown. When he was governor. He used to go out with Linda Ronstadt when she lived here."

"I brought the package you sent me," he said, only slightly concerned that he might be the victim of some elaborate hoax.

"I still don't know what you mean."

Frank reached in his pocket and unfurled the panties. He waved them in the air like a red flag between them.

"Oh, *that* package," she said with a straight face. And when Frank looked as confused as he felt, she began to giggle. "Do they fit you?" she asked.

In all the time he spent with her, that night and all the other nights, she always kept him a little off balance. He never knew what to expect. Like many politicians, Frank had a roving eye and a taste for the adulterous liaison. The women of Washington were his usual prey, the aides and secretaries, supplicants to the powerful, who would open their mouths or spread their legs on office sofas and never ask for more. Gwen was no groupie; she did what she wanted, when she wanted it. She put a Mozart violin concerto on the stereo and when the volume pleased her and the fiddle's sound floated above them, she walked back to where he was sitting and stood close to him. She said nothing, but as she looked at him he could sense that her breath was getting short. Her eyes got wide and her throat and cheeks flushed red. Frank watched her, amazed by the passion that was coming over her. She's having an orgasm, he thought. My presence is making her come. His throat felt dry and his hands were trembling. She unbuttoned him, then peeled off her own tennis shorts and moved onto his lap, straddling and plunging down on him. She gasped when they were locked together in the oldest of embraces. Then there was only the pushing and relaxing of their hips until he thought his flesh might sizzle. No word passed between them until she could feel herself about to explode. She began to whisper, "Now, now, now." Her voice got louder and insistent, demanding and harsh. "Now, now, now," she repeated, filling the simple word with meaning nearly as complex as the Mozart in the air above them. The intensity of it made his mouth open wide and his lips pull back, baring his teeth. When she collapsed against him, she began to laugh, a deep, throaty, comfortable laugh of joy and victory.

Over the next month, Frank returned to Los Angeles four times. Sometimes they stayed at her Malibu house, where they took long walks on the sand after dark when there was privacy on the beach. Once, while they were walking together in the moonlight, Frank saw three people coming toward them. They would certainly know who Gwen was and they might well recognize him. It frightened him, but Gwen, ever ready to improvise, grabbed him and pulled him down into the surf, "like Deborah Kerr and Burt Lancaster," she whispered. As they rolled in the sand, the approaching strangers stopped and applauded the lovers before turning and walking back in the direction they had come.

"They saw us," he said, amused and a little worried. But when they were gone he rolled over on top of her.

"What do you think you're doing?" she asked, giggling and knowing full well what he was doing.

"We have a saying in the Senate: In for a dime, in for a dollar. The Senate teaches you the value of getting in quick."

"That's about the level of the Senate. That place is a feminist's nightmare."

"Not me. I'm the nonsexist politician. It said so in *Glamour* magazine or *Ms.* Or one of those things."

"A lot you know about it. No more of that talk," she said, lifting her skirt and pulling him back on top of her as he fumbled with his pants. She locked her legs around his back and pushed up toward him until there were only grains of Malibu sand between them.

When they stayed at her house in Coldwater Canyon, she would send the maid away and let the machine answer the phone. After fifty times it still seemed as effortless and trouble-free as their first night in Malibu. Frank and Gwen had so little time together that they spent it in each other's arms. Although they got to know one another's bodies, they never really got to know one another.

"That's why it's so good," Gwen said to him. "Every relationship I ever had that was any good started with sex first, then it got into all the other crap and it stopped being good."

"I don't know," Frank said, trying to think about her point. What surprised him wasn't that it was good, but that he really listened to her. After five years in the Senate, which was preceded by several years of trying to get to the Senate, Frank rarely heard anyone. He met so many people every day, shook so many hands, listened to so many pleas, and fielded so many grabs at his attention that like many of his colleagues he went through his day running on a sort of psychic automatic pilot. He tried to listen to his wife and his daughter, but for the most part he listened only to his own thoughts. "I never felt anything like this before," he said. "When Barbara and I were dating and when we were first married, it was pretty good, I guess. Now our lives are so complicated, sex is this sort of occasional afterthought. Sometimes it's good, sometimes it's not, but it's never, you know, central."

"That's what I mean," she said, resting her head against his chest. "The worst way to do it is the proper way. First you play getting-to-know-you. Then you sleep together and it's a big deal. Then you're in housekeeping and it's not—what'd you call it?—central. I've never been married, but I see what happens. I'd rather have what we've got now than any marriage I ever saw. Including yours, which looks like a pretty good one. At least you don't hate her."

"No, no. It's a good marriage and I love my daughter."

"Poor Senator Frank, trapped in a good marriage."

Late at night they would lie in front of her big stone fireplace wrapped in blankets and their love and Gwen would read poetry aloud to him. He loved to listen to her read Dylan Thomas, and even though she thought the verse was too flamboyant for quiet evenings, and preferred Auden, she read what he liked and she did it quietly, more intimately than he had imagined it could be done. She was an actress who knew her audience, and she could make any poem be about the two of them.

> I have longed to move away
> From the hissing of the spent lie
> And the old terrors' continual cry . . .

After she had read to him and his heart had been stirred, they made slow, careful love in the warmth of the fire, refusing to hurry, acting unaware that planes and schedules would soon make demands.

Frank and Barbara lived in a rambling old house on Foxhall Road, where houses cost too much for a senator's salary. They also kept up a house in their home state and both places always needed more repairs than they could afford. Barbara had inherited some money and that was a help, although she wasn't rich. Frank gave speeches to business organizations for large fees. The Senate limited how much he could earn that way and it wasn't much. But without the extra money they couldn't manage. Sometimes they talked about not running for reelection and Frank becoming a partner in a law firm that would be glad to get a former senator and would make him rich. But Frank loved the Senate, the hurry and the maneuvering and the public adoration. He was good at it and he didn't want to lose his seat to some astronaut.

Each time he went to California, he told his wife he was raising money. Barbara had lived for a long time with a public man and had long ago given up trying to predict or understand her husband's schedule. But even she thought it odd that he should go to California so frequently. "One more of these trips and they'll make you a citizen of the state. If we lose, maybe we can move there."

They were in their bedroom and Frank was on the phone, while Barbara put out his clothes for the next California trip, two days away. Over the years, they had developed a packing system that always kept a nearly full suitcase at hand. At the last minute, Barbara would check it and add black tie or tennis clothes, whatever might be required. Frank was easy to pack and buy clothes for. He wore blue or gray suits and blue or white shirts. Everything came from Brooks Brothers, which rarely changed its styles, which was just fine with the senator.

"Is it fun out there?" she asked casually as she checked his shaving kit to make sure everything was in order.

"Yeah. It's not bad. Weather's great. I might get some tennis in. Sandy's got a court."

"You have free time? That's a change."

"A little," he said, sensing a problem brewing. He decided to keep talking, in the hope that it would pass. "I meet with all these movie people. They're interesting. Very smart and most of them are from New York. It's almost funny. I mean, all the palm trees and everybody I talk to has a New York accent. You wonder who's back in New York."

"I wouldn't mind going. I could use a change for a few days. I hate all that flying, but a change would be nice. We could take Karen."

"She'd be bored. These people don't have children, they have arguments and deals," he said, trying to distract her with a joke. "I thought you hated fund-raisers."

"We could go late on Friday," she said, refusing to be distracted. "If the party's Sunday, I'd have all day Saturday. Come back late Sunday." She was getting excited at the prospect of a little holiday. "I want to go."

The only person in Los Angeles who knew what Frank was doing was Sandy Keltner and he was glad to be of service. He met Frank at the airport, lent him a car, and instructed his household help to take messages as if Frank were staying there. Frank called him, explained the situation, and told him that he would have to put together a fund-raiser. Frank didn't care how Sandy did it, he just wanted it done.

"Maybe we could get a few people together and you could talk to them," Sandy said, trying to figure out who could be invited at this late hour. "Pretty much everybody's given money already. Can't you talk her out of it? Tell her you'll take her to Bermuda or something."

"Won't work. Do something. Make it look right."

The next morning, he called Gwen from his office. She was disappointed but stoic. "Shall I come and make a donation? I'd like to see Barbara in action. The senator's wife graciously launching ships, or whatever it is."

"If you're anywhere near this thing I'll come apart at the seams. I'll call you when I get in and try to see you, even for a little bit."

The only way Sandy could arrange a fund-raiser on such short notice was to call Maurice Trumpelman and if not exactly explain the situation, let him know that it was delicate on a personal level. "The senator would be very grateful, Trump," Sandy said. Trumpelman, who always knew what was going on, assumed the truth and agreed to bring a small group of potential donors to Sandy's house on Sunday afternoon.

Los Angeles didn't disappoint Barbara Talifero. On Saturday morning she played tennis and then had a look at Rodeo Drive and walked around on Melrose Avenue, where she enjoyed seeing teenagers in punk drag. She bought T-shirts for her daughter and had lunch at the Ivy.

Frank told her that he had to meet some people in the afternoon, but he'd be back by evening. Sandy wanted to take them to La Scala in Beverly Hills for dinner with some friends of his. Frank's plan was to see Gwen, but when he called, she told him she had to meet with a director about a film she was considering. "Then I'll be here all weekend and I won't even see you," he said, trying not to sound angry.

"I'm free tonight. I have a career, you know."

"Well, I'm disappointed, that's all. I think about you all the time. It's why I came out here."

"Don't pout, Frank. It sounds ridiculous. I'm going to New York on Tuesday for two days. Can you meet me? I'll be at the Pierre."

"Commerce has hearings all week. But come down to Washington. Take the shuttle. It goes every hour. We can be together. I'll show you the Capitol. It'll be great," he said, excited at the prospect.

"I'll try. I miss you. I think about you all the time. I hate you being here like this, I hate it."

During Sandy's dinner party at La Scala, Frank left the table twice to call Gwen, just to hear her voice and promise her a wonderful time when she came to Washington. He asked her what she was wearing but she wouldn't say. She told him she was trying not to be irritated with him, but she hadn't made any plans for the weekend because she was going to see him and now she was home alone reading and watching television. She wasn't crazy about the situation and he did the best he could to soothe her.

Sandy had invited a director he was trying to convince to do a picture and Barbara enjoyed a conversation that wasn't about politics. Sandy's date was an agent who flirted with Frank and dropped names so furiously that Barbara almost laughed. When the woman mentioned a dinner with the Shah of Iran, Sandy kicked her under the table. The congressman who represented Beverly Hills was dining there too. He came over to the table to say hello and kid Frank about being a carpetbagger. Sandy knew several other people in the room and he introduced them all to the senator.

It was a cocktail party, and as promised, Maurice Trumpelman delivered a small but powerful group of interested citizens. Some of them were studio executives who worked for him, but there were also bankers, lawyers, and people from Los Angeles' financial district, men and women who had nothing to do with the movie business. Frank modified his regular speech, using more statistics and numbers than usual. He spoke about the dynamics of the Senate, saying sometimes it was indeed the world's greatest deliberative body and other times not unlike the student council at a so-so high school in the 1950s. He said that it was certainly true that every senator represented one state, but in an age of instant communications it was preposterous not to recognize that each senator also represented the country. A few of Trumpelman's people were Republicans and even they were attentive.

Frank had asked Barbara to be sure to talk to Maia Trumpelman. They had gone to the same college, many years apart of course, but it gave them plenty to talk about and they got on well. Frank noticed Trumpelman watching Barbara and Maia enjoying one another's company and he seemed to approve. Frank couldn't help wondering how much this man knew about his life, but as always, Maurice Trumpelman's face was pleasant and opaque. Frank watched him ease his way around the room, smiling graciously, saying little, drinking only mineral water. His hand is everywhere, Frank thought, and never a fingerprint.

When the guests were gone and Frank and Barbara were getting ready to go to the airport, Sandy reported that the bankers had been impressed. He explained that these people didn't write out checks on the spot the way movie people sometimes did, but he knew Frank had made some important friends. Sandy said he suspected a lot of money would come in next week.

On Tuesday, Gwen checked into a suite at the Hay-Adams, and in her heart she knew it was a mistake. Should have used another name, she thought, and worn a wig. She toyed with the idea of turning around and going back to Los Angeles and forgetting the whole thing. She had been around love long enough to know that if she expected disaster, it would arrive. She tried to use her actor's skills to put herself in an upbeat mood. She pictured herself in the Senate gallery, watching Frank debate or legislate, or whatever it was he did. It made her giggle and that made her feel good enough to call him. He had given her an office number that was supposedly private. A secretary answered anyway and told her Senator Talifero was in a committee meeting but it ought to be ending soon. The woman promised to give Frank the message. In a flash of hateful insight, Gwen saw herself sitting in this hotel for hours. "I can't just go for a walk, you know," she said aloud to the empty room. Talking to herself made her feel ridiculous and a little unhinged.

It was seven o'clock when he called, but just hearing his voice made her feel better. He was very quiet when she told him which hotel.

"I'll have trouble getting through the lobby in that place," he said, sounding irritated.

"Now, you listen," Gwen said, allowing some anger to show. "If you stand me up, that's it. Don't treat me like this."

"Gwen, relax. I'm on my way."

Great, she thought after she hung up. We're already fighting. When a man tells you to relax, he knows he's wrong. It's the stupidest advice people ever give. She tried to clear her mind with a hot bath. Then she called room service and ordered champagne and waited.

It was almost nine before Frank arrived, and he didn't apologize. He kissed her at the door and said it was great to see her. He sounded like he was working a crowd, trying to get her vote, but not very hard.

"Do you know what 'indicating' means?" she asked as he sank into one of the Hay-Adams' high-backed wing chairs. "It's an acting term."

"No."

"It comes down to fake emotion. Generalities. Like some actor making his eyes go wide to show fear, or chewing your nails to show you're nervous. Get it?"

"It wasn't easy for me to come here. This is a very small town. If people see us together they won't applaud and walk away, like some places I could think of. This is probably the worst hotel you could have picked."

"You kiss better in hotels you approve of?"

"You want to give me a break here?"

"Not particularly," she snapped. "Keep your wife waiting, she doesn't have to sneak around. It's hard for me to travel alone. That shuttle plane was ghastly awful. Dirty and crowded, and if you cared, you would have made arrangements."

"Gwen, Gwen," he said, trying to calm her. He put his hands in her red hair and drew her to him. "What's the opposite of indicating?" He massaged her neck, trying to knead the anger and tension out. He tried to stroke her the way he stroked his daughter, without thought of reward, his only goal to make her comfortable.

"There's champagne," she said, starting to feel better. She took the bottle from the ice bucket to hand to Frank. "Open it."

"I better not."

"What?" Her voice was low and harsh, and she knew her fears were about to be confirmed.

"I can't stay. I'm supposed to be at a dinner in Georgetown. Barbara's there now. It's an obligation."

"Then why did you tell me to come today?"

"I'm sorry. I got excited when you said you could come. I couldn't very well check it with my office. One of the top guys from the White House is going to be at this dinner. He's already there. I have to go. It's very important."

"What am I?" she asked tersely.

"A great joy. An amazing person who teaches me and makes me feel alive and not afraid."

"In other words, good-bye."

"For tonight."

"Get out." Her voice was emotionless on its surface, but Frank could feel the anger beneath it rumbling and starting to build.

"No, no. Come on."

"Get out," she said, with such force that Frank knew if he argued it would only get worse.

"What will you do?" he asked.

"I will go to sleep and tomorrow I will go home."

"I miss you already. I want to see you again."

"Then you can buy a ticket to the movies," she snarled, and threw the champagne bottle across the room. Later, when Frank thought about it, he decided that if the bottle had smashed, her need for drama might have been satisfied. But it only made a loud noise and bounced to the floor, so she grabbed the ice bucket and threw it at him. The ice had long since melted, but the cold water sloshed over his face. He hoped if he just stood and took it, the violence and his humiliation would satisfy her. But it wasn't nearly enough. She threw the champagne glasses too, and they broke against the wall.

"Gwen, Gwen," he said, trying to be soothing. "Don't break things, it won't help."

"You're the one who breaks things." She yanked the drawer out of a desk and heaved it at him. Pens, pencils, a Gideon Bible, and a folder of Hay-Adams stationery fell at his feet. "You're disgusting," she screamed. "I hate you. You don't think about anything." She was shaking and her face was flushed. Frank's palms were damp and he felt a dull thud in his stomach. He knew it was a matter of minutes before some night manager would be knocking on the door.

"Gwen . . . Gwen . . ." were the only words he could manage, but her rage was still building. She circled the room, breathing hard, trying to decide what new pain or indignity to inflict on him. She picked a long, lethal-looking letter opener out of the debris from the desk. This is how it ends, he thought, in scandal and disgrace. He had trouble focusing his thoughts until she was charging across the room, about to stab him. In that instant he saw in his mind a photograph of his daughter. She was nine and wearing a pink sweater he had picked out for her. The image was brief but for an instant it seemed to paralyze him. Then, more by instinct than design, he put up his hand to protect himself. She slashed at his forearm and ripped the sleeve of his jacket. He could feel the warm dampness of his blood.

"I hope you die," she yelled, about to stab him again.

He seized her wrists and said, "Stop now. Stop."

"Bleed to death, I don't care. I hope you do," she hissed, and then began to cry. "You'll never forget me," she said. "You never will." She pulled away from him and ran into the bedroom, slamming the door.

Frank pushed his jacket sleeve back and unbuttoned his bloody shirt cuff. He lifted the fabric and inspected the gash on his arm. He wondered if it would require stitches as he stanched the blood with Kleenex. He left the hotel to look for a pharmacy where, recognized or not, he might buy a bandage. Then he would have to decide what story he could use to explain the mess he was in when he got to the dinner for the President's man.

"Just what is this about, Frank?" Barbara Talifero asked angrily as she handed her husband the Washington *Post,* open to a gossip item that said Gwen Carrol was going to play a senator in a movie. According to the paper, Gwen was "busy researching the role with her good friend Senator Frank Talifero, who has been spending his weekends in California."

"Damned if I know," Frank said. "She's one of Sandy Keltner's girlfriends. We all had dinner out there one night. She's been in a couple of his movies. She gave us some money. But she's certainly not my 'good friend.' Wink, wink."

"Keep it that way. I don't need this, and I don't want Karen seeing this stuff."

"I can't control the *Post* on substantive issues, let alone crap like this. I'm a public servant and a public target. I'll call Sandy and see what's going on."

When he got to his office he began calling Gwen. He left messages, but she was either away or just refusing to take his calls. Sandy was in Mexico scouting locations and it took most of the day to reach him. "That item had to come from her," Sandy said when Frank finally spoke to him. "There's no such project around that I know of. If it were real, I'd know. I'll see if I can cool her off, get her to call you or something."

"Sandy, this is very dangerous stuff," he said. "When the toothpaste gets out of the tube . . ."

"Yeah, I know. This is tough, Frank, but it can all be dealt with." Sandy's soothing words made him feel better for the moment, but later, as he thought about it—and he had trouble thinking about anything else—he envisioned Gwen going on a campaign to destroy him with gossip. It wouldn't be hard and it wouldn't take long. He was afraid of her hatred because he knew it could be as intense as her love. But there was no one he could tell about his feelings; self-recrimination or brooding introspection never came easily to him. Nonetheless, thoughts of their time together in Malibu and Coldwater Canyon came to him in unsettling moments during his day. He would be in a meeting, listening to a colleague make a pitch for one bill or another, or listening to one of his campaign aides interpreting a poll, and he would see her smooth white skin or hear her laugh, and grief would come over him. It made him feel as if he were strangling.

Sandy called him late the next day. He was back in Los Angeles and had finally managed to speak with Gwen. "She's acting very crazy, Frank. She says you treated her horribly."

"What do you think she'll do?"

"She's already called two more papers. I got my publicist on it. He took care of it. I got her to say she won't make any more calls. If the item appears again, tell your wife it got picked up from the *Post.*"

"Thanks, Sandy." Frank's throat was dry, but he kept his voice steady. "I'm going to try to call her again."

She let him worry for another day before she answered his calls. "Gwen," he said, trying to be conciliatory, "I feel terrible. You know for me to hurt you is the last thing I want. I'd do anything to take back the other night and start again." His words were a mixture of real feeling and longing, a tactic he hoped would make her stop talking to the press.

"I hope your arm's okay," she said, and she seemed to mean it. That encouraged him. He felt if he could just keep her talking and tell her about the confusion he felt, it would all be better.

"I have so much feeling for you," he said, and he meant it. "Please, don't refuse to talk to me. I never felt what we had before. It's the center of my life. I dream about you, Gwen. At night, every night, I can still smell you and feel you. I can still feel your legs on my back. Don't take that away."

"I don't want to, Frank. I'm glad you've got memories, I really am. I still have a lot of feeling for you."

"That's wonderful to hear. You won't talk to reporters about us anymore, will you?"

"No, I won't. That was a mistake," she said sweetly. "Could you speak up, though? The tape recorder didn't get all of that. The part about my legs on your back, please."

He was silent for a moment, hoping against hope that it was a joke. "What are you doing?"

"Sandy begged me not to talk to the press. Okay. Instead, I've decided to write my memoirs. And you're chapter one. Don't worry, I'll disguise you. I'll call you Senator Hank instead of Frank."

"Bitterness like this will eat you up. It'll just destroy you," he said, worrying about his own destruction more than hers.

"Oh, I'm not bitter. Actually, I'm quite amused. It's interesting to see you like this, Frank. My acting teacher used to tell me to watch people in crisis, that's when you learn about character. I'm watching and I'm learning." Then she hung up, and no matter how much he tried, she wouldn't answer the phone anymore.

"We have to calm her down," Frank said to Sandy, who was still in Los Angeles but preparing to go to Japan. "She's like a loose cannon, and I don't know what she's going to do next."

"I can delay my Tokyo trip for a day or two, I guess. The only thing I can think to do to solve it, you're not going to like."

"Is it legal?" Frank asked, feeling very desperate.

"There's a picture she wanted to do. They didn't cast her. It's prepping now. It shoots in Bali for four months."

"How do we get her into it?"

"Maurice Trumpelman."

"Jesus," Frank muttered, realizing the complexities of the situation. "How do we pull it off?"

"I'll talk to Trump, lay it out for him exactly as it is. He'll want to hear it from you, though. What do you think?"

"What's involved for him?"

"He'd have to fire Katherine Sullivan, that's who got the part.

Paying her off would cost at least four hundred thousand. The director might walk, but maybe not. Mostly it would set off weird shock waves around here. I can't say what Trump would charge you, Frank. Or when he'd want to collect it."

Frank considered his dwindling options. A the least it would buy him some time, and in all likelihood, after four months in Bali, the problem would drift away. On the other hand, his balls would be in Maurice Trumpelman's pocket forever. "Who else would have to know?"

"Probably nobody. People would assume it wasn't exactly an artistic decision, but Trump can keep his mouth shut. It might get out. There's no guarantee."

"Would Gwen know?"

"No."

"Call him, Sandy. See if you can make the deal."

Trumpelman was at the studio's New York office when Sandy reached him. He explained the situation in discreet general terms and then suggested the best solution for the senator might be for Miss Carrol to be cast in a movie such as *Shores of Paradise,* which would occupy her time for a while. Trumpelman said the senator should come to New York that evening to discuss it.

Frank got on the seven-o'clock shuttle and went directly to the Carlyle, where the Trumpelmans kept an apartment. Trumpelman opened the door himself and admitted Frank. A light supper for two had been set out in the dining room.

"Maia didn't come with you?" Frank asked.

"No. I'm only here briefly and she doesn't like these hurried trips anymore."

"I'm glad you could see me on such short notice, Trump. I appreciate it."

"Suppose you tell me about the situation."

Frank's intention was to paint himself as the victim of a crazy woman who had imagined that a meaningless flirtation meant more than it did. But as he started to tell it, he found himself explaining more than he had intended. Maybe it was Trumpelman's avuncular manner, or maybe it was Frank's own guilt about what he had done, but before he was through, Trumpelman had a pretty clear picture of what had transpired.

"Well, you know, Frank, it's an occupational hazard. I think it's easier for people in Hollywood to deal with these things. We're around so many beautiful young women that somehow it doesn't seem quite so tempting. Also, the press and the public are used to scandals from Hollywood. They expect it. Politics and Hollywood make an odd mix," he said, pouring himself a drink, the only one Frank had ever seen him take. "You people work so intensely, it doesn't surprise me that so many men in your position have an eye. If it makes you feel any better, you're in a grand tradition."

"It doesn't," Frank said with a rueful smile. Frank was fully aware that he could be signing himself away tonight, but he was fascinated by Trumpelman and impressed by his calm, reflective intelligence, a quality Frank hadn't known the man possessed.

"Hollywood is about sex and money, Frank. We claim it's about other things—art, business, communication. But in the end, it's sex and money. Washington, and certainly the Senate, is about power. Wouldn't you agree?"

"Yeah, I would. That's what it's about, all right."

"I know what your worry is, Frank. I understand it. Believe me when I tell you, I've had conversations like this before."

"I don't doubt it, Trump."

"We're practical men, you and I. You won't like everything, Frank, but no one wants your blood. I give you my word, I will never ask you to do anything that would destroy you. Quite the opposite, I'll always protect you."

Frank nodded his understanding and his assent, but his throat was too dry to form any words.

"I'll expect you to get out front on the cassette problem, reelection campaign or not. That has to have priority. I want you to make that happen."

"That it?" Frank asked, knowing full well it wasn't.

Trumpelman passed by the question as if Frank had remained silent. "You should bear in mind, it's very much in my interest for you to be reelected again and again. You're an asset to us now, Frank. You can always count on me. And I don't think that's so bad. I hope you agree."

"Right, Trump," Frank said, feeling hollow, as if his insides had been turned out for the world to pick at.

"Sex, money, and power," Trumpelman said, savoring the cadence of the words. "In the picture business, actually in the whole country, that's the real trinity. We used to say it was mom, the flag, and apple pie. But it wasn't. It's always been the same. I think I can help you, Frank. I think I can straighten out your situation. It can be done."

At first Gwen wouldn't consider it. She had already been denied the role in *Shores of Paradise* and had put it behind her. But Sandy spoke to her quietly and sensibly. He told her an offer like this was a godsend at a time when she had personal troubles. It was the right move for her career and, he pointed out, she was perfect for the part, which was why she had wanted it in the first place. This was an opportunity to shake up her life and sort out her feelings.

"Did Frank have anything to do with this?" she asked.

"Don't be paranoid, Gwen. Even senators don't say who stars in movies. You got this offer because you should have gotten it in the first place. Sullivan was a ludicrous choice. Three days of rehearsal and now they know it."

It took several days of phone calls to agents and lawyers and the writing of some very large checks to do it, but a week after Frank's visit to the Carlyle Gwen Carrol had put her memoirs aside and was on her way to Bali. Frank threw himself back into his reelection campaign and his work in the Senate. He put Gwen out of his mind and tried to spend more time with his wife and daughter. Sometimes, late at night when he had trouble sleeping, he let his mind drift back to Malibu and Coldwater Canyon, and for a moment or two he was happy with the memories. Then Trumpelman's soft and steady voice would insinuate itself into his reverie. Frank could hear him say, "You're an asset to us now," and the words lingered in his mind. He would lie awake thinking about what service he might be asked to perform. On those restless nights, he thought about what he owed, and he always wondered when Maurice Trumpelman would call to collect the next installment on the debt.

A Pornographer

❧

Studio executives fall into two categories, the ones who once considered a life in art and those who used to be agents and have a business orientation. With the first, a writer can discuss and debate story points. They might clash and argue, but each side recognizes there are no absolutes and it's finally a matter of taste and judgment. The former agents tend to accept the studio's line on scripts (usually sent down by the story department) as writ. Anyone who disagrees is being disloyal to the company.

No matter which camp they're in, sooner or later all studio executives get fired. It's built into the job. There are a few exceptions, but for the most part they're all in some state of changing jobs all the time—either hanging on to the ones they've got or making discreet inquiries about other possibilities.

Alexander was very much of the artistic school. I had known him in New York when I was covering city politics for the *Post*. When he had a studio job in Los Angeles, he called me from time to time and we'd meet or have lunch and talk about movie ideas. He was doing his job and I was doing mine.

When Alexander was a younger man, just a few years out of college and looking for his role in life, he dreamed of being in the movie business. His parents urged him to go to law school, but

Alexander saw that as doom and schemed ways to enter the only profession that counted to his generation. When he had all but agreed to take the law boards and was feeling desperate, a chum named Alan asked him for help working on a film script. Now, this was not MGM calling, but still, it was a chance. Alan said the film was a porno and he hoped Alex could put a little wit into it. Alex took the law boards on a Thursday and on Friday he began rewriting *Ball Busters,* which he renamed *Madame Ovary.* To Alex it felt like a race: get a movie made before law school started, and he could spend his life doing what he wanted; fail, and he would spend his life doing what his parents wanted.

Alexander threw himself into the production, helping to cast, raising money, and arranging to use friends' apartments as locations. The sex caused Alexander some concern, but he decided his parents would just have to make their peace with it, because he wasn't going to miss a chance to get started. Soon, in addition to being coauthor of the script, under the name "Ace Bandaage," he was also coproducer, under the name "Gian-Carlo Revulte." The last big scene to be shot was an orgy—a generic scene in movies like this, as certain to turn up as the shoot-out in a western. It was a rainy New York day and three of the actors didn't show, which made for a rather lopsided bacchanal. Alan, the coproducer, volunteered to go on so long as Alexander would join him. He agreed, and amid jokes of rising to the occasion, Alexander was filmed rolling around in a tangle of flesh, apparently having intercourse with several women.

Alexander's parents never quite knew how actively their son had participated in the movie, but they knew enough not to approve. His father urged Alexander to "take up something worth a young man's time" and managed through a business acquaintance to get his son an interview for the job of deputy speech writer to the mayor of New York. To his astonishment, Alexander was offered the position. He decided to take it, thinking it might be fun and that exposure to the ways of power would be valuable in the movie career he still coveted. He had to write a lot of proclamations and birthday announcements, but he worked hard and on his own time made himself an expert on the question of a stock-transfer tax, in hopes of being promoted to a policy-making position. His hard work impressed the mayor and it also meant Alexander spent a lot of time on Wall Street. He rarely thought about his brief career as an actor until the latest crusading reporter for the *Village Voice* got hold of the story and just wouldn't let go. Alexander was preparing his resignation, until he realized that everyone at city hall and most of the people on Wall Street thought it was quite raffish to have been in a dirty movie. Alexander was whispered about and treated with some reverence by all the stiffs he worked with. The most daring thing any of them had ever done was smoke a little pot and make clumsy passes at one another. Alexander threw away his resignation, wrote a witty letter to the *Voice,* and arranged a private screening for the mayor.

The following year the democratic process had its way and Alexander's man was voted out of office. Alex headed west to take another try at the movies. Using his Wall Street connections, he became a production executive at a film studio. His job was to find, acquire, develop, and keep costs down on anything that might make a movie. He worked hard, reading scripts and books as much as he could and romancing the stars, directors, and writers or their agents the rest of the time.

His problem wasn't the work, which was hard but possible, it was a fellow production executive. Alexander and Louis were roughly equals in the hierarchy of the studio, which made them colleagues but also competitors. Louis had heard the rumors of Alex's sordid past, and perhaps out of jealousy or perhaps because he just couldn't resist the opportunity, he got hold of a print of *Madame Ovary* and ran it at a party. Then he put it on a cassette and ran it in his office whenever Alexander was expected. Alexander knew to laugh and make some remark about Louis being an arrested fraternity boy.

After Alex went to work for the studio, the place was bought by an industrial conglomerate, a corporation whose signature product was the nation's largest-selling baby food. Several people got rich in the deal, including Pierre, the man who had hired Alex. He sold his stock to the baby-food company for twelve million dollars and kept his position as head of the studio. An intense, precise man who wore Italian suits and gossamer shirts, Pierre was one of the princes of Hollywood, a man who could say yes to a movie. When

Pierre heard about *Madame Ovary,* he professed surprise and called for a print. He summoned Alex to the executive screening room to watch the film with him. Pierre found the film murky and tedious and told Alex to have the projectionist "just show me the scene in question."

The next morning, when Pierre called him on the carpet, Alex pointed out that it was hardly a secret he had been in the film, and besides, it was made a long time ago and the scene in question was harmless. Pierre explained that the parent corporation cultivated an image of benevolent respectability because of the youth and vulnerability of its most visible consumers. "My mandate is to manufacture pap as surely as our parent company does. I am free to make whatever pap I choose, so long as it is profitable and so long as it is good clean pap." Alex, who could see what was coming, reminded Pierre that the mayor of New York and several Wall Street barons had laughed the whole thing off. Pierre laughed too, and then with regret he fired Alex.

Hollywood High

It was because of El Vitamino, my little red Porsche, that I met Neil. He had a silver Spyder, the same vintage as my Speedster, and we would run into one another at Wolf's garage in Santa Monica. Wolf specialized in old Porsches and contempt for Hollywood hotshots who didn't appreciate the complexities of German engineering. You could usually find a bunch of writers or directors hanging on Wolf's word about a clutch or a carburetor. When I first met him, Neil was on a hot streak, making films about teenagers who hung around shopping centers and rode dirt bikes. Considering he grew up in Richmond Hill, Queens, Neil made an unlikely poet of the bland land of malls and tract houses. When he was at film school at NYU, he made a film about his old neighborhood. It was good enough to make him unwelcome in Queens—until he was successful. "One hit, they love you," he said to me while we were waiting for Wolf to minister to our cars. "Two hits and they name a street after you." He'd already had two hits, and although Northern Boulevard is intact, his success allowed him to indulge himself in Hollywood. For Neil that meant cars and, later, the pursuit of unusual romance.

Neil owned three old Porsches, but he really preferred the new Toyota model that talked. If you were about to run out of gas, the big Toyota said, "The fuel supply is low." No Porsche had that.

But Neil, ever with the adolescent sensibility that had made him successful, couldn't see himself in a Toyota. He once told me that as a kid he was chubby and as a young man he was fat. By the time I met him he had dieted and exercised so strenuously that he was gaunt. But the fat boy still lurked inside and kept popping out. The teenage movies Neil was making seemed to be an attempt to correct his adolescence.

In the days when we were both hanging around Wolf's garage, Neil wasn't very communicative. Cars were the only thing he ever talked freely about. Journalists had a hard time getting him to offer an opinion on anything. In interviews, he limited his remarks to "Okay" or "I guess so." He was better with actors. On the set he'd take them aside and whisper about motivation, keeping it simple and direct. If he wanted anger from an actor, no matter what the scene was about, he'd say something on the order of "The bastard bashed in your fender and ran off. Imagine that fender, all dented up, that beautiful lacquer paint job, all shot to shit. Can you feel the anger?"

Carol Ann, who produced the dirt-bike pictures, was exasperated at her inability to get him to say anything about a script they were preparing to shoot. It was called *Wheelies* and it was another teenage picture, a lot like the last one they had made. They were working at Neil's house in the Hollywood Hills. Carol Ann had spent her Saturday morning trying to extract opinions from him. She was about to leave and Neil was walking her to her car. They stopped for a few last moments, next to the silver Porsche. As they talked, Neil patted the car, stroking it like a pet. "Do you think we ought to get another writer?" Carol Ann asked, making a last attempt to get him to speak about the script.

"I don't know. Maybe."

"Do you want to do a draft yourself?"

"Yeah. Okay. Maybe."

"I think it's a question of the girl's motivation. All she does is imitate the boys. Maybe she could do wheelies. Or something."

"Yeah. That would be good."

It went on like that, Carol Ann trying to get him to say something, and Neil just running his hand across the metal of his car.

"Is that all you give a shit about?" she asked. "What is the big deal about you and cars?"

Neil's face came alive and he began to talk, speaking in complex thoughts, astonishing Carol Ann. "I think there are a lot of reasons men in the movie business buy expensive cars. The big one is pretty basic. They get paid a lot and can afford them. Here are the other reasons I can think of. To drive fast. But they don't. I don't, anyway. To impress each other. They do. Mostly they impress kids, which nobody cares about all that much. To impress women. You might know better about this one, but I think women pretend to be impressed so they can please the men. The last reason is that it's fun. And I'll tell you something. It is, it really is."

Carol Ann laughed and put her arm around Neil. "I will never understand you. We could make a dozen pictures and I will never understand you."

"Not all that secret."

"Maybe not. You're going to talk to Sid today, aren't you?" Sid was an art director they were considering for *Wheelies* and Neil had agreed to go out to MGM to look at examples of Sid's work from over the years. "He's done some sketches for you. On spec. Talk to him, but I don't know. I think he's past it."

"I'll see him. I don't mind."

On his way to Culver City, Neil cruised around Hollywood High. He decided to stop and see what was going on. He liked to hang around with the students, just to see what they were up to. Considering the age of most moviegoers and the subject matter of Neil's most successful pictures, it wasn't a bad policy. He was particularly fond of hanging out at the basketball courts.

"Hey, what are you guys doing?" Neil said to a couple of boys playing one-on-one.

"What's it look like, dork face?"

"Can I play?"

A kid on the sidelines yelled, "Let him. Half-court." What this bystander meant was, he'd get a chance to play if the other boys allowed Neil to play. Two-on-two.

Neil ran into the game, took the ball, and dribbled downcourt. He palmed the ball and then tried a so-so version of Kareem's skyhook. For a moment or two the boys forgot he was twice their age. And that was Neil's victory. He wanted nothing more than to be accepted by these kids as a regular guy.

After they had played for a while and the game broke up, the boys saw the silver Porsche.

"That yours?" one of them asked with doubt in his voice.

"Yeah," Neil said, enjoying their confusion.

"I'd rather have a 'vette."

"Detroit plastic," Neil sneered. That was heresy to the boys. But German cars are more of an adult passion, at least in Hollywood, than a teenage one, so Neil didn't press it. He waved goodbye and drove to Culver City, feeling good.

Sid, the art director Neil had come to see, had been having trouble lately. He'd designed forty films over the last twenty-five years, but Sid's was not the first name that came to mind when the new young directors and producers were shopping for art directors or production designers. If he were to get the gig with Neil, Sid would be able to pay his kids' tuition bills. Neil looked over some preliminary sketches but didn't say much about them. "It's just some first thoughts about the picture," Sid said nervously. "I like the script," he added, trying to prompt a response. "I can feel the life in it."

"These are nice," Neil said, casually flipping through the drawings. "Did you do any of the clubhouse?"

"Isn't it here? I must have left it in the car. I'll go get it." Sid started to leave and Neil got up to go with him.

As they walked through the parking lot, Sid wondered if he was making the right move. He had left the clubhouse sketch in the car because he wasn't sure it was right. It was so hard to know what these young guys would respond to. Neil didn't say a word as they walked through the parking lot. "Is this your car?" Neil asked as Sid unlocked the trunk of his Toyota.

"Yeah. It is," Sid said, wondering if there was a better answer he might have given.

"Does it have the talking system?"

"Yes. Want to hear it?"

"Oh, yeah," Neil said, sounding excited.

Sid unlocked the car and Neil got in. When Sid put the key in the ignition, a chime rang and a woman's voice said, "The door is open."

"Far-out," Neil said, grinning. "What else does it say?"

"It'll tell you if you left the key in the ignition or if you're low on gas. A few others."

"I want to hear."

Sid put the talking Toyota through its paces for Neil, and then offered him the wheel for a high-speed spin on the San Diego freeway. When Neil hit sixty, the voice said, "You are exceeding the speed limit."

When they got back to the studio, Neil was feeling good and thinking he might look into installing a talking system in the silver Porsche. He didn't want to see the clubhouse sketch anymore, but Sid got the job designing *Wheelies*.

Movies are an unpredictable business and *Wheelies* was a failure. And the next picture Neil made didn't do any better. After four years of hits, Neil seemed to lose his touch. His failure gave him more time to reflect than he wanted. It seemed to Neil that the work he was doing, the scripts he was writing, and the ideas he had weren't any different from the ones he had when he was riding high. He could still make deals, but it wasn't so easy and he had to struggle. He concluded that in Hollywood what you succeed with and what you fail with are virtually the same. No wonder people in Hollywood are so superstitious, he thought, always going to astrologers and psychics. Neil's dark time lasted three years, during which he married and divorced, sold all his cars, including the silver Speedster, and bought a brand-new turbo-charged Porsche. It was sleek and black but it didn't make him happy. By the standards of the world, Neil was still a success, a well-to-do man. But years of writing scripts that he never got to direct had made him miserable. But he never stopped working, and finally, as mysteriously as his gifts had been taken away, they returned. He was forty and he was hot again. The difficult years had changed him. He was still interested in teenagers, but instead of dirt bikes and shopping malls the pictures had grown darker, the sex more overt, and violence was never far below the surface.

While he was out of favor, Neil developed a reputation in Hollywood for being a liberated man. It started when he hired Lila as a cinematographer. She wasn't even his first choice, but Neil was on a tight budget and Lila was willing to work for very little. Her gender didn't worry him, it was her inexperience. But it worked out and now they've made two pictures together. Lila added women to Neil's crews; now Neil is a patron of a group called Women in Film.

Lila was once married to a friend of Neil's, but that marriage is long gone and now Lila lives with Veronica and Veronica's daughter. When Neil's angry at Lila, he calls her domestic arrangements a butch commune. It's a measure of Neil's actual liberation, or maybe just his practicality, that he doesn't care what Lila's gender or her preferences are. She gets the job done right, the crew trusts her, and she doesn't take any crap from the technicians at the lab. They've become better friends since Lila decided she preferred the company of women. Lila has always been frank with Neil about her own sexuality and she's the only person he talks to with any frankness about his own.

When they're not filming, Neil and Lila meet each morning at the Fairfax High School track for a run and then they go to the Farmer's Market for fresh grapefruit juice. It's a standing date that helps keep them both trim and gives them a chance to talk about things other than the movie business.

Lila was late this morning, so Neil ran alone, lost in his own thoughts. He waved to an agent he knew, who was running with a Walkman plugged into his ears, listening to the latest rock and roll. Neil enjoyed the track and he always thought it would be fun to make a short film about it. His plan would be to just start filming the activity there, which starts at sunrise. He would get footage of the different ways people ran. The old people who sort of walk-jogged, and the hot-looking young actors and athletes who seemed to fly around the track. Maybe someday, he thought as he saw Lila trotting across the football field.

"Got held up," she said. "Domestic calamities."

"I've done a mile. I want to do at least one more."

"I'm ready for chapter two," Lila said, referring to the ongoing saga of Neil's love life.

"At the F.M. I just want to run now, okay?" She nodded her assent, and they continued their quarter-mile loops, enjoying the morning sun and one another's silent company.

By eight o'clock they were cooling off at the outdoor tables in the Farmer's Market. The tourist buses hadn't arrived yet, so the market still felt leisurely. At this hour the customers were the same each morning. Neil had picked up the trades, but they went unread as he and Lila dived into their favorite subject, which was love.

"I don't know why I tell you all this crap," he said. "I guess because you listen. You won't hate me."

"You're telling me because I'm here," Lila said. "In my position, I think about sex a lot. If the majority of the world thinks you're a pervert, it's on your mind."

"Who says you're a pervert? You have more of a regular domestic life with Veronica than most people have in suburban marriages."

"It's not easy. If people around here are bitchy about Veronica and me, I can imagine what they would say in other places. It's so obviously true it's not worth discussing," she said with a finality that didn't invite disagreement.

"I guess you're right," he said. "How's Veronica?"

"She has a new theory of show business. If nobody cared all that much about sex, if we just coupled and uncoupled, unneurotically, without any agony or guilt, there would be no more movies or TV."

Neil laughed and smiled at Lila. "Sounds like another women-on-the-march theory to me."

"Nope. She says it applies to men and women. I want to hear about your latest truck-stop-waitress fantasy."

"I'm not the only guy who has these feelings. I didn't invent it," Neil said defensively.

"Raise your finger and the most delicious actress in Hollywood would jump. But you only want bleached blonds with dark roots, too much lipstick, and big boobs. Right?"

"You forgot too-tight pants with high heels," he said, grinning. Neil's taste for trashy women was well known. He wrote them into his scripts so he could have the pleasure of casting them. Another director would be called a sexist pig, but because Neil had all those women on his crew, it was usually seen as a political statement.

"It's when you start your Humbert Humbert act that it gets sick and you should stop."

"Hey, Lila. You want to be fair, please? I'm not after twelve-year-olds."

"How old?"

"Sixteen."

"It's sick. The more impossible it is, the more you want them."

"You don't ever want the unobtainable?"

"All the time. But I leave it at that, unless it's an adult who can make free choices. It's called ethical behavior. You ought to try it."

"I didn't say I did it. I'm saying honestly what I'd like. I am trying to face my libido."

"This is all Roman Polanski's doing. Ever since that craziness, all you guys are the same. If Roman had a taste for sheep instead of thirteen-year-old girls, all the livestock in California would be in trouble now."

"You're tough, Lila."

"The ideal woman for you is a gum-chewing sixteen-year-old with too much eye shadow who lives in Canoga Park."

"Sounds good."

"You could go to jail," she said. "No court is going to be understanding about something like this."

"Calm down. Okay?"

"Don't touch any of them. Promise me that."

"Okay, okay. I promise."

"I don't believe you."

"I can control myself. I'm not Roman Polanski. I give you my word."

Neil parked the black Porsche on Sunset, just up from Highland Avenue, by the sign that says "Hollywood High: Achieve the Honorable." He let the motor purr. Hollywood High is ideal for this kind of cruising. It's not a closed-off campus, just a city school on a busy corner where there are enough street types around that one more won't be noticed. His plan, should the Dean of Propriety or some other school official come to ask his business, was to offer his card and explain he was researching a high-school picture.

By the second day of this, when no teacher had come to inquire and the students seemed indifferent—oh, the boys looked over the car, but not the girls—the only contact had been a few of the hookers in the area, asking in their quaint locution if he wanted "to go out." Some of them were probably students looking to make a buck on their lunch hour, but that wasn't what Neil wanted. During his vigil, he realized he craved the opposite of a teenage hooker. Lila hadn't seen it at all. What Neil wanted was purity and inexperience, an untouched child who could not compare him to anyone else. It was the fat boy from Richmond Hill again, he thought. The insight didn't make him happy, but he was still determined to try for one of them.

He had his eye on a sweet-looking young girl, about sixteen. She had short brown hair and although she was a little pudgy, she was prettier than the high-school boys knew. High-school boys always went for big breasts or flashy clothes, whatever was obvious. Neil had been the same. Now he was looking for a more complete package. When you're forty and shopping for sixteen, an inch or two one way or the other is not so important. She had noticed the car and smiled at him, just a friendly smile. Most of them kept their eyes straight ahead and then giggled when they were past.

"Hi," he said, trying to sound casual, which is not easy for a middle-aged man in a spectacular car, talking to an adolescent.

"Hi to you."

"Are you a student here?"

"No. I'm the principal. Yeah, I'm one. What do you think I am?"

"I don't know. Want to go for a ride?"

"Oh, God. Where'd you get that?"

"The car?"

"About a ride."

"Do you?"

"Are you for real or what?"

"No. Just your regular sex-drugs-and-rock-and-roll-crazed guy." That got a smile from her. "Come on," he added, trying to strike the right note between cajolery and indifference.

"Okay," she said, and got in the car, her chin set in a defiant show-me attitude.

He began to stammer, unable to form words. Was it possible?

The proximity of a teenage girl could still make him tongue-tied? Was it possible he still didn't know what to do around adolescent girls? Was it a life sentence?

"What's your move, Slick?"

"You like this car?"

"You giving it to me?"

"I . . . ah . . . Listen to the sound system."

"I have to go to math. See you." As she got out of the Porsche, there was a smile on her face. She had enjoyed the flirtation and the encounter. Turning this old guy in the flashy car into a bowl of Jell-O had amused her.

Neil roared away from Hollywood High, sweating and trembling a little. As he waited for the light at La Brea, he mused on it all. After all the deals and the hustle, was this what he wanted? To be humiliated by a child? He reminded himself of the festivals devoted to his movies and thought of all the magazine articles that had been written about him. It didn't help. All I get is to be constantly reminded I'm still sixteen and lousy at it. He thought about it all the way to the light at Fairfax, where he decided that it was indeed a life sentence. Permanent adolescence. He decided not to tell Lila what had happened, and he didn't cruise Hollywood High anymore, but he still had fantasies about teenage girls.

In the Desert

The more scripts I rewrote, the more were offered to me. I enjoyed the specificity of the trade. It gave me an easily perceived and remembered identity. Since selecting a screenwriter for a particular project is really a crapshoot, the people who do it—studio executives, producers, directors, and story editors—are always looking for an edge. Is it a comedy set in Italy? Then get so-and-so, he's funny and he speaks Italian. A police melodrama? Hire this one or that. No matter that the writers involved scarcely felt themselves particularly expert in cop drama or Italian farce—any shred of justification for their decision, any hint, no matter how remote, of what the script might turn out to be, was seized by the poor bastard obligated to hire a screenwriter. So I did rewrites because I did rewrites. The more I did, the more in demand I became. After a few years I found myself working with well-known actors and high-powered producers: names and faces from the gossip columns, people who got what they sought and then had to live with it, whether they liked it or not. One of them was Peter, who had a doubting streak. It's not unusual to doubt others, but Peter sometimes doubted himself. That's an uncommon quality among the Hollywood nimble.

The only thing that ever came easily to Peter was charm. That was usually enough. It got him through college and the unhappy year he spent at NYU, supposedly studying film production, but really just watching movies. It wasn't a bad education, but less orthodox than the faculty had intended. Now he was thirty-four and he had come to depend on his charm to get him through life. His fear, which was not without possibility, was that he was turning into some Hollywood lounge lizard, getting by on glibness and wit. Peter was nominally a film producer, but really only a deputy to Clare Soloway, who, whatever else he might have been, really was a producer. With Peter's help, Clare turned out one or two films each year. It made Clare an important player in Hollywood, pursued by agents and sought by actors and directors. Clare was forty-seven and he had been the head of production at a studio until the studio had become part of an industrial conglomerate and Clare was pushed out. Clare's real name was Sam, but his first wife thought it sounded common and wanted to change it to St. Clair. The marriage didn't last long enough for the name change to take legal effect, but Sam had agreed to be called Clare, and it stuck even after the marriage was over. His films still said "Samuel Soloway Presents," but everyone called him Clare, which he sometimes said was short for Clarence.

Peter had produced several films for Clare—at least his name appeared in the credits as producer. He worked hard at the job of finding material and negotiating deals, but it was Clare who decided which scripts to buy and whom to hire, the decisions that count. It was Clare who made the big money, the profits and the half-million-dollar fee for each picture. Peter got a salary, and if a picture was a really big hit, a small portion of the profits. Peter wanted the producer credit and Clare gave it to him, but what Peter really did to earn his money was help his boss sort out his thoughts. Clare prided himself on what he called his guts, and Peter made sense out of whatever Clare's guts told him. Peter did it with a light touch, knowing full well that if the situation were to take a few bad turns he would be out on the street, an unemployed, high-toned yes-man.

Clare and Peter were in Morton's late at night at a small table near the entrance to the dining room, positioned so they could see everyone who came in or out. They were eating sliced lamb and trying to unwind, when Clare asked Peter to do him a little favor.

"Kim wants to go to the Filmex opening this Friday. There's a dinner and some other usual crap."

"So?" Peter asked as he sipped a beer. Peter liked to keep Clare off balance by occasionally forgoing wine and having a beer or a bottle of mineral water with his dinner. Clare had learned a handful of facts about wine in order not to feel foolish in places like Morton's. Usually he said, "We'll have a bottle of the cabernet" if there was meat on the table, or "We'll have a bottle of the chardonnay" if dinner was anything else. He ignored any waiter foolish enough to ask him which vineyard he preferred.

"Filmex is easy," Clare said, as if he were deflecting an argument. "Come with us. The whole world's going to be there."

"The whole world's always going to something," Peter answered, not yet taking the discussion seriously. "I have Geiger that night, anyway," he said, mentioning an art director he and Clare were considering hiring. "We're going to have dinner, spend the evening."

"Geiger can wait. I'm supposed to see Joey that night," Clare said. "I promised." Joey Chakara was an actress Clare saw a lot of. Clare's fiancée, Kim, didn't know about Joey and Clare wanted to keep it that way. Actually Joey was more than an actress—the woman was almost a star—and to carry on an affair with her, Clare had to be very discreet. "Come on. You be Joey's date," Clare said, unable to keep a hint of lewdness from his face. "You'll be with Kim and me. Am I supposed to say 'Kim and I'?"

"'Kim and me,'" Peter said, glad to confirm Clare's grammar rather than correct it. "What's Joey going to say about it?"

"She'll piss and moan at first, but you can charm her. I'm in a jam here. Do this for me, Peter." Calling him "Peter" instead of "you" was about as close to pleading as Clare ever got.

Kim was just the wife Clare wanted. She was attractive, very social, and unlike his previous two wives, who were very young, she was an adult, a woman in her late thirties. Kim had been married once before and she and Clare were going into this marriage as if it were a corporate merger. Kim might have made her peace with Clare's prowling around, but she was sure to draw the line at his being seen in public with a hot number like Joey Chakara. Peter knew Clare saw a lot of Joey and he wasn't crazy about being the beard, but he owed his livelihood to Clare and didn't feel able to say no. Peter had to live with the fact that even though he knew more about scripts than Clare and usually had better ideas about most aspects of production, Clare was a success, a man who had made millions. Peter was his assistant. Peter knew full well he had his job because he was good at reacting and pleasing, unlike Clare, who just did what he wanted, untroubled by self-awareness. When Peter was starting his career, he had done a lot of script doctoring and rewriting, a skill that required him to align his mind with someone else's and still be imaginative and creative. Very few can do it, and Peter was one of them.

As Peter was trying to think of a way to wriggle out of the Filmex evening, Eleanor Taplinger stopped at the table. Eleanor had been an actress until she could no longer bear the humiliations of the profession. So she married Bill Taplinger, who was her agent. Over the next fifteen years, Bill had formed his own agency; Eleanor went to lunch and drank a lot of vodka. She was a big woman, tall and a little heavy, with cropped silvery hair. Another woman this size would be thought of as overweight, but Eleanor carried it easily. Her size and her wicked wit made her formidable. "Hi, Sammy," she said, kissing Clare on each cheek. Eleanor had known him for twenty years and was one of the few who still called him Sam. "Where's Penelope? Registering at Tiffany's?"

"Who?" Clare asked, confused by the reference.

"She means Kim," Peter said. "Penelope is sort of your basic faithful girlfriend. Mrs. Taplinger is being more literary than this joint is used to."

"Home," Clare said bluntly. "You know Peter?"

"Of course. I won't bother you. I'm sure you're making lots of important decisions or something." She smiled again and lurched away.

"She used to be such a piece of goods, that one," Clare said. "Real class act. Well, fuck her."

"Looked to me like you already did," Peter said with a boyish grin, hoping to recoup with Clare after the classical-reference incident.

"Yeah, well, it was a long time ago. Too much vodka since then."

The Filmex dinner was to be held in the ballroom at the Century Plaza Hotel, following the screening of *Passage to the Past,* a movie about kids who invent a time machine. Clare and Peter had to work late on a script so the foursome skipped the picture, which was fine with Kim because it meant she didn't have to sit through a movie in her gown and run the risk of being wrinkled for the dinner. She did insist that they get there as the movie was ending so they could walk through Century City from the theater to the hotel. That's where the photographers and news cameras would be and Kim liked the idea of going in with Joey, because then the photographers would make a fuss. Kim enjoyed complaining about the photographers as long as they were taking her picture, even peripherally. What she couldn't bear was being ignored. At the dinner, Joey kept looking at Clare in a way that hinted the arrangement was not exactly what it seemed. Joey's mind frequently raced and jumped in a way that she herself probably couldn't follow. Once she called Clare "Clair de Lune," which made Peter laugh, then she started calling him "Clare-Bear," which made Peter a little nervous. If Kim understood the implication, she was willing to let it go by. The fact that Clare was solicitous enough of her opinion to create a charade was enough for her, at least for now.

Joey's thick blond hair, teased and spiked for the evening, stuck out from her head like a picture frame. She was wearing a white satin beaded dress that fell low on her chest and was slit up the side. It was the kind of dress you couldn't buy in a store. Ann Roth had designed it for her; the next morning Joey and her dress were in all the papers.

Clare had been right: Peter had no trouble talking to Joey and playing the attentive escort. He danced with her and when the inevitable prime rib was served, Peter got her a salad, because she wouldn't eat red meat. Peter never had trouble talking to actors, since there's one all-purpose subject that always interests them, which is themselves. At the table, Peter engaged Joey in a private chat about her career. "You should stretch more, Joey," he said.

"I work out," she answered, a little indignant.

"I mean the parts you play. If you would just once play someone a little less obviously sexy, the critics would call you a genius. The sexiness, the beauty, the energy you give off that makes your audience go crazy, will still be there. If you played a more serious role, they'd talk about a great breakthrough in your work. Look at Ann-Margret. She was a Vegas dancer, now she's practically Peggy Ashcroft. She's older than you, so she maybe got pushed into it, but it worked. Look at Cher. She was some kind of joke, now she's an artist."

"I don't know if I could do it. All I ever did is what I do."

"I don't mean you should try to play Shakespeare at the Royal Court, at least not at first. I'm talking about film acting. Behavior. You could be funny and sexy, like Carole Lombard." Joey nodded, but Peter doubted if she had any idea who Carole Lombard was. "If you like," he said, "we can develop a script for you. Maybe for the first one you could be a mousy girl who becomes beautiful. It'd be a way to get your feet wet and point up your range." Joey beamed and started paying a lot of attention to Peter.

In the four years they had worked together, Peter and Clare had grown dependent on one another in ways neither of them fully recognized. They worked together productively for long hours, and a friendship had developed, but there was also a prickly and complicated antagonism between them. They seemed to be the best of friends, but both harbored resentment; occasionally each complained to friends that he was being driven crazy by the other. But for all that, neither could imagine working any other way.

Peter was aware that his position with Clare gave him a satisfying identity. Clare's dependence in intellectual matters gave Peter a sense of power over his master. For his part, Clare never quite trusted Peter to be aggressive enough in negotiations, but he loved the idea of having this intelligent young man at his side and in his service. Clare had never gone to college, and although Peter assured him he hadn't missed all that much, Clare was insecure about literary matters and questions of artistic taste. Clare wanted to be able to quote poetry and to be discerning about painting and music, but he didn't have any real sense of those things. His attachment to Peter gave him that sensibility, once removed. In script meetings, writers sometimes made reference to Othello's jealousy or Hamlet's indecision. If Peter let it pass, Clare knew the writer knew his stuff. If Peter stopped the fellow and offered a gentle correction or an amplification, Clare knew the writer was winging it. In his heart Peter was worried that after Clare and Kim got married she would supplant him. Peter didn't have much regard for Kim's aesthetic sense, but he knew eventually Clare might well come to depend on her rather than on him.

Clare was so pleased with the way Peter had handled the Filmex evening that about a week later, as they were sitting in Clare's office, he proposed they do it again. "You were great. She loved your ass and Kim didn't give a shit," he said, adjusting the framed photograph of Joey that hung on his office wall. Clare's office, which Peter had once described as being just slightly smaller than Rhode Island, contained the usual array of framed photos: Clare with various governors and senators, Clare with stars, and Clare with his family. The political and personal photos were there to provide a benign context for the ones Clare really cared about, the photos of all the beautiful women of Hollywood he had slept with. There were rows of actresses, agents, executives, designers, and writers, all pinned on the wall where Clare could contemplate them whenever he cared to. The active ones stayed just above his desk. When he was through with one of them, she was moved to the back, to what Clare always called Memory Lane. "Joey stays front and center for another round," he said, pleased with himself.

"Bimbos on parade, huh?" Peter said, with less admiration in his voice than he felt.

"It's a bigger parade than this," Clare said, gesturing to the photos. "These are the ones I liked."

"Right. Friendly bimbos."

"Come on to dinner with us on Friday. Why not?"

"Again?" Peter asked, seeing nothing but grief ahead. "Why can't you get somebody else?"

"Just do it," Clare said, closing the subject.

The second double date was a dinner at Spago, where they were eating one of Wolfgang Puck's lamb-sausage pizzas made with wild mushrooms, garlic, and zucchini and sprinkled with fresh coriander. A bottle of Stag's Leap cabernet was on the table. With Joey along, Bernard, the maître d', had given the four of them a prominent table in the front, looking out over the Sunset Strip. Joey was wearing black leather pants that looked tight enough to cause pain and a loose white shirt with three open buttons. Kim, who was much too smart to try to compete with Joey and her blowsy good looks, was in a fitted blazer that made her look like the boss. She busied herself waving and nodding hello to everyone she knew, happy to be seen at a good table. She pretended not to notice the crowded bar, where people clutched their drinks and stared longingly at the occupied tables. A few of the supplicants tried to curry favor with Bernard. One young woman repeatedly lifted her glass so Bernard might see she was drinking white wine, that she understood the drinking customs and ought to rate a table. Her companion, trying to help but apparently not grasping the subtleties of the situation, displayed a rye and soda. The others at the bar looked away as if the fellow had ordered boilermakers for everyone.

At the Filmex dinner, it had amused Joey to be at the same table with Kim. Now that Clare was doing it a second time, she felt used and she didn't like it. She got up a couple of times and went to the bathroom and when she came back she was wired and talking fast. By Hollywood standards Joey didn't have a big cocaine habit, but she used the stuff frequently and this evening was one of the times. Kim seemed oblivious, and if Clare cared, he wasn't saying. It didn't matter to Peter what Joey did, just so she didn't get so loaded that she'd do something dopey, like announce that she'd spent the afternoon in bed with Clare.

The third time she got up to go to the bathroom, she was walking very fast. Some instinct told Peter to go after her. He worked his way through the crowded room, nodding and shaking hands. By the time he got to the bathrooms, in an alcove between the front room and the less desirable patio, Joey was talking to Carla Moore, an executive at Tri-Star, who was thrilled to have what she took to be Joey's attention. "It is an absolutely sensational woman's part," Carla said, describing a script to Joey. "It's sort of a feminist prisoner-of-war story with comedic overtones. Whoever plays this part has a lock on a nomination." But Joey was so ripped that Peter couldn't tell how much she had heard or whether she even knew who Carla was. As Peter approached, Joey was running her fingers through her thick hair in a nervous, unconscious gesture. When Peter joined them, he cupped his hand under Joey's elbow in a proprietary way to let Carla know this was his date. As he was saying hello, the door to the bathroom opened and two young women in black spandex pants and identical green tube tops came out, gawked at Joey, and moved on. Joey ignored Carla, who was still trying to talk about her script, took Peter's hand, and pulled him into the bathroom, locking the door behind them.

"I haven't been in one of these in a while," Peter said with a grin. "When I was about five my mother took me into the ladies' room at Bloomingdale's. But I don't remember much about it."

"Pee if you want," she said as she fished the bottle of cocaine out of her purse. "Let's get loaded." She scooped out a tiny spoonful of the flaky white powder and held it up to Peter's nostril. He hesitated for a second, but Joey pushed his face into the cocaine and he inhaled.

"Not bad," he said, brushing a few stray grains from his lip, waiting for the rush.

"The campesinos died for your nose," she said, putting the spoon to his other nostril. Then she snorted some herself, and Peter felt the roof of his mouth go numb and his pulse start to race.

He smiled and said, "I used to take this stuff instead of Dexamyl. To lose weight." It wasn't true. When Peter wanted to lose weight he just ate less. But he knew plenty of women in Hollywood who used cocaine as a diet aid, and at the moment he was less interested in informing than in charming her with his vulnerability.

"Me too," she said, laughing. "It gets rid of what you don't need and makes flabby stuff hard." She was squirming and talking fast, too wired to stand still.

"How could you think you're overweight? One of the few things the entire Western world is in agreement about is that you're gorgeous."

"In our biz, any weight is too much."

"That's America," he said with a wry smile. "The whole goddamn country is trying to diminish itself. We think we're all guilty of something, so we're trying to make less of ourselves." To Joey that was the ideal philosophical aperçu, since it involved flesh and she could grasp enough of it to feel smart. She smiled at him and moved a little closer.

"What am I doing here?" she asked, not expecting an answer.

"Getting loaded, I guess."

"No, no. On this bullshit date. What am I doing this for? He brings her and then makes me go along."

"Yeah, well, all in a day's work, right?"

"No," she said as she snuggled against Peter. "Fuck 'em both." Then she put her arms around Peter and kissed him.

It was a difficult moment for him. She might be a little trashy, but men all over the world stayed warm at night thinking about Joey Chakara, who at the moment had her tongue in his mouth and her hands in his back pockets. If she was crazy enough to proposition him in the bathroom, no matter how casually, she might do anything. He knew if he made love to her she'd throw it in Clare's face and that would certainly cost him his job. The price seemed a little steep. On the other hand, he thought, this woman could be life-changing, or at the least, seriously deal-making. Despite his practical thoughts and concerns, Peter could sense something else, a little frisson of mutual interest between them that seemed real. In that moment, Peter wanted to believe that Joey, with her high-flying energy and flashes of wit, was a woman of surprise and magic. She relocked the door and sat on the edge of the sink and tried to take her pants off. But they were so tight, she couldn't even get the buttons open. "Not here. Not now," he said, lifting her down and holding her to him. The conflict within him, which made him say go away and stay here all at once, seemed to draw her nearer to him. In saying no and yes to Joey, at least for the moment, he was trying to say no to being a beard, no to Clare Soloway, and yes to his own future. Maybe it was because she belonged to Clare, or maybe it was the drugs, but the intensity between them was undeniable. No matter what he wanted to think or feel, they both knew that here, under the harsh lights of the bathroom and in a cokey haze, the moment had occurred when a passion is born.

"I want to go somewhere." She pouted, "Take me someplace good."

"It's Clare's car, but I'll think of something. Come on. Let me handle it."

"More blow first," she said, fishing the little bottle out of her pocket for the third time in less than twenty minutes.

At the table Clare and Kim were listening to a young agent from the Morris office. The guy was glad to have Clare's attention and determined to say something memorable. "But those woods have dark corners, if you know what I mean," is what he managed. Clare nodded as if he knew what the man was talking about. Kim smiled and pretended to listen while her eyes darted around the room seeing who had good tables and who didn't.

"Joey's feeling a little tired," Peter said when they got back to the table. "I'm going to take her home." Clare jumped to his feet and all but bowed to Joey, who had decided to affect a wan look that she must have thought showed a sudden grave illness. She smiled thinly and mumbled her good-byes.

"Take my car," Clare said, meaning the opposite.

"We'll figure something out," Peter answered. Clare looked at him oddly, but Peter pretended not to notice.

Kim smiled and said, "It's been brief but penetrating," which made Joey giggle.

As Peter escorted her through the restaurant, Joey seemed to get sicker. She might be ripped, but she was still an actress. Before they got to Bernard's station near the door, she was coughing and having trouble with her balance.

Outside, as Peter looked around for a cab, Joey announced, "I want to hear some music. Rockamole."

"What's that?" Peter said, laughing at the word.

"Mexican rock and roll. East El-Lay. Los Lobos," she said, affecting a Mexican accent. "Let's go to the barrio and boogie." Before Peter could start listing the many reasons why that wasn't such a great idea, Joey decided she wanted to go across the street to Tower Records. It was past eleven, an hour when Tower Records, a vast sign-encrusted, neon-lit building devoted to loud music and outré fashion, was most active. They walked across Horn Avenue, through Tower's parking lot, and into a rock-and-roll temple where yet another teenage anthem that Peter didn't recognize was blasting over the speakers. There were easily a hundred stoned-looking kids shopping for music and one another. A lot of the boys tried for an English-rock-star look, with feathers in their hair and denim vests over bare chests. The girls wore black lipstick and had bits of colored crinoline mesh in their hair.

"Jesus," Peter muttered. "You could get herpes just standing here."

"It's great. Let's get some music."

"Why not?" Peter answered, grabbing a handful of cassettes and heading for the checkout counter. As he was waiting to pay for the tapes, Joey's mood changed again; she was not looking happy. Peter had spent a professional lifetime around actors and knew it was because none of these kids recognized her, no one was whispering about her. To this crowd, a four-minute rock video is the outside limit of concentration and sittting through a two-hour movie was like reading Proust. A really big star wouldn't care, might even welcome a moment's anonymity, but Joey, at the top of the second tier, took it as a bad omen and wanted to leave.

When they were back in the parking lot and Peter was trying to figure how to get her home, his eye fell on the Budget rent-a-car office tucked below Spago, right on the Strip. Only in Hollywood, he thought, would a car-rental agency be open at this hour. A credit card and a driver's license later, they were driving a Mustang convertible west on Sunset toward Joey's house in Benedict Canyon.

She lived behind gates in a Spanish house filled with pillows, candles, and a lot of Laura Ashley fabric. "You like it?" Joey asked. "It's supposed to be old-world charm and upbeat colors, or some shit like that."

"Great," Peter said, trying to adjust his eyes to the sea of flowered fabric and all the ruffles and bows. There were several end tables stacked with art books—histories of impressionism, volumes of Japanese prints, books of photographs, and catalogs from museums around the world. Most of the books looked too heavy to lift.

"Actually, some decorator my agent found did the whole thing. It's sort of nosegay central," Joey said as she rummaged around for a joint. "Who cares about that shit. Let's do something alive." She slapped an old Muddy Waters record onto the stereo and waited until the smoky, urgent voice filled the room:

> You aint seen nothin' till you
> seen her do the do.
> Aint nothin' like it when
> she do the do . . .

Joey came alive when she made love, the same way she came alive on the screen. When the cameras rolled, Joey always glowed, and here in bed, it was the same. The effect was to electrify Peter and give him a sense of abandonment, of wildness, of prodigious needs and secrets revealed. Such feelings had been in his dreams, but never before in his waking life. The woman had appetites as great as her attention span was small. She liked to be athletic in bed, which meant a lot of thrashing and rolling about, which didn't particularly appeal to Peter. But he was determined to stay in bed with her as long as it took to make her need him, at first romantically, then professionally. What surprised Peter was that his cold-blooded approach to romance created something like real feeling between them. But not the first night; that was given over to sweaty, druggy sex and little else. On the second day, Peter made clear his intention to stay with her no matter what, which meant no matter what Clare said or wanted. "Is there anything to eat around here?" he asked, poking through her refrigerator and looking in the cabinets.

"I don't know. Maybe," she said indifferently, as if the idea of food in a house struck her as unlikely.

"Maybe we should go out. I tend to eat once or twice a day. Just a habit. I guess I could learn to break it."

Joey smiled, enjoying his humor, and told him where she hid the cookies, and then why she hid them. "When I first got out here, I was way overweight."

"You? The figure that launched a million wet dreams? Including mine?"

"Is that true?" she asked, taken by the idea that someone who had fantasized about her had now slept with her. "I was a fatso. La tubby. The only job I could get was for Mike Dandino. You know, the record producer?" Dandino owned a couple of rock clubs in Hollywood and managed a few singers. Even in a business as crude as the music business, Dandino's vulgarity stood out. "My job was to go around to all the diet doctors and get prescriptions for diet pills or whatever kind of speed I could. Then I'd give the pills to Dandy for his clients or whatever."

"How long did you do that?"

"Months. There were so many diet doctors, I could go to a new one every day for weeks—then start over. Sometimes I took a couple pills so the doctors wouldn't get mad. You know, to lose a few pounds to show some progress. Then Dandy would get pissed and make me eat onion rings. It was a really stupid job but I was broke and I was too fat to be an actress." Peter enjoyed her story and he even began to enjoy her. She was beautiful, famous, unpredictable, addicted to any substance that came her way, and about as stable as the rocky hills above Malibu.

Kim had refused to live with Clare until they were married, so she kept up the charade of her own address, an apartment in Beverly Hills. It might have been one of Kim's few tactical errors, since it gave Clare the freedom to pursue Joey. For a while Kim had spent nights at Clare's house, insisting on leaving about midnight, but that seemed entirely too much to Clare's liking, so now she made him come to her apartment, then threw him out if he looked too comfortable. Her plan was to make herself indispensable to him and make it difficult for him to see her in private. She figured that he'd marry her rather than commute crosstown. So when the call came very late Sunday night, Clare was alone, dozing, with a script on his lap.

"Clare, hi. Clare, Clare, Clarabell clown, how are you?" Joey said in a coked rush of words. "It's me. How are you?" She and Peter were in bed, where they'd been since Friday night. Joey had taken it into her head to report that particular bit of news to Clare. By the time Peter realized what she was doing, the deed was done. Clare was silent for a long moment, probably trying to wake up and think what to say. "We've been here for a long time, since Spago's the other night. We've been having a great time. Peter's fabulous.

He's the smartest person I ever met. And he's cute. We're in bed. I'm staying right here for the rest of my life," she said, giggling at the outrageousness of the phone call.

Peter took the phone away from her and with a laugh tried to say hello to his boss, but Clare wasn't having any of it. "What the fuck do you think you're doing?"

"Take it easy, Clare," Peter said, or tried to say, because Clare interrupted and refused to let Peter speak.

"I don't need shit like this. You can do it in the road if you want, but you can also find another meal ticket. Your card's punched around here," he said, hanging up. Peter knew that he had come to a crossroad in his life. He had expected it, but he had also hoped to time it a little better. That Joey was unpredictable was clear. That his time with her was limited was also clear. Peter knew he had better make some deals fast, a picture commitment if he could, script deals if he couldn't. Joey's name would work, and he could tie himself to her as producer. It could be worse. A minute ago he was indentured to Clare Soloway, now he was in business with Joey Chakara as a producer and, if he played it right, as Svengali.

Peter and Joey became Hollywood's new, hot couple. Army Archerd mentioned them once a week in *Variety,* and Hank Grant in the *Hollywood Reporter* called Joey luscious and Peter a deep thinker. He put them in the "New Two You" section of his column. If Kim ever suspected Joey and Clare had been involved, she wasn't saying. Clare was more attentive to her now, and she knew it wouldn't take much more for him to agree to set a wedding date. Peter was well aware he wouldn't stay in the "New Two You" column long. He organized a production company with himself as president, and by offering Joey's services in two pictures of the studio's choice, with an intervening picture of his choice, he got financing for the venture. They called it Lost Illusions Productions, and ten days after the dinner at Spago, Peter moved into the Producers Building at the studio. His hope was to get a movie into production before Joey blew up in his face.

Maybe it was because he had such low expectations for his relationship with Joey, but Peter was able to relax and take pleasure in her lunacy and enjoy the marathon rounds of sex they had embarked upon. He would spend his day at the studio listening to pitches, talking to agents, optioning scripts, books, and treatments, hiring writers to create good roles for Joey, and making coproduction deals with directors. The work wasn't much different from what he had done for Clare, except now he was doing it for himself.

At the end of the day he'd pick up Joey and they would go to screenings, dinners, and parties. Late at night, when they got back to her house, they would make love, often till dawn, and sometimes in ways Peter had only read about. At first Peter thought she had a deep kinky streak. Sometimes Joey wanted to be tied up, and other times she wanted to blindfold Peter and tie him up. But as the weeks became months, he came to see it wasn't actually kinky at all, but more like playacting. She liked to talk about whips and chains, but she couldn't bear to be hurt, nor did she want to hurt him. It was all theater to her, and what she really liked was to be held and caressed. It was as if she felt guilty for all the drugs and the public display, and if Peter would just hold her like a baby and stroke her and speak softly, she might feel okay about her life, or at least better. Then, when they were both comfortable and resting easy, she would begin to nibble on him, poking her tongue into dark corners and making love to him till they were both sore. He had never experienced anything so intense. Sometimes she would come to the studio to make love to him in his office, because she said she couldn't bear to wait till evening. On the weekends they would spend hours in bed together. Their romance might have started as a cool, calculated venture for Peter, but no longer; the intensity of their sexual connection had forged a deeper, more involving love. He was sleeping four hours a night at most and he was taking Quaaludes, cocaine, amyl nitrite, and marijuana. He loved every minute of it. Inside of two months he had gone from being deputy to a man he didn't trust and didn't even really like, to being the lover and partner of one of Hollywood's hottest, sexiest stars. He was losing weight, and bags were developing under his eyes, but he felt strong and vibrant. Joey insisted he had started walking with a swagger.

The papers often made veiled remarks about Joey's energy and her appetites, which in Hollywood was the code for cocaine. It didn't seem to bother her, until a television interviewer asked her directly if she used the drug. The interview was on tape, and Joey just got up and walked out. That night she announced to Peter that she was afraid she'd become an addict, which was like Sammy Davis declaring he was a tap dancer. Joey said she ought to go to the Betty Ford Clinic to dry out. Peter suspected the real reason she wanted to go to the clinic was that *People* magazine had done a story about all the stars who had gone there and Joey felt left out. If he hadn't been so tired from all the work he had been doing and all the drugs he had taken himself, he might have tried to talk her out of it. But instead he said that wasn't a bad idea at all. He was thinking he could do with a little rest.

With Joey in her Norma Kamali sweatsuit, a fifties fur coat, and her diddy-bop sunglasses, Peter put the top down on his Mercedes and drove her into the desert to Rancho Mirage, outside of Palm Springs, to sign up for the cure. She had a bottle of Stolichnaya vodka in her pocket and she took belts from it for the first hour of the trip. By the time they got to the desert, Joey was drunk, feeling crazy, and singing to the cactus and the Joshua trees:

> Bye bye, love,
> bye bye, happiness,
> hello, loneliness,
> I think I'm going to die . . .

Peter helped her sign into the hospital and made sure she understood she was signing on for one month. As Joey wrote her name, an orderly reached into her pocket and found the vodka bottle. "What are you, a bloodhound?" she asked, but the orderly just walked away with the bottle without saying a word. Peter wanted to see her room, but the admitting nurse said visitors were never allowed beyond the lobby. Peter felt a twinge of anxiety as he watched Joey walk away down the hospital corridor.

In the clinic, Joey lived in a simple room with a bed she was expected to make and a bureau she was told to keep clean. In the cafeteria she was assigned to clear the table and take out the garbage after each meal. She spent her mornings in group-therapy sessions. She had private consultations in the afternoons. At first

Joey threw herself headlong into the life of the clinic. Her problem wasn't with the staff or even with being deprived of drugs or alcohol. It was with her fellow patients, some of whom were celebrities, but most of whom were not. The group sessions sometimes became a battle between the celebrated and the unknown, in which those without public personalities felt free to abuse the famous.

Joey's group of seven included Tory Scoliano, who hadn't been famous for some years but who had once been a Broadway star. Tory had been an alcoholic for years and as a result her career had all but evaporated. At forty-eight she seemed pathetic, her figure gone pouchy, and worst of all, her famous flashing eyes dull and indifferent. The group also included Eleanor Taplinger, the woman who knew Clare Soloway when he was still called Sam. She wasn't exactly a celebrity, but her husband, Bill, was a big agent, so Eleanor had sort of honorary celebrity status, at least in Hollywood. Tory and Eleanor had both been around fame almost longer than Joey had been alive, and they both knew that the famous always had to remember that everything they said would be quoted for years to come. As a result, Tory and Eleanor said little in the group sessions, never criticizing the other patients. Joey couldn't keep her mouth shut.

One of their fellow patients was a streetwise junkie from San Francisco, a veteran of clinics and group-therapy sessions who had been hooked on heroin and was now addicted to methadone. He called himself Tugger and he was about Joey's age. He was slim and sinewy; there seemed to be no fat on him. He had a strong, stubbly jaw, malicious eyes, and a lot of tattoos. Tugger had needle marks on his arms, which he showed off like badges, trying to frighten the middle-class addicts who were appalled at the idea of heroin. Tugger resented the celebrities and took every opportunity in the sessions to say so. Tory said nothing and Eleanor just smiled, so he left them alone. Only Joey took the bait. In the first session, while the counselor was explaining the terms of the group therapy, Tugger was quiet. After each person was introduced, Joey made a self-dramatizing speech about how difficult and unmanageable her life had become and how much she wanted to change. She ended her speech saying, "I know I take drugs, I know I'm a drunk, and I want to stop." She put a lot of emotion into the words, more than she felt, and the others in the group were stirred. That's when Tugger made his move.

"That supposed to be your *Lost Weekend* speech or what? Everybody supposed to fall over now and kiss your Beverly Hills ass because you're so honest? Boutique bullshit," he said, almost spitting the words. "You going to disco till you get clean? Big fucking deal."

If Joey had any common sense, she would have let it pass, but no one ever accused Joey of being sensible. Tugger's words were just true enough for Joey to fight back. "What do you know about it?" she said. "You think I'm a target because you've heard of me. You're a target too, and a lot easier to hit. So don't push me, you don't want to be pushed back. I'm getting clean."

"Where'd you get that line, some television show?" He laughed derisively at her, the contempt he felt rolling out of him. "That from your hot new mini-series? That's your name from now on, Minnie Series, the dope fiend. Right, Minnie? How'd you get in this joint, anyway? O.D. on Tab?"

"You listen to me," Joey said, her voice growing quiet and dark and a little frightening. "I know your kind of low-life. Play bandido and the girls fall apart. I got news for you. It won't play with me. I think you're a two-bit hustler, a street junkie, and one of life's prize assholes. You don't interest me in any way. I wouldn't bother to piss on you if the toilets were broken. Do I make myself clear?"

Tugger had infuriated Joey; that was his victory. But she had shut him up, and that was hers. Later, Eleanor took Joey aside and explained the facts of celebrity life. "He can't control it, you know," Eleanor said, treating Joey like a daughter. "He's not so much attacking you as the idea of you."

"That guy wanted to fuck me, that's what that was all about. I know so many men like that, and they're all jerks. Big outlaw. Big deal," Joey said, getting angrier the more she thought about it.

"That's only part of it. He's angry because you're famous and he's not," Eleanor said patiently. "You have to try to understand that."

"Why?" Joey asked, with contempt and anger at Tugger in her voice. "He's a schmuck and you know it."

"Joey, a part of you is public property. You're famous, and that means people look at you like a mirror. That guy sees something he wants in you—and it's more complicated than sex. Whatever it is, he hates you for having what he doesn't."

"So what am I supposed to do?"

"You just have to take it. You have to be as nice as you can, and not fight back. My husband calls it 'passive celebrity resistance.' Try it, okay?"

"Okay," Joey said quietly, pleased to have the guidance. "Let's get Tory and have dinner. Okay?"

Eleanor smiled and put her arm around Joey. "Don't get too close to Tory. Not in here."

"Why not?" Joey asked, knowing the answer before she was told.

"She was loaded during therapy. She'll always get something to drink, somehow. I don't trust myself to be around her, and you shouldn't either."

The first week Peter tried to call Joey every evening. The clinic refused to put through his calls, repeating only that patients couldn't receive outside phone calls for the first five days. Peter tried anger, indignation, cajolery, and sweet reason, but it did no good. It made him uneasy to be so cut off from Joey, so on the sixth day he drove to Rancho Mirage to see her. He arrived about noon, hoping to have lunch with her. The clinic staff said Joey hadn't been there long enough to have visitors, but he was welcome to call. He left and phoned from a gas station and told her he was nearby and she should just come out to the lobby to meet him.

"We're not supposed to have visitors. We're supposed to form bonds with the other patients," she said, surprised to hear his voice. He was on her mind, she said, but from her tone, he suspected not very much.

"Just meet me in the lobby," he said, sounding more like Clare than he realized.

They sat in plastic chairs and sipped coffee from Styrofoam cups. She was wearing a shapeless hospital dress and there was no makeup on her face. Peter held her hand and sat close to her. He said he was proud of her and that he thought about her all the time. But she seemed distant to him and a little strange. He told her about the various scripts that were being written for her; she smiled, but it was clear that scripts were not on Joey's mind. Only when he asked her about the other patients did she light up. "Eleanor Taplinger is in here with me. Do you know her?"

"Sure," Peter said. "You two hanging out together?" He was glad to find a subject that appealed to Joey.

"She's great. We're in therapy and everything together. Then we sit up a lot and, like, talk all night. She's had a really interesting life."

"I know her husband pretty well. When you get out, we can all have dinner." The talk of life after the clinic changed Joey's mood again. Her shoulders slumped and she was quiet. Peter touched her cheek and pushed her hair back. "Joey, Joey. It must be so hard to be here." He said it as if it were a question. She didn't reply.

Later, as he was driving back through the desert to Los Angeles, he knew something had changed between them. He hoped it wasn't permanent and he tried hard to think if there was anything he should do. He was worried about her distant mood, wondering what it meant. He tried to think what Clare would do in this situation, but because he couldn't identify the problem, there was no action he could think to take. He decided to attribute Joey's remoteness to the clinic and the treatment and to put it out of his mind.

In the time Joey stayed at the clinic, she didn't take any drugs, she didn't have anything to drink, and she never wore any makeup. She never became friends with Tugger, but she did manage not to get upset when he attacked her. Just as Eleanor had suggested, when Joey relaxed, Tugger gave up and started picking on the other patients. When Eleanor's husband came to visit he wanted to give Joey a script but Eleanor said no dice, there wouldn't be any business conducted here. To Joey, that was a sign of Eleanor's true fidelity, and it assured their friendship. Eleanor was in her early fifties and had no children. She seemed to enjoy Joey without wanting anything from her, and Jocy was grateful for that. Since both of them were big drinkers and that was out of the question, conversation was their stimulant, their narcotic. Reporters had asked Joey about the story of her life so many times, and she had repeated it so often that it had become a sort of set piece that she hauled out whenever asked. Eleanor was interested in more than a recitation of how Joey had grown up on military bases until her parents were divorced. Eleanor had been divorced twice and she knew a thing or two about the problems. She didn't know Peter well, but she certainly knew Clare Soloway and she didn't approve. "You can know how your career's doing by how hard that man chases you. If he stops, look out, or change agents or something."

"Do you know Kim too?"

"Oh, sure. Clare wants a stylish wife, Kim wants a rich husband. They'll be fine as long as she gives the right kind of parties and ignores his girlfriends. As long as he brings in the money and keeps her credit cards going, she'll stick around. What a bitch."

"I don't even think I like Clare. But I just hated it that Kim could get him and I couldn't."

"When he was chasing me—and it was a long time ago—it was always dinner at this place called the Steak Pit. It was on Beverly or somewhere. He thought it was a great restaurant because he could pronounce everything. It was dark and stupid and you could always count on Sammy to grope you under the table right around the cheesecake."

"Steaks? Yuch!" Joey said. "There ought to be clinics like this for meat eaters."

"The Steak Pit specialized in guys who were cheating on their wives. Then he'd take you to a screening if you were lucky, then back to his place. He had this crummy apartment on Fountain. He always put on the same music—*Bolero* or 'Flight of the Bumble Bee,'" Eleanor said, laughing at the memory.

"Wait. I know," Joey said, getting giddy and acting out the memory, playing both parts. "Okay. You're in his house. He sits on the sofa and pats the spot next to him. 'Care for a brandy, kiddo?'" she said in a deadpan imitation of Clare's voice.

"And ninety seconds later," Eleanor added, "he'd jump you and try to get his hands in your pants. That's Sammy. Mr. Wrong," she said, laughing again. "With all his crap, women always went for him. Even before he had two dimes, you just knew he'd always get what he wanted. That was powerful."

"It still is," Joey said plaintively. "But he's still a pig," she added, starting to giggle again. "How does she stand it?"

"It's easy," Eleanor said. "Shall I instruct you?"

"Okay," Joey said, enjoying herself, quite taken with Eleanor.

"Think of the most ridiculous woman you can. Some combination of a slave and a puppy dog. Then take it farther. You know the drill: big round eyes, too much perfume, then get frilly-silly and flush your cheeks and tell him he's God. He'll do whatever you want."

"Kim does that?"

"I'd bet on it."

"How could you do that with a straight face?" Joey laughed. "It sounds like some retro how-to-seduce-a-man book."

"Right. That's what I should have done, except he bored me, so I said the hell with it. But you're a star. Different rules for you. You're a trophy, another picture for his wall. If you had really wanted him, you should have let him run your career. Then he'd be yours."

"Not a chance," Joey said. "I give my career over to that guy, I'll never see it again."

"Right! And that's why it didn't play. What you two had was secrecy and danger. Right?"

"I guess. He had the secrecy part."

"And what you got was the danger. It was okay for a while. It couldn't possibly last."

"What does he get from Kim?"

"Kim's perfect for him. I know how she operates. She's a feminist in public. At home she bats her eyes and probably wakes him up to give him head. Then apologizes for interrupting his sleep." Everything Eleanor told Joey seemed true; once Eleanor had said it, it all seemed obvious. Joey had never had an older woman friend, someone who was wiser and could give her the guidance she hadn't even known she needed. Joey didn't have any brothers or sisters and she had never been to college and her own mother was so confused as to be no help at all. So Joey told Eleanor all about Peter and their adventures in the bathroom at Spago.

"God, I was wrecked that night. It was Clare. I hated being there. Peter's nice," she said tentatively, probing for Eleanor's approval.

"I want to get to know him," Eleanor said. Hollywood men were Eleanor's favorite subject. In Joey she had found her ideal pupil, a woman sought after by men, seemingly sophisticated, but in fact sweetly naive. She was ideal for Eleanor's true vocation and art, which was counseling on the ways of love in Hollywood. "Peter's a nicer version of Clare. That's probably why he's not more successful. You be careful with that type."

"Why?"

"Peter's better than a lot of them, but if he's broken off with Clare, then he has to make it work with you or he's dead in the business."

"Should I stop seeing him?"

"No, no, darling. I can't tell you something like that. You have to stop thinking everyone knows better than you. You enjoy Peter. Is that so awful?"

"I don't know. Is it?"

"It's a young man's dream that he has. Only a bubble really, but it can be fun. You like him, and you never liked Clare."

"That's right. He cares about me. I think. Does he?"

"Joey, you just do everything headfirst and a hundred percent. I've been around Hollywood men all my life and Peter's a very specific sort. He's too smart or too literary for the business. Guys like that can get along up to a point, then all that literary knowledge gets to be baggage. He's making his move with you. He'll get you better scripts than Clare, but he'll have trouble getting them made."

"What should I do?" Joey asked, like a schoolgirl unsure of which blouse or hairstyle to wear.

"You should dry out, calm down, and remember you're the money, you're the heat, the meal ticket. As long as Peter pleases you in business, or bed, or wherever, keep him around. Otherwise it's strictly HGYC."

"What does that mean?"

"'Honey, grab your coat.'" They both started giggling at the silliness of it, getting themselves high on joking around.

Every patient agrees to stay at Rancho Mirage for a month, and Eleanor had been there for two weeks before Joey arrived, so she was ready to leave sooner. But Joey couldn't bear the idea of not having Eleanor to talk with each evening, so she decided to leave too. The counselors were disappointed and when word got around that Joey was leaving, Tugger was contemptuous but only Tory seemed upset. She didn't say anything, but as Eleanor pointed out, she rarely said anything. Tory's face sagged and she looked wounded whenever she saw Joey. It made Joey sad, but she had learned that all the clinics in California couldn't help Tory. Joey knew that if Tory could get hold of vodka in a place like this, nothing could stop her from destroying herself. Joey watched Tory disintegrate and vowed to remain clean. Once her decision to leave was made, she asked Eleanor, "Should I tell Peter, you know, call him or something?"

"If you want to. You want him to pick you up?" Eleanor asked, knowing full well Joey didn't want any such thing.

"Can't I go back with you?" Joey asked in a little girl's voice.

"Of course. You don't have to get all upset over what car you go in. It's okay."

It relieved Joey not to be separated from Eleanor and made her feel strong enough to face Los Angeles. Eleanor hugged her and smiled, and then Joey asked, "You love your husband, right? I mean, he's the right one for you to be married to and all that. And you tell him 'I love you, darling,' over the tuna fish and stuff, right?"

Eleanor laughed at Joey's idea of domestic life. "The thing is," she said thoughtfully, "I think about loving him. The idea of loving him is on my mind a lot. But I don't tell him and I don't do a whole lot to show it. It's odd and I don't understand why I'm like that. But I am."

Eleanor's husband, Bill, drove down to Rancho Mirage and picked them up. Joey had decided not to call Peter and tell him what she had done. It left her feeling shaky and uncertain. Eleanor had given Bill orders not to hustle Joey in any way, just to drive them back to Los Angeles. On the way he told them all the recent

Hollywood gossip. Who had been fired from what job, which couples were fighting, and which pictures were hits and which weren't. Joey listened to it all and she seemed fine, but when they got to Benedict Canyon, she was unable to get out of the car. "It looks so clammy," she said of her house. "Maybe I should go to a hotel."

"You just come home with us for a few days," Eleanor said. "See Peter if you want, or not if you don't. You can stay in the guest cottage."

"Okay," Joey said, relieved that Eleanor's kindness didn't stop now that they were back in what Bill called the reel world. Eleanor's interest, which seemed to have no motive other than friendship, moved Joey; she was glad she didn't have to face her empty house.

Bill, who had long ago learned to accept his wife, said, "I won't give you any scripts unless you ask, but I intend to let it drop all over town that you're staying with us."

The next day, when Peter was told that Joey had checked out of the clinic, he had visions of her drunk or stoned and lost in the desert. He drove back to Rancho Mirage, determined not to leave the clinic until he was satisfied he knew where she was. At first the clinic staff wouldn't give him any information at all, but when he threatened legal action, the clinic's chief administrator agreed to talk with him. The administrator was conciliatory and explained that Joey had checked out voluntarily and had left with Mr. and Mrs. Taplinger. The administrator, who was really very nice, explained that the experience of the clinic was sometimes difficult to absorb. He was sorry Joey had chosen to leave early and he hoped Peter might influence her to return. Peter thanked him and left to make the two-hour trip back to Los Angeles. He felt scared and shaky all the way home.

The day after that he read in *Variety* that Joey was staying at Eleanor and Bill's and that she had given up her old ways. He called several times, but she was out and there was no message for him. He tried Bill at his office, but was told Mr. Taplinger was in a meeting and would have to call him back. Peter drove over to the Taplingers' house, but the Mexican maid who answered the door said Mr. Taplinger was at work and Mrs. Taplinger was at lunch. Peter assumed she was at lunch with Joey. He considered making the rounds of the Bistro, Ma Maison, La Toque, Le Dôme, and Trumps in the hope of running into them, but the thought of seeing Joey for the first time since the hospital in a restaurant seemed ridiculous to him. Instead he left messages and waited for her to call. He was determined to stay sane through this, at least in public. At night he had trouble sleeping and his wrists and ankles ached. He recognized the symptoms as the first signs of depression. The following day another column said Joey had decided not to marry Peter but that he would always be her best friend. Since they had never discussed marriage, the interview baffled him all the more. It seemed loony even by the standards of show-business gossip columns. On the third day Joey called and explained that she was going to build a new life, and as good as he had been to her in so many ways, he was part of her old life. She told him that Eleanor had advised her to say the stuff about marriage and being best friends to the press, so that their breakup wouldn't hurt Peter's business.

"The business is the least of it," he said, trying to mean it. But in his heart he was afraid of what the studio would do if he was perceived as being without Joey Chakara. "Can't I see you? I miss you. I've been scared, I have to read the papers to find out where you are."

"I'm sorry. I've been through a lot down there. I have to have some breathing space."

"What the hell does that mean?" he said, refusing to understand what she meant.

"Eleanor says—"

"Eleanor?" Peter said, interrupting her. "Is she the bad guy in this?"

"No. She told me how it's important for the studio to know I still want to make all the movies we talked about. I'm going to do it. Eleanor'll tell me what to say. I can't help it if it hurts you in some ways, but I can try to make it okay with the business part. Okay?"

"Can't I even see you?" he said.

"In a while. Pretty ridiculous, me helping you in business. Good-bye, Peter." And she hung up.

He was relieved that she planned to help him with the studio, but Peter still felt crushed. He had grown dependent on Joey. Not just for the business advantage she provided, but for the constant, intense, out-of-control lovemaking. It might have been contrived at first, but there had been so much of it, for so long, that it was painful for him to be without it. Sex of that sort is a drug as much as cocaine or vodka, and for it to be gone so suddenly depressed Peter and gave him withdrawal symptoms. He grew edgy and more insecure than he had been with Clare. His insomnia got worse and he was convinced he had an ulcer.

He had prepared for a business disaster, which, thanks to Joey or Eleanor, never came. What he got was an emotional calamity and a heartache more intense than any he had ever felt. He felt empty and very lost and he longed to understand why he continued to feel so bereft. He looked for clues or signs in everything, and insight finally came to him while he was sitting in his car at Melrose and Fairfax waiting for the light to change. On the corner, near Fairfax High School, he saw a group he took to be Russian Jews in a heated discussion. They looked like animated fireplugs, waving their arms, trying to sort out some problem. Some of them seemed to speak English, others not. One man was translating for everyone. Only he could keep track of both sides. The others were too involved in the dispute to notice, but Peter could see that the translator looked pleased and content to be of service. He was in the fight but out of it; nothing could proceed without him. In that instant a wave of clarity washed over Peter. It had pleased him that Joey could hardly tie her shoes or fall asleep unless he was there. He had liked it that Clare couldn't read a script or judge a writer without him. At first Peter thought: I'm grieving because no one needs me. But if that's all it is, I should just get a puppy dog. It was like seeing white light as he realized: I always have to be needed by people who are more successful than I am. They have to be dependent on me and I attach myself to them like a barnacle. If they succeed, I do too. But if they fail, I can still stand outside. The truth of it made him tremble, and by the time the light changed, Peter had a new sense of what the true hole in his life was. He might feel superior to Clare, but Clare put himself on the line all the time and Peter was afraid to risk himself. He was determined to change. He still missed Joey, but now he knew his depression would lift.

True to her word, Joey assured the studio that even though she and Peter had changed their personal lives she still wanted to do all the pictures they had in development. The head of production was a little nervous at the new arrangement, but Peter pointed out that the studio had already invested so much money in Lost Illusions that it would be senseless to pull the plug based on an actress's mood change. Peter was as convincing as Clare would have been in the situation, and the studio allowed the production arrangement to continue. He threw himself back into his work again, determined to make a success of his company. He knew he would be okay by the way he reacted to the news of Joey's new romance. According to the columns, she was involved with an actor. The guy was close to Joey's age and very handsome. It hurt Peter and caused him pain in private, but in public he was able to shrug it off. As a result of the romance, Peter had become a public figure in Hollywood; people were watching to see what he would do next. He made a point of appearing at screenings and parties in the company of beautiful or interesting women. He didn't care to be involved with any of them, but the presence on his arm of so many different women made Peter the subject of gossip again. Peter knew that the new self-assurance he exhibited was his real capital and he had Joey to thank for that. Then Clare started calling again. "It's all nuts around here since you jumped ship," Clare said. "I keep hiring people to take care of the scripts. I've gone through two of them already. Some Vassar girl who redecorated your office twice in one month. Painted walls and lectured me on material. I kicked her ass right out of here."

Peter laughed, glad to hear Clare's voice again. "Who else?" he asked.

"Then there was this guy who got fired from Fox. First day, he's patting all the secretaries; second day, he asks for a raise. He didn't have a third day."

"I see the whole thing. You probably terrorized them both."

"So how's your business? I hear you got a lot of scripts and no pictures."

"My company's in pretty good shape. Why not? Look who my teacher was."

"Me! I was your teacher."

"That's right. You were."

"Let's get together, Peter. Have some lunch. I want to talk to you."

They met at Ma Maison, where Peter brought Clare up-to-date on what had happened. He spoke truthfully, feeling no need to embroider the facts or make himself appear better or wiser than he had been. Through it all Clare nodded approvingly at the way Peter had handled everything. Then Clare proposed that they start working together again. Peter started to say no, but Clare stopped him.

"I'm talking about a partnership. It's crazy to break up what we had. Together we're greater than two times what we are separately," Clare said, stumbling over the words.

"Greater than the sum of the parts, is what you mean," Peter said, without worrying about correcting Clare.

"I'm offering you half my business here." It was certainly an attractive deal and Clare was admitting he couldn't manage without him. For an instant, Clare's face looked twisted and a little ragged. Probably just can't bear the thought of giving up equity, Peter thought. Or maybe it's more. Everyone is in pain, and that's the truth. "We'll be equals," Clare said. "Because that's what we are."

"What about Joey?"

"What about her?" Clare said, unable to say her name.

"How do you feel about that? All that's happened?"

"Hey," he said with more bravado than Peter believed he felt, "if I couldn't work with my exes, I'd be totally out of business. You know what I mean?"

"Right. But that's not exactly what I mean. I took her from you, Clare. I stole her away. You have to resent me for that." As he said it, Peter knew that before Joey he could never have been so blunt with Clare. Peter also knew he had touched the only nerve that counted in this negotiation. Clare was quiet for a long moment as he considered his answer.

"I'm over that," he said finally. "I can make my peace with it if you can." Peter thought he saw a trace of what he took to be self-doubt flicker across Clare's face. "So what do you say, partner?"

"Split all the fees and the profits?" Peter asked.

"Absolutely. We'll merge the companies. We'll own the town inside of a year. Come on, Peter. Nobody says no to that." As Peter was savoring the offer, considering if he should say yes right now or give it a little more thought, Eleanor Taplinger stopped at their table.

"Well, here are two men I know a thing or two about." They both rose and Clare kissed Eleanor on the cheek. Peter shook her hand and smiled. "Sam, this is an extraordinary young man here. I have it on the highest authority."

"I taught him how," Clare said.

"You'll excuse me if I stare at your ears, Eleanor," Peter said, knowing that if ever he needed his charm, it was now. "But I can't help wondering what they've heard lately."

"Oh, that's how it is, is it?" she said, laughing. "He didn't learn that from you, Sammy. I can see why she went for you."

"How is she?" Peter asked, managing to sound sincerely interested but not heartbroken.

"She's Joey," Eleanor said with an airy wave of her hand. "You were good for her, Peter. If you don't know that, I'm telling you now."

"I think I'm the one who benefited. I really do."

Eleanor studied his face, perhaps looking for a sign of weakness. Peter's instinct told him that if anyone in Hollywood knew his secret fears about standing alone, it was Eleanor. He offered only his mask of self-assurance. Finally, seeing no weakness, she said, "Now, see here, Peter, I can imagine what you're doing these days. You work your head off, then you either pretend to go out and have a good time or you go home to be miserable. Don't deny it and don't be ashamed of it. I want you to come to dinner. By yourself. There are some people you should meet."

"You mean Joey?" Clare asked. "That's all over."

"No, no, Sammy. Don't be thick. Of course it's over," she said in a dismissive voice. "But there are other women, you know."

Eleanor took Peter's hand as if she were going to shake it. But instead she held onto it for a moment, inspecting it like a buyer who has found what she's looking for. "I'll call you. I'll organize an evening." She turned back to Clare and asked, "How's the delicious Kimberly?"

"Kim is great. Absolutely top of the line," Clare said, recovering his bearings.

"That's good, Sammy. I'm glad to hear it." Then Eleanor, the broker of romance, turned to Peter, gave him a private conspiratorial wink, and then moved away, disappearing back into the tables of Ma Maison while Peter and Clare made plans for the future.

Under the Sun

As we bounced out of Abidjan in a banged-up Mercedes, the driver, a secret Ghanaian called Kofi, was practicing his English, repeating, "Pretty soon the Xerox machine is fixed. . . . No problem, okay, okay. . . ." He was secret because we were in the Ivory Coast and the movie company had agreed to hire only Ivorians, but Kofi had the job because the Ghanaians were better drivers. He was a big, solid-looking man with tribal scars, three slanting lines carved into his cheeks. He had two wives and a lot of kids back in Ghana, so driving the movie company around was important to him. He was taking me out to look at a fishing village on the Sengha River that was to be a location in the film. About an hour and a half out of Abidjan, driving along the coast, we passed through Grand Bassam, the deserted colonial capital of the Côte d'Ivoire. "No one home," Kofi said. "Shall you see with your eyes?"

I wandered in and out of decaying French colonial houses with crumbling verandas, all empty except for the lizards and the rats that ate them. The town had been like this since 1899, when an epidemic of yellow fever killed everyone who didn't run away. A few black children played in the dusty street and sat beneath filao trees that were at least as old as yellow fever. The beaches were pleasant for seaside lunches, but the town just sat, purposeless and ghostly. There was a bit of public sculpture of the *Winged*

Victory style still standing. It had been painted in delicate pastels that had faded long ago.

I had come to work on a picture about the discovery of some dinosaurs alive in modern Africa. It was to start shooting in a month and I was here to try to polish the script. I had taken the Concorde to Paris and the next day a milk run to Abidjan, which included a two-hour layover in Ouagadougou. As the plane set down, I saw the airstrip was lined with the rusting hulks of planes that hadn't made it. I intended to get out and walk around, just to stretch my legs, but the pilot announced leaving the plane wasn't permitted. There were soldiers with machine guns on the tarmac. There had been a coup. The government had fallen. The pilot thought better of the layover. We had arrived in Upper Volta and we were leaving what was soon to be Burkina Faso. The soldiers were firing their weapons into the air and laughing as the plane took off.

That was a week ago. Now Kofi was asking had I seen enough of Grand Bassam. I nodded yes, but it occurred to me a man could spend a lifetime seeing Grand Bassam and still not understand it. It took Kofi another hour to reach the unmarked road that went inland to the village. A few hundred yards in, there was a path of sorts. Although the stroll didn't require machetes, I couldn't get Stewart Granger in *King Solomon's Mines* out of my thoughts. The village consisted of a dozen mud-tin-and-palm-frond huts spread along the river. The movie staff was already there. An Ivorian named Marcel who spoke French, English, and several tribal languages was the translator. He had lived in Paris for a while and worked on French movies there. We were glad to have him, since in addition to translating he had a sense of what was needed. He was about forty, tense and excitable, very small, compact really, with well-articulated features. He had shining black skin that seemed to give off light rather than absorb it.

The village chief thought we wanted to buy the place. He wasn't opposed if the price was right, but he couldn't understand what we would do with it. The chief, a gentle man who looked to be about fifty, was only vaguely aware that Abidjan, a city of one million, was two hours away. He and his people, sixty or so souls, all of whom the chief considered his immediate family, went where their feet or their fishing pirogues would take them. The river was the center of their lives. They ate from it, bathed and defecated in it, honored and feared it. The villagers had a good sense of money and commerce, because they sometimes walked eight miles to a public market where they sold or bartered fish. There were odd bits of Western paraphernalia around the village—a broken umbrella, pieces of string, a few tires, polyester shorts, T-shirts, and some commercially made sandals. One of the movie staff gave a little girl an American nickel. The adults knew it was money, but no more. They touched it and passed it around.

Marcel explained we would make a few alterations to the huts and we would like some of the villagers to appear in the movie, for which there would be additional pay. When the chief was satisfied with the terms, we sat in a circle on the riverbank to seal our bargain with a bottle of rum. Marcel drank first and then passed the bottle around the circle. The director had a drink, then the producer, the art director, and I had a drink. I handed the chief the bottle and he drank. Then he poured some rum into the river, so the river could have a drink.

That evening I was sitting in the hotel bar wondering how I was going to get this script written before the actors arrived, when Marcel turned up and asked if he could join me. "My pleasure," I said. "Let me buy you a drink."

"Are you enjoying our country?" he asked, and began eating the olives that were on the table. "Perhaps here and there it feels like France to you? Yes? But not Paris. No." When he had gone through my plate of olives, he reached over to the next table and started on somebody else's. "Do you live in Hollywood? It is my hope to go there."

"Maybe you will."

"When I lived in Paris it was easier to find work. But still . . ." He lifted his hand slightly in a little Gallic shrug and lit a Gauloise. His English was good, with a French accent, and to my ear without much sign of his native Baoule. He wore narrow-cut French trousers and an unvented jacket. They were a little threadbare, but I assumed it was because Marcel was as broke as everyone else in the country. The clothes were enough to set him apart from other Africans, even the Westernized ones. "You have been to Paris of course," he said, with something like suspicion in his voice.

"Yes. I was there a week ago, on my way here."

"I lived there once and I will go back when it can be arranged. I would stay in Paris always, and happily, too, but there was some confusion in legal matters. I assure you I stand guiltless, but I was accused of not paying the proper taxes. It was best to return temporarily. But Paris is my true and spiritual home. I have many friends there. In the cinema. Perhaps you know Monsieur Navelle. Didier Navelle?"

"I don't. I'm sorry."

"Didier is the *premier régisseur,* well, I mean to say, the *directeur de production.* In Hollywood you say 'production manager.' If you have worked in Paris in films you would know him," he said, his voice rising.

"I haven't worked in Paris," I said, and then added, "But I'm sure everyone who has knows him."

"I would think so. Many foreign directors, Americans particularly, will not work in Paris unless Didier is also engaged. It is a matter of contract. Cyril will attest to this. He is of course aware of Didier, although they have never met." Cyril was the production manager on the picture. Production managers are important figures on film sets, but they're like noncommissioned officers—master sergeants in the army or stage managers in the theater—tough and practical, but not usually confused with the gods. "Didier was born in Algiers," Marcel continued, about to tell me more about his friend than I wanted to know. "He grew up in Paris, in Belleville. He lives in Montparnasse, near the Boulevard Raspail. I have been there many times. I can show you the address sometime. I miss the restaurants. Didier knows them all. He is fond of L'Ami Louis in the Marais. Do you know it?"

"I do," I said, thinking it a victory to get in a word. "I remember the foie gras."

"But you have never lived in Paris?"

"No."

"So we are even," he said. "I have never lived in Hollywood." Then he signaled to the waiter for another plate of olives.

In the days that followed, the staff was busy with the problems of building the dinosaurs. Most of it was supposed to have been done in Hollywood, but there were so many problems that it consumed everyone's time. That gave me an opportunity to get started on the script. I was too busy drafting scenes and trying to find an English-speaking typist to think much about Marcel.

He would come around to my office in the hotel from time to time to say hello and ask how the revisions were coming. "Writers are everything," he said. "In Paris they are held in the highest regard. You must know that many American writers have lived in Paris. Hemingway, Fitzgerald . . . James Baldwin lives there now. Didier and I have often commented on that. We revere writers."

"Well, I'm just trying to make sense out of these scenes—it's not exactly writing the great expatriate novel."

"Oh, no," he said, rushing to the defense of my trade. "You are too hard on yourself. Didier often says, without writers there would be no scripts and no movies."

"I've heard that mentioned—usually from writers. Whatever it is, or isn't, it's hard to do, so if you'll excuse me . . ."

"Yes, yes. I don't mean to interrupt you. The writer on a film I worked on in Paris told me about the man who knocked on Coleridge's door—"

"Maybe we could talk later. It's not Coleridge's door," I said, pointing, "but please close it as you go." He left, glad to have had any conversation at all. Marcel wanted to be around Westerners, particularly me, so badly he could be oppressive. I resolved not to let him consume my time.

When the company needed extras for the film, it was Marcel's responsibility to assemble some Africans and see that Polaroid snaps were taken, so the director could look at faces. Marcel insisted on calling this "the auditions." He hired a rickety frame building near the Treichville market, where the local economy thrives. The film company was paying a few dollars a day to those selected. Many of the unemployed hanging around Treichville were from the bush, men who had come to the city to find work and had found only grief. They had no city skills and their days were spent in a hazy stupor, scavenging for food. The possibility of jobs was like an electric charge rushing through them. Security guards, off-duty policemen in military uniforms, were in place to ensure order. I went along at the last minute, more to see Treichville than anything else.

Two earnest young Brits, Brian and Rosemary, had been charged with taking the photos, a task they took very seriously. Neither of them had ever been out of the U.K. before. I sat with them on the second floor in a large room, bare except for a wooden table and a few uncomfortable chairs. Brian had never used a Polaroid camera and he insisted on taking several trial shots of Rosemary, who smiled sweetly for him. We were accompanied by a frail-looking security guard called Moussa who wore a baggy military uniform. On the street below, a large crowd of would-be movie extras waited patiently in the sun. Through the window I could see Marcel in action, moving through the crowd like a duke greeting his serfs. Before the applicants could enter the building they had to get a number from Marcel and wait while he enscribed their names in a ledger. Marcel held the numbers close, glancing imperiously at his supplicants, accepting some, dismissing others.

When Marcel gave them the word, they climbed the narrow staircase, a few at a time, uncertain of where they were going, but each one expecting to find a job at the top of the stairs. They entered our room and held out their numbered cards like offerings. Rosemary greeted each one with a cheery English hello, as if they had come for tea, while Brian snapped their pictures. Then Moussa, the guard, sent them back down to the street. Each one took about thirty seconds.

The crowd on the street was getting larger and I could sense an undercurrent of dissatisfaction as the would-be extras came back down, still jobless. Marcel had placed so much importance on the numbers that the crowd assumed getting a number meant getting a job. Some of them were holding up scraps of paper as if that alone might get them employment and feed their children. They could see that wasn't the case, but they pressed forward anyway, trying to get numbers.

From my second-floor perch, where I was sipping a warm Coke, I watched the guards stalk back and forth, getting edgier as the crowd grew. It's hard to say exactly when the crowd became a mob—but it was easy enough to see once it happened. People just suddenly surged forward, trying to get inside the building, trampling those in front. The small and the weak fell away as two dozen or so of the large and strong pushed into the building. The guards ran off when they couldn't stop them.

On the second floor, Moussa was jabbering in a combination of French and what I think was Dioula. He shoved Brian and Rosemary's table against the door and bolted it shut. The mob was trying to squeeze up the narrow staircase. It made the walls of the room bulge and the floor vibrate. Brian tried to comfort Rosemary, but she was very frightened. My thought was to give them all numbers and try to get the hell out. Then there was a rap at the window behind us. It was Marcel, with a ladder, asking Moussa to open the window. As we climbed down, I could see soldiers arriving, truncheons out. They began beating everyone. Men and women collapsed on one another and children screamed from underfoot. The soldiers stomped the bodies and beat anyone still standing. They used a simple standard. If you were white, they protected you, if you were black, they bashed you on the head. The clarity of that rule separated Marcel from the rest of us. What was left of the crowd saw him before I did. They chased him into the street, shouting and laughing in a high-pitched, dry cackle.

Kofi had brought the car around to the back to get us out and when he saw what was happening to Marcel, he said, "They will kill him." I didn't think he was exaggerating for dramatic effect.

"Can you get to him?"

Kofi didn't answer, but swung the Mercedes around, about to chase into the crowd. If I had been less scared, I might have had the sense to stay put, but it was clear Marcel was going to die because he had acted the martinet in service of the damn movie. Anyway, I got into the car, which surprised Kofi, and off we went. I don't know if Kofi had ever seen car-chase movies, but God knows I had written scenes like this enough times. The hell of it was, the cine versions of what I now found myself doing were pretty accurate. Kofi just stepped on the gas and didn't hesitate when people were in his way. They scattered, and we got to Marcel just after the mob. Two guys had grabbed him and they were pushing him back and forth, poking him with sticks. I could see their eyes. Kofi was right. They were going to kill him, but they were going to do it slowly and make it last. Kofi braked and spun into the mob. I heard the dull thud of someone being hit by the car's back end. As we skidded, I opened the door and yelled, "Marcel!" He glanced up as I reached out. He took my arm and I yanked him into the car. I tried to see if we had actually hit anyone. If we had, he was still upright, and under the circumstances, that was good enough for me. Kofi came about again and drove away.

In the car, Marcel was trembling and breathing hard. Kofi found it amusing and laughed at his predicament, now that it was solved. Marcel tried to thank me, but the terror was still on his face and he had trouble speaking. Afterward, Rosemary, who had witnessed it all, was so upset that she found it difficult to leave the hotel. She had trouble sleeping and was often in tears, until she decided she'd had enough of Africa and went back to London. It broke Brian's heart.

After the incident in Treichville, Marcel seemed to turn up everywhere I was, almost clinging to me. "You have saved my life. I owe my life to you," he said the next day in the production office as I was trying to get the photocopying machine to work.

"Kofi saved you, not me. Be grateful to him." But Marcel had no intention of being in debt to someone less powerful than he was, so he attached himself to me, murmuring, "I am in your debt." In the mornings he'd be in the restaurant waiting for me to come down for breakfast. If I was going out to look at locations, he followed behind, like a mascot. "Don't be so bloody polite to him," Cyril said. "It only encourages him. Tell him to bugger off." I couldn't quite manage that, but I did tell him my work and my temperament required privacy. Marcel nodded yes, of course. He apologized and backed away. Then an hour or two later he was back, asking if I needed anything.

After the casting calamities, Cyril, who was more of an adventurer than a liberal, declared Marcel a fool and made him the company goat. He had liked Marcel well enough at first, but Cyril had a very low tolerance for any talk about Paris. Even before Treichville, about the third time Marcel mentioned Didier, Cyril had snapped, "If you say that name one more time, you're sacked. I'd sooner learn Senoufou myself then hear about you and bloody Paris." Taking their cue from Cyril, the rest of the staff decided Marcel was faintly ridiculous. Some of them began imitating the exaggerated way he smoked his Gauloise. They held a cigarette between thumb and forefinger, wrist up, and asked for a light in a thick French accent. Sometimes they let the cigarette droop from their lips and pretended to be Belmondo imitating Bogart in *Breathless*. They would say, "Bo-geee. Dew yew know Dee-dee-yay?"

Marcel was most successful at finding unusual locations. He knew the countryside and he could improvise because he had a sense of what the movie was supposed to be. He was proud of a mined-out quarry he had secured. It was deserted, and the company was able to convert it to the archaeological-dig site the picture required. Finding the quarry and hiring laborers to build the set had helped Marcel recoup from the casting debacle in Treichville. The laborers had spent weeks digging all day in the heat. Marcel controlled their jobs, and therefore their lives, so they treated him with deference. Marcel reveled in the power, strutting among them like a tropical floorwalker.

The first scene to be shot at the quarry was in a tent. In the course of the scene, one of the characters looked out the window, and because this was meant to be a dig site, there had to be digging in the background. Extras who could handle shovels were needed.

"Why not just use the laborers?" Marcel asked. "They can continue to work with their shovels, which we know they can do, and the scene will be complete." Even Cyril said it was a good idea.

The laborers, now promoted to extras, were a few hundred

yards away from the camera, which was in the tent, focused on the principal actors. Marcel had been given a megaphone so he could speak to his men and give them their instructions. The megaphone was his badge of office and he carried it everywhere, testing it in various languages, rehearsing his extras. These men had been digging all day for the last few weeks, but now Marcel was telling them to stop and start, or move here and there, all according to the needs of an unseen camera. They were to dig only when film was rolling, or too much dirt would pile up and the shots wouldn't match. Marcel instructed them to either pretend to dig or actually dig, depending on conditions inside the tent. It would have confused anyone and the laborers didn't know what a camera was anyway. Marcel was very careful and he got every detail right. Even Cyril had to acknowledge Marcel's success. Marcel was so happy that his laborers had succeeded that he called to them through his megaphone to tell them they had done well. It pleased the laborers but it ruined the take inside the tent, where the action hadn't stopped, only moved away from the window. Cyril roared out, ready to throttle Marcel, who was unaware of what he had done. He smiled and reached for Cyril's hand. "Is it a wrap?" Marcel asked. "Shall I dismiss the men?"

"Do you think the whole bloody picture is about background extras with shovels?" Cyril snapped. "You're no better than they are, and a whole lot noisier to boot." He took the megaphone away and went back into the tent. Marcel looked stricken. To have been called no better than his laborers was a harsh judgment.

To please the Brits on the crew an English caterer had been hired to prepare meals at the quarry. Who ate what quickly became a cultural problem. Marcel said it was out of the question to offer shepherd's pie or cheese and yogurt to the African laborers. "It is not only a question of palate," he said. "It will confuse them and make them afraid." They had to be fed, so it fell to Marcel to hire local women to cook. They were called Mamas, who, despite the name, were young and attractively dressed in brightly colored fabrics. They arrived carrying caldrons on their heads, lit fires on the ground, and made a yam-and-millet stew. Their customers squatted in the sun and ate with their fingers, while the rest of us sat shaded, under canopies, and ate our English dinners.

Marcel trotted along next to me as I walked toward the tables. One of the Mamas approached and tried to give Marcel some of her stew, wrapped in a palm frond. She looked about twenty-five, with high cheekbones and the perfect posture that came from carrying caldrons on her head. Eating this food was the last thing Marcel wanted, and he snapped at her in Dioula, telling her to go away.

"What's it taste like?" I asked.

"It's not for you," he said, putting himself between the Mama and me. "You wouldn't like it." I smiled at her and gestured toward the palm fronds. "No, no," Marcel said, alarmed. "You mustn't. Even my stomach can't hold it."

Cyril noticed what I was contemplating and hurried over. "No you don't," he said. "Not till the script's done and you're on your own time."

"I told him," Marcel said, getting excited and unwittingly breaking into French. *"Ça va vous foutre en l'air,"* he said, hopping about like a little boy who needed a bathroom. "Please, please, this is not for you. We'll have a proper luncheon together, at the tables."

"That's right, mate," Cyril said, locked in an unlikely alliance with Marcel to protect my bowels. I dipped a finger into the stew anyway. It tasted like yam-flavored stones. I didn't keel over or break out in a rash. I nodded to the Mama and said, "Very nice, thank you."

"Bloody fools on this picture, every one of you. It's the sun that does it," Cyril muttered as he walked away.

For three days the company was in Treichville, in and around the market, shooting scenes I had worked on. I was there to make last-minute adjustments, extending or trimming dialogue to fit the time it took an actor to walk from place to place or adapting a speech to reflect the actual conditions in the market. The crew set up lights; the actors stayed hidden in their trailers and I wandered through the vast market. The goods ranged from monkey and bat and other local food to unmarked pills heaped in little piles and sold by color—blue, white, and yellow. Some looked like aspirin, others might have been Valium. There was no way to know for sure. Ahead of me was a group of touring American blacks from

Chicago. They were staying at the hotel and I had spoken with one of them, a schoolteacher. He was a thoughtful, reflective man and he and his friends had come to Abidjan to see and show their kids a black culture. What they saw were thousands of displaced persons trying to live in a city that was theirs in name only.

The American movie technicians greeted the tourists, exchanged hometowns, and made well-met-far-from-home small talk. As I waved across the stalls to my acquaintance, one of the children with him stopped in front of a bowl of bats. She was about nine, and when she realized the bats were somebody's lunch, she couldn't stop yelling, "Yuck-eee!" My friend the teacher waved to me and smiled, but the look in his eye said: There's far less difference between you and me than between me and all these people. He didn't look pleased with the knowledge.

Later that morning we were working outside the market. There were a dozen trucks and about sixty people, white faces every one, bustling about, tying up the streets, and creating traffic problems. No one ever accused the Ivorians of being careful drivers, and accidents were common. But today, because we were so near the market, the crowd that had gathered to watch was quite large and there was a serious accident. A driver had apparently been watching the movie crew and not the road. He struck a woman pedestrian and she was killed. The driver, a Nigerian, deserted his car and ran off. He was caught and taken to jail, but it was little comfort to the woman's family. No one held the movie company directly responsible, but the Americans felt that if they hadn't been there, the woman might well be alive. They took up a collection to pay for a funeral. When Marcel heard about the plan, he said, "You mustn't do such a thing. It's wrong. It has nothing to do with you." But the Americans were determined to do what they knew was right. They gave the woman's husband what amounted to two hundred American dollars. "He has never seen so much money. It will be on your head," Marcel said, causing the others to add "heartless" to their descriptions of him.

The next morning the company was back at the market, and another large crowd had gathered to watch. Marcel was busy translating orders and explanations from English to French or Ebrie or Senoufou. He was essential at times like this, and that made him happy, despite his misgivings about American charity. I came by in the late morning to watch the scene, but had to wait. All movie sets are similar: a lot of people waiting for something to happen. Since that is a familiar feature of African life, the crowds that gathered seemed content.

I was trying to decide if I should stick around when I heard Marcel's voice above the crowd. He was arguing with a tall, smiling African who was pushing a plump woman in an exquisitely draped African dress at him. I took her to be the tall man's wife. Marcel was yelling in Dioula while the woman just stood there, apparently the pawn in the dispute. They argued until Cyril noticed the fuss and said, "Cool it, Marcel, don't make trouble." When the tall man saw Cyril, a white official of the movie company, he smiled, bowed low, and then shoved the plump woman into the traffic. She barely resisted and a tiny Citroën 2CV hit her. The car was going too slowly to hurt her but it frightened the driver, a middle-aged Ivorian. The woman just sat down in the street, making the rest of the cars go around her. She remained expressionless.

"Good God Almighty," Cyril said, realizing the situation before I did. "Tell him there's no money in it, no matter what. Tell him quick!" Marcel tried, but the man wasn't convinced. He shouted at Marcel and walked into the street and slapped his wife. "What did the bloody fool say?" Cyril asked.

"He asks if he must get a car and run her down himself. Also he says that he will use the money well."

"I am a doomed man," Cyril said, sounding serious, but suppressing a grin. Cyril didn't joke much, but I guess the gallows humor of the situation appealed to him. Or maybe it was just that the pressures of location shooting, which is like fighting a war every day, needed a release. He spoke into his walkie-talkie, calling to his assistants in the market, asking for help. The crowd looked on with no more or less interest than when they had watched the actors or the lighting crew. They had the glazed look of American children who have watched too much television.

Then a man in a fancy dashiki with two wives in tow pushed his way through the crowd toward Cyril. When the man thought he had Cyril's attention, he started beating one of the women. She tried to run away, but the second wife held her. The husband knocked down both women and pushed the first into the street. As Cyril, Marcel, and I were trying to stop the cars, a third man emerged from the crowd, dragging his reluctant wife with him. "I told you, I told you," Marcel kept repeating.

"Tell them there's no money for them," Cyril said, shoving one of the women back at the man with two wives.

"That's the wrong husband!" Marcel shouted. "She goes to him," he said, pointing to the tall man.

"They can sort it out themselves," Cyril snapped back. The husbands were arguing, I believe, over who had the right to throw which woman into traffic. It looked to me as if the three husbands were trying to cut a deal to divide the money they were sure they were going to get.

The deputies came running from the market and halted traffic while Cyril told Marcel to explain very clearly that no one would get any money. They would all be arrested. They would go to prison and their families would starve. Marcel shouted at them, and after a few moments of argument, the men collected their wives and left. In seconds the crowd had forgotten them and turned back to watch the electricians try to start their portable generator.

As Marcel and I were being driven back to the hotel from a morning location, we sped past the usual array of women on the side of the road, walking for miles with babies strapped to their backs and bowls of water or bundles of wood on their heads. "What do you think goes through their heads when they see a car drive by? What do they think?" I asked.

"Nothing. Nothing. They think nothing. Does a cow think, or a camel?"

"Oh, come on, Marcel. You wouldn't say that about a Frenchwoman."

"No Frenchwoman, not the stupidest peasant, would walk miles for water and bring back so little." His contempt for the women at the side of the road was great. "They know nothing. They have only anatomical similarities to Frenchwomen."

"Marcel," I said, trying to choose my words carefully, "you're aware of feminism, of the changes women have demanded and gotten—"

"In Europe. In America," he said, cutting me off, one of the few times he had interrupted or taken serious issue with something I said. "It is not the same at all. They have certain tasks to perform."

"You've lived abroad. You speak many languages. You know it could be made better for them."

"Do you think it's different for the men?" he asked bitterly.

"I don't know. Is it?"

"Look there," he said, pointing to a few huts near the side of the road. "They have a well. It was put in last year by the government. Sometimes a child falls in it. That's all. The men can't learn to cover it and the women can't learn to use it. The children drown, the men look away, and the women walk to the river because they always have."

"But surely they can learn," I said, thinking I was sounding like Candide.

"Only with the luxury of money," he said, with vicious contempt in his voice. "In the villages there is none. That is more important than all the ideas about women and men."

"I'm trying to understand it."

"You cannot. It doesn't matter how much you want to. Your eyes will not allow you to see what is simply true. They have no other possibilities. None. Even the idea of change is not in them. In Europe the poorest have at least the hope of hope." He spoke with such intensity that he could only be talking about his own life and not about the people at the side of the road.

"I hope you're wrong," I said, fearing he wasn't.

"What happens every day will be painful for you to even hear. The truth will make you shudder." I must have looked doubtful, and perhaps that was a challenge to Marcel. He spoke quietly, without apparent emotion. "In all these villages," he said, sweeping his arm across the countryside we were passing, "in girl children the clitoris is cut out, sometimes at birth, sometimes later. But it is always snipped away." He watched me closely as I shuddered. Then he said, "When I return to Paris, it won't matter. Didier is trying to arrange it. Paris is life."

"When was it you lived in Paris?" I asked, regretting the question instantly.

"Nine years ago, this month."

We rode the rest of the way to the hotel in silence.

Ivorian army helicopters were to fly the dinosaurs to the jungle location. The idea was to suspend them from slings for the hour flight over the city, out past the mud-hut villages and into the bush. The male was seventy-five feet long and the female sixty feet. There were articles in *Fraternitè-Matin,* the local paper, about all this, so the city people turned out to watch. Children had been let out of school and offices and shops closed so workers might see dinosaurs over Africa.

At the airport, the latex beasts were on the tarmac next to helicopters marked "Côte d'Ivoire Militaire." The pilots, two solemn Ivorian army officers, looked over their cargo, poking at the rubbery skin. Buddy, the chief American technician, grinned an open Midwestern grin and told the pilots, "Drive careful. You got Mom and Dad there." The pilots spoke no English and Buddy spoke no French. One of the pilots touched the pistol at his hip, a reflexive gesture. He said nothing.

I had come out to the airport to watch, and as always, Marcel was behind me. "What do you think they'll make of flying dinosaurs out in the bush?" I asked, imagining that the whole business could give animism one hell of a boost. Marcel shrugged in his exaggerated Gallic way, as if to say: Who knows? The operation was taking longer than predicted and it was hot and dusty at the airport, so I decided to go back to the hotel in the hope the air conditioning was working.

On the way into the city, there were a few herds of scrawny cattle grazing in the dust. The herders had pitched tents, bedouin-style, at the side of the road. "What are they doing there?" I asked.

"Waiting to sell the cattle," Marcel said. "At the abattoir."

"Where did they come from?"

Marcel consulted with Kofi in a mixture of English and Senoufou. "They have driven their cattle down from Haute-Volta. It takes many months," he said. "When they sell them, they go home."

"Are they waiting for a good price?"

"They're waiting for any price. They want to fatten the cattle, but there's no grass. So they wait."

"Do they walk back?"

"Yes. How else would they get there?"

Buddy and the pilots didn't get the dinosaurs launched that day. The children went back to school, the shops reopened, and I went back to work. That night while I was eating dinner and reading a three-day-old copy of the *International Herald Tribune,* I found a one-paragraph wire-service item with a Los Angeles dateline: "H'wood Institution Closes Doors." It went on to say: "Schwab's Pharmacy, a Hollywood gathering place for fifty-one years, is going out of business." No more Schwab's? How could that be? Someone will buy the place, I thought. Maybe a new management will take over, but surely it can't close. I realized Hollywood hadn't been on my mind at all. Thoughts of Dorothy and Big Edith and walking over to Schwab's from the Chateau Marmont and the script for *Cry I am* that Steve Terzarian and I wrote in the corner booth floated over me. When I looked up from the paper, Marcel was standing there. He often did that, as if he had just wandered into the hotel and run into me.

"Is something wrong?" he asked solicitously.

"Not really. A place I like went out of business," I said, pointing at the *Trib.*

"In Hollywood?"

"Yeah. It's sort of a restaurant."

"The Polo Lounge?"

"No. It's a drugstore. It's not important." I was no longer hungry but I didn't want to sit there alone, so when Marcel sat down, I didn't object or make an excuse. "Schwab's. Schwab's drugstore. It's near where I live, and I go there a lot. No more, I guess."

"I've heard of it," he said excitedly, proud of his information, his connection to the West. "Didier told me about it. For the American eggs. Yes?"

"That's right. I wrote a script there once."

"Ah, yes," he said. "Like the cafés of Paris, the pleasures of the city. I'm sorry for your Schwab's." Mourning a drugstore in a culture where people are hungry is rude at best, but it had put me in a contemplative mood. Marcel was trying to be polite, but he really only wanted to talk about Paris and he thought of me as his ideal audience. In his mind I understood and approved of his dreams. Marcel had very little in this world, but he did have certainty; that was his sadness. He knew where the better life was, even if he couldn't get to it. Compared to him, I had free choice and it had filled me with ambivalence. I guess that was mine. He longed for Paris and I shuffled back and forth between New York and California, unsure of the movie business, wondering if I belonged in it. When it threatened to give me satisfaction, I would leave. Staying and leaving, embracing and rejecting. "I am sorry for your Schwab's," he said again.

"Do you know who Milton Berle is?" I asked.

"Of course," he said indignantly, hurt that I might doubt his knowledge. "He is the famous American screenwriter. Yes?"

"No. He's a comedian."

"Ah, yes. Like Bob Hope?"

"Close enough. When Milton Berle's in front of an audience, he begs for applause with one hand and says stop with the other." Marcel nodded, but there was no way on earth he could know what I was talking about.

The next day Kofi and I were on the road to Grand Bassam again, driving out to the fishing village. There were always merchants at the side of the road selling trinkets, furniture, clothing, and food. Some of them were in elaborate kiosks, others just wandered about. It was never clear who bought these things, since I had never seen any customers. We were stopped, allowing a man and some goats to cross the road, when I heard the helicopters and saw the dinosaurs high overhead. Buddy and the Ivorian pilots had managed it: there were dinosaurs over Africa. I stood in the road squinting up at them, trying to see. In seconds I was surrounded by merchants and peddlers, all indifferent to flying dinosaurs. They were tugging at me, whispering in my ear in a mixture of French and English, wanting me to look at wood carvings or jewelry, telling me of the bargains I could have. I had wanted the flying dinosaurs to be a mystery to them, a source of legend among the tribes. The possibilities had put me in a literary-colonialist mood. I wanted to say to them: Look up in the sky, look at the wonder of it. I had hoped it would be as memorable and all-consuming for the Africans as making movies was for the Americans. They were interested in selling trinkets, not in buying dreams. So instead of showing them metaphor, I bought a tiny carved ivory elephant. The idea of buying a white elephant from these people struck me as appropriate under the circumstances. As usual, Kofi told me I overpaid.

When we got to the fishing village, the art director and his staff were putting mud on the huts. About half the huts were made of tin—not an ideal building material under the African sun, but the material of choice, nonetheless. The art director was concerned that he might be distorting the way the village lived for the sake of the movie. He said he would never do such a thing in the Cotswolds and he was loath to do it here. He assured the chief that when we were through, the mud could be removed. The chief took a pragmatic view of the alterations. His concern was that his village be paid. The villagers usually stood and stared at us, but now they seemed uneasy. Their moods were as mysterious to me as mine must surely be to them, but I could feel something about to happen. Then they turned abruptly and walked to the river, where they stood in a silent line on the bank, staring upriver into the distance.

Coming around a bend was one of the dinosaurs, strapped to a barge, its long tail dragging in the water. As it got closer I heard a motor, but at first the image was silent and ghostly. It seemed one of the helicopters had been in danger of losing its load. Prudence, not a typical African trait, prevailed and the pilot had landed near the river and the dinosaur was transferred to this barge. The other dinosaur was still in the air. It's hard to tell what the villagers made of this enormous green beast or if they knew it had to do with the white men crawling over their village, spreading money around, and worrying about putting mud on their huts. It must have looked to them like the result of a very unusual hunt. When the barge got close, Buddy waved. "We'll be there in six hours if the current holds," he yelled.

"How do you get her out to the location?" the art director called back.

"Overland. They're chopping a trail now."

"I hope."

"Me too."

The easy tone of the talk seemed to reassure the villagers. When the chief realized this was part of the good fortune that had come his way, he began chanting in a high singsong voice. His people joined him and the entire village sang to the dinosaur, wishing it a safe journey as it traveled up their river into the mist.

With the filming in high gear, Marcel could see his job ending. He had complained a lot and he had often been the butt of jokes, but it was a job and it gave him purpose and, I suppose, identity. He was afraid for it to end, so he slowed down and completed nothing. Every task became impossible for him. Find a seedy café with a few outdoor tables suitable for night shooting? "Oh, it's very difficult. It can't be done on such short notice. I'm working on it, but it's not so easy." He seemed always to be making excuses or talking about Paris or Hollywood. Then he came down with a fever, the only African to get sick. The white Westerners were sick all the time—flu, fever, stomach disorder. Some had to be sent to London for treatment. Alone among the Africans, Marcel fell ill. "It's my Parisian stomach," he said.

"It's his bloody pretensions," Cyril said. But Marcel was feverish and unable to hold food. The company doctor gave him an injection and some pills and told him to rest. And then he was gone, just disappeared. "Probably gone to Paris," Cyril said. "And good riddance." No one much liked Marcel and there wasn't exactly an outpouring of concern. I wasn't sure how much I liked him myself, but I had come to know him a little and it was impossible not to feel some responsibility. I asked Kofi to find out where he was and take me there.

The hotel looked out over a serene lagoon to the city beyond. But if you looked the other way, behind the hotel, past the swimming pools and over a grassy hill, there was a shantytown of dusty roads and crumbling shacks, a few primitive shops, and a barber who would straighten your hair. A few of the buildings had electricity, stolen from the hotel, it was said. None had plumbing. There were a few skimpy gardens, and for some, a chicken or two scratched in the dirt. There were worse slums in Abidjan, but none of them were in view of a posh hotel. There were no street signs and no addresses, but Kofi knew where to go. He drove slowly while fly-covered children chased the car until we stopped at a wood-and-cardboard shack.

As the car sat there and I tried to decide what to do, a young woman, barefoot and only partly dressed, appeared in the doorway. She posed provocatively, hip thrust out and with the pouty, sullen look of prostitutes everywhere. At first I thought I recognized her from the hotel, and perhaps I did, but then I realized where I had seen her. She was the Mama whose stew I had tasted out at the quarry. Marcel's anger at the women on the side of the road came back to me, and his words, ". . . they have certain tasks to perform," echoed in my head. Kofi grinned and pointed. "In there," he said.

The only light inside the shack came through a hole that served as a window. Marcel was there, in the dark, resting on a straw mat on the dirt floor. I greeted him and said, "I hope you're feeling better." His Parisian clothes were gone now, replaced by a pair of tattered shorts and an undershirt. If he was surprised to see me, he didn't show it.

"My fever is gone now," he said. "Is the film still shooting?"

I nodded yes and waited for my eyes to get used to the dark. Aside from Marcel's mat, there was a low bedside table cobbled together out of a few boards where he kept aspirin and antibiotics from the company doctor. I didn't see any other furniture. Along the back wall there were seven or eight neatly stacked caldrons of the sort the Mamas had used to cook. On the wall near the door, pictures of Paris, clipped from magazines, were next to a fetish, an old tire studded with nails, guarding the place, like a mezuzah on West End Avenue. "There's more to do on the picture," I said. "Are you coming back?"

"More to do, but not for me. Cyril said, 'If you don't come in today, don't come in tomorrow.'" He shrugged his Gallic shrug and fumbled for a Gauloise. When he lit it, I noticed an old woman squatting in a corner. She was large and round and wore a necklace of charms and amulets made from shells and animal teeth. Her presence surprised me and Marcel said, "Ignore her, it's nothing."

She must have known he was speaking about her, because she pushed a caldron over to Marcel's mat and slathered some of its contents on his stomach. It was a concoction made of leaves floating in a dark liquid. As she put it on his belly, she shook her necklace over him and whispered an incantation. It embarrassed him to have me see it and he pushed her away, but he allowed the leaves to remain on his stomach.

"Didier may come to visit," he said, as if we were in the hotel bar drinking English gin and eating olives. "I had a letter from him."

"I hope he does."

"He may be in Dakar. On a French picture. Will you give me your address in Hollywood?" I wrote it down and handed it to him. He stared at it and said, "Sometime I will come. You'll be surprised. I'll knock at your door and tell you, 'It's Marcel. In Hollywood.' You'll see."

I didn't know what else to say, so I did what my countrymen have always done. I gave him money. I found a spot on the low table between the plastic bottles of Western medicine and the residue of the old woman's animist healing potion. I put a wad of the local currency under the aspirin. He thanked me and then looked at the slip of paper with my address. He asked, "Will you go to Paris on your way home?"

"I don't think so, Marcel." He was so disappointed that I added, "But if I do, I'll say hello to it all for you. That's a promise."

As I drove away, I glanced back and saw him standing alone in the doorway, watching me disappear.

A few days later I was out on location, deep in the bush, staying in a hunting lodge. There was no electricity or water at night but there were lovely tame monkeys playing and chattering. I couldn't sleep; with no electricity I couldn't read.

It was hard not to think about Marcel and a life that had allowed him Paris and then had taken it away. Character and anatomy might be part of it, but on this continent race is destiny. As I mused on Marcel's life and the uncertain, unknowable forces that had brought us both here, I looked up into the starry night, and the dinosaurs were there, dangling from the helicopters. The sky was so dark and the stars so white that it seemed I was watching, had become a part of, a strip of black-and-white film. When I looked down, the Sengha villagers were on the far side of their river staring at me, impassive and still. The rocks in the river were covered with phosphorus, and in their glow I saw Marcel. He was calling to me from across the water, begging me to understand and not judge him too harshly. He asked, did I know Didier in Paris and had I been to L'Ami Louis in the Marais and had I eaten the foie gras there? I wanted to put him at ease, tell him to guard his memories, but not let them consume him.

Before I could find words, the Sengha villagers pushed back the branches and Marcel went deeper into the bush. They kept the path open, like a curtain, and I could see into the darkness. The film crew had made a clearing and they were moving equipment and setting up a shot. Dorothy and Big Edith from Schwab's came to the river and beckoned to me. "Old Leon has shut it down," they said. "It's gone forever." I stepped out onto the glowing rocks so I could see more clearly. Then everyone called my name, saying, "Come on over, come on across." They were all there, standing around the camera: Teddy, who wrecked Porsches; Peter and Joey, who were holding hands; Bucky, the stuntman, and Claude, the screenwriter who could walk on fire; Sheila and her grandfather; Tommy, the exercise coach, and Olivia, the actress; and the others—the living and the dead or gone, all calling to me. Then my little red Porsche appeared in the sky, chasing and honking at the dinosaurs. I stepped over the rocks and moved closer to the opening the villagers had made. Everyone seemed serene and untroubled. No one was arguing or scheming or trying to get some advantage. The monkeys were swinging by their tails through the trees, chattering and making everyone laugh. As I stepped up out of the glowing river, I saw we had arrived at the water's source and I knew with surprising clarity that when the secrets were revealed and the story told, then the past would be understood and the future could be seen. When I was standing among them, the light had been reclaimed and a calming peace had come over us all.

After my work on the picture was done, I went to Dakar for a holiday and from there to London as I worked my way slowly back to Los Angeles. When I was finally home from Africa I found I no longer wanted to do rewrites and began to take more seriously the business of writing my own screenplays. By then El Vitamino was spending more time at Wolf's garage than with me. Rock stars were staying at the Chateau. It had become fashionable and expensive. I had been around Hollywood too long to pretend I didn't know where the freeways led.

Life was beginning to write its name on my face and I realized I was through with hotel rooms and racy, troublesome cars. I stopped telling myself I was just passing through and bought a little house in the Hollywood Hills. I found myself thinking about Marv, my old editor at the *Post,* and his ruminations about truth and lies and his prediction for me that when I'd been in California long enough I might be ready to try to get at some skinny version of the truth about the place. Marv's instruction had been to start with facts and then add whatever I felt would make the facts tell the truth. I thought I'd give it a try.